TAKING HOME THE TYCOON

BY
CATHERINE MANN

MILLS
BOON

First Published in Great Britain 2017
By Mills & Boon, an imprint of HarperCollins*Publishers*
1 London Bridge Street, London, SE1 9GF

© 2017 Harlequin Books S.A.

Special thanks and acknowledgement are given to Catherine Mann for her contribution to the Texas Cattleman's Club: Blackmail series.

ISBN: 978-0-263-92835-8

51-0917

USA TODAY bestselling author **Catherine Mann** has won numerous awards for her novels, including both a prestigious RITA® Award and an *RT Book Reviews* Reviewers' Choice Award. After years of moving around the country bringing up four children, Catherine has settled in her home state of South Carolina, where she's active in animal rescue. For more information, visit her website, www.catherinemann.com.

To Vee, Sharon, Tiffany and all the volunteers
who make such an incredible difference
through the Sunshine State Animal Rescue.

One

For self-made cybersecurity billionaire Max St. Cloud, his life as a teen on the unforgiving streets of LA—panhandling, Dumpster diving for his next meal and hot-wiring cars for cash—seemed like a distant dream. Fifteen years later, hotshot Max enjoyed the hell out of his life in Seattle.

He adored his fleet of fast cars and hangar full of planes. His state-of-the-art modern marvel of a home was any techie's wet dream. He had his pick of women equally as committed to their professions. And he was married to St. Cloud Security Solutions, his corporate computer and building security firm.

So why in the hell was he sitting here in small-town Royal, Texas, sporting one helluva hard-on for a scrubbed, fresh-faced woman wearing mom jeans?

The ginger-haired beauty seated in the wingback beside him seemed unaware of his dilemma. A good or bad thing? He wasn't sure.

Digital tablet on his knee, he shifted in his leather chair, one of a pair by the fireplace in a meeting room at the Texas Cattleman's Club's lodge. Given he'd been called in as a security expert, he should be focused on this latest interview into a cyberwar being waged on the citizens of Royal.

Those were the key words: *should be*. He stole another glance at the woman beside him.

Clearing his throat, Max forced himself to take notes on his tablet because the odds of him remembering the details of this conversation with Natalie Valentine were next to nil. He stared at his notes about her: twenty-nine years old, war-widowed mother of two, wedding-dress designer, owner of the Cimarron Rose Bed and Breakfast in the center of town.

The simple facts didn't come close to revealing how damned appealing he found her.

"Mrs. Valentine—do you mind if I call you Natalie?"

"That's fine. Of course." She scratched a finger along the flour stain on her denim-covered thigh—her empty ring finger. "Actually, I prefer it."

The flash of pain in her eyes made him feel like an ass for jonesing over another guy's wife. Even a dead guy. Especially a dead guy. "I appreciate your taking time from your business day to speak with me."

"I'm still fairly new to the town. Surely there are people better suited than I am to share about the personalities in this area." Her fitted green T-shirt only made her massive emerald eyes glitter all the more. Her shoulder-length red hair was swept up into an unfussy ponytail. Little pretense. Raw beauty. And those eyes. Damn, they were intrinsically vulnerable and full of heart, yet the tip of her chin spoke of spirit just begging to be uncovered.

He recognized grit when he saw it, a kindred spirit. "I have a different take on you being too new to help. It's my experience that newcomers can also offer an objective perspective."

But the stakes were high on this security-consulting gig. Max had been called in by his longtime friend Chelsea Hunt—Chels—to help trace who was waging cybersmears on the good citizens of Royal. Chels had been one of his few true friends back in his early twenties. They'd both been hungry hackers with a bent for justice during a time she ran to LA to get away from her overprotective parents. But Chels had a more cultured upbringing. She'd helped him smooth out his rougher edges as he sought entry into the legitimate business world. She'd believed in him when no one else did. She'd been the sister he'd never had, cheering him on.

So some wannabe troll was hell-bent on destroying the lives of members of Royal's Texas Cattleman's Club? The sorry son of a bitch had picked the wrong firewalls to infiltrate. As far as Max was concerned, once a hacker, always a hacker. He was certain he could beat this amateur...or team. He had a hunch it wasn't one man or woman working alone...

"Mr. St. Cloud—"

"You're Natalie. I'm Max."

"Yes, then, um, Max, I'll try to help, but I'm usually running full tilt at my bed-and-breakfast." Natalie fidgeted with her simple silver watch, checking the time. "I don't mean to rush you, but I have dough rising for bread and pastries that I need to check on soon."

With each breath, her chest rose and fell faster, which happened to draw his eyes to the pink rose logo in an oval between her breasts. The paneled walls with trophies and historical artifacts closed in on him. The space seemed tighter. More intimate.

Mom jeans. A T-shirt. And the thought of tasting pastry filling on her lips.

Seriously?

"I realize your time is precious and I'll try to make this quick." Quick? Quickie… Damn, she sent his mind down distracting paths. So much for logical, techie objectivity. "You would be surprised at the details you hear without consciously registering them. And there are impressions gained in passing. You have the heartbeat of the town with your B and B…and with the wedding dresses you make."

Surprise turned her cheeks pink, her eyes widening and lips parting ever so slightly. "You know about my dresses?"

"I do my research," he said simply. "Experience with individuals in your line of business leads me to conclude that people talk to you, a lot. They share their life stories—about their children, their dates, their dogs, hell, even their medical history. They even, dare I say, gossip."

"I don't think of it as gossip really. I prefer to believe they feel comfortable at my B and B, whether they're spending the night or just stopping to join in a hot breakfast." Absently, she fingered her watchband.

"And there's no counselor-patient confidentiality involved in pastry making and stitchery."

She laughed, a full-throated, sexy laugh that relaxed stress lines from her pretty face. "Clearly."

"So I would like to pick your brain about…just impressions." He hated seeing the smile fade from her lips and her eyes, but he did have a job to accomplish. "I'm not asking you to implicate anyone. It's up to me to put together a whole picture that points to the culprit or gives ideas for ways to smoke him or her out. So if you're comfortable just talking...let me do my thing."

Her eyebrows shot up. "Do your thing? Is that computer-tech talk out West?"

Well, hell. So much for the badass-businessman persona he'd cultivated from his street-rat youth. He'd just been taken down a peg by a sassy ginger rocking her flour-stained jeans.

Nearly a half hour later, Natalie was fairly certain her stomach had more fizzing going on than the air bubbles in her likely overflowing dough back at the bed-and-breakfast.

Max St. Cloud was a man. All man. A testosterone powder keg of sexuality. And after over a year of abstinence, her sex-starved body couldn't help reacting. Her military husband had died a year ago, and he'd been deployed to the Middle East for eight months when he died in an explosion.

Still, though, while her B and B, the Cimarron Rose, might be open to the public, her heart was officially closed for business. She was one hundred percent devoted to carving out a life for her and her two children. Colby and Lexie were her world now. They'd suffered too much loss and change. She owed them stability.

The insurance money had just barely paid off their debts.

Her husband had left behind an overextended double mortgage on their home in North Carolina. Doctor and therapist bills for her special-needs son were costly, but necessary. Working and paying for childcare had stretched her budget to the limit. She'd feared she would have to cave and move in with her parents for her children's sake, and then her late husband's military friend Tom Knox had insisted she move close to his place in Texas so he could help and keep an eye on her.

She hated exploiting his kindness, but truth be told, she wasn't close with her family in her hometown of Phoenix. So she'd taken Tom up on his offer. Her family had never been supportive of her decision to travel the world with her military husband, and they definitely weren't supportive of his back-to-back deployments that left her essentially a single parent for years.

The bed-and-breakfast had been a godsend that just sort of fell into her lap—the former proprietor was an older woman who decided to move to California to be with her daughter and had sold it for the right price. Exactly the amount she received on the North Carolina house.

Since four-year-old Colby had recently been diagnosed as being on the autism spectrum, running the B and B was a perfect fit for being more flexible to meet his needs as well as keeping up with her two-year-old daughter. It allowed Natalie to stay home with the kids and pursue her dreams of designing wedding gowns, and gave her the one-on-one time to work with a trainer for their young golden retriever to become her son's service dog. Miss Molly had the smarts and the aptitude, and heaven knew, Natalie needed all the help she could get.

All of which left little time for fizzy flutters in her stomach for tall, dark and dangerous.

Natalie gripped the arms of the leather chair in the Cattleman's Club lounge. "While I want to help, I'm beginning to lose the thread here on your questions. I feel as if we're covering ground you must already know from your research."

"I'm digging for nuances."

"I don't mean to be rude, but you're a computer techie. Not a detective." Okay, so she'd actually been a little rude, but only to give herself distance from Max and his striking aqua eyes with dark lashes, his dark brown, rumpled hair that her fingers itched to comb through. He was quite simply imperfectly gorgeous. This ex-hacker-turned-billionaire tech genius. Bad-boy brilliant. A potent mix.

"I'm experienced with cyberprotection, so it is a combination of both. Quit worrying about what I need to know. Leave that up to me."

"I just expected this interview to go faster."

"Your bread and pastry dough. Can't it be punched down and rise again?"

Now, that surprised her. Because he was right. "A few more minutes, perhaps. But I need to pick up my children from preschool soon."

He nodded, his booted foot resting on his knee and twitching as he took notes on his tablet. Hiking boots. Expensive, clearly, but worn in. Not worn just for show. "Of course. I'll move this along, then."

The image of those well-worn boots and faded jeans contrasted with the button-down shirt and pocket protector. God, why couldn't life be simple for once? "At least Cecilia, Simone and Naomi—they've gone from suspects to victims. Nothing seems off-limits to this creep in what secrets are revealed. Exposing Cecilia's birth certificate in spite of her closed adoption. Sharing private medical details about Simone's in vitro pregnancy. Then announcing Naomi's pregnancy and stealing her chance to share that special news? It's crazy around here. All of us feel vulnerable."

She crossed her arms against her chest, a poor attempt at a shield from all this mess. Still, it made her feel better, if only temporarily.

"You have nothing to hide."

"Everyone has secrets." And she had so many parts of her past that she wanted, more than anything, to wish away.

"You look pretty squeaky clean on the internet."

Her secrets weren't internet worthy. They just made for grief and nightmares and a difficulty in trusting in picket fences anymore. "Well, having our friends hurt is wounding, too."

"I'm not giving up until this bastard is found and stopped." His large hands clenched into strong fists along the arms of his chair.

Very large hands.

Lord, she didn't want to think about clichés about the size of hands and feet right now. She kept her eyes firmly off his boots, damn it.

But the way those hands then unfurled and carefully handled the thin tablet had her envisioning nimble touches and more…so much more.

There was no denying the conviction in his voice, and she couldn't help admiring that. He truly was here to help, and her adopted town needed that help. The people here deserved the best. They'd done so much for her, welcoming her and her children with open arms. She should be helping rather than being so caught up in her own concerns.

This town had welcomed her wholeheartedly and she wanted to feel a part of things, to make a contribution however she could. And she really only had one thing to offer.

She tipped her chin and, before she could change her mind, blurted, "Mr. St. Cloud—um, Max—you can stay at my B and B free of charge, as my thanks for helping out the town."

She might not have as much as some residents of this wealthy town, but she had her pride and she could offer something to help out Royal in its time of need. She was *not* going to fall victim to some smooth-talking player. For the next few days—or even weeks—she could hold strong.

Besides, it wasn't like she was his type of female.

"Thank you very much, Natalie. I will gratefully accept."

He smiled.

And holy hell, that gave her pause. His smile lit his eyes and made her stomach flip in a way she'd forgotten was possible.

What had she gotten herself into?

Cell phone in hand on his way to his rental vehicle, Max charged through the Texas Cattleman's Club parking lot. The old-world men's club dated back to around 1910, and was a large, rambling single-story building made of dark stone and wood with a tall slate roof. He needed to touch base with Chelsea and report on his progress with interviews this afternoon.

And let her know he wasn't going to be staying with her after all. He'd made—his mouth twitched—alternative plans. He unlocked the rented Lexus SUV—a larger car was a must to transport his gear.

Natalie's offer had stunned the hell out of him, but he hadn't even hesitated. Would seducing a suspect jeopardize his investigation? Sure.

Lucky for him, she wasn't a suspect.

Thumbing speed dial for Chels and setting the phone for hands-free talking, Max steered past the stable, pool and tennis courts, all TCC member perks. And all freshly maintained. Chels had told him part of the clubhouse roof and many of the outbuildings had been damaged in a massive tornado a few years back. The group now took special care to reinforce the roof and had added some height to the ceilings so the main building seemed airier than before.

For a club steeped in tradition, a lot had changed in the TCC lately. He might not be a member, but he'd done his research since this group seemed to be the focus of the hacker's attacks. Colors had been brightened. It wasn't such an "old boys' club" anymore, especially because women were now full members.

He accelerated out of the lot and headed toward town, toward the B and B, just as Chelsea answered his call.

"Max!" Her voice chimed through the car's speaker as he drove. "Hello, my friend. How did the fact gathering go after I left?"

"Interesting… Nothing conclusive yet, but lots of pieces to review and leads to follow once I get my gear set up." He'd come straight from the airport.

"I can't thank you enough for dropping everything and coming here personally to help."

Chels's voice filled the car as he made his way down the road. His eyes darted from the asphalt in front of him to the dusty town.

"That's what friends are for. We go way back. I still owe you for teaching me about which fork to use," he joked, tapping his brakes to let a minivan out of a parking lot. She'd taught him more than that. She'd helped him learn the nuances to moving in circles of society he needed to build his business.

She'd also given him the nod to be himself and not let those societal boundaries contain him. Heaven knows, she was an edgy original herself. They really could have been siblings, as they were made from the same mold in many ways.

Slowing, he drove past a school yard teeming with children living idyllic lives of normalcy so different from his. Adults rushed to organize their students into an efficient line for parent pickup. Each little face trusted that their parents or a car pool member would arrive right on cue.

Even from a passing glance, he saw the effort it took to contain the wildness of the children bursting with excitement to return to their home lives and after-school activities—activities that did not include Dumpster diving.

"But you surely have higher-paying clients—especially since you're doing this pro bono, in spite of our offers." She exhaled a hard sigh and he could envision her shoving back her thick honey-blond hair impatiently. "And this feels, perhaps, below your pay grade. You could have sent one of your staff."

"This is sensitive. The info this bastard is sharing hurts you and your friends. I trust my staff, but I don't want you exposed any more than is needed." The criminal had made this personal by launching slanderous attacks on Chels's friends here. Someone had infiltrated their personal data and found dirt for blackmailing—everything from revealing a man's love child, to concocting the appearance of an affair to destroy a marriage, to dabbling in land documents to threaten land holdings. Nothing was secret or sacred to whoever had it in for the people of this town.

Anger rippled through Max as he turned off the main road, eyes squinting in the glare of the September sun.

"Thank you." Her voice wobbled, full of emotional

appreciation. She'd always hated to feel like an imposition, and he never wanted his old friend to feel that way.

His pal had always been an in-your-face, indomitable spirit, ready to kick ass for a cause one moment and outrageously issue a skinny-dip dare in the next. That someone had his friend so afraid and off balance... pissed him off.

"No thanks needed, Chels. I'm here for you, and I'll do whatever it takes to see this through."

"You're a good friend. I look forward to catching up with you while you're staying with me." Even over the phone, he could picture her smile. Loyal. Genuine.

And now he had to figure out how to tell his pseudo sister that he'd made other arrangements for his stay in town.

"Um, about that. I really feel bad about putting you out, so I made arrangements to stay at this nice little B and B called the Cimarron Rose."

Silence stretched for a few heartbeats.

"That's Natalie Valentine's place. You interviewed her today after I left, right?" Her question came out quiet, noncommittal.

He couldn't get a read on her—was she defensive or enthusiastic? Chels wasn't usually guarded around him, so she must be fishing.

Well, he wasn't feeling the need to share about his attraction. While Natalie might be new to the area, it was clear she'd become the town darling. The small community had embraced the young widow, and he sure as hell wasn't the boy-next-door type of person. "Yes, I spoke with Natalie Valentine today. That's how I heard about her place. It seems like a solid fit for me, given I don't know how long I'll be here." He'd done some additional online digging into her business after Natalie left. More detailed, yes, more personal.

The house was a far cry from the penthouse hotel suites he usually frequented. The B and B looked cozy—it was a white wood home, with large porches, ferns and rocking chairs. The ancient oak spread welcoming branches casting long-reaching shadows.

And it was as far from the harsh streets of LA as he ever could have imagined. The town sprawled, buildings seemed to resist the urge to converge, to press against one another. There was space here. Places to go and exist. Places to hide, too.

"Okay, that's cool, Max," Chelsea said slowly.

"You aren't going to argue?" he asked, surprised. "That's a first."

"Nice. Not," she joked right back.

"I would just expect you to warn me off her, given you know who I am, how I am. She's a war widow with two children."

"Of course I know you. Very well, in fact. And I know someday you'll stop running."

Unease crawled up his spine. "Are you trying to push me toward her? Matchmake?"

She chuckled lowly. "I wouldn't dream of maneuvering your life."

Yeah. Right.

Staying silent, he kept on driving, noting the old 1960s' tin diner on the side of the road. A mix of old, rust-peppered cars were scattered throughout the parking lot, contrasting with newer, sleeker models. He had to be close to Natalie's place. Based on the concentration of buildings—the diner, a strip mall and a grocery store—he guessed this was the center of town.

"Max, really, I just figured you must be drawn to her

if you're staying there. You have to admit, that isn't the kind of accommodations you usually choose."

True, perhaps. But there was a time he would have considered the Cimarron Rose pure heaven and far out of his reach. In many ways, it still was. He'd chosen a different path for his life. Impersonal. Sleek.

Impenetrable. Just like his cybersecurity.

So how to deal with Chels's Cupid leanings?

Don't even take the bait. This was about him and Natalie. And who the hell even knew where it might lead? But he wouldn't want there to be gossip. "Natalie offered." Remembering that moment pleased him. She had seemed to surprise herself with the offer, but she'd been sincere. Hell, something told him she'd needed to make the offer and contribute to keeping her town safe. He liked that. "She seems to want to help. I'm comfortable with the choice, and it will give me the opportunity to get the pulse of the traffic flowing in and out of town in a way I wouldn't be able to do staying at your place."

"Right," Chels said skeptically. "Okay, so you're staying there because it's comfy. Got it. Are you sure there's enough bandwidth for you there?"

As if he would rely on anyone else's connection?

"Ah, come on, you know me better than that. Since when do I travel without remote-access capabilities?" He had his own equipment and boosters up the wazoo.

"Okay, I'll be frank. I know you too well to buy these cagey answers. Natalie is not the kind of woman you usually pursue, so I think you need to be careful, for your sake. I care about you, bro." Chels always had a knack for being blunt, even when Max didn't want to hear it.

She was worried about *his* feelings?

For real?

"Who even said I'm chasing her?" he asked too quickly. Damn it. Still, he wasn't giving ground. He pulled into the B and B's lot.

No. This wasn't the kind of place he typically stayed in. The pictures online hardly did the place justice.

The white cottage with reddish-brown trim was framed by an oak tree that seemed to use a tree branch to gesture invitingly to the front door. A warm glow emanated from the windows.

His eyes were drawn to the side yard—to Natalie. A golden retriever danced around, nuzzling Natalie's son. Her daughter stood leaning against her leg, head thrown back in a giggle, red pigtails dancing.

"I just said I'm staying at her place. In fact, she generously offered a room to thank me for helping out with the investigation."

"Uh-huh, okay, Max…"

The rest of his friend's words droned in his ears as he couldn't tear his eyes off Natalie. She'd exchanged her flour-flecked clothes for a simple, long sundress that grazed her curves. She was still earthy but fresh, and her hair swung free.

As if she could tell he was entranced, she turned, looked straight at him. His breath caught in his chest. Like a fist right to the sternum. There was no denying the impact.

He turned off his car. "Chels, I gotta go."

Time to check in to his new digs.

And check out his new landlady.

Two

Concentrate, Natalie sharply reminded herself, looking into the dark eyes of Miss Molly, the golden retriever puppy who had a very specific purpose within their family unit. Natalie wanted to make sure her autistic son had every advantage in the world. And so she'd hired a trainer to help transform Miss Molly into the model service dog. Miss Molly had a lot of potential to help her son.

But not if her mind kept wandering during training sessions like this. Max's handsome face drifted in and out of her mind. He'd unnerved her, caused a rupture in her day-to-day routine—a routine she had carefully constructed since losing her husband. The daily structure was everything she had—it gave her a sense of stability and power.

Enter Max. A big, bad, devilishly handsome tech billionaire. So much for humdrum. For a moment, Natalie couldn't believe she'd offered for him to stay at the bed-and-breakfast. Under her roof. She took a deep breath, pushed him from her thoughts and tried to mirror the movement Margie, Miss Molly's wiry dog trainer, was making.

The sound of an SUV engine mingled with Lexie's giggling at their golden retriever's head tilting at Natalie's command. Lifting her eyes to the road in front of her, she saw him.

Max St. Cloud.

Even from their limited interaction, she'd recognized his features. The door of the black SUV opened and he slid out. His booted feet thudded on the ground, causing dust to encircle him ever so slightly.

Colby nudged her with his foot, causing her to stop gaping for a moment. Her son didn't look at her and didn't touch her outright, but instead kicked the ground with his sneaker, and fidgeted with the plaid shirt he wore.

As if sensing his unease, Miss Molly bounded over to him, planting a wet kiss on his cheek. He smiled slightly, but lines of caution still colored his stance.

Margie knelt beside the dog and Colby. Her sharp blue eyes looked up to meet Natalie's. "New guest? The cyberdetective in from Seattle, right?"

"Yep. That's him," she answered, taking in his slow, confident gait, the ease and appeal of his plain white T-shirt. Natalie's stomach tumbled. With a deep breath, she smoothed her hair, tried to build the wall back up around her emotions.

He was a boarder.

A guest.

Nothing more.

And the butterflies in her stomach damn well needed to listen.

But what could happen with her kids here?

Nothing. Because they were her whole world.

Her daughter, Alexa, bolted from her side, a flurry of kicked-up leaves trailing behind her. She stopped as Max clicked open the picket-fence gate, her little dress still filled with rippled motion. Lexie pulled on the sleeves of her light jean jacket and smiled at him.

"Mister, wanna pet my dog?" Lexie's spritely voice cooed. She pointed back to where Natalie, Margie and Colby stood together.

Natalie rushed to her daughter, then smoothed back her outgoing child's hair and tucked her close. "Lexie, Mr. St. Cloud has had a long day. He needs to go to his room."

"His room?" Lexie glanced up with wide eyes and long lashes. "For a time-out?"

"No, sweetie, he isn't being sent to time-out. He hasn't misbehaved." Although the gleam in his eyes indicated he was open to the option. "He is a guest and we need to be polite."

"Yes, ma'am." She turned to Max. "You hungry? We got pastry, Mr. Cloud."

Natalie started to correct her daughter and he held up a hand.

"It's all right, Natalie." He knelt in front of the toddler. "I like pastry. I hope you'll save some for me for breakfast."

Margie crossed the lawn to join them and tugged one of Lexie's curls lightly. "Show him to his room, Natalie. I'll keep working with Miss Molly and watch these two."

"Thank you, Margie. That's very generous of you."

A blush heated her cheeks. Margie continually went above and beyond what was required of her during these training sessions. When she wasn't training dogs, Margie was part of a search-and-rescue team. A woman in her sixties, she had spent her whole life helping other people.

Margie waved a hand, a tough hand with a scar she'd gotten from a dog bite long ago. "Go on. I've got this under control."

Natalie nodded, motioning for Max to follow her up the porch and into the B and B.

"I'll show you to your room, Mr. S—um, Max." Her tongue had tripped as she remembered he insisted that she call him Max. The lack of his last name made her feel unsettled, put them on a more familiar setting, as if they were old friends or something. As if the boundaries between them were already dissolving...

It was a dangerous thought, one she could not risk.

"Your dog is quite friendly—your daughter, too." The smile in his voice felt genuine as she opened the door to the B and B, the immediate scent of cinnamon filling the air.

She appreciated the homey scent, which grounded her. It was something to focus on aside from the strong male presence beside her.

"I apologize if she talked your ear off." Lord knew, Lexie could talk for hours without much effort.

He paused in the threshold, eyes scanning the area, seeming to scrutinize and process what was before him. She followed his gaze, noting the quirks of this place that she had started to love. Like the wooden knob on the staircase that popped off occasionally. "This is a bed-and-breakfast. I expected the family-style approach."

He clicked the door behind him, making the space seem smaller just by being there.

"I'm curious why you took me up on my offer. Surely you're used to more upscale accommodations," she said, moving through the hallway, her feet soft on the plush vermillion patterned carpet.

"Did you want me to say no?" He cast a sidelong glance at her.

She felt that curious stare even as she kept her eyes forward on where they were going. They passed the door to the bright white-and-yellow kitchen, the room she seemed to always be in. "I wouldn't have offered if I didn't mean it."

They turned the corner and climbed up the second staircase in the house. The stair corridor was lit by sconces on the walls. The bath of golden light always made her think of some grand Regency-era novel. The Cimarron Rose was not the size of an estate, but this particular passage in the house always felt stately, like it belonged as a backdrop for some other time period.

"Do you need the space for paying customers? I don't want to take business away from you." His offer echoed in the stairway, accompanied by his determined footfalls.

They reached the landing and she moved away from him, a fierceness entering her voice. "I have another open room if someone needs to check in."

"I didn't mean to sting your pride." He sounded sincere. He paused again and looked at his surroundings, eyes fixating on a landscape portrait of a sunrise on the plains. Horses darted across the painting, free of all trappings of humanity. She'd bought that painting upon moving to Texas, feeling a kinship with the unbridled herd.

"You're fine. You're just being thoughtful, to me and the whole town. I want to do my part to say thank you and this is the only way I can contribute."

He laughed, a rich sound like caramel. His hand touched her wrist, the scent of his spiced cologne dripping in the space between them. "Then I'll gladly accept the room and the pastries, too."

Her stomach did back flips as she arched an eyebrow his way. "How do you know they're any good?"

"I did my research."

"Don't you let anything in life be a surprise?" She opened the door to his room. Late-afternoon sun streamed in through the old, warped glass window, casting shadows over the bed and threshold.

"Not if I can help it." He took a step closer to her. The light from the room seemed to pierce through his T-shirt, showcase his well-maintained chest. He leaned against the door frame and crossed his arms, the muscles flexing.

The electric pulse of his smile sent her reeling. She watched the way his lips folded into a smile. A spark. No—ten thousand sparks danced in the air. "I need to get back downstairs."

She took a step back, stumbled a little.

"To your children," he said with a knowing look in his eyes.

If she just leaned forward, into him, what would happen? The idea was tempting.

But it wasn't a reality she'd let herself pursue. Natalie straightened, drew herself up to full height. "Actually, the children are with the local dog trainer. She's on the clock." She wasn't going to let this man know how much he'd rattled her. She was a businesswoman. Not as wealthy as him, but her job mattered, her life was full. "I need to return to my customers. Let me know if you need anything during your stay."

A flame lit his eyes.

Ah, hell. She hadn't meant it that way. Or had she?

Either way, she needed to shut up, now, and put some distance between herself and this muscle-bound distraction.

Dropping to sit on the edge of his overstuffed king-size bed, Max surveyed the room. Over the past few hours, he'd transformed the space into a makeshift computer lab. The oak desk, which originally had a globe from the early 1900s, a stack of old novels and a vintage-inspired notepad on top of it, along with three screens, a mouse, a hard drive and an elaborate, curved keyboard. Nothing was plugged in yet, but the layout would do.

He stood and pulled out an array of wires from one of his bags. Crawling beneath the oak desk, he began hooking up the system, determined to catch the creep who had dared go after Chelsea's friends. After setting up the cords, he slunk into a plush leather chair and turned on the computer network system. An array of muted dings and computer groans greeted him, making his room in the Cimarron Rose feel a bit more like home.

While he waited for the remote access to connect with his home system, he spun around in his chair. The cream color of the walls made the room feel cozy, especially with the rich browns and oranges that made up the decor. A vintage map of the world was sprawled above the four-poster bed, and other travel accents—an old camera, repurposed suitcases—punctuated the room.

He glanced at his watch and was shocked. Somehow

the setup of his mobile workstation had taken him a few hours—it was nearing midnight. He needed to stretch.

Pacing around his room, he made his way to the far corner to the window. He scanned the area, noting the play of shadows in the yard…and someone on the wrought iron bench beneath the oak tree.

Natalie.

Natalie beneath the tree with a glass of wine looking as relaxed and natural as a wood sprite.

There. That was his opening. She sat under the oak, her strawberry blond hair soaking up the moon glow. Serene and unguarded. Filled with an urgency to talk to her, he started down the stairs.

Careful to close the door behind him without a sound, he strode toward her, his feet drawn to her before he even figured out what the hell he was doing here. "Do your guests get wine?"

A smile formed on his lips as she turned to find the source of his voice.

She tilted her head back and forth, an exaggeration that exposed the length of her neck and the grace of her movements. Eyebrows raised, she looked at him and lifted her glass. "I'm not sure my grocery-store vintage is up to your elite standards."

"How do you know what my vino standards are?" he returned, just as playfully, taking a seat next to her.

Natalie pursed her lips, folded her legs into the lotus position and turned to face him on the bench. "Seriously? Someone with your income?" She took another sip and held her glass up to the moonlight as if to examine its nuances. "You wouldn't pick this."

"Maybe it wouldn't be my first choice, but that doesn't mean I wouldn't enjoy a glass. Well, unless maybe you have beer instead."

She laughed softly, lowly. "I guess I did offer you a place to stay as my part of thanking you for helping with this cyberwacko." She started to push herself up from the bench. "I have four left from a six-pack of beer in the fridge. It was for Tom Knox when his family visited."

He put his hand on her wrist. "You don't need to wait on me. I can get my own beer. If you don't mind me reaching around in your fridge, that is."

She sank back down. "I'm more than happy to rest my feet."

Max went back inside to the kitchen. The cabinets were painted white, a vibe reminiscent of the 1970s. A beautiful orchid was placed on the kitchen table—vibrant violet.

He made his way to the stout yellow fridge and popped it open. An array of juice boxes and snacks covered the shelves. After some shuffling, he found a beer and headed back outside.

Earlier today, covered in flour, Natalie had been enchanting. Sitting beneath this tree, drenched in starlight and moonlight, she was ethereal. Her hair, loose, natural, rested elegantly on her slender shoulders.

Damn. He should have gotten two beers. No going back now. Opening the bottle, he sat down next to her. She lifted her glass and he clinked his bottle against her drink. "Cheers, Natalie. To solving a mystery."

"To altruistic millionaires." She laughed, then sipped her wine.

Billionaire. But he didn't think that would do much to advance his cause of getting closer to her.

Was that what he was doing?

Hell, yes, he wanted to taste her. Right now he wanted to kiss her more than he wanted…anything.

He took a swig of his beer, the hoppy flavor settling on his palate.

In this moment, underneath the stars and tree limbs, Natalie seemed so easygoing, so much less guarded than she had that afternoon. "Glad you found your brew."

"It was tough at first, tucked behind the juice boxes."

She laughed, choked a little on a sip of wine, then pressed the back of her wrist to her mouth. "Sorry about that. I should have warned you."

"Not a problem. You're a mom. I figure juice boxes come with the territory." Natalie just nodded in response, staring out toward the road.

A night orchestra filled the space between them. Low chirps of active crickets, the occasional rustle of a slight autumn wind through the branches. In the distance, he could hear car tires rolling over the mixture of dirt and pavement. No wonder she liked this time of night. "Your kids are cute. Your daughter sure is a little chatterbox."

"I think sometimes she is filling in the blanks for her brother." She stared into her glass, lightly swirling the wine along the sides of the crystal. "My son's been diagnosed on the spectrum for autism."

"I'm sorry." Her sudden desire to share this private moment struck a chord with Max. As if by instinct, his hand went to hers and he squeezed it reassuringly, noting the way she squeezed back. Max brought his hand back to his side, aware of the absence of warmth.

"I'm just glad we got the diagnosis. Early intervention is key to giving him the most life has to offer. Actually, that's true for any child. Proactive parenting."

"And you're doing it alone."

"I am, which doesn't leave me any free time. You need to understand that."

"You're a superb mother. You don't need to ever apologize for that." Another swig of beer. As he swallowed, he tried to push his own childhood back to the dark morass of his mind. When he was six, his mother had abandoned him. No explanation. Just gone. He became yet another child of the foster care system, cycling through homes, but never finding a permanent place. Never finding a family of his own. Unadoptable. All these years later, the label and reality still stung.

"We're training Miss Molly to help Colby in a number of ways." She combed her fingers through her hair as she turned to face him.

He shifted to face her, closer, as if the rest of the world was outside their pocket of space here. "Like a service dog?"

"Eventually. Right now she would qualify as an ESA—emotional support animal. However, there's no public access with that, but Colby's doctors can quantify how she helps ease his panic attacks. With training, we hope to hone that to where she can assist him in school, the store, and make so many more places accessible to him. My son is also quite the escape artist, so it helps having Miss Molly stick close to him. She barks when we call, even if he won't answer."

"I don't mean to sound dense, but why not just get a dog that's already trained?" Parenting, along with the world of disability and service animals, felt like a foreign language to him, but he was eager to learn more.

"The waiting list for most agencies is one to two years, if they'll even partner a dog with a child as young as Colby. Few groups will. We didn't have a lot of options left to us in this arena." He took in the slump in her spine, her downcast eyes and the pain pulsing in her tight-lipped smile.

He scooted closer to her, raised her chin. Shining emerald eyes met his, and a deep exhale passed from her lips to his receding hand. "But you investigated. You found answers."

Natalie the fighter. Natalie the woman who didn't quit. He admired that.

"Of course. We worked with the trainer and with Megan at the local shelter. They were fantastic in identifying a dog with potential for the job."

"That's impressive."

She worried her bottom lip with her teeth. "There's always the chance Miss Molly won't be able to complete the training to the level we hope. That's a risk with any dog in training. But we're already getting some help with Colby now in the way she offers comfort and sticks close to him. And we're committed to keeping her regardless of how far she progresses in her ability to learn."

"Even if you have to start training with another dog?"

"Yes, even if. For now, though, we're taking things a day at a time, doing the best we can." A stronger, more resolute smile formed on her face, as if she was replaying some scene in her mind.

"You're doing a damn fine job now," he affirmed before taking another sip of his beer, listening to the continued sound of crickets.

"Miss Molly already passed her Canine Good Citizen test. We're not taking this lightly. It's against the law to pass off a fake service dog."

"I didn't say you were." Max stretched his arms, expanding his chest, and let out a low sigh.

"I'm sorry to be defensive. People understand Seeing Eye dogs and dogs that assist with mobility. But when the animal is helping with developmental or emotional

disabilities, people can be incredibly…rude and unen-
lightened." Just as before, Natalie's gaze turned downward, pain evident in every part of her.

"Then enlighten me." He tucked the loose strands of
hair behind her ear.

She angled her head away. "I think we need to be
careful here."

"What do you mean?" he asked, wanting her to spell
it out. What they were feeling.

"I didn't invite you here as anything but a guest."

"Understood."

"An attraction is just that. An attraction. It doesn't
have to be acted on."

"Fair enough." He rested his elbows on his knees,
clasping his bottle, retreating for now. But only to regroup. "I appreciate your generosity with the room.
Your place here offers a homey feel I don't find often
in my travels. Now back to talking about your dog. I
want to know more about the training."

Even in the moonlight, he noticed a blush rise on her
neck. She sipped her wine, before talking into the glass.
"You're just being polite."

"I'm curious. Explain it so my techie mind under-
stands."

"Okay, have you heard about studies on dogs that
can sniff out cancer?"

"I have." He nodded, gesturing with his beer. "I assume it's like drug-sniffing dogs."

"Nice analogy. And there are dogs that alert to sei-
zures and diabetes glucose drops."

"Keep talking." He genuinely wanted to know. And
God, he also liked the sound of her voice.

"Those all involve chemical changes in the body,
with physical tells. Think of processing issues and stress

from autism in the same way. We can teach the dog to anticipate problems, assist in managing the environment… Your eyes are glazing over."

Narrowing his gaze, he processed the implications of what she was saying.

"No, I'm thinking. It makes sense." He leaned forward, looking past her, eyes alert on the surrounding area, always looking and observing. A calm street in a calm town, no threat to either of them present here. Old habits stayed with him, probably would forever. Including his drive to help, which was giving life to a deep protectiveness for this woman carving out a life on her own in the face of challenges that would have caused many people to crumble. "Have you got an online presence to chronicle your journey with Miss Molly and Colby?"

"In all my free time?" she asked drily.

"You could make a difference for others. Let me help set something up for you. I can make it very user friendly. And you would be surprised at the reach you can get with adding in guest bloggers like your trainer, your vet, people here in town." He grinned. "The cyberworld isn't all bad, you know."

"Why would you do that for me?" Her slender fingertips traced the rim of her wineglass, and she tilted her head in wonderment.

"Because what you're doing is important. You wanted to help. I like to help. I'm a lucky man. I can do what I want with my time. No worries about income. It's not a huge sacrifice really. I'll get one of my techs to work with your trainer. Free publicity for her, since she's volunteering her time at a discount to you. Call it paying things forward."

Her eyes lifted in surprise. "That's really kind of you. Thank you."

A crooked smile spread across his face. "I'm not doing it just to be kind."

"Then why are you?" She leaned into him, desire flashing in her eyes.

"It's a good thing to do…" He angled closer, unable to resist. "And because I really, really want to get on your good side so you'll let me kiss you."

Three

Determined to put a hint of space between them even if she couldn't will herself to just walk away, Natalie flattened a hand to his chest.

The hard, muscled wall of his chest.

Gulp.

"I'm complimented you want to kiss me, but that's not included in the bed-and-breakfast package."

He chuckled, the rumble of his laugh vibrating against her hand. "That's the nicest put-down I've ever received."

Gaining strength, she let out her own low laugh, arching her eyebrows, taking him in, trying to focus on the crisp September air instead of his musky scent. Or the way the shadows played up his bad-boy mystique. "I imagine you don't often get told no."

"Another compliment. For someone who is rejecting me, you're doing it very nicely." Voice still throaty, he swallowed, eyes fixed on hers.

"So you hear me saying no to your advance?"

He shook his head, the line of his lips growing taut. Sincere. "I hear you. *No* is *no*. I just want you to remember I still feel the same way. I want to kiss you. Very much. And if you decide you want to act on this attraction, I'm not going anywhere anytime soon."

The courtyard dimmed ever so slightly. The moody stars seemed brighter as the lights from the B and B went out one by one. People were making their way to bed. She ought to be moving in that direction, too. Away from Max. Away from the way his aqua stare sent her reeling.

"You assume the attraction is mutual." A lame defense. She knew it as soon as the words flicked from her tongue into the night air.

He stayed quiet and held her gaze.

She sighed and rolled her eyes. "Fine. Attraction exists. But I think it's fair to say people don't act every time they're attracted to someone." She looked past him, toward the street. A neighbor walking a border collie shuffled by in a half daze. The sound of gravel shifting beneath paws and feet gave her something else to focus on besides the tempting muscled man in front of her.

"Touché."

"You're conceding?" Narrowing her eyes, she tucked a few strands of hair behind ear, unconvinced.

Max passed the now-empty beer bottle from hand to hand, the green glass glinting. "Not giving in. Just noting your point, since you noted mine. We are attracted to each other. I consider that a huge win. I'm a patient man, especially when the stakes are important." He leaned forward, a devilish twinkle in his eyes. "Very important."

"A kiss? Really?" She'd never met a man patient for a kiss.

He leaned close, so close his breath caressed her face. "Yes, really. What I believe is going to be a *really* amazing kiss."

He smiled at her, collecting his empty bottle and her glass as he stood. His absence allowed for the light breeze to brush her exposed skin, leaving her aware of just how close they'd been sitting. How easy it would have been to act on any of her feelings and temptations. How she simply could not allow herself to do that.

As if she needed another reminder. Watching him walk back to the B and B, Natalie swallowed hard.

Just a boarder. Maybe if she repeated that enough times, it'd be true. Glancing up at the muted stars, Natalie realized it would be quite some time before she would find sleep.

Next to the kitchen, the craft room was Natalie's favorite place to spend time creating—everything from her dresses to accessories she sold in The Courtyard. The little artisanal mall was a big hit in town, and a nice source of extra income for her stretched budget.

She knew she was lucky to have a creative outlet that blended with her life as a single mom. In a house drenched in color riffs of reds and yellows—remnants, in some ways, of a Texas sunset—the craft room boasted a lighter, airy setting. The light sea-foam-green wall stood in contrast to the other cream walls. Tufts of tulle, lace and silky fabrics huddled in the corner, sparking whimsy into Natalie's life.

She ruffled through the half-finished sketches of bridal dresses on the glass desk rimmed with gold, nearly knocking over the arrangement of blue hydrangeas—her favorite.

The room itself, such a stark contrast to the rest of her house, made her feel like she'd stepped into a fairy-tale land. A place outside the reality of her existence. A place where she channeled the grief of losing her husband into more productive, selfless endeavors.

Like running a small, custom-wedding-gown business. Sewing was threaded throughout her entire life for as far back as Natalie could remember. Great-grandmother Elisa had taught her to crochet, and after that Natalie found the act of creation comforting. She'd soon transitioned into sewing, sketching and eventually designing her own clothes.

Natalie had always found art in these moments of baking and sewing. These weren't merely goods to be sold, but pieces of her soul she sent out into the world.

Turning away from the desk after consulting the sketch, she tried not to think of the man staying in the room above. Focus on the here and now. In a slight state of disarray, she noted the piles of airy fabric in her three sewing machines—evidence of her works in progress. More than just her work, it was her creative outlet. A piece of the world just for her.

In the very back corner behind the white couch accented with gold pillows, where her two friends were sipping mimosas, she smiled at the completed gown—a wispy lacy dress with a sweetheart neckline. Perfect for a boho bride. Their figures formed a silhouette against the drawn blind to keep prying eyes out. No one needed to see the masterpiece until after it was complete and the bride made her debut.

Even with the blinds drawn shut, an expansive skylight allowed golden September light to wash over the room, adding to the otherworldly airiness.

Sketch in hand, Natalie made her way to the white couch where Emily Knox sat, green eyes rolling back as she bit into one of the apple turnovers. She swallowed and dabbed her pink lips with a napkin, a smile forming on her whole face. "You have outdone yourself this time, Natalie." Emily placed the turnover back down on the glass-and-gold coffee table, her nimble, long fingers finding the champagne flute.

Natalie couldn't help thinking about the drink with Max, how easy it had been to talk to him, to lean into his touch. How quickly he'd filled her home, her thoughts, her life.

Emily took a sip of the mimosa and then raised her glass to Natalie, appreciation radiating from her eyes and her *yum*. After she set the glass down on the table, Emily carefully arranged the knickknacks and uneaten pastries, pulled out her camera and snapped a picture. She fluffed her honey-brown hair, content to review her image. Emily saw photographically, and her ranch-based home provided a continual canvas of inspiration.

"Please. It's nothing." Natalie shoved her left hand into her pocket, searching for her misplaced measuring tape.

"No, honey, this is delightful," Brandee Lawless offered, staring at her reflection in the ornate mirror. Her dress wasn't quite finished.

A pit of guilt welled in Natalie's stomach as she examined the state of Brandee's dress. She was a mashup of the girl next door and a woman who would fight for her ranch and dreams with every fiber of her body.

Brandee was set to marry Shane Delgado, a rancher and millionaire real-estate developer.

The wedding was approaching, and Brandee's dress was more of a suggestion at this point. Classic lines that felt just right for Brandee—and that was about as far as Natalie had this dress figured out. Silk skimmed over a more structured underdress, and while Natalie imagined lace integrated into the design, the exact positioning was still a work in progress.

Brandee licked a hint of cinnamon from the corner of her mouth. "I'm praying Max St. Cloud can find the person responsible for these cyberattacks. It's just…deplorable what this person is trying to do to the people of this town."

Emily nodded, her normally sunny features darkening. "So much hatred in one person. It must be personal, which is scary because if so, the person could be close." Her voice grew taut, as if the words had to climb over a lump in her vocal cords. "But to try to destroy my marriage. How can a person have a vendetta against so many of us?"

The cyberattacker had sent photos to Emily trying to make her think her husband, Tom, was cheating on her with Natalie. Someone had taken photos of Tom helping Natalie and her children, photos so strategically taken one could almost believe he had a second family. Tom had just been trying to help, had been suffering from a hefty case of survivor's guilt over her husband's death. Life had been hard on all of them.

Thank goodness the Knox marriage had survived and was stronger than ever.

Now Emily and Natalie were even friends. Truth was stronger than hate.

Natalie strategically hugged Brandee, careful not to

press any of the loose pins into her. "Let's not allow that awful person to steal anything more from us by taking our joy. We can't stop him or her—not yet anyway—but we don't have to invite that negativity into our lives. There are so many reasons to rejoice."

Brandee nodded. "Did you hear? Nick and Harper's latest ultrasound showed the twins are both boys. It seems like the population is exploding in our little town."

Emily snorted on a laugh. "Isn't that the truth? It'll be your turn, Brandee, soon enough. We need to keep that joy in mind."

"You're right." Brandee smiled widely. "Nothing should taint every *moment* leading up to my wedding." She twirled around on the pedestal, recalling a lithe ballerina. Even in the half-finished dress, she was a swirl of bridal beauty.

Shoving off the couch, camera slung around her neck and mimosa in hand, Emily strode over to them. "Mimosas and friendship and photos. To weddings. And gorgeous gowns."

"I'm sorry the gown isn't complete." Wringing her hands, Natalie stared at the heap of fabric, beads and lace. At all the yet-to-be-realized potential.

"This is a custom job. I understand that, love that and adore the idea of photos of the gown in progress, fittings and changes." Brandee shrugged, another smile lighting up her face, brightening her eyes. "It's a metaphor for life. The joy and process doesn't stop on the wedding day."

The work.

Natalie blinked back tears. Damn it, she usually didn't let her armor crack this way.

Emily glided forward and wrapped her in a gentle hug. "Oh, God, Nat, I'm sorry."

Natalie willed in one steadying breath after another. Comfort almost made it tougher, but she practically shoved the tears back into her body. Another steadying breath, and she patted her way free of the hug. "Please, don't. It's been a year. I'm moving forward with my life. I'm beginning to remember the happy times that deserve to be celebrated."

Her attraction to Max had been a mixture of relief, in that it assured her she was moving forward, and wariness, because now she needed to figure out if she was ready.

Reaching out to her friend, Brandee gave Natalie's hand an encouraging squeeze. "You're incredible."

Natalie choked on a laugh and sniffled back the last hint of tears. "I wish. But thank you. Making these dresses brings me happiness." She didn't need a man—didn't need Max—because she was happy and fulfilled with the life she'd built.

"And about this moving forward... Would it have something to do with Max St. Cloud staying here?" Shifting her weight from foot to foot, Brandee exchanged a glance with Emily, who offered her a mimosa.

Natalie made notes in her sketchbook, not that she needed to, but it was easier than meeting their eyes.

"Why would you say that? He's just a boarder, staying here while helping the town." Natalie worked to keep the heat from rising to her cheeks.

Brandee snorted halfway through a sip of her mimosa. "Seriously? I saw you two out front playing with the kids and when you walked past each other in the hall on our way in here. The two of you all but launch electric static snapping through the air when you're in the same room." She turned to Emily. "Am I wrong?"

Emily refilled her crystal flute. "Just the looks you two exchange damn near singe my hair."

Natalie conceded the obvious, making her way to the sewing machine. "He's an attractive man, Emily." Arranging the material, she began to work, hoping the sound of the machine would disrupt this conversation.

"And you're an attractive woman." She swept both hands through the air to form Natalie's shape.

Clutching satin, Natalie sagged back from her sewing machine. "I'm a tired, overworked mom."

"Hmm…" Brandee clapped her hands together. "Maybe you need a spa day."

Natalie's spine stiffened defensively. "I'm not going to launch some Cinderella-vamp makeover to snag a man."

Tut-tutting, Brandee shook her head. "No argument. I'm going to schedule it for next week. This is for you. Just for you. You deserve it."

Emily smiled knowingly. "And in case you haven't noticed, you already snagged his attention."

Natalie shot to her feet. "I'm going to get us more pastries and something to drink without alcohol."

With quick steps, she made her way to the kitchen, popped open the largest cabinet and extracted an ornate crystal pitcher—her great-grandmother's. Absently, she tossed the already-sliced lemons from the fridge into the pitcher, filled the bulk of the container with ice cubes and added water. As the impact of water caused the ice-cube cluster to melt and disperse, she heard a steady, almost undetectable sound.

The pitter patter of a slight drip. The sink was leaking ever so slightly. Another thing to fix—after she finished this gown session, of course.

As Natalie began to make her way back to the craft room, the scene from outside the oversize window arrested her gaze.

Max.

But not just Max. He sat at the pink-and-white Little Tikes picnic table across from Lexie. Her chatterbox daughter was serving him imaginary tea, and had just extended a feather boa to Max, who good-naturedly rested the bright purple boa on his shoulders.

As Natalie clutched the water pitcher, she swallowed.

Trouble.

Maybe that spa day wasn't what she needed. Maybe instead she needed the frumpiest burlap sack and chastity belt money could buy.

For the past three days, Max had been holed up at the Texas Cattleman's Club. The beginnings of investigations were always the same. A blur of faces, words, files. For Max, the initial phase of the investigation was at once the most frustrating and most fascinating.

All the contingent possibilities took shape before him—the various paths seemed to reveal themselves as he met with the key town players.

Max had to continue to watch how the men postured, wait for nuggets of information to be dispensed. Analyze. Repeat several more times until something like a lead developed.

After a long Wednesday of scanning through the files of the Texas Cattleman's Club, his eyes demanded some rest, craved home.

He corrected himself. He craved his makeshift bed in his transitory space—the theme of his life. Home was never locatable, and this dusty town was not home, either.

Max barely registered the drive back to the Cimarron Rose. Flashes of leaves turning from bright green to yellow and the lack of cars on the road both gave Max a feeling of timelessness. Ironic, considering everything except for this car ride had turned his world on its head. Max's time at the bed-and-breakfast had been a surprise, to say the least. Not just because of a certain auburn-haired bombshell with sweet, sad eyes that melted his soul. But he'd been surprised how drawn he was to two of the cutest rapscallions on the planet as they rode their tricycles and played ball. Max usually avoided interactions with children, but now it seemed he was living under the same roof as two of them. He should be irritated. Or avoiding them.

Not having freaking tea parties, for God's sake. He laughed to himself, recalling the way Lexie had sidled up to him, her invitation to have a cup of tea was the most earnest request he'd ever heard.

Just like that, two-year-old Lexie—who had inherited her mother's eyes—had him, a big, bad billionaire, eating out of her hand in no time. He'd even worn a boa at her tea party, much to Lexie's delight.

It seemed, though, that four-year-old Colby would be a tougher nut to crack. Could a kid that age be brooding? This one was. How much was the autism and how much was the boy's personality? Max wasn't sure, but he definitely had felt an instant kinship with the boy, who appeared to be a tech geek in the making with his video games and his aptitude at the computer.

But the kinship went deeper. Though their experiences were inherently different, Max knew what it was like to always be positioned on the outside of "normal" routines. As he made his way to the door, he found himself wondering what he could do for Colby. He would figure something out, a way to connect with the kid.

Now, though, he was having a harder time processing his reaction to Natalie, and the instant twinge of arousal that kicked through him every time she entered the room. Hell, even when she was bent over her sewing machine working on a new design for a wedding dress. So Max had decided to give himself a breather by spending some time working on the case these past three days.

But for now, there was no avoiding the need to go back to his room to compile his latest round of interviews and some data he'd gleaned from the Texas Cattleman's Club's files.

As he pulled into the parking lot, he noted the stillness of the air, the lack of guests. So many of the guests who had been there over the weekend had checked out, leaving him largely alone in this place.

As he was turning the doorknob, a scream assaulted his ears. Heart hammering, ratcheting into overtime, he dropped his things at the front door, his body posed to launch in the direction of the distress.

Worry coiled around bones, and an unsettling image of Natalie cornered in the kitchen seemed to permeate every nook and cranny of his mind.

But then another sound.

A squeal of wicked laughter. And another. Suddenly, the bed-and-breakfast was filled with the sound of hysterical laughter, emanating from multiple people. Heart steadying and curiosity rising, he followed the sounds.

His inner investigator egged him on.

The squeals and peals of laughter intensified as he neared the bright kitchen.

Nothing could have prepared Max for the sight in the kitchen. Water pooled everywhere on the tile, and more water continued to bubble from underneath the sink, creating a kind of indoor, shallow water park. Lexie theatrically splashed around, combining water stomping with something that looked like ballet. Her laughter and antics even incited the ever-reserved Colby to motion. Miss Molly ran circles around them, barking and wagging her tail in a golden fan.

Natalie's rich laughter warmed the kitchen, made the disaster seem less like a crisis and more whimsical. Water soaked her shirt and her loose hair dripped, clinging to her.

Those radiant green eyes were calm—she was just as carefree as she'd been under the tree several nights ago.

Stunning.

In every situation—flour dusted, bathed in moonlight, drenched in water—Max felt drawn to her.

Intruding felt wrong. He might have stayed at the threshold for ages if not for the thrum of voices behind him.

Glancing over his shoulder, he saw Tom and Emily Knox approach, hands intertwined.

"Oh, uh…hello," Max said with a surprising semblance of manners, since right now he really wanted them to go away.

"Hello, Max," Emily cooed with half a laugh. "We're picking up Nat's kids and bringing them to our ranch. They are staying with us while she gets all this—" she pointed to the water spewing "—under control."

"That's a real nice gesture. It's heartwarming to know that Natalie has such good people looking out for her. Especially in light of recent events going on around this town."

Emily smoothed back Lexie's hair. "We're friends, happy to help however we can."

"So, Max," Tom said with a knowing grin, "you're playing Sir Galahad with the sink as well as the computers? I would have expected you to be over at the Cattleman's Club."

Emily elbowed her husband in the side before turning to Natalie. "Are the kids ready to go?"

"Practically, other than being soggy—"

Emily waved away Natalie's worry. "We have blankets in the car for the seats. It's a beautiful day for opening the sunroof to dry everyone off. No need to waste time or it'll get too close to their bedtime. Wouldn't want to upset their routine."

"If you're sure…" Natalie nibbled her bottom lip before turning to her kids. "You are both going to behave for Miss Emily and Mr. Tom, aren't you?"

"Yes, Mommy." Lexie bobbed her head. "They have cows!" Lexie's eyes widened as she spoke. Colby simply nodded, then picked at his shirt.

"That sounds fun, sweetie. Now, go get your bags with Miss Emily. They're by the front door away from all this chaos." Natalie's children sloshed through the water.

Tom's brow furrowed as he looked at the mess. "Do you need me to stay and help with the sink and water?"

"You're taking my children. That's honestly the best way to help me because I can focus on clearing up this mess."

Max placed a hand on her shoulder. "Tom, I've got this. Thanks, though."

The whole lot of them made their way to the front

door. Tom scooped up the overnight bags. Lexie wrapped her mother in a hard hug, and Colby even leaned into her, shoulder-to-shoulder, before the two children walked out the door with the Knoxes.

Max swallowed hard and scratched the back of his neck, doing his damnedest to look anywhere but at her wet T-shirt. "You've got quite a mess here."

"Thank goodness I'd already made breakfast pastries for the week. We'll all need to eat breakfast picnic-style." She sagged into a chair with a sigh, a wrench in her hand, and glanced out the window. "I'm praying it won't rain."

He pulled a chair to sit close to her, their knees almost touching. "Temperatures are cool in the morning. It will be perfect. You handle everything with ease."

Max stretched his arms wide, and the buttons on his green polo shirt pulled slightly. He'd opted for comfort today. One of his tactics as an investigator was to come across as unassuming—less like a suit. Which was why he'd worn a polo, cargo shorts and boat shoes today. Respectable without any hint of superiority. People seemed more candid with him that way.

"Ease? I don't think so. I'm holding on by a thread, one day at a time." Her eyes seemed to examine something he couldn't.

"I really do want to help."

She shook her auburn hair and sighed. "You're not paying for my plumber."

"I'm insulted you would think I can't handle a simple plumbing fix." He put his hand on his chest for added drama.

"I really don't expect you to fix my sink."

He shoved himself to his feet in a smooth sweep. "Consider it in the realm of driving along, seeing someone on the side of the road with a flat tire in need of help. It's minimal time and the right thing to do."

Standing as well, she eyed him skeptically. "Are you going to wreck my plumbing?"

He laughed. "If I do, then you can let me pay for it. Now, step aside and don't challenge my manhood, woman."

Pushing the toolbox closer to the sink, he squatted down to investigate what was going on. The leak wasn't too bad—it had just expelled a lot of water.

He noted the tools he needed, and she passed them to him. Natalie sat next to him, eyes watching…learning. With every pass of a tool, their fingers would brush. Slightly. Enough, though, to continuously remind him of how damn attractive she was. Of the mutual draw tugging at both of them relentlessly.

Silence had overtaken them. Max cleared his throat, craving the soothing sound of her voice. "No critiques or advice?"

"Nope. You look like you've got it under control." She laughed, silky hands touching his forearm.

"Hmm…" He emerged from under the sink to stare at her, gesturing for her to take a look.

"What does that mean?" Natalie drew closer, looking at the state of her kitchen sink, inspecting his work but not commenting.

"You're a strong-willed woman. I expected your, um, feedback."

"And risk dinging your manhood when you're fixing my sink for free? I'm quite content to pass wrenches on this." She leaned back on her heels, coy and sexy as hell.

"You look hot doing it, by the way." The words tumbled out. But at least he was being honest. Wrench in hand, he went back under the sink to make the final adjustments, drying things off before he sealed up a couple of joints with plumber's tape.

"I thought you weren't going to hit on me anymore. That any further move was up to me."

"I said I wouldn't kiss you. I didn't say I wouldn't try to make you want to kiss me."

Still, the word *kiss* hung in the air, until he could imagine caressing her ear with his mouth as much as his voice. Someday. Yes, definitely someday.

She crossed her arms over her damp chest, over her breasts pebbling from cold—or desire? "And that's why you're fixing my sink?"

He shrugged, biting off another piece of tape with his teeth. "It's a way to spend time with you." Ah, there. Perfect. The sink cabinet was bone-dry, as were the pipes. "And I'm not fixing your sink. It's officially done."

"And is that why you had a tea party with my daughter? To soften me up? Because I want you to know I absolutely draw the line at you using my children to get to me."

He pushed out from under the sink, and holy hell, they were close. So damn close. He tucked a hand behind her neck and looked her directly in the eyes. "I would never, never use a child to manipulate any situation. That's wrong on more levels than I can count. Believe that."

Her eyes searched his for so long he was tempted to talk, encourage her to speak, but God, the chance to touch her, to look into those deep green eyes of hers was…just damn good. So he held on to the moment that was intimate in a way he couldn't remember feeling before with a woman.

Then she nodded slowly. "Okay."

His throat was raw, his thoughts sluggish. "Okay what?"

"I believe you." She touched his temple with the softest fingers, wiping away droplets of water. "Now that we've cleared that up, I think it's time you kissed me."

Four

Natalie had stunned herself with that proposition.

But she wasn't sorry.

And she wouldn't call the words back.

She couldn't deny the truth to herself or to Max. She wanted him to kiss her. She burned to feel the press of his lips against hers. Her body hungered for a man's touch after so long. After all this time alone, however much she yearned for contact, she hadn't acted. She'd resisted. Until now.

The draw to Max St. Cloud couldn't be denied.

Would he question her?

She barely had time to form that thought before he angled toward her. He slid his hand behind her neck, his broad palm cupping the nape of her neck. His fingers thrust up into her wet hair and she felt the tingle all the way to her roots. Her lips parted and…yes.

Max kissed her. Oh, how he kissed her. His mouth

slanted over hers with a skim, then another as he settled into a fit that only belonged to two specific people. A kiss unique just to them.

His tongue traced along her lips slowly, deliciously. And she was surprised at his careful finesse. He was such an immense and bold personality, she'd expected a more…audacious, forceful even, approach. Yet he took his time. Her fingernails dug into his chest and she wriggled closer, leaning into him.

A rumble of approval vibrated in his chest against her touch and she slid her arms around his neck.

As he leaned back against the cabinet, he pulled her across his lap. She held tighter to him, twisting her body to press her chest to his, her legs draped to the side. Max's mouth returned to hers with a soul-drugging allure that seeped into her senses.

Their wet clothes sealed to each other, the heat of him radiating into her already-combusting body.

The attraction was every bit as strong as she'd thought, dreamed, even feared a little. Because she was a mature woman who knew her wants and desires. This level of chemistry was rare.

Incredible.

If one kiss could set her on fire so intensely, what more would she find in bed with him? And, damn, how fast her mind had skated to there, to images of them naked together, moving and pleasuring each other.

Already she could tell from the brush of his hands and his attention to detail in noting what she liked—yes, that pause to kiss along the tender flesh of her neck— that there was a generosity that would bode well in bed.

He seemed to hear and react to her every hitch of breath, just as she went on alert for clues from him. How when she stroked along the edge of his ears he inhaled deeply, a tug on his earlobe… Yeah, he liked that. Although her wriggle in his lap launched an all-out groan from him. And a throb. A hard, steely throb that made it abundantly clear how much he wanted her.

Pulling away from the warmth of his kiss, she rested her hands on his hard chest for balance. The steady rise and fall of intrigued breathing. The warmth of his eyes searching hers.

Desire pulsed through her, enlivening her joints, her bones. She didn't even seem to register the way her waterlogged clothes clung and hung off her body. Barely noticed how wet his polo shirt had become from the press of her body.

What she did notice was the flame in his eyes, the palpable hunger resting on his lips.

She took a steadying breath, attempting as much as possible to collect herself.

Moments of silence ticked by as they stared deep into each other's eyes. She broke the stare, willing her tongue to form words as butterflies rose in her stomach. "Aren't you going to ask me why I did that?"

"Uh-uh." He tugged lightly on a damp lock of her hair, then traced down the length of the strand.

"Why not?" She couldn't resist leaning her cheek into the cradle of his palm.

"I'm just glad you did." His eyes skimmed over her face, as if he was learning and taking in every aspect of her.

Her face. Not her body. And somehow that felt even more intimate.

"Max, this is complicated. Maybe we need to talk—"

"Who says everything has to be analyzed or discussed? This attraction between us just is."

"I don't want you to think it's an invitation to—"

"Shhh. I don't." He pressed a finger to her mouth. "Quit the overthinking. Stop with the overanalyzing. And yes, I understand. A kiss isn't an automatic invitation to sex."

"I know that."

"I wanted you to understand I know that, as well."

She nibbled her bottom lip, aware of the press of her bottom against his thighs even as she remained with her arms looped around his neck in a fit far too comfortable for her peace of mind. "We're talking a lot, considering you said we aren't going to discuss this."

He rested his forehead against hers, their noses close, their breaths filling the thin space between them. "Then let's make out."

"Make out?" Just kiss? Maybe even heavy petting? But no sex? It sounded…appealing and frustrating all at once. She'd never expected to be single and dating at this stage in her life.

"Yeah, make out… Well, not now, exactly, since we're soaking wet." He plucked at her shirt lightly with a familiarity that teased without going too far. "The kids are gone for the evening. Let's put on some dry clothes. I'll take you out to eat…then we'll go park somewhere."

The plan smoked through her mind and curled in her chest with an appealing swish. Still, she couldn't afford to be impulsive. She needed for things to be clear between them. "That sounds like a date."

"It sure does." Clasping her waist, he lifted her and stood in a smooth move. He set her on her feet and kissed her nose. "Wear a dress. I want to pamper you… and see your legs."

Without another word, he sauntered out of the kitchen, his soaked jeans riding low on those narrow hips and drawing her eyes to his fine ass.

Damn. He was so arrogant and sexy…and yes, irresistible.

For the first time since high school, she was going on a date.

Max slipped out of the kitchen, knowing that if he stayed in there to make this next phone call, Natalie would protest and reject his assistance. The water-filled kitchen needed to be cleaned up, and after a quick search on his phone, he had identified a local cleaning service.

"I'm going to check on a lead really quickly, but you should head upstairs and change into something dry," he called from the threshold, gesturing to his cell.

She nodded. "I do feel a little like a drowned rat." Glancing around the floor, she let out an audible sigh. A weary sigh.

All the more reason to make this call.

Making the arrangements to have the kitchen dried and mopped didn't take too much time. Natalie worked so hard—mothering her children, baking, running a B and B and designing wedding dresses—that he wanted to make just one aspect of her life easier.

While he was on the phone, he watched Natalie swish upstairs to get changed.

For their date.

Which he also needed to get ready for. He headed upstairs, phone in hand—multitasking like a pro. A lot had to be accomplished in a short amount of time.

Next on the agenda: dinner reservations at a five-star steak house.

Max shucked off his drenched clothes and ran his hands through his thick brown hair. Going on this date with Natalie had his heart pounding. He grabbed his favorite sports coat—the one he'd bought when his company made it in the industry. The tie he chose reminded him of his persistence, loyalty and dedication. All things he needed tonight.

After getting dressed, he knocked on her door. She stepped out, a radiant whirl in a silky lavender dress, her hair in loose flowing curls. A simple silver chain with a solitary pearl adorned her neck. But most beautiful of all, her chin tipped with confidence that flamed the fire inside him.

Breath caught in his chest, like warm molasses in his windpipe. All of him was warm. Because of her.

Damn. He was in a helluva lot of trouble. "Shall we?" He extended his arm, eager to have her fingers on him any way he could.

With more of that confidence, she met his gaze with sure bright eyes and slipped her hand on his arm. "We shall. Where are we going?"

A low laugh rumbled deep in his chest. "It's a surprise."

Brows raised, she looked at him sidelong, an easy smile tugging on her cheeks. Her smile outshone any makeup or jewelry.

Seeing her happy… Yeah, he could get off on that all night long.

They walked down the stairs to the SUV. The drive wasn't long, not nearly long enough for him to get his fill of looking at her slim legs. But then he wasn't sure how long would be enough soaking in the appeal of her.

About twenty minutes later, they reached their destination—the Society, a five-star steak house Chels had raved about. He trusted his friend's taste would not steer him wrong tonight in his quest to impress Natalie.

He eyed her across the table, the low lighting playing

with hints of gold in her auburn hair. Her body swayed ever so slightly to the riffs of live Spanish guitar as they talked, reminding him of the way she'd moved in his arms during that kiss that had been spontaneous combustion. She had a dancer's grace, a musician's ear for the rise and fall of the notes. It might not be the right time to make a move for sex, but dancing? Yes, he decided he would dance with her, feel her body against his before long.

Meanwhile, easy conversation flowed, about favorite books, movies, foods, recreation… He couldn't get to know enough about her. He certainly wouldn't have expected she was into hiking. He envisioned dozens of places around the globe he would like to show her… with her kids? Hell, sure, why not? He could imagine her and the kids in a private jet, the dog, too, and maybe the trainer as sitter when he and Natalie wanted time alone—

Holy hell.

The thought caught him up short. Who the hell was he to think of himself in some kind of parental authoritative role? He was far from qualified for that job. And he needed to tread carefully when it came to her children, keep things light, not let them get too attached to him.

Or him to them.

This was about Natalie. And him. And exploring the attraction while he was in town. It couldn't be more, for either of their sakes.

Still, even watching her eat was a total turn-on. She seemed relaxed and was enjoying herself as she finished off her caprese salad with Texas goat cheese. And wine. He already knew she enjoyed her wine…

He added hiking through a French vineyard to his list of possible dates. With a wine-tasting dinner after...

Max found himself wondering when the last time she'd been out like this had been. Or out, period. Natalie seemed to give everyone around her comforts, but didn't seem to allow herself to indulge.

And how he wanted to indulge and spoil her.

The table was small, intimate...and probably too tiny to properly house the amount of food they'd ordered. That didn't matter, though. They were together and that had been the goal.

He held her hand, felt the surge of her pulse increase at his touch. A flush spread over her skin, perceptible even in the dim light of the restaurant. Her eyes moved past him, skimming over the decor. The place, to his eye, looked like a living sunset. Stately paintings of the open Texas terrain hung on the walls, candlelight cast orange hues in the space—the feeling of twilight. Like Natalie.

Her slender fingers twined with his, calling his attention fully back to her. To the present. She raised her brows at him, and the strap of her silky lavender dress slid just off her shoulder as she speared a tomato with her fork.

The image sent him reeling. In the flickering light, he felt like he really saw her. Natalie the caretaker, the tenacious spirit. Her soft hair pooled on her shoulders, the wildness of her curls tamed by a vintage hair comb pushing her hair from her face, revealing her slender features.

Normally he charged ahead and ordered for his date, but tonight he'd found himself settling back, daring her to order for them, wanting to hear what she would pick. She chose filet mignon topped with lemon-butter sauce, steamed asparagus and portobello mushrooms. In between all his questions, she'd eaten with relish— she wasn't one of those three-bites-and-leave-the-rest kind of people.

She savored the meal and, God, he found that sensual relish appealing. When she set down her fork with a satisfied sigh, arousal sent a bolt of heat surging, making him hard with desire.

He tempted fate—and his tenuous hold on his control—and took her hand firmly in his. "I've enjoyed this."

She laughed, shaking her head but not pulling her hand away. "Hearing about my favorite color and top ten movie picks? Surely you have more exciting things going on in your fast-paced life. I've researched you, too, you know."

Plates were cleared to make way for dessert. He lost track of the foods they shared and tasted, well, except for the dessert. That couldn't be forgotten.

Huckleberry sorbet and chocolate ganache.

Still holding her hand, he cut into the dessert and wanted to feed her a bite. Someday. In bed. Together. Yes.

For now, he watched her eat. She smiled deeply, eyes fluttering shut as she tasted the flavors.

A crescendo from the live Spanish guitar cut the silence between them. Natalie cleared her throat, her eyes flickering with a hint of self-consciousness. "I've really indulged tonight. Thank you. This dinner has been lovely, truly." She eased her hand from his and sipped her wine. "But I can't help wondering. Why are we out together? I didn't mean to give you the wrong impression with that impulsive kiss. I think one look at me would make it clear I'm not a fling sort of person."

"We're here because I like you and I admire your tenacity." And yes, he wanted to work his way into her bed.

A fling? Maybe. But not a one-night stand. One night wouldn't come close to quenching the fire he felt for her. And he could swear he saw that same fire in her eyes.

"Tenacity?" She twirled the stem of the crystal glass between her slim fingers, her nails were trimmed short and glistening with clear polish. "How do you know so much about me from such a short time?"

"I'm an observant man. I recognize a survivor when I see one." No matter how comfortable he'd made himself, he'd always carry the memories of foster care with him. He'd always recognize the souls that had been tried by fire. For a fraction of a second, a collage of memories pushed themselves on him—the ammonia-cleaner smell of the group home, the nights spent in an alleyway instead of a bed.

"*Recognize?* That's an interesting word choice." She leaned forward, homing in on the one word that betrayed so much about his life. The life he never spoke of.

He was losing control of the conversation. Time to steer it back to her. "Tell me about your parents."

"They've retired in Arizona." Her face closed off, her smile not reaching her eyes any longer. "I was an only child and had an easy, lucky traditional childhood. They love me."

The normal sparkle in her tone was absent, nothing at all like the glimmer when she talked about her children. There was more to this story. Much more. "And...?"

"That's it." She waved away his question.

"There's always more to the story."

Chewing slowly, she set aside her fork, then swallowed and dabbed at her mouth with her napkin. Weighing her answer? "My parents didn't approve of me marrying Jeremy. They didn't want me moving away. They didn't like how much I was on my own with the children."

"That's the military lifestyle."

Shadows shifted through her green eyes, like lush grassy earth being darkened by clouds covering the sunshine. "They thought he should have served his country for his enlistment commitment and then gotten out."

He clasped her hand in his, squeezing lightly and grazing up to her elbow and down again. "I'm sorry they couldn't have been more supportive of your choices."

"Me, too." She watched the movement of his caress along her arm, but didn't stop him. "They wanted me to move to Arizona to be near them for help after Jeremy...died."

The heaviness of her tone gut-punched him.

"Why didn't you?" A bold question, but Max had never been one to mince words or avoid the uncomfortable aspects of life. He wanted to know, wanted to be there for her.

"They want to parent my children, not be grandparents." Her gaze rose swiftly and her throat moved, hard. "And I really can't bear to live my life hearing them say if we'd listened to them, he would still be alive," she said emphatically.

"That's... God, I'm sorry." The words weren't enough. He knew that. It was all he had for her, though.

She shook her head. "Thank you, but no need. The past is the past." She gripped his hand once, firmly, before letting go and leaning back. "So, survivor, tell me about your parents."

So she wasn't going to let his misplaced word go. He would share the streamlined version. Better than the detailed crap, for sure. "Parent. I never knew my father. My mother was a junkie and I went into the foster system young."

"Max, I'm so sorry. I feel...ungrateful for what I had." She looked down at her plate, her hair obscuring her features.

Nope. He wasn't letting her go down that path. His turn to shake his head. "Don't. This isn't about you. This is just my story of how I became me. My mother fought for custody, I'll give her that. But she didn't fight to get clean, so she eventually lost her parental rights. By then, I was too old to be a cute, chubby adoptable baby or toddler. And I was definitely too much of a delinquent pain in the ass to stay in with one foster family for any length of time." He kept a don't-give-a-damn grin on his face, but his voice felt rusty in the telling, given how few times—never, actually—he'd shared so many details from his past with anyone.

"So you went from foster home to foster home until you were eighteen?" She gripped his hand.

"I was in the LA foster system. It's full. I ended up in a group home, which made it easier for me to slip out and do my own thing."

"What was your own thing?"

He grinned. This was the part he didn't mind talking about. This was his moment of rising. The way he'd come into his own. "Computer hacking. Nothing big-time illegal." For the most part anyway. More like, well, boundary pushing. "I helped people out with cyber and home security, made some money, pulled myself up and out of my less-than-affluent circumstances."

"You're more than a survivor. You turned your journey into something amazing." She set aside her spoon, her dessert only half-eaten, and as if by habit, nudged the plate toward him.

In case he might want to finish the rest?

Had she done that with her husband? Max sure as hell didn't intend to ask and wasn't going to give her time to question the action. He simply dipped his spoon into the sorbet, his eyes on hers. That electric spark was pushing them together.

"Max?" she whispered, her voice husky. "We were talking about you building your business."

He swallowed, and shrugged dismissively. "So I made some money. I was lucky to have a brain for computers."

"That isn't what I meant." Her thumb stroked along his wrist as she studied him through narrowed eyes, her lashes long.

"What do you mean, then?" He clasped her hand in a firmer grip, stroking up to her elbow and then back over the tops of her fingers.

Her throat moved in a low swallow, her chest rising and falling a hint faster. "You've devoted your life to making other people feel safe. That's admirable."

He didn't want her to have any misconceptions about the kind of man he was. "You're overthinking things."

"Or else I'm observant, like you," she said firmly, meeting his gaze steadfastly. Unflinchingly.

Damn, she was amazing. And he wanted her more than… He couldn't remember when he'd been this hungry.

"Well, you can believe whatever you want if it gets me back to kissing you and closer to second base." He gave her his best Boy Scout smile—ironic really, since he'd never been anything close to a Boy Scout. "Are you ready to go drive around the city and find a scenic mesa perfect for parking?"

* * *

Before Natalie could gather her thoughts for a witty answer—and will her jittery nerves to settle—a clearing throat interrupted them.

Natalie glanced over her shoulder to find Sheriff Nathan Battle standing alongside Gabe Walsh, who also happened to have some hefty PI skills that proved helpful with the Royal Police Department on occasion.

"Hope you don't mind if I interrupt your dinner for a moment." The sheriff stood just behind her, his dark brown eyes narrowed, full of intent. The poster child of a man on a mission.

Not that Natalie found any of this surprising. Sheriff Battle, a kind man who'd poured his life into the community, always had a way of strengthening connections in seemingly strange settings. He was devoted to his community in a way that Natalie deeply appreciated, particularly in the wake of the recent cyberattacks by the maverick character.

"Evening, Max. Natalie." Nathan gave them both a curt nod as he approached the table, eyes resting on Max as hard lines formed in his brow. Worry.

Gabe's eyes showed the same concern, although he stayed silent and nodded in greeting.

Natalie noticed Nathan's wife, Amanda, a few tables away, talking on her cell phone, pen and pad in hand. Multitasking. It must be a trait they shared.

Max pushed back his chair and stood to shake hands with Nathan. "Hello, Sheriff. Gabe. What brings you two to our little table?"

Nathan began, "After we spoke yesterday, I had a thought about..."

The conversation launched into cybertech talk that soon turned into mostly a droning blend in Natalie's ears. Her thoughts fell far from the conversation at hand. Instead, she found herself openly surveying Max, and noticed the way the dim light illuminated his dark features. Could shadows really make a man hotter?

An awareness in her stomach—something like butterflies on steroids—answered an unequivocal yes.

Suddenly hungry again, she scooped into the dessert, letting the cooling sensation of the huckleberry sorbet ground her. The bite allowed her a pause—a second of reflection and distraction as she appreciated the fruit and chocolate flavors.

This had been a helluva night.

Natalie had known Max was charming. But he hadn't seemed real. But after tonight, the narrative offered to her... Well, resisting him seemed more difficult. The rawness and pain in his voice had taken him from being an untouchable sexy data analyst to a human.

What in the world was she going to do with their deep discussion? Did it change anything about her situation at home, her responsibilities...her past? And even on a somewhat lighter note, how did she feel about going "parking"?

"We should arrange for..." Max's voice called her back to the present.

She blinked as Nathan's warm brown eyes reflected excitement.

Max angled forward and planted his hand on the table as he became more invested in the case planning. His fingers brushed hers, so close were their hands on the tablecloth. Jolts of electricity spiked through her bloodstream as she thought about the possibility of parking with Max; carefree, romantic, sensual. The drumroll thought of his body touching hers, of his lips... Anticipation blossomed in her chest.

Scooping into the dessert again, Natalie became aware of another sensation rising in her chest. The unmistakable mark of apprehension twined with her previous desire to go for it. Throw caution to the wind if even for a brief time.

It had been a while since she was intimate with a man—well over a year now, given how long her husband had been deployed even before he died. That wasn't quite the total issue, though.

Conversation—deep conversation—had fallen away long before Jeremy had died. True, their marriage had been in trouble. Rocky times were to be expected. Silence had become the language they spoke. Increasingly withdrawn, Natalie had started to feel like she and her now-deceased husband had occupied different temporalities that never seemed to sync up.

Yet somehow tonight, she was reminded of what it was like to be in the same moment. To share. In her gut, Natalie knew the comparison of one date to years of comfortable routine in a marriage was not fair. Not even close.

But the act of exchanging stories tonight connected her to Max in a way that being physical couldn't. The interweaving of past tragedies left her heart raw, scarred from the weight of multiple losses.

And if she reached out again to touch him, would she be able to pull away? Or was it already too late just from that kiss, from being here tonight?

Because truth be told, she feared she might well have already set something in motion she didn't know how to stop.

Five

Clicking her seat belt into place, she threw a glance at Max as he started the engine of the SUV. The luxurious leather seat creaked as she shifted her weight. Loose curls fell into her face as the familiar feelings of nervousness and desire pulsed in her blood. "You were serious about going parking?"

No taming the rampant thudding in her chest.

As he caught her eye, a smile formed on his lips. A devilish one at that. "If that's what you want, we absolutely can. But you'll have to tell me where the good spots are."

He put the car in Reverse, his right arm went to her headrest so he could see as he backed out of the steak house parking lot. Musk and spice emanated from his sports jacket sleeve. A dizzying effect.

Looking shyly out her side window, she muttered, "How would I know? I'm new here."

"Good point." He winked, the SUV lurching into

motion as they exited the parking lot. Silence passed for a moment as he got onto the main road, heading away from the safety and certainty of Cimarron Rose. Of her carefully constructed life and fortress against feeling. He took them north, the lights on the road scattering, allowing the open Texas sky to be punctuated with flickering heavenly bodies.

Clearing his throat, he added, "I actually took that into consideration and came up with a different plan that didn't involve me asking my friend Chels where the great make-out spots are around here."

She folded her arms across her chest, intrigued as hell. "Oh, you did? And what is your plan, then?"

He shrugged, eyes glued to the road. "I thought you might like to go dancing."

Natalie's shock took the form of a head tilt. "Dancing?" She couldn't even remember the last time she'd cut a rug. Years. It had to have been years. Perhaps her wedding...

She silenced the thought. Brought herself back to the present moment. To movement in sync with this man.

Turning his face to her, he flashed a smile and raised an eyebrow. "Dancing can be every bit as...connecting as making out."

Her thoughts exactly. And didn't the thought cause a rush of heat through her despite the perfectly moderated temperature in his expensive car?

"You're really taking me dancing and not going to hit on me?" Based on the look in his eyes, Natalie didn't quite buy that.

He shook his head and threw on the turn signal. "No, unless you tell me you prefer not to dance."

She gripped his hard-muscled arm. "We can dance."

"Are you sure? Do you want to go back to your

place to make out…maybe get away from the crowd at a hotel? Because if you do, just say the word and I will make love to you well and long through the night. But I got the impression that wasn't something you're ready for." He reached to squeeze her hand. A seriousness seemed to wash over his body, and she sat up straighter. "And I want you to be ready."

Gulp.

Words jumbled in her throat as she attempted to formulate her next words. Her next sentence mattered. She needed to be as precise as possible. The pressure of having to know what she wanted made her ribs tight with tension and the weight of her decision.

Yes. She felt attracted to Max. His ease with words, compliments. That ready, lopsided smile that hinted at his mischievous side. And he was damn sexy with his tousled dark hair and bright, inquisitive eyes.

Losing Jeremy had left her raw. Giving herself away to Max would take time. Trust.

But dancing. She could manage that. Dancing could live in a box, be compartmentalized. "I believe dancing is the wise choice. Thank you."

He turned up the heat in the SUV. "Wise. Hmm… Okay, we'll be wise for tonight."

After a few more minutes on the road, Max navigated the SUV into a spot in Jackson's Honky-tonk. After he parked, Max opened her car door, offering a steadying hand as she stepped out into the graveled parking lot.

"This is not what I expected," she said, looking at the building. Even from the car, she could hear the sounds of country music—big guitar melodies and the echo of twangy voices.

A bitter September wind swept through the area,

sending a shiver down her spine, making her step closer to Max. He rubbed her shoulder.

Opening the heavy wood door to the honky-tonk, he whispered, "I'll be fighting off the cowboys who want to steal you away."

"You're such a talker." A laugh formed on her lips as she surveyed the room. Men in cowboy hats led women to the dance floor. Couples shared drinks, clinked beer bottles together.

Dim yellow lights hung suspended from the ceiling over the bar area. The lighting only seemed to deepen the color of the wood, making the place feel out of time, like a relic from decades ago.

"Is that a challenge?" He shucked off his sports coat and draped it on the back of a chair at an unoccupied high-top table. His lips thinned to a confident line.

"All right, then. I hope you are prepared for this." She pulled her heels off, becoming substantially shorter but growing in confidence.

They made their way to the dance floor. Bright spotlights illuminated the area. She leveled her gaze at him, remembering the times she and her college friends used to frequent a country bar, learning all the line dances and smiling at cowboys. Her roommate, Jessie, made them go week after week. She was a Georgia girl, through and through. Weekly visits had made Jessie feel more at home during that scary time of transition. Natalie picked up the steps to the various dances quickly, found a way to lose herself in the music and movement.

This was her turf.

A square dancing song began and the crowd let out a variety of emphatic whoops. Max and Natalie began as partners, but soon the movement of the dance swept them from each other.

No matter which partner she found herself with, her eyes found Max's. Even from across the room, the stare electrified her.

Eventually, the song ended and he closed the distance between them. Suddenly, she took in how tall he was, noticed how the other women dressed in cowboy boots eyed him. He didn't pay them any mind.

His steady gaze seemed to see her—only her. As if they were alone in this space.

The Texas two-step began, and his arm instinctively went to the small of her back. Taking his hand in hers, they swayed together. Bodies melting into one another.

For four more songs, they stayed like that.

A country ballad replaced the more active tunes. Sweat had pooled on her brow and his. The lights dimmed, became cooler. Natalie's hips swished in time to the slow music. Max's agility surprised her, thrilled her. She pressed closer to his chest, looked up at him.

His lips were so close to hers now. They tasted the same breath.

Max's hand tangled in her hair. He lowered his mouth to hers. A kiss unfolded, exploded her sense of control.

What had started as a gentle kiss soon deepened to pure passion. Electricity still surged and hummed beneath her skin.

Her tongue explored his mouth, drawing them somehow closer together. All sounds seemed to fade.

Nothing else existed.

Except for a faint ringing. A literal vibration.

Her imagination? She felt disoriented at the sensation, distracted by the taste of him.

Slowly, the sound registered. Her phone was in Max's pocket. Pulling away, she said breathily, "I need to take that. My kids…"

Heart still pounding, she waited as he fished the phone out of his pocket. She answered it, rushing off the dance floor.

She'd been too late—no one was on the other line. Stepping farther away from the dance floor, she went to return the phone call. A text buzzed through.

Lexie was crying. She wanted to come home now. Natalie's heart sank. Guilt washed over her. She needed to be there for her kids. Not gallivanting with a mind-numbingly sexy man at a smoky honky-tonk. How could she have thought otherwise for a second?

I'll be there in a half hour.

She sent the text. Max had reached her now, concern washing over his features.

"I need to go pick up my kids." She needed to get her head on straight while she was at it. Remember that she wasn't in a position to indulge herself with a wildly sexy newcomer to town.

He nodded. "Of course." Turning on his heel, he went to collect their things from the table.

What she didn't add—couldn't add—was that she also needed to process this whole night. The moment. The spark.

Everything.

She needed to salvage more self-control before she spent any more time alone with Max.

For Max, the morning crawled. There wasn't a moment that hadn't been filled with movement, but since picking up Natalie's children last night, things with Natalie had cooled.

She'd barely spoken to him.

In her rushed "good morning," he'd felt her defenses reforming. She avoided his gaze, pushed past him and mumbled something about work.

To be fair, Max knew she was an overachiever—a woman pulled in too many directions. Or at least, too many directions for the hours in a day.

Still, after that dinner and the slow dance…the distance felt calculated. Stress radiated from her as she passed him in the hall, making her way to the craft room. He could see it take hold of her shoulders, enter her stance.

She'd served her B and B guests an elaborate spread of a breakfast picnic. Brie cheese, fresh croissants, an assortment of breads, apple turnovers, grapes and strawberries covered the table on the outside porch. The cool temperatures provided an inviting backdrop for guests as they piled fruit and pastries onto plates, grabbed picnic blankets from the stack and arranged themselves on the lawn.

Sipping fresh coffee that she'd also brewed for the guests, Max found himself wondering how she managed all this. Determined to make a difference for this kind, selfless woman, Max put himself to good use. He'd help her out this morning. As guests finished their breakfasts, they dispersed. Natalie had done a quick cleanup before Margie spent some time playing with the kids and dog, canine socialization more than training.

Chaz and Francesca, a young couple Max had met while standing in line for coffee, began looking a little antsy. Francesca's inquisitive brown eyes scanned the area, looking for something. Based on Chaz's glance at his watch, Max surmised they were waiting for Natalie.

Chaz folded and unfolded the receipt, the kind Max

had seen Natalie slide under doors of departing guests each morning.

Rather than disrupt Natalie, he took their checkout form, looked it over quickly and confirmed they'd paid. Nothing more needed doing, no need to get Natalie to run payment. He couldn't help but notice her computer was open, not password locked. He really did need to upgrade her security—internet and building.

After tapping a message into his phone about her system, Max glanced at his watch. It was 11:45 a.m., and he noticed how both Lexie and Colby watched television, sharing a little bowl of strawberries while Miss Molly napped on the floor in front of them. Margie had ducked out a few minutes ago, and asked him to send a shout-out to Natalie. Which he'd decided to delay. He could watch the kids while they sat in front of a television.

And there was another way he could help Natalie, since not many realized he knew his way around a kitchen.

He walked into the common room and stooped to be eye level with the kids. His heart hammered. This was a new space, and part of him couldn't believe how easy and natural this instinct was. But then again, as much as he didn't like to address it, kids spoke to him in a way.

His years in foster care had made him more empathetic, more in tune with what people needed. Max supposed it allowed him to literally see the world differently. To be attentive to details, how people interacted. What they weren't saying. All of this made him a good detective now.

And what he saw when he looked into the TV room was two well-behaved but hungry children.

"Hey, kids," he called out. "Whaddya say we make some lunch?"

Lexie's green eyes lit up as she clasped her hands over her mouth. "Yeah! Yes, yes, please, Mr. Max. You cookin'?"

Her squeals and giggles reassured him that he'd made the right decision. Even Colby nodded, a faint trace of a smile forming as he pushed himself off the big red couch.

The trio made their way to the kitchen. Other guests milled around. Snippets of conversation filled the halls.

"I wub pancakes for lunch." Lexie teetered back and forth as she opened the pantry door, pointing to the pancake mix. She grabbed a jar of sprinkles from one of the lower shelves. "With this, too."

With a light nod, Max picked up the pancake mix, and grabbed the sprinkles from Lexie's extended hand. Not a stretch for his cooking skills, but if that was what they wanted, then he was happy to comply. "What about you, buddy? Do you like pancakes for lunch?"

Colby considered Max's question. The young kid seemed to hold a microscope up to Max, examining him in that quiet way of his. For a moment, Max felt Colby wasn't going to answer him, and he'd learned that sometimes the boy refused to talk. And in those cases, there was nothing to be done to force him. In fact, pushing the issue could cause the child to have a meltdown or retreat into hiding.

Just when Max was about to give up, Colby spoke in a small but confident voice. "Yes. But plain. No sprinkles. Three small pancakes. Circle. But don't stack them."

"Gotcha. Circles. No sprinkles," Max replied, pulling out bowls from the cabinet. He opened the fridge and extracted eggs, milk and butter. He found two pans and started heating them up. "We should probably make more than pancakes, though. Like healthy stuff. Do you like bacon or sausage?"

"Bacon," Lexie said, climbing a three-step ladder by the counter so she could see better. Her blanket trailed from her fist.

"Sausage, please," Colby said, his wide eyes hesitant as if choosing differently from his sister would cause trouble.

And in that moment, Max's gut clenched. Sure it was just bacon and sausage. An easy enough request to fill. Nothing like the tougher stuff of dealing with children—the more intense needs they deserved to have met by responsible adults in their lives.

So he would stick to food, because the Valentine family in this simple B and B was far from simple at all.

Panicked, Natalie rushed into the kitchen, swiping perspiration from her forehead.

It was just past noon, and she didn't know where the morning had gone. So much had to be done, and one of her guests had let her know that Max was starting lunch for her kids. Embarrassment burned her cheeks as she saw the array of cooking supplies Max had gathered.

He didn't have to do that. Shouldn't have to. Damn it, but she was coming apart at the seams trying to manage everything. And that no doubt showed in her appearance.

Her hair was tucked up into a messy bun she would have liked to call chic. Ha. Were snug jeans sexy when they were tight? Because the ones of hers that fit were all dirty. She'd dug these out of the back of her closet, a pair from prebaby days, along with a simple V-neck T-shirt tight around her breasts.

Yet he made low-slung jeans and a soft T-shirt look…yum.

Swiping back a loose lock of hair, she drew in a steadying breath. "I can't believe I worked into lunchtime."

Natalie opened the back door and called to Miss Molly with the proper commands and gestures, sending her into the fenced area of the yard where guests weren't allowed. "I'm so embarrassed and so sorry to have imposed on you." She clasped her daughter by the shoulder and touched her son lightly on the hand, just a fingertip brush. "Let's have some soup and PBJs."

Her daughter's bottom lip quivered. "Want Mr. Max make pancakes."

"Lexie—" Natalie began.

"Natalie, really," Max interrupted. "It's no big deal. Either I can cook for myself here or I'll have to go out to eat, which will take longer. So, free pancakes for me in exchange for my work?"

He was being nice in making this face-saving excuse, but still… She shook her head. "They're children, *my* kids."

"Kids?" He raised an eyebrow, egg in hand hovering over the bowl. "Are you insinuating I can't handle feeding young palates?"

Damn, he was charming. No wonder he'd taken the business world by storm, amassing a fortune beyond anything she could comprehend.

Rich or not, though, that didn't make him the boss of her domain.

She stood her ground. "I'm saying thank you, but I'm not your responsibility. I'll even cook the pancakes and you can have some, since you're a guest—"

Colby pulled her hand. He so rarely touched her any

contact instantly stopped her cold. "Mom, please. Color with me. He can cook."

And oh, God, that tugged at her heart with memories of family meals with Jeremy. She needed to separate the past from the present. And in this present her son's needs and wants came first.

It was just pancakes. And a coloring page. If it made her children happy… "Okay, Max, if you're really sure you don't mind."

The familiar roguish smile returned to his face, sparking him to movement. With a bold flourish, he grabbed a towel, wrapped it around his waist and winked at her. "I don't mind at all. I enjoy cooking, and I travel so much I don't get to do it nearly often enough."

Instantly, the dance from last night rushed back into her mind. How close they'd been. How easily they'd kissed.

Oh, that kiss.

Her knees went a little wobbly and she held on to the table's edge as she sat with her children while Max began cooking. The sound of eggs beating and the soft hum of the oven filled the kitchen, mingling with the sound of colored pencils touching down on paper.

Colby had a blue pencil in his hand and he carefully colored in a large fish—his obsession. Natalie picked up a green pencil and joined her son in coloring, half watching Max move about her kitchen with a smooth efficiency and confidence.

Did the children remember the old days when their father had been home, in the kitchen with them? He hadn't been much for cooking, but he'd played with the kids while she prepared meals. Her gaze skated back to Max.

He managed multiple pans at once. Bacon. Sausages.

Pancakes and even crepes in another. He'd grabbed the leftover caramel and apples from this morning's pastries. He caught her eye and mouthed "crepes for the lady" with a wink in her direction that sent a tingle of awareness along her skin, prickling in her breasts.

She couldn't help it. She smiled. Although she quickly tucked her head to color and tried to hide how far that smile reached, deep inside her. The smells of fresh food—food she didn't have to prepare—felt good. Damn good. This whole moment did and all because of Max.

After washing the pans, he dished up the kids' food and placed it on their small, plastic table tucked in the corner. "Coloring break and time for grub."

Max ruffled Lexie's hair and yet was careful to keep his hands off her son, clearly aware Colby preferred to call the shots on hugs.

Natalie said softly, "Thank you."

For more than the food. For the thought. For being here. For the three perfect, sprinkle-free circles on Colby's plate that weren't stacked.

Max spread his hands. "All under control. And as much as I would like to stay here and, uh, dance with you, I need to head over to the Cattleman's Club to meet with some members."

He started grabbing the cooking supplies to put them away, eyes flicking to the B and B guests that stood at the threshold of the kitchen. She joined him, gathering more supplies in her hands, and they went into the pantry. Together.

Away from people, he set down his supplies, leaned in for a kiss.

A deep body sigh had her melting into him. The

kiss wasn't as feverish as last night, but it was every bit as hungry.

Maybe it was she who was hungry. Despite all her talk about self-control, she allowed herself just a moment to touch him. His strong chest and arms. The corded neck. His warm jaw, where the skin bristled ever so slightly against her palms.

Just one kiss and she felt like she might come out of her skin.

"Why are you pursuing me so?" She eased back to look into his eyes.

Not his talented lips. Nope. Not looking there.

She struggled to catch her breath, and staring at his sexy-as-hell mouth would not help matters.

His eyes narrowed. "I'm not sure I understand the question."

Didn't understand? Or didn't want to discuss it?

For her part, she'd rather lose herself in the feel of his mouth on hers again. The feel of his hands on her waist. Her back. Her everywhere.

But she couldn't go on like this, kissing in pantries. "I'm not exactly your type," she said to clarify.

"Natalie," he whispered into her ear, his breath hot. "Stop with Googling stuff about me and get to know the real person."

Her thoughts scrambled at the feel of his lips against her neck. "I Google everyone who stays here—for safety purposes."

"Sure. You like me, though." He skimmed his mouth back around to hers, his grin decidedly devilish.

Handsome. Hot. Charming.

He wasn't wrong. But maybe that didn't matter.

Still, she felt compelled to repeat what she said. "I'm really not your type."

He angled back to look at her, his expression solemn, as if he sensed how important this mystery was to her. "You're so sexy I've been on fire for you since the second I saw you." He tugged at the loose band holding up her hair, sending it free around her shoulders. His fingers combed through. "That makes you my type."

Okay, that brought another question, perhaps an even more important one. "What if you're not my type? I'm not talking about attraction. I'm talking about type, what's good for me."

Or good for her children. She had to think of them. Especially with Colby's special needs. Sure, Max had figured out not to pat the boy on the head and to keep sprinkles out of his pancakes, but that wasn't the same as dealing with the challenges of parenting a special-needs child day in and day out.

"If you don't want me in your life, Natalie, then tell me to go." Silence hung between them. He nodded once. "And that's my point."

"But as you said, this is about attraction. And yes, maybe I'm attracted to a bad-boy type, and as much as I loved my husband, I'm not saying that marriage or love guaranteed happiness." Concern burned in her belly.

He drew closer, ran a hand up and down her arm. "Okay, so you're saying you don't want a relationship and there's no replacing your husband." He kissed her forehead. "Let's stop talking about types and the past. It's not about trying to logically explain what's happening between us."

"You're a cyberguru. Doesn't that make you the epitome of logical?"

His low laugh rumbled his chest against hers. "I like to think I'm a Renaissance man, in touch with my emotions. I'm here for now. Let's go with the flow."

In the moments before the next kiss, she searched his eyes and wondered if, and how long, she could take him up on that dare?

As Natalie cracked open the door, a long yawn of hall light winked into her daughter's room, illuminating Lexie's sleeping form. At the threshold, Natalie watched the steady rise and fall of her daughter's breathing.

With silent footfalls, Natalie crossed the room, and made it to her daughter's bedside. She planted a kiss on Lexie's forehead. Lexie didn't stir, seemed content in whatever sweet dreamscape danced before her closed eyelids. A small stuffed animal—a unicorn named Mrs. Agatha—was snuggled up next to her daughter, whose little fingers were twined in the purple mane.

Content with the scene at hand, Natalie left Lexie's bedside and made her way to Colby's room for their nighttime ritual.

The last rays of the sun had melted away, and the hall no longer boasted a cool autumn glow. Instead, the manufactured light of the hall—dim in comparison to the natural amber of a few moments ago—guided her to the other end of the hall, to the blue door that led to Colby.

Clicking open the door, she let herself into the plain white room. Paintings of fish lined the walls, an array of end-of-the-rainbow colors dancing before her eyes. She'd made a gallery wall for him—hung up his meticulously colored pages of deep-sea fish. He seemed to enjoy the soothing nautical world.

She stretched, eyes meeting the now-familiar scene of Colby underneath his blanket, reading. He had his own flashlight, one she'd bought him with the barrel decorated in magnifying glasses and microscopes, part of a science kit.

The weighted blanket draped over his head, thick enough to give him the pressure he preferred, but thin enough for remnants of the flashlight's beam to penetrate the fabric as he read underneath. A silent fan whirred, cooling him. Miss Molly was stretched out beside him, pressed up against her charge.

Miss Molly's deep brown eyes seemed to spark with interest as Natalie made her way to the bedside. Tail thumping, the golden retriever let out a small whine but didn't move away from Colby.

He let the blanket slide down, exposing himself to the air of his room and to her. Natalie's heart fluttered a bit, as she wondered how to connect and engage with her son—her deeply kind son—even more.

Hugs were on his terms, but they had developed another language of affection. She softly tapped her fingertips along the top of his hand, then his forehead. A smile pushed up his lips, reached his eyes.

Not a hug, but a connection. A genuine connection. These little moments meant everything to her, and she imprinted them into her memories to draw comfort from in tougher times.

He closed his book and set it aside, then turned off his flashlight as a yawn shook his whole body. Blinking at her, he lay down. "Good night."

So matter-of-fact and confident.

"Good night, Colby." She stroked a hand along Miss Molly's swirls of fur, the dog being the link between them; then she closed the door after her.

She sagged back against the hall wall and let out a hard sigh. Glancing down the hall, she noted—how could she not?—that a warm glow emanated from under Max's door.

He was still awake and here.

Not that it should matter to her.

Still, she envisioned him in the room, casual and relaxed in her home. More than just a guest?

Silly thoughts. Shaking her head, she pulled her phone out of her pocket. It had been a few weeks since she'd spoken to her own parents. An overdue conversation.

Natalie glanced over the railing and down, nodding at the guests sitting in the landing area on an overstuffed couch. They were huddled under a fluffy blanket with the staples of movie watching—popcorn and candy. The thirtysomething man, Albert, balanced a laptop on his lap while his wife, Beth, rested her head on his shoulder.

The thing about running a B and B was that Natalie continually had access to private moments. And many—like this one—made another tear in her barely healed heart. Which made it all the easier to respect the couple's privacy. She went quickly downstairs on soft feet to make her phone call.

Natalie rounded the corner into the kitchen, sat at the table and dragged in a couple of bracing breaths before she hit the speed dial for her mother.

Five rings.

It had taken five rings for her mother to answer. Already, a knot formed in Natalie's stomach.

"Hey, Mom. How are things?" Staring hard at the table and scratching her finger along a scar Colby had worn into the wood with a compulsive scratch when he was three, she waited for her mother to respond.

"Hello, Natalie. It's nice to hear from you after all this time." The dig chipped away at Natalie's heart. "Things are just fine here. Your father and I are planning a vacation."

"Oh? Where are you two going?" Natalie asked, winding her hair around her fingers. Nervous habits died hard.

Her mother, Georgina, let out a long, exasperated sigh. "Clearwater Beach vacation. In Florida. We might as well."

Not a word asking about how her grandchildren were doing. How she was doing. Not that she expected or needed it. But still...

"How's Dad?" Natalie asked, hoping to talk to him. She seldom heard from her father on the phone.

"Just fine. Though we are about to have dinner out on the balcony. Hope you and the kids are well," Georgina said tightly. She'd made it clear long ago that if Natalie wasn't willing to do things their way, then she didn't have their support.

As a mother, Natalie found that tougher and tougher to accept or understand.

"Well, enjoy your meal, then. We can speak another time. Bye, Mom. Love you and Dad." She said it out of habit, but meant it even as she wished for more. God, was she destined to always be wishing for more from people who were supposed to be partners in this life journey—people like her parents, like Jeremy?

"Love you, too."

And just like that, the connection went dead, leaving Natalie feeling hollow and raw.

Lord knew that hadn't been their worst conversation. When Natalie had decided to move to Texas, the conversations were laced with distaste and annoyance.

But things hadn't warmed up between her and her mother. The connection between them felt strained. It always had. So different than the connection she felt with her own children.

The tendrils of anxiety inched around her heart. Restlessness entered her limbs, and she found herself walking back up the stairs, past the couple watching movies, toward her kids' rooms. The lights were still out in Colby's and Lexie's respective rooms. She laid a hand on Colby's door and took a deep breath, vowing to always be there for her children.

As she turned, the glow from underneath Max's door caught her attention.

He was still awake. Still up. And yes, from the rustling sound inside, he was still here.

The prospect excited her. And while life hadn't turned out the way she'd hoped or given her what she might have always wanted, she couldn't control what others did or felt. She only had control of her own decisions and actions. In this exact moment, she knew what she wanted.

She wanted something just for herself.

She wanted to sleep with Max St. Cloud.

Six

His eyes strained while he reviewed the code sprawling on the laptop screen in front of him.

Dissatisfied with the machine language, Max shifted his laptop to the edge of the bed. His hand reached blindly to the wooden end table, and he felt around for the mason jar full of sweet tea. Not exactly a protein shake—his normal ritual—but apparently sweet temptation abounded everywhere here in all forms.

A few hours ago, he'd left the room, needing movement to rejuvenate his senses. As far as the case went, he knew a piece of information escaped him.

That frustrated him. Rather than spend a few hours falling through rabbit holes, Max had changed his environment. Foot-to-pavement time always allowed him to clear his head. Or at least it had.

Every stride he took looped his mind back to Natalie. And while he didn't actively think about the case, he did think about the smile of appreciation she'd given him earlier over pancakes and crepes.

He'd run harder than usual. As if running would not only reveal the origin of the cyberattacker, but also reveal a way for Max to proceed with Natalie.

The postrun shower renewed him. Max had felt ready to dive back into this work. Ready for a break in the case. He needed it, really.

But the backdoor code analysis hadn't revealed anything useful. He blinked, sipping the tea, noting how the cool liquid soothed his throat. Satisfied, he set the tea back on the end table next to the fresh-cut flowers from the yard, a nice touch that Natalie made all around the B and B.

Amazing how often she slid into his thoughts.

Time for another change of scene. He made his way to the desk, leaned against the plush chair. A new angle—one that focused on the members of TCC.

Max ran a hand through his hair, sighed deeply. On the edge of his four-poster bed, just to the left of where he'd placed his laptop, a large spread of papers loomed. He picked up the stack and the laptop, made his way back to the main workstation and settled into the chair.

Ready.

He'd been looking into members who had been outspoken about allowing women in the Texas Cattleman's Club and compiling a list of people who'd been denied membership. Maybe someone had a grudge against members after being excluded. This list was damn long. He would have to farm out some of the names to employees in his firm. Once they found identifying markers, he could dig deeper into the cyberworld and with human intel here.

He leaned back in his chair, the floorboards creaking beneath.

When he closed his eyes, his thoughts went right back to his date with Natalie. Kissing her, the way she felt pressed up against him. How freely she'd given herself over to dancing. No matter how many showers he took, he could still smell the flowery scent of her hair.

A rap on the door forced his eyes open. His heart rate accelerated as he cleared his throat to answer.

He swiveled in his chair and faced the door. "Come in."

Natalie in the flesh, not in his memory. Looking as sexy as ever. Maybe even sexier.

She held a plate with a slice of pecan pie à la mode. A loose cotton dress draped along her curves and brushed the tops of her bare feet. "I saw you were still burning the midnight oil and thought you might like a late-night snack."

Oh, he was hungry all right. Looking at her sent a gnawing ache straight to his gut.

"That's incredibly thoughtful of you."

She stayed in the doorway, not walking in but not passing over the plate. He tried to get a read off her and what she wanted. She scrunched her toes, and he noticed her nails were painted green. Interesting. Not the conventional choice he would have expected.

And damn, he was in a sad shape if he was obsessing over her toes. He scratched his chest over his heavily thudding heart and realized he wasn't wearing a shirt.

Max cleared his throat. "I'll grab a T-shirt and we can go downstairs to get a second slice of pie for you to join me."

Natalie looked over her shoulder at the empty hall

and then took a step closer to him. "How about you leave the shirt off and we share this one in your room?"

Whoa.

Just holy hell, whoa.

That was not what he'd expected her to say.

As much as he wanted to haul her in without hesitation, he was starting to care about her. He wanted to be certain she wouldn't regret this and boot him on his ass five seconds later. "Are the kids with Tom and Emily?"

She held up her phone, a low hum of music emanating. "I have a monitor going between their bedrooms. They're next door. I'll hear if they need me. I figured that out for keeping them safe and separate from boarders."

"Of course. I should have realized you would have that figured out." He didn't know much—anything—about parenting. His mother sure hadn't kept track of him at that age and his foster families were usually overwhelmed by the sheer number of kids around. Natalie was…incredible. Beautiful and giving. He should tell her to go. Should. But couldn't. "Are you certain you want to share that pie?"

"Absolutely certain." She met his eyes without hesitation, and with her free hand placed a condom in his palm.

Not much stunned him anymore.

Well, not until Natalie had walked into his life.

His hand closed around the condom. She couldn't be any more obvious than that.

He stepped aside, clearing the way.

She looked back over her shoulder at him with a toss of her hair. "Aren't you going to ask me why?"

"And give you a chance to talk yourself out of being here? I don't think so." He closed the door with a decisive click. All the doors locked automatically, like at a hotel, an upgrade to the place he appreciated right now.

She glanced at the desk and he nudged aside the computer, clearing a space for the plate. Natalie put down the pie, pulled two spoons from her pocket and held them up. "I'm hoping you'll share?"

"My pleasure." He plucked a spoon from her hand and clasped her wrist in his other hand. "One condition, though."

She tipped her head to the side. "What would that be?"

"We get to feed each other," he said, grinning as he sat and pulled her into his lap.

Laughing, she sat sideways across his legs. She swept her spoon through the ice cream and started toward him, only to snatch the bite for herself at the last moment. Her green eyes twinkled.

He chuckled, surprised at her playfulness. She was always so serious. But then she was always overworked. He'd been drawn to her before. Now he was…mesmerized.

Scooping up a taste of ice cream, he brought the spoon to her mouth and didn't play.

She closed her lips over the spoon and moaned in appreciation. "I'm not being much of a hostess, and this really is tasty, if I do say so myself. The ice cream is home churned."

This time, she didn't play, but offered him a taste with some pecan pie mixed in. He'd eaten at the best restaurants around the world, but damned if he could remember ever having had homemade ice cream before. Either it was the best ever, or being with Natalie made it the best ever.

To hell with food. He kissed her. Really kissed her. And hell, yes, she really kissed him back.

While savoring the taste of vanilla on her tongue, he set aside his spoon with a clink of metal against china and plucked her spoon from her hand, as well. The curve of her hip pressed against him in a temptation even sweeter than the dessert. Having her in his arms was better and better every time.

He didn't know what he'd ever done in his life that was good enough to deserve this moment, but he was grateful. And was going to make sure she didn't regret whatever made her decide to take this leap. He considered himself savvy at reading people, and he suspected her fast move into intimacy was out of character for her. He didn't want to ponder too much on the why of that.

He just wanted to ponder on…her.

He slid an arm under her legs and along her back, lifting her as he stood. She sighed, her hands clasping his shoulders. He closed the four steps to the bed in record time, lowering her to the mattress without breaking contact. He'd dreamed of having her here, planned, but the rush of excitement at holding her in his arms, in his room, exceeded his imagination.

And his imagination had been mighty damn amazing.

Stretching out over her, he groaned with pleasure at the feeling of her under him. The mattress gave ever so slightly as he did his best to keep his full weight off her while still enjoying the fit and match of their bodies aligning. Of seeing her fiery hair splayed across his pillow. Her emerald green eyes were sultry with want.

She snapped the waistband of his running shorts with a sass that sent a bolt of desire surging through him. He sketched his mouth along her jaw, down her neck to her shoulder and then the soft length of her arm until he could reach her ankle. He inched his fingers under the hem of her dress and bunched the fabric up, up, up her silky leg to her hip.

Arching her back, she bowed upward and stretched her arms overhead in an unmistakable invitation. An invitation he fully intended to accept. He swept her dress up and off...exposing breathtaking curves encased in white lace.

She looked like one of those timeless models painted on the side of an aircraft in the prior century. Pinup luscious and all his for the taking. Or maybe she was taking him, because the way her fingers were caressing his chest, then moved lower still to cradle his erection, had him throbbing to be inside her. Deeply. Fully.

The feel of her hands on him numbed his mind to rational thought. Instincts took over, his whispers of encouragement mixing with her moans as they swept aside the remainder of clothes until—yes—they were skin to skin, heated flesh to flesh. The length of his hard-on pressed on her stomach in a tempting precursor of what it would feel like to have her all around him.

Soon.

Not soon enough, if her eager hands were anything to judge by, as they touched him, explored him...and sheathed him in the condom.

Damn. She was tight... *Tight* or *tense?* Either way, he intended to take care of her.

He slid his hand between them, touching and circling the nub of nerves. Her hips rocked in response, urging him deeper even as he perceived a wince. He didn't consider himself an ego dude about size, but clearly there was an issue here. Possibly she'd been abstinent for a long while? He'd heard of that being an issue for a woman who'd gone for long periods without, but he could also see in her face that talking was going to be a serious mood buster. So he ramped up the foreplay.

And truth be told, taking his time with her was no sacrifice. A bit torturous, but incredibly so.

She grazed her nails down his back to dig into his buttocks. "Why are you waiting? I want this."

He nipped her earlobe and whispered, "And I want this to be good for both of us."

"I know what I'm doing. I'm not naive." She rubbed a knee along his hip.

"I can tell." He smoothed back her hair, smiling. "We're just having some logistic issues here, and taking my time with you is in no way a hardship."

He kissed her neck, devoting his undivided attention to gently licking and tasting along the creamy patch of skin running from her ear to her shoulder. Her pulse picked up speed under his mouth.

Every inch deeper inside her was sweet torture, but he was determined to make sure she didn't regret this. He wanted to be invited back into her bed and he intended to use every touch, taste, instinct in his arsenal to make sure she issued that invitation.

She writhed under him, arching her breasts against his chest. The sensation of her softness against him threatened his tenuous control, but what a sweet temptation. He dipped his head and took a pebbly peak in his mouth, teasing and tugging. And yes, her breathy sigh of approval sent a rush of victory through him. He shifted his attention to the other creamy mound while sliding his hand over the breast he'd abandoned.

Moments melded into each other and he reveled in her relaxing. An interesting dichotomy as her passion rose but her muscles melted. His thrusts slid deeper,

deeper still and he searched her face for the least sign of discomfort and found she was watching him. Which meant she was thinking. He wanted her feeling.

He stilled, angled his mouth over hers and held, then teased the seam of her mouth. She parted quickly, their tongues thrusting, her arms holding tighter to him.

Her knees fell open wider, her feet sliding up higher.

Yes, and in this moment he realized her body was starved for touch. She'd been alone for so long, and he suspected she'd devoted herself totally to her children and not to any kind of social life. With that thought, his hands went into motion. He was bolder, stroking, caressing and massaging along her shoulders, arms, sides, hips, along her thighs. She hugged him closer, tighter, her breathy moans mingling with his groan. Release—his, hers—was so close.

When hers hit, she took him right with her.

Wave after wave of pleasure pounded through his veins.

His arms clasped her closer even as they rolled to their sides, panting. Wordless. Her forehead pressed to his chest.

And words were scarce because while he'd expected sex with Natalie to be amazing, he hadn't expected it to be the best sex ever.

Natalie stretched, luxuriating in this moment. In her choice. He'd brought the dessert to her, along with his sweet tea.

His low-slung running shorts were back on, but his muscles still tempted her. Max's messy hair made him seem somehow even sexier. Plopping down next to her, he traced his fingers along her thigh.

The scents of perspiration and his body wash mingled into a perfume that was just…them.

She was sated. Her body relaxed and her senses hummed. And thank goodness her children slept, the monitor still playing the music softly, no sounds other than an occasional sniffle in their sleep.

She had this pocket of time awhile longer, an incredible, unexpected encounter even though she'd come prepared. She couldn't deny, she was also a little embarrassed at the awkward start as she'd discovered those big hands of his fulfilled every cliché and combined with her abstinence had made for a rather uncomfortable start.

"You're a patient man," she offered, by way of a delicate acknowledgment.

"You're a sensual woman."

Only because he'd made her feel that way. Wow.

"I feel like we should talk about how things started, how I… It had been a long time…"

He pressed a finger to her lips. "I understand. We figured things out, I believe, and when we recover our energy, you'll keep communicating." He kissed her once, twice. "Tell me what you like and don't like, what you want and don't want…"

Her hand behind his neck, she drew him closer. "I want more of you—" she nipped his bottom lip "—and more of the pie."

A moment of the past threatened the present. An image of blond-haired Jeremy entered her mind—their budding relationship. The flowers, the hotel where she'd first slept with her husband. A marriage. A life. Two kids. So much love and it still wasn't enough to keep any of them safe from darkness.

Swallowing, she closed her eyes, willed herself to

stay in this moment. To not slip back to the source of so much pain.

"Yes, ma'am." Laughing, he skimmed his mouth over hers once more before they both dug in to share the rest of the pie and pass the tea back and forth.

Chewing through her last bite, she studied him, wondering...so much. "I don't understand you. Surely there are more experienced, less complicated women out there."

"Less complicated sounds...boring." He leaned forward, resting his chin on his hand.

Swallowing, she tilted her head, trying to understand. "So I'm a challenge to you?"

"Lady, I have challenges in my life all the time and I'm not hopping into bed with them. I just know I want you. And seeing you happy, seeing your face flushed with pleasure, brings me pleasure. That's worth being patient for." His tone was so simple. So measured and assured.

"You and I, together, we don't make sense. Can't you argue with that fact?" And they didn't. Their routines, goals. All those things were worlds apart. And she couldn't take another fissure, another fracture in her life.

There it was again. The past running to overtake her. A flash of her dead husband again. How they stopped talking because it was easier than arguing. That distance made more resonant after his death.

"This last thing I want to do is argue with you. I will say, I can't claim to understand this draw I felt from the moment I clapped eyes on you. But it's real."

Tears gathered in the corners of her eyes, and part of her just wanted to make love again and say to hell with talking, with this sharing that was somehow so much more intimate. But just as she started to lift her hand, something in his eyes gave her pause and bolstered her. Encouraged her to take another chance here.

She breathed. Once. Twice. Willed the tears away. In a small voice, she pressed on. "He was my first love, my first…everything."

He stroked her face with tender fingertips, the rasp of his calluses so gentle. "I'm sorry for your…loss? *Loss* seems like such an inadequate word."

"*Loss*… It's a fair word. One I understand well."

"What do you mean?"

"I was a military wife. I am the mother of a special-needs child. Those two things alone put my marriage under tremendous stress."

A lifetime flashed before her eyes. All the hardships that came with the military life. The disruption of daily life—their routines that had to be started and stopped continuously.

"You and Jeremy had problems?"

"Long deployments. War scars. A child with challenges. Yes, my marriage was going through a rocky patch, and that broke my heart. His, too, I believe. And we both felt helpless to fix things." Natalie released a shuddering breath, the air almost punched free by pain. The aftershocks of his death rocked her still. She knew they always would.

How could they not?

"And then he was deployed again," Max offered, filling in the gaps of the story.

She shook her head, lips thinning to a line. Eyes closed, she willed her tongue to form the words she scarcely uttered. "He volunteered to go."

"He did what?"

"He voluntarily went on this deployment. He said

time apart would be good for us…and now he's…" The word couldn't come out, became lodged in her throat. Threatened her ability to breathe.

"You can't possibly blame yourself."

A bitter laugh accompanied by another wave of threatening tears. She swallowed, finding her voice again. "I understand intellectually, but I'm human. I can't help thinking if he hadn't been trying to put space between us…" She pushed her hair off her forehead. "And then there were the bills from all the specialists for Colby. Deployments come with hazardous-duty pay."

"Sounds like you both had a heavy load on you."

"Sometimes, in my darkest moments, I wonder if he was distracted…or worse, if he put himself in harm's way."

"You think he could have been suicidal?"

She shook her head emphatically. That was a possibility she couldn't bear to entertain and could never know for certain. Still, she found herself whispering words she'd never said to anyone. "I don't think so. But grief is irrational. We weren't communicating. And if in some flash of a moment he thought insurance money would… God, I can't even say it, it hurts too much."

His voice lowered an octave. "I wish there was something I could do to ease this pain you're carrying around."

And just knowing that he wanted to comfort her… that meant so much. A tiny piece of her grief unknotted for a moment.

"Just having you listen helps. There's no one here I feel comfortable telling." She cradled her head between her hands, her voice breaking. This secret—this knowledge—weighed her down every day. She'd had no one to speak to about this. Not her friends. And certainly not her parents, who already blamed her for making poor decisions in regard to her marriage and family.

"I'm glad you feel you can talk to me."

"There's a connection between us." She watched his eyes lift. "I realize that… What? You're surprised I would say that?"

"Yes, I am. I know about this…draw between us, but your standoffish vibes have been strong." He stroked a finger down her cheek. "At least they were until tonight."

"I'm trying to move on. I *want* to move on. But it's easier said than done." She rubbed the spot where her wedding ring had been.

He touched the bare spot. "Seems to me that you are taking steps forward with your life."

"You're just saying that because you have me naked." She tried to lighten the moment, lighten her heart.

"I'm talking about your B and B, the dresses you make, your incredible kids and even that funny, sweet dog you're having trained. From where I'm sitting, you've got life locked and loaded." He leaned forward. "And yes, you're here in bed with me. Beautifully naked."

Her emotions were raw from memories of the past, but those same memories made her all the more certain. She would make the most of this night with Max.

Because life had shown her well that tomorrow was never guaranteed.

The smell of asphalt after the rain entered Max's nostrils. The acidic smell felt like the only constant in his life.

He'd been passed over again by another family.

Fine. He didn't need them.

He didn't need anyone.

Standing beneath the streetlight, he surveyed the city—he had no need to go anywhere, since the group home thought he was at some camping trip. He was good at dodging places that didn't care about having him around anyway.

Out here, crappy as it was, everything and nothing were simultaneously at his fingertips.

The sun sank low on the horizon, setting fire to the skyline. The whole world seemed to be drenched in fire-red hues as a cold wind stung the edges of his exposed cheeks. A hunger rumbled deep in his stomach, and his eyes shifted to the Dumpster behind the Italian restaurant. Every night, they dumped perfectly good bread and pasta.

So what? He wasn't adoptable. Not every kid had the run of the streets like this. The future was as open as this Dumpster. Rules were made for some other people. He'd make his own standards.

Another growl rumbled from his stomach. Light seemed to stream at odd angles from the streetlight as he moved toward the Dumpster.

Flipping open the Dumpster lid, he began digging, looking for a hunk of bread.

Instead, his hands found a soft sheet. The scent of lavender replaced the wet asphalt. Wrapped around him. Felt like home, a concept he hadn't ever really explored...

He flinched, finding himself miles and years away from that Dumpster. The city scene was gone, replaced by a domestic one. Natalie slept next to him, the soft sounds of her breathing grounding him in the present. She'd shared so much about herself, her past, making herself vulnerable to him. And he couldn't help being moved by that. He couldn't fix her past and her heart, but he could give her ease, pleasure, a moment's forgetfulness.

Watching her sleeping body, he tugged lightly on the edge of the sheet, gathering one deliberate handful at a time toward him and off her. She squeaked once, gripping a fistful, then slowly unfurled her hand and released the crisp white cotton so that… Yes…

He revealed her shoulders, then more as the sheet glided over her breasts, farther, farther…until he unveiled creamy skin with a sprinkling of freckles.

Irresistible.

Angling forward, he pressed his mouth to a smattering of freckles on her hip. She moaned, rolling ever so slightly. He sketched his hand down her leg, sweeping the sheet the rest of the way to the floor. He nuzzled her stomach, feeling the hitch and catch of her breaths, encouraging. Arousing. He kissed his way lower, and lower still until his shoulders nudged apart her legs.

The scent of her was an aphrodisiac he would never forget. Her sensual nature fed his own. Kissing her intimately, he felt a delicate shiver tremble through her whole body. Anchoring her hips in his hands, he tasted her fully, greedy for more but careful not to rush the slow build for her.

She was impossibly sweet and soft. Her fingers skimmed through his hair, a new restlessness in her touch as she arched beneath him.

A flush spread over her skin. A warmth he felt under his palms right before her body quivered.

She writhed and shuddered with her release. Her head pushed back into the pillow and she pressed her wrist over her mouth to hold in her gasps and moans of pleasure. He burned to take her somewhere private, where she could revel in her release with full abandon.

And he would, he vowed. He would find a way to have her all to himself. Soon.

Seven

After stacking the orange pottery plates together, Natalie made her way to the sink, careful not to spill any of the toast crumbs on the floor. Her children had just left for preschool and the guests were already all checked out, leaving her in relative silence.

Peace seemed so rare these days.

She turned on the water, letting it heat up as she put the plates in the deep sink. Pumping soap onto the sponge, she thought back to the taste of Max—the night they'd shared together.

For a moment, she imagined his hands around her, craved that touch. Being close to him had been surprising in more ways than she could have expected. The connection she felt to him was more combustible than she would have predicted. She'd been looking for more of a simple release, a way to deal with this crazy obsession.

But his touch had been…electric. Surprisingly tender. Beautifully intuitive.

The night would have been perfect, if only her body hadn't carried a betrayal. She'd expected a bit of adjustment after so long without sex. She had not expected quite so much, from the combination of abstinence and his size. His skill as a lover had brought her to completion, but her body was definitely tender. She almost felt as if she was revisiting the morning after losing her virginity.

And that frustrated her. She wanted to just lose herself in a wild, simple, brief affair. Something that wasn't going to happen until she figured out this issue with her body.

As she scrubbed the plates, the sound of heavy footfalls sounded behind her, cutting short her thoughts. Glancing over her shoulder, she saw Max approach. Stomach fluttering, she turned back to her work.

Max slipped behind her, his arms drawing her to him. Hot breath curled around the nape of her neck. He kissed tender skin there, reminding her of all the ways she'd come undone in his arms the night before. His intense attention to detail, always apparent in his job, had been a delicious gift in bed. Just thinking about that made her breath quicken, and she melted into that moment.

But something else worked its way into those sensual thoughts. Though the guests had all checked out for the day, there was still a chance that she and Max could be spotted.

Swallowing, she spun around, grabbing a dish towel before she placed her hands on his muscled chest. "We need to talk."

She took a deep breath, willing her pulse to slow down. Her brain to catch up with her senses.

He squinted, as if trying to analyze her words like

computer code. She could see his detective gears spinning. "That sounds ominous," he said.

"It's not…" Her shoulders sagged a bit, and she seemed to shrink away from him.

"About what?"

A long sigh gave her enough time to gather her thoughts. And courage. "About how we're going to handle things now that we're sleeping together and living under the same roof."

He reached out to touch her arm. Careful. Enough to send a shiver down her spine. "To be clear, we're not living under the same roof. It's your roof. I'm a guest, a boarder. I understand that. So, if you were panicking that I expect to move into your bedroom, then put your mind at rest."

She'd never even considered the possibility. The idea of nightly access to Max was enough to send her imagination into overdrive. But, of course, that wasn't happening. "Okay, I'm glad you realize that. But that wasn't what I was going to say." A sad kind of smile tugged at her heart as well as her mouth as she stared at him. Took in his dark features and the concern that splintered across his eyes.

"Well, hell. You sure put me in my place."

"I apologize. It's not my way to make someone uncomfortable. But I do have to say, you don't look particularly wounded."

An uncomfortable laugh escaped his lips. Raising his eyebrow, he gestured. "Say your piece, woman."

"I need for you to be careful outside the bedroom."

"Clarify that?"

"I don't want gossip among the guests. I have a professional reputation to maintain. We may have gone on a date, but I have to live in this town afterward." That was the reality. Whatever existed between her and Max was temporary. He would leave because, as he pointed out, he was a boarder. This transient relationship could not impact her standing in this town.

"After I leave, you mean," he said, eyes burning into hers.

She raised her chin, leveling him with a stare all her own. "Yes, that's exactly what I mean."

"You're writing me off awfully fast."

She chewed her lip, pulling away from him. Needing to remember to build space between them and guard her heart. "You know you're going home, more likely sooner rather than later."

"Still, gone isn't exactly…gone." He wiggled his hand around above his head. "I have an airplane. I could be here more often than planned."

"That's all hypothetical. I'm talking about today. About this town…about my children."

"Even if I were to stay somewhere else, they already know me separate from you. I—and others—enjoy being part of their lives. It's about more than helping you. They're good kids who've been through a lot."

"I realize that. And I believe the more people who contribute positive moments to their lives, the better. Truly. I'm grateful for the way people rally around them." She leaned back against the counter, her T-shirt brushing against water, dampening her back.

"They're great kids. You're a great person."

"Thank you. Just… Let's not be a couple around them." She couldn't enter this casually for the sake of her children. Bringing a man into their lives was a big deal. Natalie needed whoever that man was to be a stable force.

He nodded, understanding the implications of her

statement. "It's not about gossip. It's about your children hearing gossip and making assumptions."

"They may not really remember Jeremy, but they know they lost their dad. They know other children have fathers. They feel the loss and I can't have them creating false expectations because you're nice and you're here and they assume we're a couple."

He took his own step back now, vision seeming to travel back, away from the moment. Max took a measured breath before answering. "I understand what it feels like to be a child wanting a father, then wanting any family at all. I would never put any child through the pain of having those hopes dashed."

The ache in her stomach screamed. Heat flooded her cheeks and she reached out for him, seeking his hand. Needing to connect. "Max, I'm sorry. I should have thought that and realized you would understand. I—"

"You have nothing to apologize for. You're looking out for your kids. That makes you a good mother, and quite frankly, it makes me like you all the more."

"You like me?" She couldn't resist the urge to flirt, just a little.

"Yes, I do like you. You're an incredibly likable woman." He leaned in and whispered, "And I really like you with your clothes off."

"Well, the guests have checked out and no one's due in. The kids are at preschool…" Temptation pulled at her. She felt the connection in the air between them.

"Hmm… I would take that as an invitation, but then I know this place well. There's always traffic."

"I do have a dress client coming by in a half hour."

A devilish grin spread across his face as he squeezed her hand. "Then how about we make out in the pantry?"

With ease, he lifted her off her feet and brought them to the kitchen pantry—away from any and all prying eyes.

The last two days had unfolded at a breakneck speed of work for him and an uptick in business for Natalie, as well. Max attributed that to the lack of time together, the distance.

Or rather he could have.

But her standoffish vibe was clear, granted it was in an understated way. She was never rude to anyone. But there was no mistaking that some of her busyness was self-inflicted.

Morning sun streamed through the front windows of the sitting area, and Max pored over documents in the common area of the B and B, enjoying the generous amount of natural light the two huge windows provided. He thumbed through a St. Cloud Security Solutions company report on an overseas project. His business partner and the company's chief technology officer, Will Brady, had been keeping him up-to-date on details from the main office. Balancing all his contacts and projects the last few days had drained him. Keeping up with business back in Seattle and working late here when people were most often free for interviews was more challenging than he anticipated.

That didn't leave him much time to spend with Natalie, especially given how early she woke to prepare breakfast for her customers. His and Natalie's paths weren't crossing much privately—only a few stolen kisses that she clearly enjoyed, but there hadn't been a chance for anything more. And certainly not an opportunity for any lengthy discussion. Was that deliberate on her part or accidental?

Stealing a glance across the room, he watched Miss Molly curl around Colby's feet. The dog let out an audible sigh, her soulful brown eyes shifting around the room, head tilting to look at Margie and Lexie.

Natalie's words echoed in his mind, along with her step back when it came to going to bed together again. He didn't so much sense a no, but more of a "not right now." Maybe she was figuring things out in her mind in regard to her children. He respected what she'd said. Her children had been through a lot very young. His life on the streets had made him even more empathetic to struggles. And he wasn't going to be here long... something that should be a relief, since no one could get overly attached to him.

Right? The thought didn't bring him as much comfort as it should have.

Lexie stood up, tapped Margie on the shoulder. She cupped her hands together and leaned on the woman's lap, whispering in her ear. Margie's face softened and she nodded.

"Yes, you can go see your mom, sweetie." Margie gave her a hug, eliciting a squeal of delight from Lexie. She scampered away, disappearing from view.

Margie handed crayons to Colby, and he began to color another fish. Colby's fish drawings were all around the house, hanging on the fridge, in the common room. He was actually quite good, his details precise with scales and gills.

The little boy popped a Goldfish cracker into his mouth and chewed thoughtfully. Max wondered what it was about the water that intrigued Colby. Even his room was sea themed.

Closing his laptop and shoving his documents into a manila file folder, Max followed what his gut instincts were telling him. He walked over to the corner table with his hands in his pockets and cleared his throat. "Margie, if you want to take a break, I can hang out with Colby."

The older woman glanced up, smiling. "Well, if you're sure you don't mind, I would like to stretch my legs and refill my glass of tea."

"Take your time. I'll send a shout-out if I get in over my head," Max said and nodded. Then he shifted his attention to the four-year-old, who carefully picked up a pretzel stick, dipped it in peanut butter, then dabbed a small fish cracker with the sticky end.

Ingenious.

But then he'd seen dozens of ways Natalie multi-tasked as a mother while managing her B and B and wedding-dress-design business. That humbled him more than a little as he considered he had only himself and his company to think about. Hell, some days he barely had time left over to eat away from the computer.

He glanced at Colby again, the boy so silent, such a mystery to Max still. The child pretty much only let Miss Molly near him for any extended length of time. The golden retriever's tail thumped on the floor as she leaned against Colby's legs.

Maybe there was a way to accomplish a few goals at once. Give Natalie a break. Show her he knew how to let the kids have fun without them growing too attached. And yes, give Colby a nice outing, one of the child's choosing. "Do you want to go fishing?"

Colby chewed thoughtfully, then set aside his peanut butter–covered pretzel stick. "Gotta ask my mom."

"Of course." He should have thought to reassure the boy of that right away, but he hadn't spent much time with kids since leaving foster care. "But if you don't want to go, then there's no need to even ask her."

"I don't understand."

"I want to know that it's something you would enjoy."

Colby nodded. "Fishing is quiet. I like quiet."

"Good. I like quiet, too." There weren't many silent moments in crowded group homes and overcrowded foster families. But Max had had one foster father who'd always woken up earlier than the others to cook breakfast and he'd let Max join him. They hadn't spoken much, but Max had learned more, gained more confidence, in those near-silent exchanges than during any other time growing up.

"I don't like taking it off the hook. It feels weird."

"I can handle that part. Are you okay with eating the fish?"

Colby grinned and held up his cup of crackers, rattling them. "I like all kinds of fish. But I mostly like the real kind grilled. And corn on the cob, too."

And right there, the boy had said the most words at once in Max's presence.

The sense of victory rivaled winning a multimillion-dollar contract. The feeling gave him a moment's pause. This simple outing was supposed to be about Colby... not about Max. He was supposed to be careful the kid didn't grow too attached to him.

Max hadn't considered he might actually become attached to the child.

Clearing his throat and shaking off the unsettling feeling, Max stood, careful not to move in too close to the boy and encroach on his personal space. "Let's talk to your mom."

They made their way to the sewing room. Glancing around, he realized how busy she was with the client. An explosion of lace and patterns seemed to occupy every spare surface. Chaos contained, but only barely.

Somehow amid all this chaos, Lexie managed to find sleep. She was curled up on the nap mat and did not stir.

He waited for a break in her conversation with the customer, then asked softly, "Natalie, do you mind if Colby goes fishing with me?"

She glanced at him, then at the customer and over at napping Lexie. He could see her independence at war with her need for help. "Max, are you sure you don't mind?"

"I wouldn't have offered if I didn't mean it."

Colby stepped inside the room, shuffling his feet, eyes darting. "Please, Mom."

Her face melted into a smile. "Of course, son. But you have to promise me you'll listen to Mr. Max and don't wander off. Okay? Promise?"

Colby nodded solemnly. "Promise."

Her smile growing, she gazed at Max. "Thank you so much for the generous offer. There's fishing gear in the shed out back. And please be sure to use the extra car seat in the mudroom."

Max nodded, already planning a quick trip to the store because he wasn't using her dead husband's gear. "We'll do our best to bring home food for all."

He drove them to the local fishing store for an array of supplies. Colby picked out two poles and Max chose one. They loaded up his SUV with tackle and bait. Colby seemed excited by the lures, and his smile grew as they approached a nearby river.

An hour had passed by in a whir of activity. They'd managed to catch three sizable fish. Colby clapped after he brought the first fish to shore, excitement wriggling through his little body. Three fish were chilling in the icebox they'd brought, certainly enough for dinner.

The silence of the last twenty minutes felt soothing.

Max felt himself decompress as they sat side by side, listening to the softer sounds of the river as it whirred by. He'd purposely chosen a spot away from some local picnickers, and enjoyed the view of the houses on the other side of the water and the big live oaks shading a bend in the river. Every now and then, a fish jumped, the splash making a wet plunk. Other than that, the day was quiet. The silence had attracted him to computer work. He liked the self-reliance that silence forced.

Colby seemed to enjoy the quiet, as well.

To make the boy feel as comfortable as possible, they'd brought Miss Molly. Max had been concerned the dog might bark and scare way the fish, but the golden retriever was as quiet as a church mouse. She simply rested her head on Colby's leg, her wide brown eyes watchful, alert, but calm. Max was starting to buy into this whole service-dog angle for autism. It had seemed kinda fuzzy wuzzy before. Not very scientific. But Max had been watching. And the dog employed techniques to keep Colby calm that went beyond the boy just feeling comfortable with his four-legged companion. Pressure at just the right moment to stop a meltdown. Alerting Natalie when Colby was growing agitated. The list went on and every time Margie came by for lessons, they fine-tuned training, increment by increment.

Colby cast a quick glance Max's way, then turned his face back to the water. "My dad isn't coming home."

The air whooshed from Max's lungs. This conversation had gone deeper than he'd expected. Deeper than he thought Natalie would want. But right now Max had to handle this as best he could for Colby's sake. "I'm very sorry about that."

He nodded, his head moving like the jerky fishing bobber. "Mom's sad."

Of course she was. Could that be a part of her pulling away? And how damn wrong was it to feel jealous of a dead man? "And what about you?"

"Lexie's sad."

"And you?" Max asked again.

The grief in the boy's normally rather flat tones tore at Max. "I don't like when people are sad."

"I don't either, buddy."

"I'm not your buddy."

"Why do you say that?"

"You don't know me."

"All right. Fair enough." More silence sprang up, allowing Max to contemplate the boy's words. Max knew what it was like to be wary of trusting other adults—part of why he'd been so drawn to the logic of computers. An idea tugged at him. He cranked his reel in, then cast again. "Colby, when we finish up here, would you like me to show you some fishing games on my computer?"

"Yes, please." He nodded eagerly, still keeping his face forward. "But we're still gonna grill our fish, right?"

"Absolutely," Max said without hesitation, pumped at the boy's enthusiasm over the computer idea. "Absolutely."

And he was unsettled at how much this victory meant to him.

The sun had already receded from the horizon as Natalie stood at the sink and cleared off the supper dishes. She'd tucked her children into bed, and sleep had found them quickly.

Colby had gone to sleep so quickly and deeply he hadn't even needed his weighted blanket that helped him with sensory issues. He'd clearly enjoyed his afternoon with Max. Which, of course, made her happy.

But, God, it worried her a little, too. She hated that she had to worry about that, since she wanted desperately to see more signs of him connecting with people.

"You're quite the chef." She scraped the traces of grilled catfish, corn on the cob and a raisin-and-rice salad into the garbage disposal.

"You should see me in my own domain." He sprayed cleaning solution on the kitchen table. The gesture didn't go unnoticed by her. Receiving help wasn't something she was accustomed to, and she appreciated it.

Moving from the trash can to the sink, she pressed on. "Your house in Seattle?"

"Condo actually, in my company's St. Cloud Tower. It keeps me close to work."

"A condo. In Seattle." She couldn't imagine living without a yard for her children and Miss Molly to run in.

"I haven't had much use for a yard with all the time I spend away from home. But I can see the benefits of a porch swing." He winked. "I'll have to look into installing one on my rooftop garden."

For a moment, her mind wandered to the rooftop garden. What it would be like to nestle next to him in the cold Seattle air on that yet-to-be-installed porch swing. "I imagine that would be a lovely view."

"You should come see it."

She just laughed softly. Like that was even possible.

"You should," he said with unmistakable sincerity. "I could cook for you there. My kitchen is a sight to behold."

"Unlike here?" She waved around her kitchen. Homey, sure. Up to code. Clean. But a long way from the high-tech sort of place a billionaire could afford.

"That's not what I meant. It's up to the chef to create. I was simply stating what I could do, and what I would like to do for you." He moved toward her and kissed the nape of her neck.

Her throat bobbed as she swallowed, breathing in his scent. Musky temptation. But she had her reservations…like how to figure out a way to make things more comfortable between them. Hell, how to even tell him. "You have already done so much—cooking me dinner, fixing my sink and all you're doing for the town."

He ran soft fingers up and down her arm, sending shivers through her body. "We're talking about you and me."

"This is strange territory for me, this whole dating world. It's been so long I've forgotten the rules." Her fingers found his.

He lifted her hand to his lips. Kissed her, maintaining eye contact. "There are no rules. Only what you and I want."

"If only it could be that simple." She sighed, avoiding his gaze, along with telling him her thoughts. Aside from her being embarrassed, men could be so…sensitive, when it came to how things went in the bedroom. Her hair obscured her vision.

"It can be."

"How?"

"I pour a glass of wine for you and grab a beer for myself and we go outside, sit on your porch swing. We can talk, look at the stars, make out a little."

"What if I want more?" At some point. Because she really did.

"Oh, we're going to have more. But I can sense from you that tonight is not the right time for that."

"Seriously?"

"Yes." He touched her hair. "You still have things going on in your mind, and there's the issue with not wanting gossip."

She swallowed hard to give herself time to weigh her words. To be sure of what she wanted to say. "I guess it's unrealistic for me to think the town expects me to never see anyone. And you did an admirable job with Colby today." She felt like she was standing on the edge of something…important. "So as long as I'm not making a spectacle of myself and you can handle that I need a couple of steps back to regroup…?"

Natalie left the thought unfinished rather than continue her nervous ramble.

He stepped close to her, closer still until their bodies brushed if not their lips. "Lady, I hear what you are saying and want to reassure you. I am in control of myself. You could take off all your clothes here, now, and nothing would happen tonight. I want everything to be right for you."

At the sound of his syllables, a rush went through her. Her heart beat out of time as she considered his control.

And she found she did trust him at his word. As much as she would enjoy being intimate with him again, this was all moving so quickly between them, at warp speed, actually. And an old-fashioned evening date in her backyard could give her the info she needed to help protect her heart.

Or would it sink her deeper into temptation's way?

Eight

As Max approached Natalie, who was sitting on the porch swing, his breath hitched. The night was perfect in a way he could barely quantify. The whole vibe, the moment, was just right there in the pocket with a rightness he couldn't deny. From the woman in front of him, to this idyllic haven she'd created on her property.

The hooting of an owl mixed with the gentle creak of the porch swing. He extended the glass of chardonnay to her, his fingers grazing hers.

That awareness returned to his limbs, his chest. Damn. Her emerald eyes were grateful as she took a sip of the wine.

Sitting next to her, he stretched his arm around her back. Natalie settled into him, that limber body pressed up against his chest.

It was a perfect contrast of warmth to the increasingly cool September air. The B and B had dull lights at best, providing a somewhat uninterrupted view of the stars in the sky.

Taking a swig of his beer, he embraced everything—the sounds, the air, the potential of the ridiculously sexy woman next to him. Her soft curls cast shadows across her face in the shuttered porch light, making her look alluring. Mysterious. Sexy as hell.

Next to him, Natalie sighed deeply, swaying more into the rhythm of the swing. Tempting him and testing his resolve.

He'd meant his vow not to take her to bed tonight. He was a man of patience and she clearly needed space to process what had happened between them.

And he had to admit, their night together had moved him more than he'd expected.

She was right. They were moving fast—both of them.

No question, he wanted to be with her again, and he wasn't sure where this crazy draw was headed. He didn't know where it could go. He couldn't ignore the importance of being careful for her kids. Great kids who were fast becoming more than just Natalie's children.

They were people in their own right.

Lexie.

Colby.

The dinner tonight had tasted better than any in recent memory and he had to be honest with himself. It was the company that added the special seasoning that flavored the meal to perfection.

So where did that leave him? He understood her concerns and reservations. Maybe it was time to help her understand more about what made him the man he'd become. A man who wasn't right for her but wanted her all the same. A man who wasn't good at denying himself what he wanted except he had to be that man. For her, tonight at least.

But tomorrow? Away from here and prying eyes?

He rested his beer on his knee and tucked her to his side. "I know how to cook because of this one foster home I lived in. It was a really good home. People talk about the bad ones so much, and sure, there are some." He shook his head. "But there are some good and amazing people out there opening their homes to children in need. Not enough of them. But plenty."

"And you learned to cook in one of those homes because of the foster mom?"

Memories flashed before his mind's eye. A montage of baking in the well-lit kitchen. Lessons in cooking fettuccine alfredo, lasagna, chimichangas and frittata. Eliot, his foster dad, arranging all the supplies on a faded laminate countertop. "Because of the foster dad. He did all the cooking and made a point of teaching us kids. He told us his wife worked hard and this was his way of pulling his weight. He also told us we would likely live on our own at some point in our lives and that the best way to save money was to cook for ourselves. Eating out was a treat, but not always the financially wisest or the healthiest move."

"Valid points and smart of him to teach you kids that." Her voice was soft and soothing, stroking along the edges of those memories.

"He was a wise man. I learned a lot from him." And back then he'd been hungry to learn and daring to hope he might, just might, get to stick around there long enough to learn a lot.

"Like what?"

A hefty sigh damn near deflated him. Of all the foster homes, that one with Eliot had been the closest he'd ever gotten to having a family. The memory of what-if still pained him. "How to change a tire. How to use crap to make things, which ultimately led me to build my first computer by Dumpster diving behind a few business offices and a computer store."

"How old were you while you were there?"

"For a little over a year when I was thirteen." He'd learned a lot in that year, things that had stuck with him long after he left. He'd just been too mad then to realize it.

"What happened?"

A knot formed in his chest. "He had a stroke, a really bad one. His wife couldn't take care of him and all of us foster kids. She wanted to." He believed that now, even though then he'd been so angry he'd doubted her. "But the system thought otherwise about her ability to juggle his care with raising fosters and they moved us all."

"I'm so sorry." She clasped his hand and rubbed lightly.

"That's life. It's not always fair and a person has to accept the things beyond control—or go crazy." He shrugged, swirling the beer in his bottle.

"You figured that out at thirteen?"

"Hell, no. My foster dad told me that, slowly, with drool pooling in one corner of his mouth, his left side almost totally paralyzed from the stroke. I just didn't fully accept it until later."

She angled her face to see him, her eyes searching his. "How is he doing now?"

"He died when I was nineteen." He tore his gaze away from hers and tipped up his beer for a long swig. "But I think of him when I cook and I feel like I'm honoring his memory. The way I see it, the foster system isn't perfect, but I made it through. I can focus on the good, and do what I can to help fix the broken."

"Fix the broken?" she asked sympathetically, lifting her wineglass to her lips. "How do you do that?"

"Ah, that's a story for another day."

Her eyes went wide and she lowered her glass. "You're a secret philanthropist."

He laughed lightly and tugged a lock of her red hair—God, it was silky. "If I talk about it, then it's not a secret, is it?"

"Magazines call you a billionaire playboy, but then go around doing all these nice things for people."

He shifted in the seat, uncomfortable with the turn of the conversation. "Don't romanticize me, Natalie. I've lived a footloose life as an adult, living my way. It's easy to be nice with all this money and freedom at my disposal."

"Max, you're trying to paint such a bad boy—"

He kissed her. Held her lips with his, not pulling away for even a second as he set aside his beer bottle, then filched her crystal glass to put it down. Hands free now, he wrapped his arms around her and hauled her close, giving his all to kissing her. The taste of wine on her tongue was almost as intoxicating as the woman herself.

And yes, having her in his arms was better than being tempted to talk more. She had a way of drawing things from him he hadn't thought about in years, and wasn't sure he wanted to think about now.

Losing himself in her was far preferable to visiting the past. And damn, he would like to completely lose himself in her body.

And Natalie swayed closer to him, her breasts flat against his chest, her fingers thrusting up and into his hair. She breathed a husky moan against his mouth. "I thought you said you're okay with my need for a bit of breathing room. That we weren't going to sleep together tonight."

"We aren't." He grinned, enjoying the sound of temptation in her voice. He could have her, but he could still sense the reservation in her. She might have come to his room, but clearly something about that gave her pause and she had the right to say no. And he would respect that, even as he gently pursued her. He wasn't going to risk spooking her altogether. "But I never said I wasn't going to kiss you absolutely senseless. Which now that I have done, I will say—" he kissed her lips, then the tip of her nose "—good night."

Training days in the yard with Margie always gave Natalie hope.

Hope for a fuller life for her son. Hope that somehow she was managing to give her children what they needed to grow into productive, happy adults. Listening to Max talk about his childhood reminded her of the lifetime of emotional scars that could be left on a person from their youth.

Hearing her son and daughter laugh was the sweetest reassurance of all. Today, Margie had been playing hide-and-seek with the kids and the dog, what she termed one of the early foundations of teaching K-9 search-and-rescue. While Miss Molly wouldn't be taking that path with her working life, she could be called upon to find Colby if he wandered off—not an unheard of occurrence for her brilliant, reticent son.

Lexie and Colby had spent the past hour hiding in different places around the yard, giving Miss Molly variations of clues to find them—anything from whispering, to squeaking a toy, even wearing a shirt from the dirty laundry pile to give Miss Molly an extra whiff of their scent on the breeze.

Miss Molly was a natural.

Natalie leaned against a tree, taking in the sight of Miss Molly tunneling under an upside-down kiddie pool, where her children were curled up together, giggling.

Lexie wrapped her arms around Miss Molly's neck and hugged gently. "Love you, my puppy." She glanced up at Margie. "This is fun. I like this game."

Margie adjusted the treat pouch strapped around her waist. "I'm happy to hear that. We'll play that some more in the future, all right?"

"Yes, yes, yes, yes!" Lexie wriggled farther out from under the baby pool.

"Yeah," Colby said simply, but his enthusiasm showed in how he leaped to his feet, upending the plastic pool.

Natalie pushed herself away from the tree and knelt by her children. "Margie's going to work on leash walking now, so would the two of you play in the sandbox? I'll be right here in eyesight and you can call me if you need me."

"Okeydoke." Lexie hugged her mom hard and pressed a sticky kiss on Natalie's cheek.

Colby nodded, following his sister to the wooden sandbox full of shovels and buckets and toy trucks.

"Miss Molly, come." Margie issued the command low and firm, her alpha-style authority a fun contradiction coming from the slight, wiry woman. Miss Molly stopped dead in her tracks, pivoted on her paws and trotted back toward them.

Even after these months of training since Natalie had

adopted Miss Molly from the Royal Safe Haven Animal Shelter and started the golden retriever's training, Natalie still found Margie's ability to command the dog with such ease impressive. That was why she was the professional, after all.

Miss Molly still had a lot of training to accomplish, but Margie assured them all was on track. Kneeling, the trainer hooked a service-dog-in-training vest on the yellow dog.

Glancing to the left, Natalie checked on her kids in the sandbox. Lexie and Colby had constructed a rather lopsided sand castle. Her daughter's infectious laughter mingled with the sounds of birdcalls and the hum of conversations on the front porch. Even Colby seemed relaxed today. Her heart squeezed, returning her attention back to Margie and training. Natalie hoped that Miss Molly's training would give her son every advantage in the world.

As Margie passed over a treat from her pouch, Natalie took a deep breath. The scent of fallen leaves filled her. She loved this time of year.

Her mind wandered a bit, picking up a well-worn trail in which she stored the recent memories of Max. His confident grin and mischievous eyes. The way his kisses hinted at his duality. Every kiss with him fused strength to passion, abandon to control. An addictive combination, if she were being truthful.

Last night had been a bit more of a high-stakes moment. The evening had unfolded with perfect ease. A combination of everything she needed. His kiss, his measured ability to keep things from escalating too far. Respecting her wishes and boundaries.

He'd been great with her kids. Especially Colby. He seemed to understand how to engage with him. Max was different than a lot of her friends in town, who, at first, tried to smother Colby with well-meaning affection. It had taken her closest friends some time to understand physical touch had to be dictated by Colby. But Max fell into a pattern with Colby. For that she was grateful.

He'd even shared more about his life last night, become more real by the hour. Her mind again returned to the kiss at the end of the night.

She'd wanted to go further...but there was still an awkwardness she couldn't get past.

Giving Miss Molly a hand and spoken command— *let's go*—Margie started a brisk walk toward the gate, Natalie walking alongside. They would walk the yard, and the perimeter, the children always in sight, while still working the training.

Margie made Miss Molly wait at the gate, then proceed forward on command. A few steps later, the trainer glanced at Natalie. "Honey, what's wrong?"

"I'm fine, really," Natalie said quickly. Too eager. The words betrayed her.

"You're actually a really a bad liar." Margie's eyebrows shot heavenward.

"Look around you. My life is complicated. I'm exhausted and sad and overworked. That's all." Natalie walked toward the cars. The dog seemed to be getting the message that when she wore her vest during an outing, she wasn't allowed to sniff. This had proven to be the hardest part of working with Miss Molly, but they were making progress.

"You've been that before and something's different. I want to help if I can. If you want me to. Does it have something to do with that hot, young boarder of yours?" Margie walked alongside Miss Molly, her eyes on the dog's movements but she was still concentrating on the conversation. "If he's messing with your heart, there are people in this town who will knock him down a peg or two."

"He's not playing with my heart at all. He's been completely forthright. I've been upfront with him, as well…"

"Then…?"

"It's too embarrassing to say." Natalie lowered her voice, eying her neighbors pushing their toddler on a swing hanging from a fat oak branch. Her heart squeezed with the beauty of all that promise.

Margie ducked her head conspirator-style. "Then I'm guessing it's about sex?"

And there it was. She'd slept with Max. He'd made sure she was satisfied. She wanted to go to bed with him again—needed a passionate affair. Her body was on fire every time he came near. Still… "How crazy is that? I've been married, but…" She shook her head. "It's kind of embarrassing."

"Can you talk to your mother?"

"Heavens, no." Natalie shuddered at the thought. What a way to make things more embarrassing. At best she would get either a lecture or encouragement to pursue Max because of his wealth.

"Well, honey, you clearly need to speak with someone. We girls have to stick together and talk. Too much is kept secret out of embarrassment, and that makes me sad."

Natalie lengthened her stride to keep up, each breath shaking free thoughts through her mind like the rustling trees shedding leaves. "I want to be with him, I want an affair. I need an affair, something just for me."

"What's stopping you?"

"My husband was my first, my only, and, um, there's a size difference. Max was patient…and wonderful, but still, things were uncomfortable."

"Oh, my. That puts a damper on a moment, doesn't it? Could also be your extended period of abstinence making the situation even more complicated?"

"I considered that."

"These things happen. Happened to me when I went through menopause and my body went into seventy kinds of crazy changes. I learned from my sister that it can happen to cancer patients after treatments or surgery."

"That's so sad. How did I not know that?"

"We women need to talk more. It's silly to be embarrassed about our bodies and finding what feels good."

No one had ever been so candid with her. Not even her friends in college had talked about these matters so openly. A blush heated her skin. She couldn't control it, and it deepened into what felt like a bad sunburn.

"See, why are you blushing? Your man was gone a lot. My Terence was a traveling salesman. The week on the road could be long. I invested in some toys and the separation was less stressful."

"I really can't believe we're having this conversation."

"Fair enough. Boundaries should be respected. How about this? Do some reading online. There's a wealth of information on all the subjects I mention and ways to help ease that discomfort. You deserve to enjoy yourself and enjoy that hot, young man of yours."

Could it be that simple? Some practical answers to helping her body along and then going for what she wanted?

Take something for herself?

Take Max.

Damn, that had such an exciting sound she couldn't imagine saying no. If only life wasn't so complicated by her history with her dead husband, by being a single mother with children who deserved to be her priority.

And still, she couldn't deny, against her better judgment, she wanted Max.

Eyes growing heavy, Max forced himself to concentrate on the content on his tablet. As he sat on his bed against the overstuffed pillows, sleep tugged at him.

Stretching out, he readjusted. Propped his head in his hand. He needed to learn just a little bit more.

Max had never backed down from a challenge yet. After today, he wanted to ensure that he could be more helpful to Natalie. Which was why he'd spent the last two hours reading articles about dog training.

Max was a self-taught hacker—it had launched his cybercareer. He possessed a confidence that, given enough reading and research, he could figure anything out. It was a useful trait in his line of work. It probably was why he was so successful at his job. His need to know and understand things drove him to keep pressing on in spite of hitting brick wall after brick wall in investigating this maverick cybercreep.

A knock reinvigorated him, causing him to snap his attention from screen to door.

"Come in." As the words left his mouth, he hoped it was Natalie.

Sure enough, as if some magic prayer had been answered, she appeared at the threshold.

Damn.

Her damp hair fell in waves, adding to the feminine softness in her features. As she held up the phone that allowed her to listen to her children, her green eyes were filled with hope. And something else. Something he was sure was also present in his hungry gaze.

A faint smile played on her lips as she pulled innocently on her loose yellow sundress. Stepping all the way into his room, she shut the door behind her. Took a deep sigh and stared at him.

He took in the sight of her. From the damp hair and bare feet, it was clear she had just showered. She had come to him renewed, that electricity stronger than ever before.

She shut the door and leaned back against it. "I've been doing some reading myself."

Where was she going with this? "Reading is good."

"Informational reading," she said with extra emphasis, biting her bottom lip.

"Okay." What was he missing?

"On our issue."

"What issue might that be?" He placed his tablet on the bedside table and sat on the edge of the mattress.

"This is embarrassing to say—" she scrunched her nose and braced her shoulders, creamy shoulders bare with just the straps of her sundress "—so I'm going to spill it all really quickly and I need you not to interrupt so I can just get it out there. All right?"

He nodded, staying silent, curious as hell as to what she was going to reveal. She looked so serious and intense.

And nervous.

The last thing he wanted was for her to feel apprehensive around him.

"Clearly you had to have noticed that when we had sex, there was some discomfort. We talked about abstinence being an issue. You're also, um, I don't want to sound disloyal, but there's a size issue, too."

Size? His brain went on stun for a moment, not sure he'd heard her correctly; then he thought back to their night together, needing to go slow, to give her time to adjust and realized, holy hell, she'd been more than a little uncomfortable.

He wanted to launch from the bed and close the space between them, cradle her close and make sure she was okay, but she had a distinct stay-back expression, her eyes filled with the unmistakable need to say more.

But he had something to say first. "Natalie, if I hurt you, then, God, I'm so sorry—"

She held up a hand. "No, you didn't hurt me and you have nothing to apologize for. You're...more. So I read up on how to help make things easier for us and I have ideas. Why are you smiling? I'm being serious here."

Was he grinning? Hell, yes. "You want to have sex with me again. Of course I'm smiling." And he was doing his best not to just jump her, because she was here and he was throbbing to have her under him.

Over him.

Beside him.

"I'm trying to be serious here."

"Okay, I can be very serious about having sex with you. Tell me more about your research."

"You don't look very serious."

"Oh, I can assure you." He stood and moved toward her. "When it comes to making sure you are thoroughly, completely, blissfully satisfied, you have my one hundred percent undivided, serious attention."

Her eyes flicked to his as he closed the distance between them. Her eyebrows rose, anticipation showing on her face. Inviting.

Max's hands went into her hair, and he let a soft triumphant laugh roll free as he brought his face to hers. He could feel the smile in her cheeks.

They stayed at the precipice of a kiss for a moment, sharing breaths. Natalie's hands wrapped around him, tightly, urgently.

Kissing her caused his whole body to pulse with life. Quickly. Fully. Because, there was no denying the truth. A kiss from Natalie topped anything he'd felt with women in the past.

Right now he couldn't even bring their names or faces to mind.

His thoughts, his gaze, even his breath, were all focused on *Natalie*.

Nine

Max's skilled tongue and roving fingers had Natalie's toes curling. With a heavy inhale, she soaked in his hot breath on her skin, the subtle nudges pushing her closer. And closer.

They'd barely begun, and this man had somehow already had her pushing on the throes of total passion.

"Hold right there." His deep voice rumbled in her ear.

Her eyes fluttered open as she stared at him in amazement. Her body was still ablaze from his touch. "Excuse me?"

"Don't move." He sprang to his feet, crossed to the oak dresser and opened the top drawer. "Close your eyes."

"Um, I'm not so sure about that." Angling her head to the side, she studied him in the dull yellow light of the room. God, he was so starkly handsome. "That requires a lot of trust."

"You're here, so I hope that means you trust me." He

winked. "If that's the case, I promise to do my best to make sure you won't be disappointed." He tapped her eyebrows one after the other, encouraging her.

"Okay, then." She shut her eyes tight, resisting the urge to peek, though curiosity gnawed at her. Nerves pulled at her, along with anticipation. She wanted this. She was determined this time she could lose herself without reservation. She'd done her best to prepare, to absolutely make the most of this moment.

Which would be helped tremendously by taking control of her nerves.

One deep breath at a time, she pushed away concerns and sank into the present. Only here. Only now.

Natalie began to enjoy a sensation of sounds. She could hear his muffled footsteps on the carpet as he worked around the room. From the thuds, he never seemed to linger in any one place for long. The drawers opened with the creaking only old wood produced.

The sound of hurried assembly mingled with a match strike—a subtle smell of fire entered the air. Natalie felt twin to the match flame as it found the wick. Light vanilla and jasmine scents wafted through the room.

She smiled without opening her eyes. "You have candles? I assume you weren't planning for a power outage."

"I was planning—hoping—for this." His footsteps came closer, closer still until his breath caressed her face. He took her hand. "You can open them."

The world, blurry at first, was ablaze.

One blink. Two.

Then her eyes adjusted, revealing a fairyscape of winking, twinkling candles scattered all around the room, seeming to occupy every available surface.

Pink and white rose petals decorated the floor,

around the bed. Decadent chocolates swirled in elaborate designs on a silver plate, and imported sparking water glimmered in the light.

She was touched that he'd planned this—and curious. "You were mighty certain we would be back here."

"I wanted to be prepared, just in case, since options for pampering you have been limited." He held her face in both palms. "And trust me, lady, I very much want to shower you in meals and travel and gifts and a million other ideas, if you would just let me."

The thought of that made her head swirl with the complications and problems that would arise from juggling that lifestyle with her children. Sure, people with kids lived fast-track lives, but she didn't. And Colby also thrived on routine. Each thought made her more tense. She had to stop thinking about tomorrow if she expected to enjoy tonight.

She cupped his mouth. "Sweet, but not necessary. I'm not here because of what you can buy me. It's not about money." She waved a hand around the room. "All of this is thoughtful. That's what makes it special. That's what makes *you* special."

"I take that to mean you'll get naked with me." A crooked smile spread across his face. He breathed the words onto her skin, plucking the already-loose dress.

How ironic that he was a cyberguru and after her confidential chat with Margie, the internet had proven to be a helpful source of info on how to relax.

And the best part? The more she slept with Max, the more her body would accommodate him, the more pleasure she would find—and being with him had already been mighty damn satisfying.

Now that she'd done her research, she felt freer, ready.

"I consider it a race to see who can get their clothes off first." She couldn't work fast enough to liberate herself from her sundress, nerves pushing her onward. Delighted by his gesture. By the candles. She'd raced into intimacy headlong in a selfish need to indulge herself after the year of hardship and grief. But now her focus was on Max and the step they were going to take... together. Natalie unzipped her dress as he flung his T-shirt to the far corner of the room, revealing that muscled chest. Damn. Desire pulsed in this momentary pause of appreciation.

"I'm a competitive man. Very competitive." A deep, throaty laugh. With ease, he kicked aside his shorts and boxers, the discarded clothes joining his exiled T-shirt.

She pulled in a breath scented with his aftershave and vanilla candles, savory and sweet. Her heart raced at the sight of him. Endlessly masculine. Impressively confident.

He made her feel more sure of herself, too. His ease with himself. His generous touch. All the ways he was comfortable in his own skin helped her to relax. She knew from her research that was the key to being with him. To resolving the sensual issue that had worried her the first time.

"Lucky me." She arched against him, wiggling out of the gold-toned panties until the two of them were flesh to flesh. Her breasts took in the sweet, gentle abrasion of his chest hair, which teased her nipples to tight, sensitive peaks.

His calloused hands slid down her back to her bottom and lifted her against him.

She viewed that as the very best kind of invitation to wrap her legs around his waist.

"Sweet," he growled against her mouth.

She melted against him, breathing into the moment, determined to wrest every amount of pleasure from this night. And yes, giving pleasure had its own rewards, better than any chocolate treat.

Natalie dug her heels into his back as he walked them toward the bed, her loose hair swaying along her spine.

"Hurry," she urged against his mouth. "We can have slow with flowers and chocolates, too."

She reached down to snag a condom off the bed-side table.

He growled in approval and backed her against the door, freeing one of his hands as she clamped tighter with her legs. She couldn't resist watching as he rolled the sheath down the turgid length. A shiver of antici-pation—and yes, even a hint of apprehension—rippled through her. She breathed, willing the tensed muscles to ease. Max pressed his hand to the door, his legs braced, his erection nudging against the moist core of her.

Breathing, sighing, her head back against the panel, she welcomed him into her body, gravity gently working its magic as he lowered her, filling her. She hooked her ankles and pressed him the rest of the way home. And oh, yes, this was good, so much better than good. Each slickened thrust sent shimmers of sensation through her starved senses.

Tremors began quaking soon, all too soon. Even knowing she would have him again tonight, she wanted to draw out this wild moment as long as possible. It seemed that the past couple of days had been a pro-tracted foreplay leading to this. He eased away and stared deeply into her eyes with an intensity that built her need to a taut point that just…couldn't…be…denied.

Finally—thank goodness, finally—he kissed her,

fully, thoroughly, and thrust into her with a thick abandon that sent her over the edge without warning.

She bit her lip to hold back a cry of bliss with each wave cresting through her. Her heels dug into his butt as she angled harder into the sensation. His breathing was ragged, urgent. Max moved faster, launching aftershocks. His shout of completion spurred a final wash of pleasure through her. Goose bumps prickled along her flesh, sparks shimmering inside, as well. His forehead fell to rest on the door, his cheek against her hair.

Replete, her body went limp. She kept her arms locked around his neck as they stood together silently for more heartbeats than she could count.

Then he released her and her feet slid to the floor. She started to lose her balance, her body still too sated to hold her.

Smiling, Max scooped her into his arms as he had before. "I have you. Relax."

Her body humming with approval, she kissed his chest just over his pounding heart. Later, they could talk.

As he lowered her to the petal-strewn bed, her senses lit at his thoughtfulness. The petals were satiny, but scented. He'd done such a lovely thing in preparing without assuming. She was taking one day at a time—and today was amazing and filled with passionate hope that for the moment edged out her concerns about protecting her children, her independence, her heart.

He smoothed stray locks back from her face, his eyes flaming over her. "You're so beautiful. Touching you turns me inside out. Hell, just the feel of your silky hair gliding through my fingers makes my teeth ache from wanting you."

Clearing her throat, she stretched out beside him, their legs tangled. "You don't have to speak and convince me." Her hands fell to rest on his broad shoulders, then she looped her arms around his neck. "I'm here and, yes, I can't deny we've both had chemistry from the moment we first met. I don't understand the why of it all. It just is."

"Some things don't need to be analyzed." His thick thigh nudged higher between her legs, a delicious weight and pressure.

"That's ironic coming from a techie." She chuckled lightly against his kiss.

He combed his fingers through her hair again, light crackles of static snapping through the air. "Business, computers, codes are the last things I'm thinking about when I'm with you."

"Hmm." She savored the feel of his bare skin against her, his hard, muscled body pressing her into the mattress.

"You know what I want now?" She linked hands with him.

His body tensed, his fiery eyes full of determination. "Name it. I'll make it happen."

She lifted his hand and kissed the back of it, then nipped his thumb. "I want that chocolate over there—and more of you."

Warm water streamed down Max's face, steam filling the shower stall, and he gave a prayer of thanks for the tankless water heater that made it possible to stay in this shower with Natalie even longer still. He'd come a long way from the kid who'd waited in line for his turn in the bathroom, often behind a half-dozen other people. Yeah, he liked hot water. A lot.

And he liked being under that spray with Natalie even more.

It had been a natural progression, from bed to shower. All in the effort of cleaning up.

Sex had been great before. But after tonight...

A line in the sand had been drawn—their rhythms and chemistry syncing.

Heart pounding, he recalled when they'd eased into the stall in his private bathroom. He'd guided her in with a strong, stable arm, made sure she didn't slip on the beige tile as her smile—demure, once upon a time—turned feral with that arching eyebrow. She'd immersed herself in the water, enjoying every moment.

No one had ever been sexier. He was convinced of that.

Max wanted this borrowed time to last longer. Especially when she kissed him thoroughly like that.

As she leaned into him in the shower, Max took in a deep breath, the sensation of steam filling his lungs. Chest expanding, he wrapped his arms around her, spun her around to meet his still hungry stare. She seemed just as eager, just as awake as he was. Thick spirals of red hair settled on her back once she stopped spinning. He felt the wild abandon in her green-eyed gaze and it damn near singed his hair.

He kissed her deeply, his tongue grazing hers. Her kiss was literally sweet—chocolate still present in her breath.

They'd moved to another level, one where he suspected a two-week affair wasn't going to be long enough. Which presented a problem. He had to go home, back to work, while her home and work were clearly here.

Sure, he could return to Royal, Texas, every now

and again, but that wasn't sustainable. And she wasn't a booty call. So he needed to start exploring other ways they could see each other. And if she wasn't comfortable with those options outside her newly adopted hometown?

He refused to entertain the notion of defeat. He hadn't built a multimillion-dollar corporation from pure sweat and grit by thinking negatively or admitting defeat easily.

He stroked back her wet hair. "Now, let's figure out where you want to go for our next date. New Orleans? Miami? Or maybe you'd like to go west? Las Vegas? Chicago?"

When she was quiet for a long moment, he acknowledged maybe those spots weren't the most kid-friendly. He tried to think of what would appeal to a young mother and came up with a new angle. "An RV trip to take in some national parks? I hear Yellowstone is something to see."

"Why so far-flung?" she asked him at last. "There are plenty of local places we could go." Switching spots with him, she leaned against the tile, arms crossed over her chest.

He regretted putting her on the defensive even more than he mourned losing the view of her beautiful breasts. Gently, he untwined her arms and stepped back into them. "I have a personal jet. Anywhere is local. Would you like to go overseas? We can do that as well with an extra day's notice if you need to arrange things with the kids. Surely you take an occasional day off from work."

A dismissive smile appeared on her lips. "You're overwhelming me. I'm a simple, small-town girl."

He lowered his lips to her face. Kissed her cheek,

nose, forehead. In a too quiet voice, he made his plea. "And you also moved around the country. I grew up simply, too. If you don't want to do a tourist kind of date, we could go to Seattle...my home."

The water pattered on the stall floor. Otherwise, their steam-filled world stayed silent for more than a few heartbeats.

Finally, she swiped shower spray from her eyes and said, "You're moving things along at light speed when I think we've already moved mighty fast."

"Okay, I'll concede this is a quick step forward, but, Natalie, you have to know I can't stay here indefinitely. I have a business to run back in Seattle. But I'm not ready to call our time together just a fling."

Natalie was worth so much more than such a flippant description. "What if that's all I can give you?"

Her words slapped over him in an icy wave as if the hot-water tank had just run out. He forced himself to stop and think, to study her face rather than just react. As he looked deeper into her eyes, he saw the contradiction to her words.

He saw vulnerability.

Protectiveness pumped through his veins. He was right in pursuing her. He just needed to persuade her. "Trust me on this, Natalie. We can have more than a couple of nights and one dinner out."

Her throat moved in a long swallow. "When I wake up each morning, it's all I can do to think through twenty-four hours. And that's because dough has to rise for the next day's breakfast. I don't have the energy to think longer than that. Maybe it's because hope saps my reserves. Perhaps that makes me a coward—"

"You're one of the strongest people I've met, and I

have come across some of the toughest of the tough in the business world."

"Thank you. Regardless, though, I can't promise you anything more than one day at a time."

He needed to retreat for the moment, and he knew it. He wouldn't push his luck so hard that it cost him this woman. He straightened, finding that familiar devil-may-care smile that had gotten him this far. "Twenty-four hours at a time? I can live with that."

"Seriously?"

"Yes, give me twenty-four hours to convince you we can enjoy twenty-four more on our own, away from here, just the two of us." He sealed his mouth to hers, water sheeting down his back, trickling over them as he backed her against the tile wall. "Mmm…" He moaned against her mouth, then said hoarsely, "Can you arrange an overnight sitter? Or would you like to take the kids? I can hire a nanny."

She leaned her head back against the tile, water clinging to her eyelashes as she blinked them open, full of passion. "I think it's best the kids stay in familiar settings for now. You're new to their world. For that matter, you're new to my world. I don't usually—"

He pressed a finger to her lips. "You don't need to explain anything. I understand. Now, where do you want to go?"

She kissed his fingertips, staring at him. "Vegas sounds fun."

"Vegas it is."

A shift in her eyes matched the twitch in her lips. "But I was actually thinking perhaps Seattle. If it's not an encroachment on your space, I would like to see your home."

Not at all what he had anticipated. But a home-turf

advantage? He could handle that. "I would like to show you my home and my offices."

"What about the investigation here?"

"Actually, I've hit such a brick wall on that, I'm thinking fresh eyes would help. I had already been considering consulting with my CTO—chief technology officer—Will Brady. This would be the perfect time for him to scope out the town and data collected with objective eyes, without me here to skew his impressions. Then when you and I finish our date trip, Will and I can put our heads together."

"You are quite the multitasker." Her words barely registered as she pressed her mouth to his with another kiss.

He'd won the battle here, if not the war. A victory. For now, he could accept that much.

But for how long?

Tall snowcapped peaks stood as sentinels, providing a backdrop for Seattle that seemed, to Natalie's eyes, magical. The jutting mountains and deep green pines bit into the clear blue sky. An impossible blue rendered crisper from the cool weather in the Pacific Northwest. She had no doubt she would experience Seattle's infamous gray skies, but for now, in the moment of her arrival, the sky stretched before her. Endless possibilities.

Or perhaps that more accurately described her feelings about this trip.

She hoped her time here could help reassure her of ways she and Max could be together, ways they could blend their two very different lifestyles.

She vacillated between hopelessness and total optimism and back again, over and over. Perhaps because she'd had too much time to think while traveling on her own. Max had flown out early on a chartered jet because of a work emergency while Natalie had settled her children, and tried hard not to chicken out over flying on his private jet.

At least no one had outright questioned her. The knowledge in their eyes was clear, though. Gossip spread like wildfire in a small town. Everyone in Royal had known she was dating Max, so she gave up trying to keep their relationship quiet.

Both the town and her B and B were abuzz with her news. Even her friend Brandee had called the trip "serious."

Settling deeper into the limo's leather seat, she bristled at the word *serious*, turning the weight of the word over in her mind. Natalie's heart was still heavy from the loss of her husband and the marriage that had started to fray. Her children at least seemed to accept that Max was a "friend."

Her eyes flicked from the mountains to the buildings, noting the way bookstores, tech companies, music venues and coffee shops pressed into each other. It was a spread of literary and tech culture merging together.

Undeniably beautiful. A place she could enjoy visiting...but living here? She shook off the thought. She needed to be in the moment and not make decisions quickly either way.

Fluffing her scarf around her neck, she caught a glance of her reflection in the dark window of the limo Max had arranged to be waiting for her when the flight landed. Her skin glowed brighter—the result of some serious pampering at a spa. Much needed, she'd realized, during the massage.

Her dear new friends—Brandee and Emily—absolutely insisted on treating her to a spa day. They said she worked too hard, spent too much energy on everyone else. "Where is that attention to you?" Emily had asked, her brows arched heavenward. When Natalie didn't respond, they had arranged for a sitter and whisked her away to the day spa for relaxation.

And a makeover.

Her friends had recruited fellow TCC member Naomi Price, a stylist with her own local TV show, who'd brought in racks and racks of incredible designer duds. They'd even commandeered Royal's St. Tropez Salon. It had been a fun and magical experience. She would be lying to herself to think otherwise.

Gazing at the shadowed reflection in the window, she realized that her apprehension didn't just stem from being whisked away to Seattle, or having so many people so publicly aware of her dating life. Those were factors, of course.

But the brimming tension in her tummy came from wondering what he'd make of her new haircut—the shorter strands of strawberry that framed her face called more attention to her green doe eyes.

She touched the silky strands that still seemed slightly chilled, despite the warmth of the limousine.

As Natalie surveyed the skyline, she smiled. Bold buildings—as bold as the mountains in the background—seemed to erupt into the sky. Nothing demure or subdued about this space.

It suited him, she thought to herself.

Much like the small B and B suited her and her children. How strange the way people took on the qualities of their geographies.

Natalie inhaled, absently drinking in the way couples huddled to each other in the cold weather. Texas had yet to become this chilly—it was still only late September.

She wondered how her children were doing without her, even though she knew they were fine thanks to constant text updates and photos.

Margie had offered to watch the children while Natalie visited Max. Over these past few months, the dog trainer had become family—a mother she didn't have. A mother she self-selected. There were no words to convey her level of appreciation for that, or for how wonderful she was with both of Natalie's kids, especially with Colby. Margie even offered to stay at the B and B, which would be the least disruptive to Colby's routine. And if anything were to go wrong overnight at the B and B, Margie could attend to that, as well.

Brandee, Emily and Max's good friend Chels had offered to run the B and B in her absence. Her heart squeezed as she realized how lucky she was to have such friends in her life.

Small gestures were all she had ever had to offer. Small, intentional gestures. Natalie left Margie a fresh-baked casserole for breakfast, tons of fruit already sliced and diced and her to-die-for strudel. She'd also made Emily, Brandee and Chels strudel, as well. A small thank-you, but she'd poured her soul into the baking.

As they drew closer to the St. Cloud tower, her heart beat wildly, disrupting her normally steady demeanor. Shiny black glass dressed the spire in a dark elegance. Power seemed to cling to every aspect of the building, which was as mysterious and seductive as its owner.

The limo driver pulled up to the sidewalk, hopped out of the car to let Natalie out. Cold air caressed her cheeks, deepening the newly acquired blush—another result of Brandee and Emily's makeover.

The driver helped her out of the car and handed off

her luggage to the doorman, who ushered her inside, out of the wind.

Max lived in the penthouse. As the elevator rose, her heart sped up, butterflies returning to her stomach. She wondered as they passed the floors that housed his company what he'd be wearing, how he would react to her new look.

The door to the elevator opened with a ding. Her stomach turned with nerves.

There he was. Waiting for her. It looked like he might have been pacing, the way his muscled frame seemed to lurch forward as she met his gaze.

His lips parted ever so slightly. Eyes turning wide, growing with delight. His smile was genuine and deep as he took her hands and looked her up and down. "*Well*, hey."

"Well, hey," she teased back, his obvious pleasure warming her inside and out.

With a quick head shake, Max picked up her bags from the doorman, eyes staying fixed on her as she stepped through the threshold. And the second the door closed, he took her by the hand again and swung her into his arms. His kiss was fast, intense, deep.

Familiar.

They'd crossed into a new realm. A relationship. This was real. Toe curlingly so. She kissed him back with a familiarity that strummed her senses.

His hands skimmed down her spine and up again. "I missed you."

"I saw you this morning."

"Hours ago. Too long." He kissed her nose.

She felt her nerves settling at the rightness of being with him. She winked and then looked past him to a huge two-wall corner window sprawled in front of her, revealing a perfect view of the Space Needle. A small gasp leaped from her lips. "You have to know your home is incredible. The view is…indescribably gorgeous. No wonder you love it here."

"It was the logical place to make my mark. A techie mecca, home to companies like Amazon and Microsoft."

Max shrugged in his flannel button-down shirt. A casual look for a casual answer and a man who she was realizing didn't have a typical billionaire glitz she would have expected.

Her mind skated back to his words about Seattle. So he didn't feel attached to the town?

As quickly as she formed the thought, she tossed it away. This was about taking things twenty-four hours at a time. To think about him calling somewhere else home implied something she wasn't able to consider.

Just being here alone with him at all felt…surreal.

He placed her suitcase and his computer bag on the sleek black leather bench by the door. She immediately discarded her scarf, but elected to keep her jacket on. A chill lingered.

"I thought we could eat here tonight, on the balcony. Unless you would prefer to go out and see the city?"

Even though his private jet had been tricked out with every luxury she could have asked for, she'd been too nervous to eat or nap, which left her famished and drained. "Let's eat in tonight. Tomorrow you can give me a quick tour of the city before we fly home."

At least they would get to return to Royal together.

For how long?

She shushed her thoughts again before they could ruin their time together before it even started.

"Supper here, then."

She wondered if he planned to call in a catered meal or if there was something already here. He seemed so in control and not concerned she figured he must have plans A, B and C.

He strode toward the kitchen. Envy for a space like this tugged at her baker's heart. The counter space alone made her drool. But the top-of-the-line steel appliances were stunning—paired perfectly with the industrial aesthetic of the concrete. A chef's stove—gas with additional burners. A wine refrigerator.

What she could do with a kitchen like this at her bed-and-breakfast!

Max opened the refrigerator, eliciting a hiss from the mingling of air. She leaned on the countertop, the concrete cool against her fingertips. He pulled out a parcel wrapped in butcher's paper. "I had the ingredients delivered for me to cook supper for you." He grinned over his shoulder. "I do enjoy my kitchen, so I gotta confess I'm glad you opted to eat in. I ordered beef, since you appeared to like our dinner out."

"I did. Very much, thank you." She appreciated his thoughtfulness in noticing her preferences. "What would you have done if I'd chosen a restaurant instead?"

"I had my assistant make reservations as a backup at two different places." He opened the paper to reveal two generous portions of filet mignon. "Once I get this rib eye seasoned with porcini mushrooms and a rosemary rub, I need to head down to my office briefly. I hope you don't mind. You can make yourself at home here."

"If you don't mind, I would enjoy seeing where you work. Heaven knows you've seen every inch of my place, even the sewing room. If I won't be disrupting employees?" She had to admit, his world intrigued her. A lot.

"There's a private elevator from here to my office. But since it's Saturday, you won't have to meet a bunch of strangers. Most likely just my partner, Will, if he hasn't already left for Texas."

"I'm glad you'll have some help with your partner in Royal." She shifted her weight from right to left. The allure of the window called to her, and she found herself staring at the backdrop again.

"I will appreciate the fresh perspective. I feel as if I've hit a wall with uncovering who's behind the blackmail cyberattacks. After interviewing damn near everyone in town and scouring through all available internet data on them—including some backdoor searches it's best we don't discuss—I've hit a dead end. If I'm, uh, distracted, and missing something obvious, I need to know and I trust Will." He finished seasoning the meat, the spicy scent of garlic lingering in the air.

"Distracted?" She couldn't resist crinkling her nose at him playfully.

As he washed his hands, he tossed a wicked grin over his shoulder. "C'mon. Let me give you the grand tour of my company. I will warn you, it isn't as cozy as your setup."

"I would enjoy seeing your offices very much. And I totally understand that you're unlikely to have crayons and coloring books all over everywhere." She clasped his hand, electricity sparking between them with every touch.

The squeeze he gave her hand confirmed that he felt that connection, too.

He walked to the fireplace and keyed in a code. A large mirror slid to the side, revealing a private elevator. Definitely a different world than her homey bed-and-breakfast.

The elevator moved smoothly down ten floors from his penthouse condo, the doors sliding open to…not what she expected. She'd thought they would step into a lobby, but this elevator led straight to his office.

He shrugged. "It's a time saver. I'm able to slip into the office after hours and I'm able to step into work other times without people stopping me with a million questions. It's efficient."

She raised a hand. "You don't have to defend your wealth to me. You've made a huge success of your life. You should be proud of yourself."

"I do love high-tech toys." He pulled what appeared to be a small remote from his pocket.

Halogen bulbs winked on, flooding the room in bright white. Like his apartment, the space was sleek, embodying the bold architectural flair of Seattle. But with hints of color, hints of him…

A mixed-media Sherlock Holmes–themed painting depicting *A Study in Scarlet* hung behind his desk. No pictures, though.

She made his way toward his desk to inspect whisper-thin computer screens and touch pads. A neat pile of paper. An abacus. Orderly. So different than the chaos of the sewing room. Natalie heard the door click behind her.

She let out a low whistle, taking a turn about the room as she shrugged out of her sweater. "It suits you. What do you have to get done tonight?"

Natalie watched his eyes follow the descent of her fluffy sweater onto the desk. The temperature hadn't changed, but her body was heating.

"Um, I just wanted to show you the place and get, um—" His throat bobbed, eyes lingering on her curves.

Feminine power flamed inside her and she welcomed

the distraction from all the conflicting thoughts tumbling through her mind, jockeying for dominance. She angled back against his desk, crossing her legs at the ankles and holding his gaze. She tilted her head to the side as he approached.

He drew her in, their first embrace since she had arrived. For a moment—an infinity, it seemed like—they shared each other's gazes, drank in the nuances in each iris.

He angled his face toward hers, and his lips grazed her neck. Small kisses. A deep sigh pressed hot air onto her neck as he said, "Actually, I have a lot to do here in my office tonight."

Ten

Max had intended the trip to his office to be a quick stop to pick up work and then return to his penthouse to romance her with dinner on his balcony. Followed by an evening of lovemaking.

Apparently, they were mixing the order of his plans.

Leaving little time for conversation or regrets, Max flattened her back against the door. He kissed her, hard, fast, fully. Reasonable thoughts fell away as fast as her purse thudded to the floor. Heat poured from her lips, pulsing through his veins into a throbbing need.

Now that she'd made it clear she wanted him, he couldn't resist. Finally, he had her here, on his turf, in his domain.

And they were alone. Completely.

She grinned against his mouth. "Here?"

"If that's agreeable to you."

She took a step back, slipping her arms through the sleeves of her dress. "Very agreeable."

As Max watched her dress glide to the floor, he imprinted the memory of her in his brain. Hell, he knew full well, it was seared there for eternity. He would never forget the vision of her perched on the edge of his desk wearing nothing but heels and a do-me smile.

Control was shaky at best. But as he'd learned from her bold approach, her drive matched his. They could do slow later. And later again.

Keeping his eyes on hers, he made fast work of his polo shirt, before kicking off his shoes and slacks. He tugged free his wallet at the last second and placed it beside her on the shiny metal desk, flipping it open and spilling out a couple of condoms.

Damn, he should have put more than two in there. But then there were more in his condo.

He silenced her with his mouth, or maybe it was his hand sliding up a silken thigh, between her legs and finding her damp and ready for him.

Her hand slid down to clasp around him. A shudder rocked through him.

He tucked his arm behind her and swept the desk clear before lowering her back. Her hair spread in a stunning red fan along the stainless steel surface. He knew he would have a damn near-impossible job concentrating on work the next time he sat in that chair.

Natalie lifted a shapely leg and traced a toe down the center of his chest. Manicured red toenails grazed his pecs. His abs. His heart hammered in his ears. She was…incredible.

He tucked his arms under her knees and parted her legs, spreading her, all the while watching her eyes for any hint of protest.

She inched her heels behind him, pushing against his

butt and urging him nearer, nearer still until he slid…
home inside her.

His eyes closed at the warm clamp of her, and then
he angled forward over her, holding his full weight with
his elbows.

She clasped hands with him, linking fingers, squeezing.

And then he couldn't think beyond moving inside her,
holding her hands and restraining his release for as long
as possible. Praying she would find completion soon because he wasn't going there without her and the need to
finish roared through him like engines at full throttle.

He dipped his head to nip along her shoulder. A
groan whispered from her kiss-swollen mouth, filling
the space between them with her breath, faster, fuller,
a flush along her pale skin broadcasting how close she
was to unraveling, until…yes. Her arms flung wide to
grip the edges of the desk. She arched up, her body
tensed, moans of pleasure unrestricted. Yes, she had
found completion.

A good thing, since his orgasm was tougher and
tougher to withhold.

Finally, he allowed himself to plunge deep and hard,
his hoarse growl of completion echoing through the
empty office. His domain. His world.

And his woman.

He couldn't ignore the primal declaration echoing
through his mind, his body, his soul. And in spite of
all the reasons he was wrong for her, he began to think
the time had come to figure out how to make their
worlds merge.

The air didn't chill Natalie as she sat on Max's balcony while he leaned against the rail, thumbing through

work text messages. Despite the colder Seattle weather, she felt comfortable, seemingly heated from within. The passionate night had left her ablaze.

Though Max's portable heater certainly helped reinforce those thoughts.

The Seattle skyline was flecked and twinkled not with stars, but soft lights of buildings, a living constellation. The sounds of traffic echoed from far below, a distant beat that felt dreamlike. This whole night felt like the unreality of the border between sleep and consciousness, that temporality of potential and magic.

She sat on a plush lounge chair close to the orange glow of the heater, belly full from a five-star-worthy dinner.

That Max had cooked himself.

He was every bit the chef he'd claimed, his rib eye as fine as anything from a Texas steak house, and the kale salad and Asiago macaroni had both been delectable. And the chef had been every bit as enticing as the food. She'd enjoyed watching him deftly move around the kitchen in simple gym shorts and a T-shirt with a hand towel draped around his neck as he prepared their meal.

Most of all, she enjoyed the new ease that had developed between them. He was still his charming self, but in a more relaxed way with less of an aggressive push.

Although she couldn't deny that the speed of their developing relationship left her head spinning.

A slight wind rustled her loose hair. Strands stuck to her cheek. She pushed them aside and picked up her dessert bowl. The gray dish felt heavy and cold in her hand, a chill finally permeating the heat inside her. She scooted closer to the heater. Wearing Max's shirt might not have been the warmest choice, but she'd indulged, enjoying the sense of being closer to him. Savoring the scent of him clinging to the fabric.

Hunger for him stirred in her anew, and she spooned in the vanilla bean ice cream smothered in berries, feeding at least one appetite. She couldn't help being touched at how he remembered her love of ice cream. The fact that they were learning each other's preferences spoke of a growing intimacy beyond sex.

Was she okay with that? She glanced sidelong at him, watching as the wind stirred his dark hair. He gave her a full-out and genuine smile.

For the first time she really let herself consider the notion of attempting a longer-term relationship.

His phone lit up on the side table with a text, and his smile turned to half wattage as he tapped the cell. "I need to check in with Will soon to make sure he arrived in Royal."

She swallowed, the tart blackberry lingering on her tongue. "Okay, sure. The ice cream and I will keep each other occupied."

Exhaling hard, Max set his own bowl down. Sadness touched his features, carving a line of worry into his brow. "Will's had a rough run of it. He's a new widower and *way* out of his element as a single daddy to an infant girl."

"That's so sad. Single parenting is tough, no question." Flashes of another time, just over a year ago, scrolled through her mind. Of a fateful knock at her door. Somehow the sound of it had held a foreboding before she'd been able to confirm with her eyes what was being delivered. A military notification.

When she'd approached the door, baby on her hip, she'd known answering that knock would forever change her world.

A chilly wind blew across the balcony, almost as cold as the chill inside her from those memories.

She closed her eyes for a moment, willing the painful past away. "How is Will managing his trip to Royal?"

Standing, he looked down at his phone. "He has a full-time nanny for his daughter."

"That's good that he's able to travel with his child." She didn't know how she would have made it through without her children. Those days she'd wanted to curl up under the covers forever, she'd pulled herself from bed each day to take care of Colby and Lexie.

"I didn't mean to say the nanny and baby always travel with him." He scrubbed his hand over his chin. "He's having trouble with grief. I'm sure you understand that."

"Are you saying he's having trouble bonding with his daughter?" Jeremy had had difficulty connecting with Colby. She'd credited that to their son crying so much from colic. Then over time, it had become clear there was more than colic.

Another pang shot through her heart.

Max turned the cell phone over and over in his hand. "Will is a good friend, a good person. He won't abandon his child. Parenting is—and should be—a lifelong commitment." He held up his phone. "I need to check in with him. It won't take long."

She waved her spoon. "Don't rush on my account. I have plenty here to keep me occupied."

Natalie turned her attention back to the night skyline as she heard the sliding glass door rumble open, matching Max's baritone voice as he spoke into the phone. His voice faded, leaving her once again to the quiet of Seattle's night viewed from a penthouse height.

Taking in the magnificence of the Space Needle,

she turned his words over in her head about parenting. She appreciated that he understood that responsibility. Which, of course, he did, given his childhood that had left him abandoned by both his father and his mother.

But parenting as just a responsibility?

There was more. Another element. Love.

It was so important for children to feel their parents' love. Jeremy had tried with Colby, but he'd clearly felt a closer bond to Lexie and it had broken Natalie's heart to see the disparity.

She couldn't help noticing how Max tried equally with both of her children. He didn't give himself credit, but she could see his ease with both children, feel that he genuinely cared about people without reservations or judgment.

He was a good man.

A good man who lived in Seattle in a concrete palace. The balcony had an idyllic view, but the small space confined by rails clearly wasn't designed with children in mind. But there was so much space beyond here, out there in Seattle. Could she live here? Could he move his business to Texas?

Could he open his heart to her children?

Her stomach knotted and the spoon rattled back into her bowl. Had he imagined Max's connection to her children? Because when he was with her family, she couldn't deny that it felt right. Good. She owed it to herself—and her children—to at least give this relationship a serious chance. She could always invite him back to Cimarron Rose one last time just to see where it led…

What the hell was she thinking letting her thoughts travel those kinds of paths? Visiting Max was about having a fling. Wasn't it?

She'd just started to find her way in the world again,

learning how to build a good life for her children on her own. After the heartbreak of her marriage, did she have the courage to try for more again?

Back in Royal less than a week later, Max juggled two juice boxes in one hand while he held open Natalie's refrigerator, looking for the fresh apple turnovers that Natalie had left in the fridge. A surreal wave washed over him.

She trusted him. Implicitly. After being hesitant to allow him to be around her children, Natalie had left them in his care while she went to Brandee Lawless's house for a fitting. He'd helped load the car full of lacy material, measuring tapes and a sketchbook.

He smiled inwardly, recalling the way her nose had crinkled as she showed him the toy cabinet and location of all the supplies he would need for his childcare adventure. She'd kissed him deeply, been so appreciative of his help.

And he would not let her down. Picking up the apple turnover platter with his other hand, he turned to face Lexie and Colby.

Lexie twirled and twirled and twirled in her little pink dress.

"Mr. Max! Mr. Max! Look." She leaped, almost like a ballerina.

"That's perfect, kiddo. What do you say we eat some apple turnovers in the living room? Maybe watch some TV?" He smiled at her. So much energy out of one little body. He had to give Natalie even more credit than ever before. Taking care of two little kids was tougher, more exhausting, than any day he'd put in at the office. And she managed this while running a business.

He couldn't even claim that distraction, since the

B and B was empty for the morning, a slew of new guests due later in the day, the reason Natalie had opted to do the fitting now. She'd figured watching the kids would be easier.

Ha.

"Yeah, TV, TV, TV," Lexie squealed, clapping her hands as she bolted off to the living room in a blur of pink.

Colby shifted on his feet, looked at him. "Can we watch *Fishtales*?"

The question had caught him off guard, the way the boy was warming to him rather than just answering questions. "Of course we can, Colby."

"Cool." A rare smile tugged at his little mouth. Miss Molly nuzzled her charge's hand. Colby patted the side of his leg. "Come, Miss Molly. Let's go."

The trio walked to the living room. Lexie and Colby sat on the couch and sank into the cushioning. Max placed the plate of turnovers in front of them. Miss Molly, who had lain at Colby's feet, eyed the plate. Praying for crumbs probably.

Max thumbed the television remote, pulled up *Fishtales* and hit Play. He settled into the armchair, content. They could blend their worlds, bring them together. Natalie had spent time with him in Seattle, and now here he was back in Texas, figuring out the domestic scene.

Things could actually be this good. He swiped one of the apple turnovers, enjoying the spice of the cinnamon and the fresh apples. Calm. Everything was calm.

Until his phone vibrated three times in a row. Retrieving it from his pocket, he saw he'd just missed a call from Will.

A break in the case? Looking back at Natalie's children, he watched as they stared intensely, enthralled by a cartoon movie.

He would only be gone a few moments. He quietly excused himself, careful not to disturb their TV time.

Max made his way into the hall and pressed the call-back option on his phone. The phone rang once before Will's gruff voice answered.

"Hey, I just wanted to let you know we've gotten a significant amount of data from the algorithm you designed. I think that we might be onto something," Max's friend said by way of answering. Will was no-nonsense, always down to business.

Though Max could barely hear his friend over Miss Molly's whining. The dog came, nuzzled his hand. Whined again. Ran to the door and barked, distracting him from what Will was saying.

"I'm sorry, Will. Could you hold on a second?" Max asked, looking at the dog. Then back to the living room.

And only seeing Lexie.

He tamped down worry that threatened his focus and started walking through the downstairs, checking the bathrooms while his friend repeated whatever he'd said before. But Max couldn't think about the conversation or the case. Each step through the Cimarron Rose only hammered home that he didn't know where Colby had gone and there were no guests around who might have seen him or could help him look.

Miss Molly's scratching grew more frantic, and was now partnered with barking. Max jogged back to the kitchen and looked out the windows. Still no sign of Colby.

To hell with calm.

Panic surged through him. "Will, I have to call you

back." He hung up, moving to the door where Miss Molly scratched.

Damn. He'd turned his back for a minute. Maybe two.

But it had been enough time for Colby to leave, slip out the back door. Maybe if Max had paid attention to Miss Molly's whining sooner...

The thought chilled him. Grabbing Lexie by her hand, he ushered her outside, his heart pounding as they walked out the back door. His trained sleuth eyes scanned the horizon for any sign of the boy.

All the while, fear knotted in his chest. This was absolute failure. Never had he sunk so low, lost so much.

This wasn't a failed case. He couldn't locate Natalie's child. He'd let her down more than he could articulate. He'd made a mistake in thinking he could step into this family and be a positive influence. He'd hurt the woman he cared about in the worst possible way.

"Colby. Colby," he shouted, voice bellowing and echoing in the cool September air.

His heart hammered harder, faster. He called for Colby again and again, searching around the yard, in the bushes. The street was clear, but, God, he couldn't even stomach the thought of Colby out on a busy road.

"Colby," he shouted again.

Still, nothing. Not a sound came back. Except for the distinct sound of car tires on pavement. Natalie had come home, parking in the back as she usually did. He didn't even want to think about how terrified she would be. Right now he had to focus on the possibility that Colby would come out of hiding for his mother.

Hitching Lexie up to hold and be sure he didn't lose this one, too, he started toward Natalie. Saw her process the scene, the fear on her face registering as she exited the car. She knew, even before he opened his mouth.

Leaving the car door open behind her, Natalie ran toward the next-door neighbors. "The Albertsons. He likes their cat."

Max sprinted to catch up, a few steps behind her. He'd scanned the neighboring yards and hadn't seen the boy…but had he looked where a cat might be?

His gaze tracked up and…

"There," Max said, pointing at the Albertsons' tree, where Colby lingered. He was holding a branch, his feet braced against the trunk, ready to climb. Natalie rushed to her son and pulled him down. She hugged Colby hard, her fear for him clearly having overcome her normal restraint in giving the boy his space.

Miss Molly bounded over and nudged the mother and son. To comfort Colby? Or for Natalie? Either way, thank God, Colby had been found.

Max gripped the picket fence, more than a little unsteady. Relief washed through him.

Miss Molly pushed between Natalie and Colby. As Natalie rocked back on her heels, the sun glinted along a tear streaking down her face. That lone droplet clinging to her chin gutted Max.

Her devastated face said it all. She'd trusted him with her children and he'd failed. Failed her and failed the children.

"God, Natalie," he said hoarsely, setting Lexie back on the ground. "I'm sorry. So sorry."

Sorry for more than the moment. Sorry he couldn't be the man this family needed.

Eleven

As the door to Lexie's room clicked shut, Natalie let loose a breath she hadn't realized she'd held. The air expelled from her lungs, her chest deflating, taking with it some of the tension.

She ran a hand through her hair, letting the silken strands slip between her fingers, gaze shifting from Lexie's door to Colby's.

Thank God he was safe.

He'd slipped away before. A few times. Each time brought more panic to her lungs, to her limbs. She'd have to watch him more carefully—and warn newcomers about his tendency to sneak off.

Panic had held her chest in a tight knot in those few moments they searched for him. Now she crept to the door, just to make sure one last time that he was there.

Cracking the door open, she peered inside. She was comforted by Miss Molly's perked ears at the sound of her intrusion, and by the sight of Colby's sleeping body.

Satisfaction. Relief. Both those sensations filled her until her breath returned to a normal cadence.

As she turned the corner into the kitchen, her heart sank when another scene of departure greeted her, leaching the warmth from her fingertips. Deep down, she'd known this was inevitable, but still, she'd dared hope. And that hurt like hell.

Max sat at the kitchen table. Lines of anguish and, yes, defeat were carved in his face. His normally easy smile was replaced with a thin hard line. His eyes were downcast, seeming to examine the two leather bags off to the left of his feet.

He met her gaze, noticing her presence. Or maybe he had registered her sharp intake of breath.

While, yes, defeat colored his features, so did a kind of somber resolve. "I'm going to Chelsea's. I've already packed my computer gear. I think it's best."

Natalie blinked. Once. Twice. Tried to discern if this was indeed her reality. "That's it? After chasing me like crazy you're just leaving? I'm not a challenge anymore?"

His broad shoulders braced, his eyes pained but his jaw resolute. "It's not that at all. I'm not right for you, Natalie. I never was. I should have been honest with myself. I'm just not wired for being a part of a family lifestyle and routine."

Natalie couldn't speak, her throat was too clogged with emotion. She could only watch him scan the kitchen, his gaze pausing on Colby's fish drawings that hung haphazardly on the fridge. Total quiet descended, pressing down on the room.

On her.

Finally, he looked back at her, his eyes full of guilt on top of that pain. "Look at what happened today with

Colby getting lost. Who knows how long he could have been out if Miss Molly hadn't alerted me?"

The self-recrimination in his voice tugged her forward a step. She reached to him, her hand shaking, her nerves still rattled. "I should have told you he's an escape artist. I shouldn't have expected you to be a mind reader."

"Don't make excuses for me." He ignored her extended hand. "God knows, I can't make an excuse for myself. I'm sorry, Natalie, so damn sorry." He shook his head, seeming so distant now. His gaze turned inward, examining something she couldn't see. "You deserve better and I'm going to step out of the way so you can have it."

His words hurt, more than she would have expected, given how often she'd thought about how wrong they were for each other. Still, she'd dared to hope—he'd insisted she should. He'd made her live for more than the day. He'd renewed hope and confidence in her.

She was worth more than what he was giving her right now. He'd wanted her to take a risk, and now that she had done so, he was bailing.

Well, damn it, she wasn't letting him go that easily. "That sounds like a cop-out excuse to me. I told you I don't blame you. No one expects you to be an instant child expert in a few days. You're selling yourself short and just giving up. Giving up on us, giving up on a chance at the family you were robbed of in your early years." As she said the words, she found herself voicing the possibility in her heart, too. Yes, she'd dared to hope maybe they could work this out into a future that promised more. "There's a real possibility you could have that if you weren't so willing to walk away."

His jaw worked as he held her gaze for so long she

thought he might actually have heard her. She could see the war in his eyes, see that he was moved. Then he tore his gaze from hers and looked away, shaking his head. "You've been hurt too much, Natalie. And your kids deserve better. I'm a techie, a man of facts and probabilities, so I can calculate odds. All that training tells me, in no uncertain terms, I'm just not worth the risk."

Without meeting her gaze, he picked up his bags and walked out of her life.

Tension had been her constant companion since Max left four days ago. Her decision to call him out on running away still was the right one. Of that she felt certain.

Living with her parents' disappointment in her had finally given her the strength to see that she was a good parent. That she could raise her kids on her own and do a damn good job of it. She wouldn't settle for a man in her life who wasn't ready to shoulder the normal fears that came with parenting. But knowing she'd made the right call didn't do a damn thing to soothe the ache of missing Max.

Four days. It seemed like such a short amount of time.

And she missed him a helluva lot. Felt that longing in her chest, in the way her eyes absently, yet actively searched the parking lot for his rented SUV.

Even now, with Margie, she still found herself occasionally diverting her eyes from the yard. To the room where he'd spent so much time. To that other life she had glimpsed.

"I miss seeing Max around here." Margie tossed the tennis ball to Lexie, who giggled as she half caught, then dropped it. The golden autumn sun provided just

enough warmth to warrant a light jacket, even beneath
the shade of the tree.

Miss Molly barked in excitement as Lexie scooped
up the ball and tossed it with a strong pitch born of much
practice at the game.

"Max and I are no longer an item. It was…a risk.
That happens. Not every relationship turns into forever. Our lives are in different places," Natalie said in
a cool voice that made her seem much more collected
than she felt. Miss Molly dropped the ball at Lexie's
pink sneakers.

Margie looked at her sidelong, that knowing expression in her keen eyes. "Your boyfriend has a private
airplane. You're never far out of reach."

Boyfriend. What a surreal word. It sounded like a
word of days gone by, a time of innocence before so
much pain and loss. "Whatever he was, it's over."

Colby darted in front of them, the golden retriever
close at his heels, tail wagging in delight. Her heart
pulsed at the sight of her son's smile. Lexie threw the
ball back to Margie, catching the pup's attention.

"Oh, sweetie, I know you too well. We're your family now. That's how this town works, making family
connections out of strong friendships." Margie took
a turn at the game, lobbing the ball farther to give the
dog more of a workout. "I guess that's what makes this
hacker's attacks hurt all the more, since it means someone in our 'family' betrayed us. We all have secrets, so
we're all vulnerable."

A gust of wind rustled the yellow and red leaves that
peppered the still-green yard. The scent of pinecones
and the distant scent of a bonfire carried on the wind.
This small town offered her a haven. "Margie, I'm finding it tough to believe you have any dark secrets."

A deep laugh shook the older woman's shoulders. She tugged on the sleeve of her red-and-black-plaid shirt, eyes wide and kind. "Oh, honey, there are some, how shall we say it, boudoir photos I had made for my husband's birthday about twenty years ago. I never could find the negatives when I went through his belongings after he passed away."

"Oh, my." Natalie couldn't help grinning—and she also couldn't help marveling at the way Margie managed to smile over memories of her dead husband, to even joke over going through his things.

"Exactly." Margie let out a low, exaggerated sigh. "Every time I see a pink boa, I have twinges of fear of those pictures popping up."

"Pink boa?" Natalie asked, feeling more attached to Margie for her boldness now. A kinship, something like family. The family one chooses.

"And bubble-bath pictures." Her eyes twinkled for a moment. "My Terence sure did love that gift, though."

"Sounds like you had a wonderful marriage." Her heart squeezed at being denied that dream not once, but twice.

Margie's gaze went to the street, to a passing yellow truck. The sputtering sound of the engine filled the conversation for a few heartbeats. In a quiet voice, she nodded, blinking back tears. "We did."

"You were lucky." Was it so wrong to want a happily-ever-after for herself? A family life for her children?

Natalie's eyes flicked to the scene in front of her. Happy dog, happy children. This small town that provided them shelter. And yet...she wanted more.

"Some of it was luck. A lot of it was hard work."

Natalie bristled, ruffled to think that Margie was suggesting she wasn't trying enough now.

"Hard work isn't always enough." She and Jeremy had struggled. She liked to think they would have made things work, but she would never know for sure.

"I realize that, honey. But without the work, even luck won't pull you through. By giving it your one hundred percent, you do have the reassurance of knowing you did everything possible. And that's all we can ever control in life—what we do." She patted Natalie's cheek. "Be at peace with yourself about Jeremy, dearie. You deserve it."

How had Margie read her mind so clearly? The woman sure hadn't been joking about forging a family bond out of friendships. But then hadn't Max said the same about the foster father who taught him how to cook? That had been a family for Max.

A family Max had lost.

And in that thought, realization sank in. Max did know how to be a part of a family. And just as she had lost, so had he. That big bold man really was afraid of being hurt again.

Like she'd been doing, he was protecting his heart. Because yes, she loved him and she suspected he was falling in love with her.

Margie's words reverberated in her mind, about the only way to escape regrets was to give her all. She'd let Max walk out that door. She'd let the man she loved walk away.

And the only way she could be at peace with how her future played out was to know she hadn't left anything unsaid. She was strong enough to stand up for herself, for her children, for Max.

And for a chance at the future they deserved to have. Together.

A plan formed in her head, a way to start at least.

Parenting an autistic child had taught her she couldn't wait for problems to work themselves out. She had to be involved in positive change. To make the world a better place for her child. She needed to act. Maybe now she needed to take action for herself.

"Margie, did you mean what you said about us being family?"

"Of course, dear." Margie squeezed her hand. "What do you need?"

"Can you take the kids for the evening?" She reached into her pocket for her cell phone. "Given Colby's tendency to wander off, I need to upgrade my security system. And I believe St. Cloud Security Solutions has just the right person to install the best of the best."

In spite of his resolution to do right by Natalie and keep his distance, here he was again, at the Cimarron Rose.

Max thumbed the strap of the leather bag that he'd slung over his shoulder, taking comfort in the security gear inside. Most of his work focused on cybersecurity and grounds security for large corporations. But keeping Natalie and her kids safe? His most important job.

He'd leaped at her request that gave him a reason to be right where he'd been longing to be every second since he'd left. Even working like hell with Will and with Chels's brother, Daniel, hadn't provided the distraction he sought. Will and Daniel had all but thrown him out when the call came for a basic security-system install at Natalie's.

He approached the white picket-fence gate, drawing in a deep breath. He looked at the constellations in the night sky, taking reassurance from their twinkling as he did when he'd been on the street.

The night sky had always called to him, giving him constancy in a turbulent life.

He knew this wasn't his wisest move ever coming here. But when Chelsea told him Natalie needed a security system to keep Colby safe? There'd been no way Max could turn his back, or even send over Will. He would make Natalie's house as safe as it could be. Make her kids safe.

The past days without Natalie had been hell. The hole in his life a gaping wound. He still wasn't sure what to do—an anomaly for a man like him—but he also knew he couldn't keep hiding out at Chelsea's while he looked for the hacker.

He made a move to go to the door, then noticed the spotlight on in the backyard.

An awareness coiled in his stomach. Natalie was in the backyard. Probably on that glider with a glass of wine. Just as she'd been his first night.

He adjusted his course, made his way to the backyard. Needing—not just wanting—to see her.

His chest tightened as his eyes found her and took in the familiar sight of Natalie, feeling like it had been months since he'd seen her rather than days. Looking at him without speaking, she tapped the glider back and forth, her silver sandals glinting in the moonlight. Her sapphire-blue dress grazed her ankles, and strawberry curls fell loosely over her shoulders. She held a narrow goblet and rested it lightly on her knee.

A beer waited for him on the tree-stump end table. She'd taken a huge risk to her pride for him. Her giving heart and her confidence were…stunning.

Her calm face called him closer.

He made his way across the lawn, crunching leaves,

and then dropped his computer bag at her feet. "I hear you need a security upgrade."

Not his best opening line.

She gestured to the longneck bottle. "Have a drink and let's talk about what I need."

Had she meant the double entendre?

He took the beer and sat beside her. "I got your message from Chelsea." He glanced at her. "What would you have done if I'd sent Will?"

She smiled. "You didn't."

"I have trouble saying no to you." He took a risk and tucked a lock of her hair over her shoulder. His fingers ached for the familiar softness of her skin. "It's been like that since I first saw you. I want to give you everything. You deserve it, Natalie."

She took his hand in hers, looking at him with those clear green eyes. "That's ironic, since you're taking away the one thing I want most. You."

Hers words pierced right through him. Even more than the wind that whipped and rustled the trees. God, he wanted to cave right now, but he loved her too much—

Loved?

The word stopped him short. *The* word. The one he'd been hiding from since the first second he'd laid eyes on her.

He'd fallen in love with her at first sight. Which was why he was so damn afraid of letting her down. The stakes were the highest ever.

"Natalie—"

She pressed her fingers to his mouth. "I believe you that you would do anything for me. I do." Her fingers grazed down until her palm rested over his pounding heart. "And I don't want to take advantage of that. Instead of us spending so much time seeing how you fit into my life, I think it's time for me to be more open to discussing changes I could make. Seattle was gorgeous. I enjoyed my time there and can imagine spending time there, much more time."

Her willingness to compromise, to give up so much for him, humbled him. Max leaned in, his face so close to hers he could feel her breath on his skin. "And your kids?"

"They have fish and computers and crayons in Seattle. Maybe the kids would enjoy a trip to a cabin as a starter." She held his face, those tender fingers stroking ever so slightly.

God, she totally humbled him with her forgiving, giving, beautiful heart.

"You're really offering this after the way I walked out on you?"

She eased back, resting a hand on his chest again and looking deep into his eyes. Searching. "You're here. That tells me a lot."

A shudder of relief rocked through him, all the way to his core. "I meant it when I said I'm afraid I can't do this, be a parent, be a part of a family. Not after the way I grew up." His life on the streets had left him far from prepared for parenthood. "What if I screw up again? What if I can't give you and the kids enough?"

"Oh, Max—" she smiled, no doubts in her eyes "—we all screw up. That's life. As for your other worry? You're one of the most giving people I've ever met."

"I'm not a role model for your children, not after the things that I've done. I've broken the law more than once in my past." He needed to be sure she didn't see him through rose-colored glasses. He had to be certain *she* was certain, because he didn't think he could scavenge the will to tell her goodbye again.

"What are you doing now? How are you living your life now?" She asked the pointed questions firmly. "You're a good man. I can see that."

"I don't need to survive that way. The choices are easier now."

"I've known plenty of people with money who made less-than-moral choices. Money doesn't determine a person's character. If so, that would make for a sad world." She slipped her hand into his again and held firm. "I've seen the kind of man you are, and everything I've observed is so admirable it takes my breath away."

"You're letting me off the hook too easily." He wanted to believe her, believe it could be this simple. But he was still so damn afraid of hurting her, of letting Natalie and the kids down.

"What do you want for your life, Max?"

"That's too simple a question." He didn't understand how that would fix the problems between them. Didn't see how his wishes did a damn thing to make him the kind of father she needed for her children.

Those cool green eyes seemed to turn to fire. Her gentle features darkened, her brow knitting. "Actually, it isn't. It's a very complex, important question. You're such an ambitious man, such a kingdom builder on a professional level. Why is it so difficult for you to make wishes on a personal level?"

"Because," he admitted the truth through gritted teeth, "losing people hurts more than losing any fortune. It's not worth the risk."

She clasped both his hands in hers and squeezed hard. "Max, I've lost, too. I'm scared, too, believe me." Her exhale was shaky, but her gaze was steady. "But

I'm more afraid of the regrets I'll have if I don't take this risk and ask you. And I'm asking you, what do you want for your life?"

He told himself he wasn't going to do this. Still, he found himself speaking the deepest truth of his heart.

"I want you." The need *was* simple, after all. So damn straightforward and true. "I want to be the kind of man Colby and Lexie deserve to have bringing them up."

"That's an amazing start. What else do you want?"

He cleared his throat and dared say what he wanted most of all. "I want your love."

Her eyes went shiny with unshed tears that glistened with joy. "You have that. Completely." She leaned toward him until their clasped hands touched, heart to heart. "I am absolutely, completely in love with you, Max. St. Cloud."

Relief rushed through him and he kissed her hard, holding, sealing this moment in his mind forever before he whispered against her lips. "And I love you, Natalie Valentine. I swear to you, I am going spend every day of my life proving to you how much I adore you and your children. I'm going to work—"

"Shhh." She kissed him silent. "I know. I believe you. Let's get back to talking about what you want."

Her words surprised him, but the answer was so clear, so right, he wondered why he hadn't dared trust it before. "I want to find a way to be a part of Royal, Texas, and build a cabin home in Washington."

She grinned, surprise coloring her eyes. "A cabin home?"

"A place with a yard and a kick-ass kitchen. A good spot to fish with Colby. A private landing strip on the property so we could fly back and forth with the kids and Miss Molly."

"That sounds like more than a cabin."

He wrapped his arms around her and slid her onto his lap. "When I dream, I dream big, Natalie."

Her arms draped over his shoulders, her fingers toying with his hair. "Big dreams are a good thing."

He grazed his mouth over hers. "And making them come true is even better."

* * * * *

TAKING HOME THE TYCOON
by USA TODAY *bestselling author Catherine Mann*

and

October 2017:
BILLIONAIRE'S BABY BIND
by USA TODAY *bestselling author*
Katherine Garbera

November 2017:
THE TEXAN TAKES A WIFE
by USA TODAY *bestselling author Charlene Sands*

December 2017:
BEST MAN UNDER THE MISTLETOE
by Jules Bennett

"My feelings for you haven't changed."

"You can't seriously believe that's true," Melody said.

"I want you in my life. I want to be there for our baby. How do you see your future?"

"Honestly, I sort of go back and forth—wanting us to be a happy family but thinking it might be better if I raise this baby on my own."

"Because…" If he asked her whether she was in love with someone else and she told him yes, Kyle wasn't sure what he'd do.

"Because it hurts too much when I think how much I love you and wonder if you'll ever feel the same about me."

* * *

The Heir Affair
is part of the Las Vegas Nights series:
An exclusive club for men
who have it all and want more.

THE HEIR AFFAIR

BY
CAT SCHIELD

First Published in Great Britain 2017
By Mills & Boon, an imprint of HarperCollins*Publishers*
1 London Bridge Street, London, SE1 9GF

© 2017 Catherine Schield

ISBN: 978-0-263-92835-8

51-0917

Our policy is to use papers that are natural, renewable and recyclable products and made from wood grown in sustainable forests. The logging and manufacturing processes conform to the legal environmental regulations of the country of origin.

Printed and bound in Spain
by CPI, Barcelona

Cat Schield has been reading and writing romance since high school. Although she graduated from college with a BA in business, her idea of a perfect career was writing books for Mills & Boon. And now, after winning the Romance Writers of America 2010 Golden Heart® Award for Best Contemporary Series Romance, that dream has come true. Cat lives in Minnesota with her daughter, Emily, and their Burmese cat. When she's not writing sexy, romantic stories for Mills & Boon Desire, she can be found sailing with friends on the St. Croix River, or in more exotic locales, like the Caribbean and Europe. She loves to hear from readers. Find her at www.catschield.net and follow her on Twitter, @catschield.

To Patty and Fred

One

Kyle Tailor sat on the couch beside his business partner and best friend from high school, Trent Caldwell. It was Thanksgiving. On the great room's sixty-inch television, an interdivisional grudge match was happening between the Detroit Lions and Minnesota Vikings. Kyle wasn't following the action. His gaze was locked on Trent's sister.

Until she came along, solitude had never bothered him. In most ways it was simpler to live on his own without someone else's physical or emotional clutter. To find himself needing Melody had been a shock to his system.

Now, he didn't sleep well without her beside him. Since she'd been gone, he slogged through business meetings and routine activities in a foggy daze, unable to concentrate or care. He missed her hugs. Her way of teasing him. He'd lost weight, had stopped working out and lost an unacceptable amount of money in the casinos in the month since he'd come to Las Vegas to temporarily take over the management of Club T's.

Trent elbowed him in his ribs.

Kyle ripped his gaze from Melody and arched an eyebrow at his business partner. "What?"

"Go talk to her."

"I tried earlier." When he'd first arrived, they'd exchanged a stilted "Happy Thanksgiving" and an awkward half hug. "She's avoiding me."

"Did you perfect your world-famous curveball on your first attempt?" Trent countered. "Try again."

"She's on the phone."

Trent grunted and returned his attention to the television. His infant son sat on his lap. His matching blue eyes were on the screen and every time the Lions scored and Trent cheered, Dylan would respond to his father's enthusiasm with clapping. From the love seat, the child's mother watched the pair with such fondness Kyle's gut twisted.

Laughter rose from the kitchen. Nate Tucker, the third partner in their Las Vegas nightclub, was in the process of putting away the leftovers from dinner, helped by Mia Navarro, a fellow songwriter he'd been dating for several months.

Thanksgiving was a day for families. A chance to celebrate what they had. Nate had Mia. Trent had Savannah and Dylan.

Frustration ate at him. Kyle should have had Melody except five months ago the paparazzi had captured her and famous DJ/music producer Hunter Graves coming out of a New York City nightclub hand-in-hand. The way Melody and her former flame had been smiling at each other had eaten at Kyle day and night until he'd accused her of cheating on him. Although she'd denied it, Kyle couldn't find a way to believe her.

After all, hadn't it been Hunter with whom she'd been so deeply in love that she was prepared to do almost anything to get him to love her back? Even engage in a crazy scheme to make Hunter realize he was taking her for granted. But playing like she was in love with Kyle to make Hunter jealous had become real awfully fast. That was probably why the plan had worked so well.

Seeing that he had real competition for Melody, Hunter had realized the error of his ways. But there was another outcome that neither Melody nor Kyle had seen coming. They'd actually fallen for each other. Kyle remembered back to the moment when all three of them had stood in her apartment, with Melody between the two men who loved her. The seconds were burned in his mind. Her choice could have gone either way. He'd experienced a heart-stopping range of emotions while he waited for her decision.

And in the months since, Kyle would be lying if he claimed he'd never wondered if she was happy with choosing him over Hunter.

His heart gave a sickening lurch as he regarded Melody. She was in great spirits at the moment. Her blue eyes sparkled. The corners of her mouth were turned up in a wry smile and her cheeks flushed with color.

Was she on the phone with Hunter Graves?

Disgusted with himself for jumping to that conclusion, Kyle turned to the television and forced his attention back to the game, but it was all just a swirl of purple, white and blue on a green background.

Falling in love with Melody had been the most incredible experience of his life. No woman before her had ever consumed his thoughts like this, and their lovemaking was exhilarating. Yet he had a hard time trusting the joy and found himself unable to shake the ever-present doubts that lurked in his subconscious, fears that nothing that felt so good could last forever.

Based on how his former love life had gone, he'd braced himself for the inevitable end of their relationship, prepared himself for loss. But the months stretched out and things between them had just gotten better. He'd loosened the reins of control and started to open up. And then she'd gone on tour and their physical separation had created an emotional gulf.

The damning photo of her and Hunter in New York had come at a point when too much time apart had demonstrated just how vulnerable their fledgling relationship was. Neither one of them had had enough confidence in their connection to weather such an emotionally charged situation. Pain pierced his temple. He dug his thumb into the spot.

There was another jab to his ribs. "She's off the phone."

"Thanks." Kyle got to his feet and headed for the terrace.

Melody was on her way in. They met at the sliding glass door. Kyle stepped into the opening, blocking her from re-entering the house.

"Look," he said without preliminaries. "I came here tonight so we could talk."

"You didn't come for Nate's cooking?"

Kyle didn't crack a smile and Melody sighed in defeat. He knew she hated when he shut down like this, but he'd grown up building walls around his emotions. The strategy blocked pain and disappointment. Unfortunately, as his therapist liked to put it, it also kept him from "welcoming joy."

He'd started seeing Dr. Warner when his baseball career abruptly ended a few years earlier after a string of shoulder and elbow injuries led to surgery and he was unable to make a full recovery. Needing to see a shrink filled him with shame and embarrassment. In fact, he'd let himself sink into some pretty dark mental territory before he'd made his first appointment. But the fact was, he'd needed help. Losing a career he loved left him feeling more vulnerable than he knew how to handle.

His dad would say a real man would suck it up and deal with his problems instead of running to some head shrinker. In Brent Tailor's world, men didn't talk about all that touchy-feely crap. A real man made decisions and if things went wrong, he fixed them. Kyle often wondered if his father thought a real man didn't have feelings.

"We need to sort out what's going on between us," he said, stepping outside, herding her away from the family room and the safety of their friends.

"I don't know where to start."

"Your stuff is still at my place in LA, but you haven't been there since the tour ended. Are you coming back?"

"I don't know."

"It feels like we're over."

Melody's voice sounded rough as she asked, "Is that what you want?"

"No, but I can't remain in limbo, either. We either need to move forward or be done." Giving Melody this ultimatum hadn't been part of his plan tonight. He hadn't wanted to fight with her at all. "The decision is up to you."

"I need to think about it."

Impatience snapped along his nerve endings. "The tour ended two months ago. You've had plenty of time to think."

"Things are a little more complicated than they seem."

She didn't elaborate even though Kyle gave her the space to do so. Once upon a time Melody had been able to talk to Kyle about everything. Now, it was as if they were strangers.

"How complicated can it be?" he finally asked. "Do you want to be with me or with Hunter?"

"With Hunter?" She shook her head in bewilderment. "What are you talking about?"

"That was him on the phone a little while ago, wasn't it?"

"No. It was my mom calling to wish me a happy Thanksgiving." She paused and her expression grew incredulous as she stared at him. "Why would you think that it was Hunter?"

Kyle didn't respond right away. "He wants you back."

She huffed out a laugh. "That's ridiculous. Why would you think something like that?"

"He told me so."

"You spoke with him?" Melody looked aghast and confused that Kyle and Hunter had talked. "When?"

"After the two of you met up in New York. I called and warned him to back off. He told me to go screw myself." His fist clenched at the memory. "Apparently that night you said something to him about how being on the road can put a strain on a relationship." Kyle had no idea what had prompted Melody to divulge such private details to her ex-lover, but hearing Hunter repeat the confidence had cut deep. "He took that to mean we weren't getting along. And he told me he intends to make you fall back in love with him."

"He wouldn't do that."

"Don't you mean he can't do that?" Kyle blew out a breath and struggled to calm his pounding heart.

"Hunter can't get me back…" She didn't meet his gaze. "Because I still love you." An undertone of doubt marred the declaration.

"You don't sound as if you believe that."

Shivering, she glanced toward the sliding glass door.

When her eyes widened, Kyle followed the direction of her gaze and realized four pairs of eyes were watching them. As soon as their audience realized they'd been spotted, everyone looked away. Melody covered her face with her hands and groaned.

"They all want what's best for us," Kyle said.

Everyone in the house was pulling for them with the exception of one-year-old Dylan, who had no idea what was going on, and perhaps, Melody herself.

"I know." She let her hands fall. "I don't want to have this conversation here. Can you take me back to Trent's? We can continue our discussion there."

Getting her to talk to him was all he'd wanted these last few months. Well, maybe not *all* he'd wanted. If the tour had never happened. If she'd never gone to New York City and met up with Hunter in the nightclub. If he'd never let jealousy get the better of him. If he'd been allowed to express his emotions growing up.

His list of ifs went on and on.

But for now, he was happy that they were communicating again. Even if what was being said had the potential to hurt.

Kyle nodded. "That sounds good to me."

Ten minutes later, after they'd said their goodbyes, Kyle was negotiating the streets of Las Vegas, heading to the two-bedroom guesthouse on her brother's property where Melody stayed whenever she visited Las Vegas.

Kyle kept his attention fixed on the road, his hands tense on the wheel as if something was eating at him. Every so often he flicked an unreadable glance her direction. It wasn't like him to look so grim around her. The Kyle she'd grown up with had been quick to smile and tease. Even though he'd been her brother's best friend, he'd treated her like she mattered to him. Mattered to him like a sister. She'd never imagined he'd ever see her as a woman he desired.

It had taken almost half a year after he'd told her how his feelings for her had changed for her to stop marveling that they were in a relationship. She kept thinking about his track record with women and expecting things to go south. She wished she'd been surprised when things became strained.

Maybe they never should've taken the step from friends to romantically involved. It made her heart ache to think this way, but their inability to connect and work out their problems these last few months demonstrated that they'd rushed into a relationship that neither one was ready for. Could it be that Kyle felt the same way? Was he grappling with the same doubts she had?

Melody searched his expression, unable to discern what was going on in his mind. She thought back to the party, and how she'd tried to assuage everyone's curiosity and concern when she and Kyle left. At this point, aside from Dylan and Kyle, they all knew her secret. A feeling of dread slid down her spine. This wasn't going to be easy.

About three months into the tour with Nate's band Free Fall, Melody had begun to worry that the explosion of desire that had sustained her and Kyle through the beginning months of their relationship wasn't a solid foundation to build a future on. They'd only been a couple for nine months when she'd left LA to open for the award-winning pop band. Weeks and weeks on the road, with only occasional long weekends back in LA, had created an unsettling disassociation between her and Kyle that text messages and Skype calls hadn't been able to bridge.

Maybe if her track record with men had been more extensive she'd have had more confidence in her ability to keep Kyle's interest from thousands of miles away. From an early age she'd thrown herself into music rather than boys. Sure, she'd dated, but until Kyle came along, the guys she attracted were mostly like Hunter and way too much like her father: selfish and neglectful.

And then there was the fact that before her, Kyle's longest relationship had lasted four months. As a former pro baseball player, he had a pretty high profile lifestyle that women flocked to. Kyle was one hell of a catch and Melody recognized that every woman he met could be hotter and more famous than the last. So, she'd enjoyed their time together, never really expecting that it would last.

Before she'd realized it, they'd made it six months and he'd asked her to move in. Trent had been concerned when he'd learned about this escalation in their romance. He'd been Kyle's best friend for fifteen years and recognized that his friend was in deeper than he'd ever been before. Despite her brother's advice to slow down, Melody had taken the plunge and moved into Kyle's Hollywood Hills home.

Kyle's voice broke into her thoughts. "Why have you been avoiding me since the tour ended?"

"I've had a lot to think about," she said.

"Like what?"

Before they'd started dating, Melody had only ever seen Kyle as funny, sexy and supportive. He never demonstrated fear or anxiety or displayed a hint of vulnerability. His father had done a number on his psyche when Kyle was a young child, demanding his son stay in control of his emotions at all times. So it came as no great surprise that Kyle's first reaction to any little problem in their relationship was to shut down.

And yet, she'd been the one who'd taken a huge step back after his first big show of emotion. When he'd asked if she was cheating on him with Hunter, he'd been angry and hurt. His strong reaction to the paparazzi photo had caused her own emotions to flare.

Growing up the daughter of Siggy Caldwell hadn't allowed her to develop an understanding of healthy relationships. Her father was a hard man to like, much less love. Misogynistic, arrogant and selfish, he'd alienated his wives and his children with his disrespect.

So many times her father had declared he loved her right before launching into criticism, invalidating the claim while impressing on her that she was unworthy of his—or anyone else's—love.

While Kyle was nothing like her father, his accusation had awakened the same feelings of injustice she'd suffered as a little girl. As she'd done with her father, she'd shut Kyle out and walked away.

But that hadn't stopped her from loving him.

When she didn't answer him right away, Kyle spoke again. "Like what? Hunter?"

"No." She gave her head a vehement shake and followed it up with a weary sigh.

"Are you back in love with him?"

"No!" She stared at him in frustration. "Would you please let that go. I want to be with you."

His expression grew stonier. "You sure haven't been acting that way these last few months."

"It's not the same between us as before I went on the tour," she blurted out.

"I agree."

"Maybe if we go back and figure out where we went wrong," she said. "Or start over."

Was that even possible given the secret she was keeping from him?

"And if we can't?"

She didn't answer and their conversation didn't resume.

As Kyle drove into the gated community where Trent had his house, Melody wished she had some idea what he was thinking about. Her stomach was in knots. She pressed her sweaty palms against her coat and took deep, calming breaths, hoping to coax her confidence out of hiding.

Her nerves weren't under control by the time Kyle pulled into Trent's driveway and stopped the car. She had her door open and feet on the pavement before the silence could get any more awkward. He was seconds behind her as she keyed in the four-digit code that opened the side gate leading to the backyard.

A paving-stone walkway led to her front door. Melody fumbled with her keys until Kyle pulled the ring from her clumsy fingers and slid the correct one home. His body brushed hers, awakening her longing to be held in his arms, and she was a split second from throwing herself against his chest when he took a deliberate step away from her.

"After you."

Melody bit back a miserable groan. "Thanks."

Knowing it would be dark when she returned, Melody had left the lights burning in the living room. The heavy scent of roses hit her as soon as she entered. An enormous bouquet of fat red blooms occupied the center of her dining table. The arrangement had appeared at the studio the prior afternoon. She'd been thrilled as she'd read the accompanying card.

I'm thankful for you.

There'd been no signature and Melody hadn't recognized the handwriting. This hadn't surprised her. She suspected the order had been phoned in and the florist had written the message. But when she'd studied the card and the roses, she wasn't sure Kyle had sent them.

And now, as he helped Melody out of her coat, Kyle didn't seem to notice the flowers. Which left her wondering if Hunter had sent them. If so, that was going to complicate things between her and Kyle.

"Do you want something to drink?" She indicated the kitchen, but Kyle didn't spare it a glance as he shook his head.

He seemed glued to the floor in the space between her living and dining rooms. Melody wondered what it would take to get him to sit down.

"Who are those from?" Kyle had at last noticed the roses.

"I'd hoped they were from you."

"I didn't send them." If Kyle noticed her rueful tone, he gave no indication. He moved toward the table. "Wasn't there a card?"

"Yes, but it wasn't signed."

"Are they from Hunter?"

"Sending me roses was never his style."

"Things change." His lips tightened. "Did you call and ask him?"

"No."

Melody had left the card on the table beside the crystal vase. Kyle picked it up and read the message.

"'I'm thankful for you'?" He shot her a frown. "What does that mean?"

Irritation rose at his sharp tone. She thought it was pretty obvious. "It's Thanksgiving. Maybe someone thought it was a timely message."

"Someone?"

"I don't know where the roses came from," she snapped, wishing Kyle would stop talking about the stupid flowers. She needed to tell him that she was pregnant, but had lost control of the conversation.

"You're sure?" He reread the card. "This seems awfully personal for it to have been written by a stranger. Did you ask Trent or Savannah if they sent the flowers?"

"Yes. They didn't send them."

"Red roses are a romantic gesture," Kyle murmured to himself, tapping the card against his knuckles. He frowned at the plump red buds. "It seems like something a man in love would send."

Which was why she'd wished Kyle had sent them. Of course, despite being together for nine months and the fact that he'd invited her to move in with him, Kyle had never actually come out and said he loved her. He'd always been a cool customer when it came to women. The one who decided when it started and when it ended.

It was this tendency that had made her hesitate before choosing him over Hunter. She'd been worried about stepping from one relationship where she didn't feel safe and secure into another similar situation. Even so, in the end she'd following her instincts and taken a leap of faith. And despite their current problems, she still wouldn't say she'd been wrong.

"Why didn't you call Hunter and ask him?" Kyle asked, watching her through narrowed eyes as if waiting for her to slip up.

A thousand times in the last five months she'd regretted hanging out with Hunter in that New York City nightclub and then leaving at the same time he had. The whole thing had been innocent enough. There had been a crush of people outside the club and he'd grabbed her hand to avoid being separated as they'd run to the limo that had been waiting at the curb. Unfortunately, the media was obsessed with Hunter's love life and had blown up the incident, speculating that Hunter and Melody had reunited.

"Can you please forget about Hunter for two seconds."
Melody didn't want Kyle's thoughts taking him there.

Since she'd run into Hunter in New York, Kyle had mentioned several times that she might have unfinished business with the DJ. That couldn't be farther from the case,
but there were things she'd had in common with Hunter,
like them both being in the music business, that she didn't
share with Kyle.

Melody set her hand on his arm to bring his attention
to her. "I have something I need to tell you."

When his hazel eyes shifted her way, she released the
breath she'd been holding. It was long past time she got
this off her chest, but now that the time had come, saying
the words out loud was way harder than any speech she'd
prepared in her head.

"Earlier I said things are complicated."

Cool eyes watched her from a face made of granite and
Melody longed to be anywhere but here. Given Kyle's family background, he wasn't exactly emotive. He played his
cards close to his chest. She had absolutely no idea how
he was going to react to what she had to say. She could
only hope the anticipation was worse than the outcome.

"I'm pregnant."

Kyle's flat expression vanished. Instead, he looked like
the floor had dropped from beneath his feet. "Pregnant?"

"Yes. I know it's a shock…"

They hadn't anticipated this. The topic had never even
come up. Nor had marriage or anything having to do with
the future. Their relationship had been new and untested.
They'd both committed to taking things one day at a time.

"You're having a baby." His gaze went past her shoulder and roved around the room as if he was in search of
something to help him understand. Like a lodestone, the

vase of red roses snagged his notice once more. His body went rigid. "And the father?"

Melody shook her head and took a step back. Had she heard him right? "What do you mean?"

"The father." Kyle flung out his hand in the direction of the flowers as if they explained everything. "Do you know who it is?"

Two

At his question, Melody blinked several times in rapid succession and then just stared at him in shock. As the impact of what he'd asked sunk in, Kyle realized he'd just made a huge mistake. His heart clenched in misery. The last thing he wanted to do was hurt her, but that was all he seemed capable of these days.

"What I meant was…" he began, but she was having none of it.

"You're the father," Melody said, her voice raw with disappointment and anguish. "How could you think anything else?"

"The flowers." He slashed his gaze toward them, unable to face the judgment in Melody's eyes. "It's the exact thing Hunter sent you last year when he was trying to get you to reconsider picking me over him."

"Hunter and I are friends." Her stiff tone brooked no argument. "Nothing more."

"The same could've been said about us before we got together," he reminded her.

For several seconds she stared at him in silence as her chest rose and fell in response to the large quantity of air she was moving through her lungs. Her blue eyes were overly bright as she assessed him.

When at last she spoke, her words thudded like hammer blows on his psyche. "I can't believe you could think that I would cheat on you with Hunter or anyone else."

The urge to fold her into his arms flooded him, but so much resentment lay between them. He doubted she'd be open to any attempt on his part to touch her.

"I don't."

"Then why would you ask me something so ridiculous as whether I know who the father is?"

"It came out wrong." But it hadn't. In the back of his mind was that ever-present image of Melody and Hunter hand-in-hand.

"I don't think it did. You've been looking for an excuse to break up for months." Her voice was ragged and raw. "I'm not going to fight you any longer. We're done."

"What?" Although he'd been dreading this outcome for months now, Kyle wasn't prepared for the actual ending. His thoughts reeled. "Just like that?"

"You just accused me of being pregnant with some random guy's baby—"

"Not some random guy," he reminded her, hating the words coming out of his mouth but unable to stop the flow. He needed to get his suspicions out in the open. That was the only way they could move forward. His tone was bleak as he finished. "Hunter's."

"I can't keep doing this." Melody stuck out her arm and pointed toward the door. "Go."

The numbness that had momentarily gripped him

burned away in a rush. "Aren't you forgetting something?" He gazed toward her belly where, now that he knew what to look for, he detected the tiniest roundness. "That's my baby you're carrying."

Muscles bunched in her cheek as her arm fell back to her side. Her eyes were sapphire-hard as she demanded, "So, now you're sure?"

If he wanted to save their relationship, he had to get over the doubts clouding his judgment. He loved Melody and they were going to be a family. He'd won her away from Hunter once. He could do it again. And again. Whatever it took.

"Yes."

She crossed her arms over her chest, not giving an inch. "And I'm supposed to forget every terrible thing you thought about me and be glad you've finally decided to come around?"

"I made a mistake."

"You made a series of them." Abruptly, the fight drained out of her. "This isn't how I wanted things to go."

"What did you expect?" He took a half step toward her, intent on making some sort of a peace offering, but let his hand fall back to his side when she shook her head.

"I don't know." Her shoulders rounded with exhaustion. "I thought maybe it would magically fix things."

"We've had too much time apart."

"And that's my fault?"

Although she'd been the one who'd pulled away rather than stay and fight with him—for them—he'd meant it as an observation, not a criticism. Her distance these last few months had awakened a fear of losing her.

"I told you to go on the tour," he reminded her. "And if I had to do it all over again, I'd make the same decision. It was the right step for your career." And if he was honest with himself, he hadn't been ready for the level of commitment their relationship had reached.

It still boggled his mind how fast he'd gone from being her friend to inviting her to move in with him. Cohabiting with Melody had been the most natural thing in the world. It hadn't required any significant shift in his beliefs or habits. The transformation from bachelor to boyfriend had been seamless and rewarding. It wasn't until she left on the tour that he'd noticed disquieting thoughts creeping in.

"How far along are you?"

"Twelve weeks."

He did the math. The last time they'd been together. It had been a rocky weekend. "How long have you known?"

"Since shortly after I returned from Sydney."

"Six weeks." He rubbed his eyes while disappointment flowed through him. Why had it taken her so long to share such important news? Could it be that she was afraid of how he would react? And hadn't he just demonstrated that she'd been right?

Her vehemence caught him by surprise. "You don't get to do that." She pointed an accusatory finger at him.

"Do what?"

"Make me feel bad for not rushing to tell you that everything in your life was going to change."

She was so obviously afraid of what his reaction would be. And perhaps with good reason. He hadn't exactly swept her into his arms and spun her in a giddy circle while crowing his delight.

"I'm sorry."

"It's fine." But she appeared anything but okay. She seemed as shell-shocked as he was. "I'm sure we're both overwhelmed at the idea of becoming parents. At least we have six months to get used to the idea."

"Have you started to think about what you're going to do?" he asked.

"What do you mean 'do'?"

"For where you're going to live." Where did he figure in her plans? "Are you staying here?"

"In Las Vegas?" Melody looked like a cornered rabbit. "I don't know. Nate is here. And Mia. Trent, Savannah and Dylan will be coming back as soon as she's done filming the movie."

"It doesn't much sound like you plan on coming back to LA."

Or back to Kyle. His home was in LA. Although, at the moment he was renting a place outside Vegas for the next few months. He'd offered to take over as temporary manager of Club T's for two reasons. To be closer to Melody while she finished her album and to free up Trent to live in LA and take care of his son while Savannah worked.

"I feel as if I have a really good support system here." The subtext was clear. She didn't think he was going to be there for her. Was this opinion recently acquired or something that had occurred to her over a period of time?

"How do you figure? Trent and Savannah are in LA at the moment."

"They'll be coming back as soon as Savannah is done with her movie. And you're here."

Something loosened in his chest. "So you do want me around."

"Of course. I want us to be a family." Nothing sounded better, but in his peripheral vision a dozen red roses stood like a stop sign on her dining room table.

Then she shook her head. "Is that possible? Can we get back to where we were before the tour?"

"I'm not sure we can." Although Kyle doubted it was the sort of answer a pregnant woman wanted to hear from the father of her child, he had to be honest with her. "Go backward, I mean. I'm sorry. All this has caught me by surprise. I never imagined myself a dad."

"We never talked about it. I was a bit afraid to, knowing how you and your father get along."

"You mean don't get along."

She gave a little shrug. "You aren't him. You're going to be a great dad."

He wanted some time to assimilate all he'd learned, but she was staring at him like she needed him to fix everything. He just had no idea how to begin.

He considered her remark about his relationship with his father.

Suck it up, kid.

Be a man.

No one's going to help you unless you help yourself.

The clichés went on and on. Maybe if Brent Tailor hadn't been such a successful businessman and dedicated philanthropist, his opinions would've been easier to ignore. Instead, he was someone Kyle looked up to professionally. And much of what his father drilled into him had enabled his success as a major league pitcher.

The downside to what his dad had drilled into him all his life was that it didn't enable Kyle to celebrate all he'd achieved in his baseball career or convey to Melody how he felt about their relationship.

"And you're going to be a great mother."

She blew out a huge breath. "I hope so. It would've been better if it happened later rather than sooner."

"What's done is done. What do you need from me?" He saw her answer coming and spoke quickly to head it off. "And don't say nothing."

From her frown he knew he'd struck the truth. She'd grown up watching her father and brother butt heads and depending on the situation, tended to either retreat or take on the role of peacekeeper whenever she caught a whiff of conflict.

"I have a doctor's appointment tomorrow." Her voice came across as tentative as if she half expected him to refuse.

"What time?"

"Three o'clock."

Excitement trickled into his awareness, diluting his dismay. She was pregnant with his child. It wasn't great timing, nor was becoming a father something he'd imagined happening any time soon, but he'd watched Trent with Dylan and was pretty sure he'd never seen his friend this happy. Maybe there was something to being a family that made the big problems smaller.

"Where do you want me to pick you up?" he asked.

"You don't need to come."

"Oh, I'm not missing this."

Trent and Savannah had overcome bigger obstacles to find their way back to each other. Surely Kyle and Melody could get past what stood between them. Of course, he was assuming she wanted to. What if she didn't love him anymore? She might not have cheated on him with Hunter, but he'd treated her as if she had.

He'd broken her trust, lodged unfair accusations at her. The person in the wrong hadn't been her, but him. Just that morning he'd been all set to forgive her. It had never occurred to Kyle that the one in need of pardoning would be him.

"Thank you," Melody said, but the words were perfunctory as if her thoughts had traveled elsewhere. "I appreciate your willingness to be involved."

"I'm going to be there for you every way I can."

* * *

Melody sat in the small, utilitarian lobby of Ugly Trout Records and stared out the front window toward the parking lot. For the fifth time in ten minutes, she checked the time on her phone. Kyle had three more minutes before he could be considered late. Since last night, she'd regretted caving in to his offer to take her to the doctor's appointment. Unlike Hunter, Kyle counted punctuality as one of his virtues. He'd never left her waiting and wondering if he was going to call or show up. He'd always been very clear about his intentions and then followed through.

So why was she working herself into such a frantic mess? Practicing patience, Melody smoothed her sweaty palms down the legs of her skinny jeans. Thank goodness the denim had some stretch to it. Thanks to the severity of her morning sickness these last few weeks, she'd lost weight, but today her baby bump seemed more pronounced than the week before.

This change—more than the pregnancy test, her constant nausea and fatigue—had made her all too aware that she had a baby inside her. Sweat broke out. Most days she was happy about her impending motherhood. The timing could be better. She was on the verge of dropping her first album and the stress wasn't good for her or the baby. But now that she'd broken the news to Kyle, more than just her and her baby's future weighed on her mind.

"Hey, Melody, what are you doing up here?"

She turned at the sound of her name and smiled at the man who was detouring toward her. Craig Jameson was one of the top sound engineers working at the label. He'd been involved in eighty percent of Melody's recording sessions and been instrumental in helping her produce most of her songs. He had a knack for knowing exactly what each song needed.

They'd spent hours together in the studio, talking about music and the industry. He had great stories about various artists that had come to Ugly Trout to record. Many had involved some pretty outrageous behavior—drunken jam sessions, a party with strippers and several fistfights.

"I'm waiting for Kyle to pick me up." Although her relationship with Kyle was pretty well-known around the studio thanks to their public personas, Craig knew more details due to all the time he and Melody had spent together.

"It's a little late for lunch."

"Actually, we are heading to…" She'd held off mentioning her pregnancy around the studio until she told Kyle, but now that he knew there was no reason to keep the secret any longer. "The doctor."

"You okay?" Craig's concern touched Melody.

"Fine. Actually more than fine." She forced bright happiness into her tone. "I'm pregnant."

"That's great news. Then things between you and Kyle are better?"

During a particularly low point, she'd confided in Craig. At the time she hadn't considered that Craig was a work colleague. A few days earlier, he'd told her that he'd just broken off with his girlfriend of a year. She hadn't hesitated to offer him a sympathetic shoulder. Maybe it had crossed a line, but Craig was a decent guy who'd needed a friend.

"We're working on it." She smiled, but there wasn't a lot of joy in it.

"He'd be a fool to let you go."

"That's sweet of you to say." Tears surged to her eyes but Melody blinked them away. It seemed as if everything set her off these days. Hormones. They were driving her crazy. She'd never been moody, but since becoming pregnant, her emotions were all over the place. "There's Kyle now. I should be back in an hour or so. Would you have some time later to sit down with me? Nate wants me to get my album done and I could use some help narrowing down the songs."

"I'd be honored to help."

"Let me know what time you're free." She headed toward the front door and paused with her hand on it. When she looked over her shoulder, Craig was still watching her. "And thanks."

"For what?"

"Everything." Feeling a little as if she'd said too much, Melody pushed the door and blinked in the bright sunlight.

Kyle had parked his car and was heading toward her along the front walk. His long legs ate up the distance between them, demonstrating his upbeat mood. Today he wore a pair of khaki slacks and navy V-neck sweater over a white button-down shirt. His thick brown hair had an artfully disheveled look she loved. With a long, square face, firm chin and well-shaped lips, Kyle had the sort of good looks favored by fashion designers looking for sexy, rugged models.

When Melody saw his unguarded smile, a weight lifted off her shoulders. For a second she was catapulted back in time to when they'd first been living together in LA. It had been a heady, exciting, romantic three months. Kyle had been super supportive of her career and interested in learning her process for writing music.

His fascination had drawn Melody out of her shell. When it came to songwriting, she'd learned to be exceptionally protective. Back when she was still in school, her father had belittled her talent and broken down her con-

fidence. He'd wanted her to pursue classical violin and
made her attend Juilliard. When she'd quit halfway through
her third year, choosing instead to pursue the contemporary popular music she loved, Siggy had pretty much dis-
owned her.

"You ready?" he asked as he neared.

It seemed the most natural thing in the world for him
to wrap his arms around her and drop a kiss on her cheek.
Although she longed for a proper kiss, the affection in the
gesture sent warmth rushing through her.

"I'm ready," she countered. "Are you?"

Kyle's smile was ever so slightly crooked as he opened
the passenger door and ushered her inside. "I am."

"I'm glad." She studied him as he walked around the
car and slid behind the wheel once more. "I'm a little nervous about the ultrasound."

"Why?" Kyle got the car started and pulled out of the
parking lot before glancing her way. "I thought this was
just routine."

"It is. But they look for certain things. I can't help but
wonder what they might find."

"What are they going to look for?" Kyle's brow creased.

Melody instantly regretted sharing her concerns. The
last thing she wanted to do was freak out Kyle. He'd only
just learned about the baby and probably hadn't yet come
to terms with becoming a father and now she was heap-
ing new concerns onto the pile.

"They'll check the heartbeat and determine my due
date."

"None of that sounds too bad."

"Nooo." She drew the word out. "And then they'll look
to make sure everything looks normal. Two arms. Two
legs. That the organs are developing okay." There were
just so many things that could be wrong. And so many

things that could be right. When had she become such a pessimist?

"Is there any reason to think anything will be missing?"

His faint note of teasing as he asked the question lightened Melody's mood. She was being anxious for no good reason.

"Of course not. I guess it's just going to be more real after today."

And Kyle would be beside her as they both saw their baby for the first time. It roused all the things she so badly wanted but was afraid she might never get. For the last several weeks, since she'd learned she was pregnant, she'd been so focused on what was wrong with their relationship that she hadn't thought about all the things that had once been right.

She'd braced herself to be a single mom, not even giving Kyle the benefit of the doubt. Because of the way her father had often treated her, she'd been quick to expect Kyle to disappoint her. If she anticipated Kyle not wanting to be a father, then it wouldn't hurt as much when that was what happened.

Automatically going on the defensive certainly wasn't fair to Kyle. Or herself. Or their baby.

"There's no going back," she said.

He shot her a curious look. "Do you want to go back?"

"You didn't ask for this."

"Did you?"

"You mean did I try to get pregnant?" Melody wasn't sure how to take his question.

"I wasn't asking if you deliberately became pregnant," he said and then sighed. He reached for her hand. "I was merely reflecting your question back at you."

His matter-of-fact reaction to their situation should be

the perfect balm for her agitation, but for some reason she was finding his encouragement annoying. At the same time, his fingers gave a little squeeze and she found herself torn between wanting to fight with him and needing to give in to his attempt to connect with her.

"If I've learned anything in the last year it's that it's really hard to maintain relationships while on the road. I thought a lot about what would happen if I decide to take my career seriously. I'd be traveling a lot on tour and making appearances. That sort of life is hard on everyone."

"And you're worried that you can't have your career and a baby." He didn't voice the obvious question: whether she'd intended to choose between her career and continuing her relationship with him. "I think you can do it all." A pause. "If you want to."

This was the decision she was dreading. Did she want it all? A family? A career? Her feelings for Kyle hadn't changed, but things were so much more complicated these days.

"Do you want to give us another shot?" she asked, her heart thudding hard against her ribs.

"I think we owe it to ourselves to do so, don't you?"

"I do."

He didn't seem all that happy with her answer, however. "Just tell me one thing. Would you have been willing to work things out if you weren't pregnant?"

"Yes, because if I didn't, there would always be something unfinished hanging between us."

He waited a long time before answering. "That's fair. But you should probably know I wanted you back before I knew you were pregnant."

"Even though you didn't trust me?"

And there was the crux of their whole problem.

"I was wrong to think you and Hunter got together."

She could tell that declaration had required a great deal of effort, but it wasn't enough. "And yet last night you were wondering if I knew which of you was the father of my baby."

Three

Kyle knew he deserved her sarcasm and let it slide off rather than get defensive. "It was the roses and that weird card that threw me off."

"It was pretty weird, but it was probably just a screwup on the florist's part. Maybe they neglected to add the person's signature to the card. It could be from any number of people."

"You don't think it's unusual that someone sent you a dozen red roses?" The last thing he should be doing was arguing with her.

"Okay, it's freaking me out that I don't know who sent them. But it was a nice gesture."

Melody might not think the roses came from Hunter, but Kyle was pretty sure he'd sent them.

"Can we forget about the flowers?" Melody continued, smoothing her hands over her knees. "I want to focus on this appointment. I'm really glad you came along today."

"So am I." But even as he spoke, Kyle recognized it was going to take more than accompanying her to a doctor's appointment before the tension eased between them.

He would have to make an effort to put his doubts to rest and get back in Melody's good graces. If that required romantic gestures like flowers and candlelit dinners, he would do whatever it took.

"You can take a right at the driveway coming up." Melody pointed the way into a parking lot beside a plain five-story building.

"You've been here before?"

"A couple times."

"So, you are planning to have the baby in Las Vegas."

Melody's mouth opened, but no words came out. She bit her lip and stared down at her hands. "It makes sense."

"But your life is in LA. With me." Or at least it had been before she'd gone on tour.

"We haven't really lived together these last nine months," she said.

"When I encouraged you to go on the tour, I thought you'd be coming back. All your stuff is still in my house."

"I just need a little time."

"How much time?"

"I don't know."

Kyle parked the car before responding. "I don't like living in limbo."

"Then maybe we should break up."

This wasn't at all what he expected her to say. "Where is this coming from?"

"I just don't know where we stand anymore. We're not dating. We're not living together. Are we even still friends?"

Her bald statement of the facts as she saw them swept his feet out from under him. It was as if his world had tilted and his head connected with the pavement. His thoughts grew foggy and indistinct.

"My feelings for you haven't changed."

"You can't seriously believe that's true." Melody opened her car door and slipped out, leaving Kyle staring at nothing.

She was halfway to the building before he roused himself and chased after her. "Okay," he said as he caught up with her. "Maybe we're not in the same place as we were before you left on the tour, but that doesn't mean I'm done. I want you in my life. I want to be there for our baby. How do you see your future?"

"Honestly, I sort of go back and forth between wanting us to be a happy family and thinking it might be better if I raise this baby on my own."

"That's not going to happen." His father hadn't been there for him. Kyle intended for his child to have a loving, attentive father.

"Because it hurts when I think how much I love you and wonder if you'll ever feel the same about me." They stopped before the elevator and she gave him a long searching look. "I'm afraid to have my heart broken."

Kyle wished he could tell her he'd never hurt her, but he already had when he'd assumed she'd hooked up with Hunter that night in New York City. And again just yesterday when he jumped to the wrong conclusion about the baby's paternity. Why couldn't he just put his faith in her and in their relationship?

Because he didn't know how.

His parents hadn't given him the emotional tools to be successful in a romantic partnership. His father had ruthlessly controlled all feelings good and bad, preferring to navigate through life's ups and downs with logic. Kyle's mother on the other hand was a fearful, anxious woman who loved her son almost too much. Trapped between an emotional storm and an impassive granite wall, Kyle had stopped expressing how he felt and let everyone think he was okay all the time.

His teammates in school and then in the major leagues called him the Iceman because he was always chill. But it was a mask, not a true representation of how he felt. No matter how relaxed and unaffected he looked, inside he seethed with doubt, desire and sometimes disappointment.

But thanks to his father's tutelage, Kyle's first reaction to everything life threw at him was to slide on his aviator sunglasses and summon an enigmatic smile. No matter what the stakes, how bad the loss or how well he pitched, he was the Iceman. Even after his first no-hitter, he'd given only a sly smile to the mass of reporters who'd come to interview him in the aftermath.

"I don't want to hurt you," Kyle said and meant it, but he knew he didn't always behave the way she needed him to.

Sometimes it was as if what made him so happy in their relationship was the exact thing that caused him to regress back to the self-protective behaviors he learned in childhood. He retreated from strong emotion instead of owning it. These last few months since he'd thought he lost her to Hunter had been some of the worst of his life.

Instead of reaching out and telling her how afraid he was to lose her, he'd shoved down his fears and made it seem as if he was okay. But he wasn't okay. In fact, he was a mess, which was why he'd jumped to the wrong conclusion about her feelings for Hunter.

While Melody checked in with the receptionist, Kyle glanced around the waiting area, seeing women in various stages of pregnancy. This was really happening. He was going to be a father. Time to step up and take care of the mother of his child. Whatever that meant.

"I think we should get married," he said as she took a seat beside him.

Her eyes widened. "You're kidding, right?"

"Not at all. It makes sense. I don't want to be a part-time father and we are good together."

"Good together?" She looked at him as if he'd sprouted a second head. "We've barely spoken to each other these last few months. Neither one of us is very good at communicating how we feel." Like Kyle had, she regarded the other expectant mothers in their various stages of pregnancy. "I don't think we're ready for marriage."

Although her answer frustrated him, Kyle reminded himself that it wasn't always going to be like this between them. He would find a way to make things all right again.

"So we work on our communication," he said, hoping she grasped how determined he was to make things work.

"How are we going to do that?"

"We'll go see a couples counselor. Someone who can teach us how to express ourselves in a positive way."

Her stiff posture highlighted her discomfort. "I don't know."

"Look," he said. "We might have been able to walk away months ago, but things have changed. And I'd like to point out that while we've hit a rough patch, I don't see either one of us calling it quits." He chose to ignore that not ten minutes earlier she'd suggested they break up.

"I agree we should make an effort to be friends again for the sake of the baby." She looked flustered and unsure what she planned to say next. "But marriage is a huge leap."

"Let's table that for now." Now that he'd suggested they marry, he was convinced it was the best idea. He didn't want to be his child's part-time father. "We'll have dinner tonight and talk about it."

She shifted on the cushioned chair as if it was made of

hard plastic. "I can't tonight. I'm working late. Nate has given me until the fifth of December to finish my album."

"Good for him. You've been working on it on and off for a year. I know you're a perfectionist, but at some point you have to let it go."

And maybe then he'd be able to refocus some of her attention on their struggling relationship. He knew her music was important to her, but there had to be a way for her to be a success in her career and still have room for her personal life.

"I know, but it's my first album and I want everything to be the best it can."

He understood her quest for perfection. As a teenager he'd spent hours learning how to place a pitch over the center of the plate. The familiar repetition of wind up and throw allowed him to forget his troubles and focus on the here and now. Watching Melody get lost in her songwriting process, he'd recognized the same need to make something flawless and beautiful.

"And yet you won't know how good it is," he said, reaching for her hand, offering her both support and encouragement, "until you put it out there."

She squeezed his fingers and gave a little laugh. "Or how much people are going to hate it."

"Stop channeling your father. If the man knew good talent when he heard it, he wouldn't have run his label into the ground."

"You're right, but it's hard to ignore all the times he told me to stick with the violin because I didn't have what it took to be a songwriter or a singer."

Kyle wondered what it would take for her to believe she deserved to be successful. He'd tried to reassure her, but often felt as if she couldn't accept his uplifting words because he didn't have any musical cred.

"And yet you've proved him wrong so many times," he reminded her. "This album is going to do great. You'll see."

"You've always supported me and I really appreciate it."

The warmth in her eyes aroused a pang of longing so acute he almost couldn't breathe. Damn. He missed her.

"Melody?" A blonde woman in pale blue scrubs appeared in the doorway.

Melody practically sprang to her feet and shot him a worried look. "Are you ready for this?"

Kyle gave her a reassuring smile as he tucked her hand into the crook of his arm. "Absolutely."

Melody followed the nurse into the patient room. Kyle's broad shoulders and strong presence filled the small space. He sat beside her in attentive silence while the nurse took her blood pressure, frowning over its elevated status, and asked routine questions. She answered automatically, trying to ignore the doubts that flickered on the edge of her awareness brought on by his shocking proposal.

What was he thinking to ask her to marry him without forethought or fanfare? Not that she needed a whole huge production made out of getting engaged, but it would've been nice to be proposed to in a romantic setting by a man who adored her instead of in a clinical setting by a man who just learned the day before that he was going to be a father.

I think we should get married.

His blunt declaration had been more practical suggestion than impassioned plea. Once the shock faded, her first impulse had been to hit him. How dare he presume she would agree to marry him because she was pregnant? And then tears had threatened and she'd had to grip the edge of her chair to keep from bawling her eyes out in reception.

"Your blood pressure is a little high," the nurse said, glancing at her with a thoughtful look.

"I'm nervous about the ultrasound," she lied. It was the conversation with Kyle that had upset her.

He might not have told her he loved her, but she knew that he was committed to her and their baby. Whether that meant they would find their way back to being happy with each other was the big question.

"That's not unusual, but we should check it again before you leave."

The nurse finished adding Melody's data into the computer and then showed her the gown she needed to don for the ultrasound. Kyle's stoic expression gave away none of his thoughts as he watched the nurse exit the room.

"Close your eyes," Melody told him as she began to work the buttons free on her shirt. She was already feeling vulnerable enough without adding to her stress by stripping in front of him.

One corner of his lips rose in that sexy half smile that made butterflies erupt in her stomach. "I've seen you naked before." His heavy-lidded gaze slid over her body, cataloging her curves with deliberate possessiveness.

Melody ignored the ache that flared between her thighs. Over these last few months, she'd deluded herself into thinking she was a practical woman who didn't need a man. She was perfectly capable of making rational decisions about her future and sticking to them.

Yet, a single flirtatious grin from Kyle swiftly showed her how erroneous her assumptions had been. She actually took a half step in his direction, intent on cupping his strong face in her palms and sliding her open mouth against his in a sizzling kiss.

"Just do it," she told him, wrenching her wayward hormones back under control.

Without saying another word he let his lashes drift downward, but the smile didn't drift from his lips. For a moment she stared at his familiar features with such longing she thought she might start to cry. Her hands shook as she slipped off her low boots and set them beneath her chair. Despite being confident he wouldn't peek, Melody quickly stripped down and put on the front-closing gown.

"Okay," she said, paper crinkling beneath her as she sat on the exam table.

"How about Amelia if it's a girl?" Kyle's voice was heavy with intent. "Austin if it's a boy."

She couldn't stop the grin that twitched on her lips. "You've been thinking about baby names?"

"I didn't sleep very well last night." He pulled out his phone and stared at the screen. "I'm also fond of Aubrey and Addison."

"Did you get out of the A's?"

He scrolled down some sort of list on his phone. "Colton for a boy?"

Her throat locked up as she stared at him. Damn the man for driving her crazy with his unromantic proposal of marriage and then twisting her heart into knots with this sweet demonstration of how excited he was to be a dad. Before she could respond, the door opened and the doctor appeared.

"How are you doing today?" Dr. Sara Evans asked, advancing into the room and taking quick stock of Melody's state of mind before glancing toward Kyle, who'd gotten to his feet. "And you are?"

"Kyle Tailor, the father."

Dr. Evans gave a quick nod before getting started. Almost as soon as her doctor had entered the room, Melody had calmed down. She liked the obstetrician's keen gaze and brisk manner.

"I'm going to spread a little gel here." The doctor applied the clear goo to her belly and chuckled as Melody shivered. "It's a little bit chilly. You'll forget all about that in a second."

Melody stared down at the slight bump just below her belly button where her baby lay. When she glanced toward Kyle, she noticed his eyes were glued to the monitor where an image had begun to develop. And there it was. Their baby. Head. Arms. Legs. A whole little person inside her.

While both she and Kyle had been gaping at the screen, Dr. Evans prattled on about the development of the fetus and the fact that the organs were developing.

"About this time," Dr. Evans said, "your baby will begin to open and close his or her fingers and his or her mouth will begin making sucking movements. He—or she—is about the size of a lime. Do you want to know the sex?"

Kyle spoke up before Melody could even open her mouth. "Can we?" His eyes sought hers. "Do you want to?"

"I guess." In truth she hadn't really thought about it. Didn't the pregnancy have to be further along? "Sure."

It would make planning easier if she knew she was having a boy or girl. She'd have to get the nursery ready and buy clothes. Of course, this brought up something that Kyle kept asking her about. Where was she going to live? She'd given up her apartment in LA to move in with Kyle. Trent's guest cottage was for guests. Up until now, she'd stayed for a couple days or a long weekend here and there when she took a break from the tour to work on her album.

She could justify living there while Trent was in LA with Savannah and Dylan, and she'd considered what would happen when they came back. They were family now. They would want their privacy.

When Kyle had asked her where she planned to live, she'd frozen up. With everything that was going on with her album and telling Kyle that she was pregnant, she'd been taking things one day at a time. Today, staring at the image of her baby on the monitor, decisions she had yet to make rushed at her.

Pressure on her fingers brought her back to the present. She winced a little at the bite of Kyle's grip, but his eyes were glued to the screen and he didn't seem to notice the way he was holding her hand. She squeezed back, bringing his focus to her.

"Looks like you're having a girl," Dr. Evans announced brightly, her smile broad. "Congratulations."

Melody was numb. "Are you sure?"

Dr. Evans nodded. "No question. This little girl isn't one bit shy."

"Then she'll take after her father," Melody murmured.

Her head spun. A girl. She glanced at Kyle to see his reaction, half expecting his expression to reflect disappointment. Had he imagined himself teaching his son to pitch? Instead, he was staring at her stomach and looking dazed. And delighted.

She waited until Dr. Evans finished with the ultrasound and left the room before she voiced the concern burning a hole in her stomach.

"You're okay with a girl?"

"Of course." He blinked several times and seemed to have trouble focusing on her. A line appeared between his brows. "Why would you think it wouldn't be?"

"Because you're a guy, you love baseball. I bet you woke up this morning thinking you needed to run out and buy a mitt and a ball."

"Actually, I woke up this morning thinking how empty my bed was without you in it."

She hadn't expected this angle of attack and wasn't prepared with an evasive maneuver. Holding the gown closed as best she could, she sat up and spun so that her feet dangled. "Close your eyes. I need to get dressed."

Kyle braced his hands on the exam bed and leaned forward so he could peer directly into her eyes. "We're having a girl."

Placing her hand on his cheek, she whispered, "We are."

His grin was infectious and she found herself smiling back. He was close enough that all she had to do was lean forward a few inches to bring their lips into contact. He covered her fingers with his. The connection made her heart race. It would be so easy to just forget how hurt she'd been these last few months. Through passion and desire, they could start again. She didn't really need to return to the studio today. Instead, they could go to his house and make love all afternoon. Her toes curled at the thought.

She gathered breath and summoned her courage to suggest they do that, but the opportunity was lost when his phone began to ring. He pulled it out and frowned at the screen.

"It's the club. I need to get this. How about I meet you in the lobby."

"Sure." With a sigh, Melody watched him go, and then got dressed once more.

It was for the best, she decided. Part of the reason they were in this mess was because they'd rushed in before determining if they were really compatible. They'd been dating for too short a period of time before she'd moved in and the decision had been made out of convenience rather than a thoughtful evaluation of whether they could work as a couple.

And why was that? Because Melody had been afraid to put the brakes on. To ask the questions that might drive

Kyle away. Now she realized that had been a mistake. And no matter how hard it might be to keep from falling back under Kyle's spell, until she knew for sure that he truly loved her, she couldn't move forward with their relationship.

Four

Kyle caught himself grinning as he negotiated the Las Vegas traffic on his way to Ugly Trout Records. The entire afternoon, since finding out they were having a girl, he'd been floating in a bubble of optimism. Now that the initial shock of his impending fatherhood had faded, he was feeling as if everything that had gone wrong with his and Melody's relationship was just a series of misunderstandings that they could sort out with a little work. They were going to be parents. Their daughter deserved to grow up in a secure, loving environment and he intended to provide that for her whatever it took.

Which was why he'd decided to start his campaign by bringing dinner to Melody at the recording studio so she could see he intended to take care of her. On the passenger seat sat a bag filled with several items that topped Melody's favorites list. It would have been better if they'd been in LA and he could've gone to Mama Rosa's for the

Bucatini Alla Carbonara, but he thought what he'd found would pass muster.

He'd also discovered a place that made the most fantastic cheesecakes. He'd brought a sampler for her to gorge on. She'd lost weight these last few months and he couldn't imagine that was good for the baby.

Ever since seeing that tiny profile and hearing that his daughter was now moving her fingers and toes, he'd been filled with optimism. He was going to be a dad. The thought held nothing but joy. Sure, he had no idea what he was doing, but that didn't mean he couldn't learn. After all, he'd seen the way Trent had taken to being Dylan's father.

Trent, who'd sworn all his days that he'd never get married and have kids. His best friend had grown up with a terrible role model for fatherhood. Siggy Caldwell's ruthless tyranny in business carried over into his personal life. He had picked favorites among his children, choosing to lavish praise on his firstborn while criticizing both Trent and Melody. No matter how successful they were, neither one could do anything right in Siggy's opinion.

And yet both of his younger children managed to become affectionate, caring people. In Trent's case it had taken becoming a father and admitting he was in love with Savannah before his true nature emerged.

Melody hadn't learned to guard her emotions the way her brother had. She was more inclined to throw herself into a relationship with little regard for her self-esteem. That was how she'd been with Hunter. While she'd been dating the DJ, it had driven Kyle crazy to see her always making excuses for the way Hunter treated her. And yet that was not how she'd reacted when faced with problems in her relationship with Kyle.

Instead of laughing off his assumptions about her and Hunter, she'd been furious and they'd had a terrible fight.

He couldn't remember her ever arguing with Hunter. Was that because her feelings for the DJ had been deeper and more profound? If so, why had she chosen Kyle in the end?

The driveway leading into the record label's parking lot appeared just ahead of him. He couldn't wait to see the look on Melody's face when he surprised her with dinner. She loved it when he was spontaneous.

Grabbing a parking space near the front entrance, he exited the car. It was close to six o'clock, and the lot was half full. Nate made the studio available twenty-four hours. The rate for off-peak hours was significantly cheaper, which made recording sessions affordable for up-and-coming artists. Melody took advantage of the quieter evenings to work on her album.

Kyle was reaching for the glass front door when he spied two people approaching through the lobby. His chest tightened as he recognized Hunter's tall form alongside Melody's slim figure. They were engaged in an animated conversation and hadn't yet spied him. He yanked open the glass door with more force than necessary.

"Kyle." Melody's eyes widened as she noticed him entering the building. "What are you doing here?"

He held up the bag. "I brought you dinner. I thought you'd be working."

His gaze flicked to Hunter. The DJ's lack of concern caused Kyle's annoyance to spike. Why was Melody leaving with him?

"Oh that's so…nice." She glanced at Hunter. Was it guilt that flickered in her eyes? "We were just going to grab something."

"And now you don't have to." Kyle pushed down his irritation and smiled. "I brought all your favorites. I thought you could show me what you've been working on while we eat."

When Melody hesitated, Kyle's gut twisted. He must not argue with her. Not today. Not after what they'd shared at the doctor's office. Seeing their baby for the first time had brought them closer than they'd been in months. He would not ruin that new beginning because he was annoyed that she was heading out to have dinner with Hunter.

"Sure. You don't mind?" she asked Hunter.

"It's fine." Hunter took in Kyle's tense expression before flashing a knowing smile. "You kids go have fun. I'll catch up with you later."

Kyle didn't bother to watch him go before catching Melody's elbow and turning her in the direction of the hallway that led to the various recording studios. He could feel a trace of resistance and noticed her glance over her shoulder in Hunter's direction. He tried not to let it bother him, but something about seeing Melody with Hunter made it hard for him to be rational.

"So were you two working on something together?" He thought the question came out sounding neutral enough.

"No, I was working with Craig when Hunter stopped by to ask me to dinner. I didn't even realize I was hungry until he mentioned grabbing a burger."

They entered a control booth. She snagged a couple bottles of water out of the mini-fridge, and then sat on the couch and watched while Kyle unpacked the food onto the coffee table.

"I brought pasta, salad and a cheesecake for dessert." He eyed her to gauge her reaction. She didn't seem overly thrilled by any of his choices. "I didn't realize you were eating red meat these days," he added, wondering what else about her he didn't know.

"It's being pregnant, I think. I've been craving all kinds of weird things. And there's some stuff I can't stand the smell of anymore."

"I hope shrimp isn't one of them because I brought you lemon Parmesan garlic shrimp over angel hair pasta."

"No, shrimp is fine. It's weird but I can't stand the smell of peanut butter." She popped the top off the plastic container and rolled her eyes in pleasure as the sent wafted from the bowl. "I ordered a salad with Thai peanut sauce a few weeks ago and it sent me scrambling for the bathroom."

"But you love peanut butter." They'd once taken a jar to bed and enjoyed licking the sticky stuff off each other.

"And hopefully I will again once the baby comes." She shuddered. "In the meantime I'm staying far away." Her eyes widened when he brought out dessert. "Whoa, is that cheesecake?"

He nodded. "I brought you several kinds to choose from. Or you can eat them all."

"You went to a lot of trouble," she said, giving him a soft smile that made his pulse race and his mouth go dry.

"It's not any trouble taking care of you. And that's my plan from now on. You and the baby are my top priority."

"That sounds really great." Suddenly there were tears in her eyes. She laughed as she dashed them away. "I swear everything makes me cry these days."

"Not everything, I hope."

"Mostly when people are nice to me."

"Then you must be crying a lot because you're someone people want to be nice to."

Melody stopped eating and stared at him. "That's really sweet of you to say."

"I wasn't trying to be sweet," Kyle said. "I was just stating a fact."

"What time are you heading to the club?"

"I plan to get there around nine." He surveyed her features, gauging the level of her exhaustion. "How late are you planning on staying here? You look like you could use some rest."

As if on cue, she yawned. "I thought to stick around for another couple hours. Hunter offered to help me with the bridge for one of my songs."

"Do you think it's a good idea that you're working with him?" The question slipped out before he could stop it.

"I don't understand what you mean." She frowned at him.

"He still has feelings for you. Why else would he have taken a job at Club T's and come to Ugly Trout to work with his clients?"

"Because Trent offered him a ridiculous amount of money to DJ?" Her blue eyes glittered as she regarded him. "And me being here isn't why he is using the facilities."

"He could just as easily record in LA." And oh how Kyle wished he would. "I'm sure most of his artists would prefer that."

"Hunter likes the vibe at Ugly Trout. And you know how fantastic Nate is to work with. I'm sure he's hoping to do a little collaborating with him."

Kyle stared at his penne in spicy vodka tomato cream sauce and found his appetite had vanished. Somehow this delightful surprise for Melody had led to a disagreeable revelation for him.

"You really need to get over this antagonism you have toward Hunter."

"I'll get over it when you convince me he doesn't want you back." And when she convinced him that she was going to stop running from their problems.

"He doesn't. In fact, he's been seeing Ivy Bliss."

"I thought he was just producing her new album." The pop princess had been recording her latest album with Nate at Ugly Trout Records up until a couple weeks ago when artistic differences caused Ivy to walk away.

"Apparently they've been involved professionally and personally. So you can see there's no reason for you to worry."

Kyle nodded. Upsetting Melody with his suspicions was only going to drive her further away. The smart thing to do would be to figure out a different way to get the DJ to back off. Except that Hunter wasn't the whole problem.

"There's just one last thing that's been on my mind," he said in careful tones. The question that had been eating at him for a long time could no longer be contained.

"What?"

"When things started to go wrong. First between you and Hunter and later between us." His heart thundered as her full attention became locked on him. "Why did you fight for Hunter and run away from me?"

At Kyle's question, Melody found herself opening and closing her mouth like a fish out of water. Her brain seized like an overtaxed computer. He was right. She had done that and it wasn't at all fair. She couldn't explain why for a year and a half she'd put up with Hunter taking her for granted, but when Kyle challenged her on one thing— granted it was a pretty huge thing—she'd shut him down the same way she had...her father.

"It was different with Hunter." Immediately she saw this was the wrong thing to say. She shouldn't compare the two relationships. Yet how else to explain? "He neglected me. I was always chasing after him, never quite knowing if he wanted me or not."

"And I never did any of those things. You know I want you in my life."

She gave a reluctant nod, unsure how to explain herself.

Maybe it was that her relationship with Kyle felt more important than what she'd had with Hunter.

"You hurt me."

Kyle's eyes widened. "How many times did Hunter make you cry?"

"Dozens."

The media had linked him with several women while he'd been seeing Melody. Hunter had claimed they were just friends, but she'd never known if things were truly innocent. And then there were all the times when he'd forgotten to call when he promised he would or to show up for a date. He'd even forgotten her birthday.

"And yet you hung in with him."

"Okay, I see your point," she grumbled. But it was different. Somehow. She recognized it in her gut. "I don't have a reason I can point to."

The way his lips thinned as he pressed them together infuriated her. What did he expect? She couldn't explain to him something she didn't understand herself.

"We could get to the bottom of it if we went to see someone."

Again, his offer made her blood freeze. She couldn't understand why. "Can it wait until after I've finished my album?"

"Of course." He sounded agreeable, but worry shadowed his expression. "But I think we need to do something in the meantime. That's why after we left the doctor's appointment earlier, I called a counselor in LA I trust."

Feeling ambushed, Melody demanded, "You talked to someone about our problems?"

"Relax," Kyle said. "She's someone I've been going to for years."

This bit of information came at Melody like a wrecking ball. "You see a therapist? How did I not know that?"

A muscle jumped in Kyle's cheek. "It's not something I'm proud of."

She knew what he meant. Because it made him look weak to need help. She opened her mouth to tell him that she didn't expect him to be strong all the time, but was that true? When he'd given her a glimpse of his insecurity where Hunter was concerned, she hadn't exactly been understanding of how he'd felt.

She liked being able to lean on Kyle. Appreciated how he took charge, made her feel safe and cared for. Since he rarely discussed his own troubles or difficulties, it never occurred to her that he might need to count on her support in return.

"Why didn't you tell me?" It worried her that she'd failed him. "Is it because of your dad?" His father had taught him to appear strong.

"It's the sort of thing that would make him crazy." After a heartbeat his lips curved into a dry smile. "I'm not sure what would be worse for him. Having a problem or admitting there was something wrong. I'm sure he'd rather have his leg cut off than agree to see a therapist."

"That's pretty dramatic." Yet it wasn't much of an exaggeration.

"It's pretty indicative of how determined my father is to not show any weakness." Kyle's voice lightened despite his pained grimace. "So now you know one of my deep dark secrets."

"One of?" She smiled through her heavy heart. "How many more are there?"

"You'll have to take the next fourteen days and find out."

He'd just done exactly as she'd often longed for him to do and opened up. And not just with a little something. He'd admitted something deeply personal and all in the spirit of improving their communication. At the same time, he'd issued a challenge: *I'm all in, are you?*

"What do you mean the next fourteen days?"

"Dr. Warner gave me a step-by-step fourteen-day relationship revitalizer. I thought we could start with this right now."

Melody blew out a breath. Why was she so resistant to what Kyle was trying to do? Didn't she want them to get back together? Kyle was obviously making an effort. Shouldn't she as well?

"Okay," she said before she changed her mind. "Let's do this."

"I'm glad you're on board." And there was a little softening in his manner that suggested relief.

"Where do we begin?"

"Here is the list of what we do each of the fourteen days. I think it spells everything out pretty well." He handed her a seven-page document. "It looks like a lot, but when I explained about your album deadline, Dr. Warner said we don't have to commit to doing something fourteen days in a row."

Before starting to read, she flipped through all the pages. For some strange reason her chest tightened. This was a huge undertaking. Much more than she was ready to handle. When she thought of going to a couples counselor, she imagined just sitting in a room and talking around their problems. Not this.

"Day one," she read. "Praise and appreciation. Write thirty of your favorite things about your partner and share them."

This she could do. There were hundreds of things she appreciated about Kyle. Maybe this whole task wouldn't be as bad as she thought.

"How about we take the rest of today and tomorrow to

make our lists and then have dinner tomorrow night and talk them over?" Kyle suggested.

It was on the tip of Melody's tongue to say she could fire them off in an hour, but then she considered that maybe he needed more time to find thirty things about her he liked. Her insides clenched at the thought that he might struggle with what to put on his list.

"That sounds great," she said.

After Kyle packed up the remains of their dinner and left the studio, Melody picked up her notebook, turned to a fresh sheet of paper and started to write thirty favorite things about Kyle. The first ten were easy. His eyes, smile, gorgeous body, his long fingers, deep voice, toe-curling kisses, his listening skills, the fact that he wanted to work on the relationship, his strong work ethic and support of her music career.

She sat back with a happy sigh and reviewed the list. Now, for the next ten. She wrote down several more of his exceptional body parts, his inability to carry a tune and his laugh. Her list had expanded to seventeen. Only thirteen more to go.

Melody stuck the pen in her mouth and worried the plastic until it was covered with teeth marks. Her mind was suddenly blank. Surely there were dozens and dozens more things about Kyle that she appreciated. Why couldn't she think of any?

Instead, she was bombarded by all the things that were wrong with him. The way he could talk endlessly about baseball stats, how he often worked with a game playing in the background. How he sometimes came home from business meetings and didn't want to talk. He insisted on maintaining a close connection with his family despite how much they frustrated him.

The door to the studio opened and Mia slipped inside.

Her cheeks glowed rosy and her brown eyes sparkled. She'd obviously just come from seeing Nate. The two were so in love and for a second Melody struggled with envy.

"What are you working on?" Mia asked, coming to sit on the couch beside Melody.

"I'm supposed to be writing thirty of my favorite things about Kyle." She went on to explain about the relationship revitalization journey they were on.

"That sounds amazing. Nate and I should do that."

Melody gave her a wry look. "But you two are deliriously happy together. You don't need to revitalize anything."

"I think every couple could stand to deepen their connection no matter what stage the relationship is in."

While she mulled this over, Melody handed Mia the instructions Kyle had given her. Maybe if she and Kyle had done something like this in the beginning, instead of just counting on their sexual chemistry to drive the relationship, they wouldn't have drifted apart during those long months she spent on the road.

"'Day six,'" Mia read, her voice filled with delight. "'Sex—a spoiling session for her.' Now that sounds fantastic."

Melody's stomach dropped to her toes. Three hours earlier she'd been ready to have sex with Kyle again and yet now, instead of the idea sending thrills through her, she was awash in apprehension. Because day six wasn't about the physical act of sex, but about intimacy. And she sure wasn't ready for that.

Mia continued, "'Your partner gets to have a totally selfish block of time.'" Her eyes widened as she kept going. "'Thirty minutes to three hours. She gets to be totally in control of the environment and actions.' Oh, you lucky girl."

"Let me see that." Melody wanted to snatch the pages from Mia's hands and read it all herself. Instead, she stewed impatiently while Mia finished reading the instructions.

"And at the end are suggestions for what can happen during the spoiling session. If you don't mind I'd like to make a copy of this."

"Sure." Melody fell into a thoughtful mood as Mia left the control booth.

She turned her attention back to the list she was supposed to make. After adding some of his cute quirks and business acumen, she'd reached twenty. Well, at least she had another twenty-four hours before they were supposed to get together. Surely she could come up with ten more things she liked and appreciated about Kyle. And if she couldn't, maybe she was kidding herself that they could make this work.

Five

Instead of picking up Melody at the studio, he agreed to meet her at Batouri's restaurant in Fontaine Ciel on the Strip. He was already waiting at the bar when she walked in. The chandeliers dangling from the ceiling cast faceted light over her dark hair as she slipped onto the barstool beside him.

"Nice place," she commented, her gaze touring the gold pillars and black tables set with white china and crystal.

"Wait until you taste the food. Chef Croft is a culinary genius."

"I'm glad I brought my appetite."

Kyle frowned. "Did you eat today?"

He wasn't happy about her weight loss. She claimed it was because of her morning sickness, but he wouldn't be surprised if stress had added to the problem.

"Breakfast, lunch and several snacks."

"Healthy ones?"

She gave him a stern look. "I'm not sure if you fussing over me is delightful or annoying."

"It's delightful," Kyle said. "Just like me."

"You're delightful?" Her lips twitched.

"When I put my mind to it." And he'd decided that was what he intended to do. "Come on, let's go see about our table."

Taking her hand, he led her to the hostess. He liked the way Melody's fingers curved around his. The contact reminded him of a time before the gap between them had grown so broad. Settling into a cozy booth, they placed their drink order, listened to that night's specials and waded into the shallow end with some small talk about her album.

"It's crazy, but now that I'm nearing the end, I'm in a love/hate relationship with every song. I can't be objective about any of them. Mia thinks I'm struggling to finish because I'm in love with making the album and I don't want the process to end. I keep telling her that I'm eager for it to be over."

"All of that makes sense. It's a huge undertaking. Have you given much thought to what you're going to do to celebrate?"

"Not a clue. I've been so caught up in putting all the finishing touches on everything that I haven't pictured what the coming weeks will hold."

"Some much-needed rest and relaxation," Kyle suggested, hoping she'd consider returning to LA with him.

Savannah's movie was wrapping in the next few weeks and she and Trent would be returning to Las Vegas. That meant Kyle's stint at Club T's was over. He had his business interests in LA to return to.

But he wasn't going anywhere without Melody.

"How did you find our first exercise?" Melody asked as the waitress delivered her salad and Kyle's steak.

"Are you asking me if I had a hard time thinking up thirty things about you I like?"

In fact, the exercise had been remarkably easy.

"Yes."

"Not at all. There are hundreds of things about you that I appreciate."

She scowled at him, but he could tell she liked what he had to say. "Are any of them not sexual?"

"Quite a few. Would you like me to pull out my list and get started?"

"Sure." She got her own list out of her purse and flattened the folded sheet on the black tabletop beside her plate. "Do you want to start or should I?"

"Ladies first." He thought a second before adding, "Why don't we alternate."

"Let's see." Her eyes scanned down her list as if searching for the perfect place to begin.

He shook his head. "From the top. I want to know what your first thoughts of me were."

Her cheeks grew pink and she squirmed in her seat. "Your eyes. I never know what color they will be from one moment to the next. It's something about the light or what you're wearing. And there's nothing I enjoy more than looking up and catching you watching me from across a room."

Kyle decided this was an excellent beginning. "Your determination," he said, taking his turn. "Since you were a teenager, you've written music, despite your father's attempts to dissuade you. Even though it hasn't been easy to overcome Siggy's negative attitudes, you chose your path and you've been successful."

His words made her smile. Good. That was what he was going for.

"Your smile," she said after a quick glance at her sheet. "Sometimes you come home and I can tell your day has been trying. But then you look at me and smile and it's as if the sun comes out."

Kyle made a note to smile around her more often. "Your talent. Both your songwriting and your singing. I am constantly impressed by your lyrics and music. Makes me wish I could carry a tune."

"That's farther down on my list," she said excitedly. "Your inability to carry a tune."

He made a face at her. "Why would someone with perfect pitch find that attractive?"

"Because it means you're not perfect." There was such an eager note in her voice.

"I'm the farthest thing from perfect and you know it."

"Well, but..."

She rolled her lips between her teeth, a sure sign she was thinking hard. Was she struggling for a way to spin his flaws in a positive light? Kyle waited her out. When Dr. Warner had spoken to him about the exercises in this relationship revitalizer, she'd made sure to point out that he needed to listen to what Melody had to say. It was something he hadn't done after finding out she'd been in New York with Hunter.

"You are handsome, rock a sexy body, have a full head of soft wavy hair, kissable lips, great legs. Don't get me started on your abs." Her words tumbled over one another as she rushed on.

As she listed off his physical attributes, he couldn't help but chuckle. It was nice to know the sexual chemistry was alive and well. He didn't plan to rely on sex to save their relationship, but maybe their desire for each other would compel them to work through all the tough stuff.

"Your voice on the phone gets me hot and in person…" She shook her head ruefully. "It's nice that you can't sing. It makes me feel like I can keep up with you."

"How many things on your list did you just read off?" he asked.

She scanned her list. "I might've gotten a little carried away. But there are lots of other things about you that I appreciate. Your sense of humor. Your business acumen. That you are such a good friend to my brother. I know things would've been a lot harder with my dad if Trent hadn't had you to talk to."

When she paused for breath Kyle jumped in.

"I admire how you've coped with a father as difficult as Siggy. And I remember what a hard time you had when your mother left you with him after the divorce."

Melody grimaced. "We've both been through a lot with our families."

"It's made us pretty gun-shy." Was it any wonder that neither one of them reacted well to their first major dustup.

"Can I tell you something without you getting upset?" she asked him.

"Of course." No matter what she had to say he would not take offense.

"When I was making this list, I got sidetracked into some things that I didn't like about you."

Kyle was amused by how horrified she was to admit this. "You don't think I know there are things about me that drive you crazy." He paused, thinking about his jealous reaction to her continued connection with Hunter. "Like everything baseball."

"You are obsessed." She exhaled as if his reaction, or lack of one, was a huge relief. "I just found it interesting that even though I didn't mean to I couldn't think about the good without thinking about the bad."

"Nobody is one thing or another. Although I think it's human nature to dwell on what's wrong rather than focus on what's good or right." It was something he'd done a lot of while they'd been apart.

"I'm glad we did this exercise. It really opened my eyes to who you are and why I fell in love with you."

"And also why you stayed away?" he prompted.

"A bit. I've been pretty overwhelmed these last few months. The tour took more out of me physically and emotionally than I realized and then I was nonstop writing, recording and producing my album." Her smile came and went. "Not to mention the fact that I'm pregnant and that has made me a little more reactionary than usual."

Kyle reached across the table and took her hand. "So shall we consider this exercise successfully accomplished?"

"I think we should." Her beautiful smile bloomed. "I'm happy with the results."

So was he. Kyle only hoped the next thirteen exercises went as well.

A huge yawn seized Melody just as she was pulling into the third stall in Trent's garage and she almost bumped up against the back wall. She shouldn't have stayed at the studio so late. In the last hour and a half she hadn't accomplished much of anything. Her mind kept wandering back to the prior evening with Kyle.

After the dinner had gone so well, neither one had been in a hurry for the night to end. They'd strolled through the extensive grounds behind the three interconnected Fontaine Resort hotels for almost two hours, talking about everything and nothing. She'd told him about her favorite

parts of the tour and how much fun she'd had watching
Nate and Mia fall in love. They rehashed what each knew
about Trent's clever takeover of his family's company, West
Coast Records. After seeing her back to her car, Kyle had
given her a friendly kiss on the forehead and she'd driven
away feeling achy and unsatisfied.

Now weariness dragged at her as she slipped through
the door that led into the side yard, following the softly lit
path to the guest cottage. Trent had spent a fortune landscaping the nearly one-acre backyard, tucking lights in
every nook and cranny. Pathways, shrubs and trees were
softly illuminated. The Monday after Thanksgiving, he'd
hired a crew to wrap colored Christmas lights around the
palm trees and fill the empty spaces on the lawn with
lighted reindeer pulling Santa's sled and a train. For the
past two days workers had been bustling around like elves.

He was pulling out all the stops both here and in LA so
his son would have a memorable Christmas. Melody had
refrained from pointing out that Dylan was only a year old
and wouldn't remember any of it. Why spoil anything for
Trent. He deserved to be happy. So did Savannah. Melody
wanted nothing but the best for both of them. They'd traveled a long path to arrive at their destination.

Melody wondered if she and Kyle would ever get back
to a place where they looked at each other with the sort
of dreamy lust that marked the nonverbal exchanges between Trent and Savannah. For her part, she couldn't stop
guarding her emotions. She wanted to trust Kyle, but was
afraid if she opened herself up, he would say something
that disappointed her. It was no way to build a relationship.
But she couldn't figure out how to move on.

A large basket, wrapped in cellophane, sat on the porch
beside the front door. She stared at it in wonder. How had
he gotten here? Kyle had keys to Trent's house as well as

the gate code to let himself into the backyard. Had he put it here as a surprise for her? As she drew closer, she could see baby items through the clear plastic wrap. Her heart gave a funny little leap.

She unlocked her front door and brought the basket inside, setting it on the dining room table where the roses had sat until Thanksgiving night when she and Kyle had argued over them.

A ribbon held the plastic wrap closed. The knot wouldn't yield to her fingers, so she fetched a pair of small scissors. Until she told Kyle about the baby, Melody hadn't been able to start planning for her future. Once they'd gone to the ultrasound and she'd seen the child growing inside of her, her nerves had transformed into flutters of excitement. But still, she hadn't started buying any of the multitude of things a baby would need. It was too early. Besides, shopping would be more fun if she shared the experience with Kyle.

The wrapping fell away and Melody admired the collection of onesies, bibs, tiny socks and books. And there was an adorable teddy bear. All the clothes were in neutral shades of yellow and green as if the giver didn't know the sex of the child. Did that mean Kyle hadn't given her the basket? Surely he would've chosen something in shades of pink to celebrate their baby girl.

She quickly checked over everything, but still didn't find a card. Another anonymous gift like the flowers. What the heck was going on? Should she be worried? Especially the way the basket had appeared on her doorstep. On the other hand, there could be a simple explanation. Savannah and Trent knew she'd told Kyle. Maybe they'd had the basket delivered. A quick way to find out would be to give them a call. Melody dialed Savannah's number. She didn't want to upset her brother for no reason.

"How is the filming going?" She asked when her sister-in-law answered.

"Pretty good. Just a few more scenes before we wrap. It's been a lot of fun. I really miss acting."

Savannah had been working in New York City first as a model and then an actress on a soap opera for several years before giving it up and returning to LA. She'd put her career on pause when she'd become pregnant and married Melody's brother Rafe. Now, two years, one baby boy and a deceased husband later, Savannah had accepted a supporting role in a movie and married Melody's other brother, Trent.

"I imagine I'd have a hard time giving up singing now that I've gotten a taste for it." Was that a choice she was going to have to make? She could name several women with huge music careers and families.

"Maybe you won't have to. I'm sure you and Kyle can work something out."

Would Kyle expect her to stay close to home? Before going out with Nate and Free Fall she'd never imagined herself a big star. And it would take a lot of hard work and personal sacrifice to get there. Was she ready for that?

"It's going to be a lot more complicated now that I'm having a baby. I guess if I tour, I'm gonna have to go for shorter periods of time."

The thought of being on the road and tearing apart her daughter and Kyle even for a few months made her queasy. And what if he sued her for partial custody and it was her separated from her baby. Her thoughts returned to his proposal. It had been more practical than romantic and so unlike him. While they'd been dating and even after she'd moved in, he showered dozens of sweet gestures on her.

It was why she'd thought he'd sent the roses. She'd been shaking with excitement as she opened the card. That it hadn't been signed by him had snatched away her delight for the briefest of seconds. He'd given her roses before, although his romantic style was more low-key and subtle. A handwritten note stuffed among her lingerie. A case of her favorite bottled water delivered to her while on tour.

Kyle made his feelings for her known in practical ways. The biggest one being how he supported her career and acted as a buffer between her and her father. She didn't need big drama to prove how much he cared for her.

But wouldn't it be nice if the baby basket was from him?

"Something showed up on my doorstep today," Melody said, "and I was wondering if you or Trent had anything to do with it."

"I didn't, but Trent might have. What was it?"

"A basket of baby things. There was no card. I thought maybe..." Melody felt foolish.

"Kyle must've sent it. No one else beside us knows that you're pregnant, right?"

"I said something to a couple people at the studio." Melody relaxed. Maybe Mia had organized something and sent the gift. But why no card?

"That is very nice of them. Now I feel bad that Trent and I haven't done anything for you."

"Don't be ridiculous," Melody said, gazing around the beautiful guesthouse. "You've been supportive and Trent is letting me stay here rent-free."

"You know you're welcome to stay as long as you need." Savannah's voice took on a note of concern. "Now that Kyle knows about the baby, have you thought about moving back in with him? Not that we want you to go, we just want you two back the way you were."

"We talked about it a little." Melody huffed out a laugh.

"In fact he proposed. Before you get all excited, I turned him down."

"Why? You love him and you're having his baby."

But did he love her in return?

"It was more in the vein of *hey, you're pregnant, we should make it legal*. He hadn't thought it through. And before he found out about the baby he was pretty clear he thought we should break up."

"That's not the impression I got."

"He jumped to the conclusion I was cheating on him based on a paparazzi photo," Melody reminded her. "He's known me over ten years. He should've realized I would never start one relationship without ending another."

"You sort of started something with him while you were dating Hunter."

"We were pretending. Our feelings might've gotten out of hand, but Kyle and I never kissed or did anything that crossed the line."

"I think he loves you and doesn't know how to handle such strong feelings. His dad is such a control freak. Kyle never really had a chance to be open and intimate with anyone before you came along."

"I know. He was an emotional fortress. Still is sometimes." Most of the time, Melody thought, wishing she'd stayed in LA and nurtured their fledgling relationship instead of taking off for nine months. "Some of it is his dad. Some of it is the women he met when he was a ballplayer. They wanted the lifestyle his money could provide. When we first started dating and I was trying to get him to open up, he often mentioned that they were disingenuous. He didn't know who he could trust."

"Well, he knows he can trust you," Savannah said. "Oh, dear, looks like my boys need me. Give Kyle our love and you stay strong. And if you ever figure out who gave you the basket, let me know."

Melody hung up with Savannah and stared at the phone for a few minutes before dialing Kyle's number. Maybe it was time she stopped making excuses for keeping him at arm's length and start figuring out if they had a future.

Six

Several days passed after their dinner to exchange their favorite things about each other, before Kyle and Melody were able to get together for the second exercise: romantic massage. The thought of getting to put his hands on Melody and vice versa had preoccupied him for the last couple of days. Seeing the way she'd been logging hours at the studio he'd expected to wait. Therefore, he was delighted when she phoned him from the studio one day—Nate had found her sleeping in one of the control booths and told her to go home. She'd called Kyle to ask if they could meet and he'd quickly agreed.

She'd chosen to come to his house in the early afternoon before he had to be at Club T's. When his doorbell sounded, Kyle hadn't yet settled on what part of his body he wanted her hands on. They'd agreed that each got to choose one part to massage on the other person and also which part they wanted massaged on their own body. He'd decided to lavish his attention on her hands.

"What all do you have there?" he asked.

"It's a foot spa." She carried a large plastic tub and had a heavy tote bag slung over her shoulder. "I'm giving you a pedicure and foot massage." She said it like she expected him to argue.

"Okay." The notion of her kneeling at his feet was a definite turn-on. Unfortunately that wasn't what this particular exercise was about. "And what part of you am I massaging?"

"I haven't decided yet."

"Maybe we should put body parts in a hat and draw."

She smiled at his suggestion. "That's not a bad idea." She carried her supplies into his living room and placed everything in front of a chair. "Do you mind putting some water on to boil?"

"Are you planning on cooking my feet?"

"No, but I want the water to be extra warm so you relax." She cocked her head and looked at him. "Have you ever had a pedicure?"

He shook his head. "One of the guys on the team used to get them all the time and got the nickname Twinkle Toes because of it."

"That's terrible," Melody said, but her scolding would have been more effective without the amused smile. "You shouldn't ignore your feet. They deserve to be pampered just as much as every other part of your body. More so, because they take the most punishment, lugging around our weight all day."

"I see your point."

From his vantage in the kitchen, he watched her pull a perplexing collection of items out of her bag, from clippers to lotions to some sort of scrubber. He was half expecting her to produce a bottle of red nail polish. No, she wouldn't do that to him.

"How's the water coming?"

"Almost ready to boil. Do you need me to fill the tub with warmish water?"

She was arranging a towel on the tile to soak up any spillage and glanced up with a smile that caused a spike in his heart rate. "That would be great."

Ten minutes later, she had things arranged to her satisfaction and made him go put on shorts. Soft instrumental music poured from the speakers set into the ceiling, adding to the spa-like feel she had created. He sat down and slipped his feet into the spa tub. As the hot, bubbly water enveloped his feet and the vibrating massagers worked their way along his arches, he got a sense of what old Twinkle Toes had been about.

"Relaxed?" she asked, adding something fragrant to the water that had an immediate impact on his blood pressure.

"That smells great." A low noise left his throat as tension he didn't even realize he'd been carrying fell away. "What is it?"

"Lavender." She tapped his right shin. "Let's start with this one."

He lifted the foot free of water and she dried it off before setting it on the towel in her lap. While she got to work with clippers and some sort of manicure scissors that tickled his skin, he stared at her bent head and let himself appreciate her.

Once she had his toenails trimmed to her satisfaction, she began to work lotion into his feet and calf muscles. From playing the violin and piano, she had strong fingers. And she knew exactly where to apply pressure to best effect.

"That's amazing," he groaned, closing his eyes and letting his head drop back. "Where did you learn to do that?"

"On tour," she said. "I'd come offstage after a set and

my feet would be killing me. One of the guys in Free Fall gave the most incredible foot massages."

"Should I be jealous?" In truth, at the moment he couldn't conjure the tiniest flicker of concern.

"He was happily married with three kids. Apparently his wife runs marathons and he's learned how to take care of her feet."

"Lucky woman." However, her comment made him aware that he and Melody hadn't been the only two people separated by the tour. Maybe they'd just been the least prepared to deal with the lengthy time apart.

He considered asking her how the other band members and their significant others coped with the separation, but that was a question for another time. Right now, he just wanted to sit back and enjoy the feel of her soft, strong hands turning his bones to oatmeal.

"How do you feel?" She asked him twenty minutes later. Her eyes glowed as she observed the effect of her ministrations on him.

"Call me Twinkle Toes," he said. "I'm sold."

She laughed and there was such delight in it. More than the relaxing massage, this was his reward.

"Next time," she promised. "I'll give you a facial."

If he wasn't careful, she'd turn him into a hedonist. On the other hand maybe that wasn't such a bad thing. Maybe he should arrange for a couples massage as a special treat when she put her album to bed and could relax enough to enjoy it.

"Thank you." He pulled her into his arms for a quick hug that quickly escalated into something more as she wrapped her arms around him and held on.

In the early days of their relationship, he'd been so caught up in his body's need for her that he hadn't taken the time he should've to get to know her romantic side. Instead, it had been easier to learn what made her body writhe and where to touch her to tear moans from her throat.

At the start lust had a fierce hold on him. But as the months wore on and his craving for her didn't so much diminish as change, he'd realized for the first time in his life he was caught up in something dangerous and delightful.

"This feels amazing," he began, wondering how to extricate himself without upsetting her. "But after three months without you, I'm more than a little hard up. And we have to get to day six before there's any sex allowed." He cupped her butt and held her firmly against him, letting her feel his arousal. It wasn't a request for sex, but a way to seek her sympathy.

"Are you sure you want to wait?"

At his fierce growl, she laughed and arched her back, rocking her hips and lightly grinding herself against him. The sharp bite of desire caused pain to flare, but not where Kyle would've expected. When her softly rounded stomach grazed against his lower abdomen, his heart gave a mighty wrench. This so shocked him that he stepped back instead of going in for a mind-blowing kiss.

Cursing, he rubbed his hands over his face.

"Kyle?" Melody caught at his hands and pulled them down so she could see his expression. Her eyes darkened as she regarded him. "Are you okay?"

"Yeah," he said, cursing the uncertainty in her gaze. The last thing he wanted was for her to feel less than safe with him. Summoning a lopsided grin, he rubbed his chin. "It's just that I go from zero to a million around you." He glanced down at the front of his shorts. "You deserve better."

"There's nothing wrong with a little down-and-dirty sex." Her lashes fluttered down to hide the glint in her eyes. "Once upon a time we fell on each other like hormonally charged teenagers."

"That was before you got pregnant." And before he'd overreacted to her being with Hunter in New York instead of talking through the situation.

"What does my being pregnant have to do with anything?"

He made a vague gesture in the direction of her stomach. "It's more than just the two of us now."

"Kyle, are you telling me you're going to be shy in front of our unborn baby?"

This conversation was not going the way he wanted it to. "It's not about being shy. It's about being careful."

"Careful?" Now she wasn't even trying to conceal her amusement. "How exactly do you plan on being careful?"

Damn her. He didn't have an answer. Mostly because he hadn't thought the whole thing through. When he remained silent, grappling for how to respond, she made a rude noise.

"Pregnant women have been having sex since the dawn of time. I read that during the second trimester as the nausea fades, hormones increase our sex drive."

"Please stop."

"In fact," she said as if he hadn't spoken, "many women engage in sex to stimulate labor."

Kyle was desperate to put an end to the topic of sex. His shorts were uncomfortably tight and thinking about naked Melody, sprawled on his sheets, her belly round with his child, wasn't helping matters one bit.

"Your turn. Have you figured out what you'd like me to do for you? We could refill the basin and I could return the favor."

She shook her head. "I had a pedicure the other day." Her lashes came down to shadow her eyes. "I suppose you could do my shoulders. They're pretty tight at the moment."

"How about I start with your hands and work my way up to your shoulders?"

Her eyes brightened. "Sure. That sounds nice and I have some really great cream I just bought."

He drew her to a chaise longue and sat down with her between his thighs, her back to him. While she relaxed back against his chest, he took the cream and utilized some of the techniques she'd demonstrated on his feet, sliding his thumbs deep into the flesh of her palms.

"That feels really good," she said, her head falling back against his shoulder.

She'd stripped down to a tank. Her breath slipped out in a happy sigh as his fingers traced up her arms and over her shoulders. He loved the way she fit against him. All soft, yielding curves and warm, enticing energy.

He thought they were getting somewhere until her phone rang. The discordant sound caused her to tense.

"Ignore it," he murmured, kissing the side of her neck. "This is our time."

"I really can't." She shifted forward and quickly moved beyond his grasp. "There's this one song I really love, but I can't quite get it right." She checked her phone's display and turned her back to him. "Hey, thanks for calling me back. Do you have some time later?"

Now Kyle was the one growing tense. From her body language and tone he knew exactly who was calling. Hunter. She shot a look over her shoulder in Kyle's direction.

"Ah, sure, I can meet you in an hour. Thanks, I really appreciate it."

"I thought Nate told you to take the rest of the day off."

"He did, but there's a really small window of opportunity…" She slipped her shirt over her head and once again donned her sweater. Moving with more speed than grace she began to gather up all that she'd brought.

Kyle stood with his arms crossed and watched her. "That was Hunter, wasn't it?"

"Please don't make a big deal out of this," she pleaded. "It's really just about my album."

He couldn't help but think she wouldn't be running off if it wasn't for Hunter. "Why aren't you going to Nate for help?"

She wouldn't meet his gaze. "I have gone to him. And to Mia. I just want another opinion."

It was obvious that she was drowning in self-doubt. This album was her chance to prove to herself and the world she was a talented singer and songwriter. But more than that, deep down, part of her would forever be that starry-eyed teenager whose dreams had been trampled by her father's brutal words.

"I understand." She would never know what it cost him to say that. "But before you leave, can we please agree we'll do date night on Wednesday?"

"Wednesday is perfect. Nate has given me a deadline of noon. After that…" She smiled through her anxiety. "I'm all yours."

When the door to the rehearsal studio opened, Melody looked up and spied Nate. He frowned at her.

"Weren't you supposed to be out of here two hours ago?"

"I've been working on this song for Ivy Bliss."

She'd gotten caught up in working on something she shouldn't be. Hunter had called around noon and asked for some changes to a song Ivy Bliss had started to record before switching to work with Hunter a month ago. Apparently, thanks to Hunter, she was back to being interested in the song again. But she wanted two new verses. Melody had been fiddling with the song all afternoon instead of working on her own album. Hunter was in LA tomorrow to work with Ivy and wanted the song today so they could look it over.

"Wait," Melody said, as something Nate had asked just penetrated her creative fog. "Did you say two hours ago? What time is it?"

"Nearly four. I thought you and Kyle had some big dinner planned for tonight."

"I lost track of time." This was not good.

Today was day three of their relationship revitalization and they were supposed to have date night. The plan had been for her to head to his house at two. They were going grocery shopping and then would return to his place to prepare a four-course dinner. The point of the exercise was spending time together engaged in something fun and cooperative.

"What song?" Nate asked, bringing her thoughts back to the moment.

"The one you and Mia suggested she do. She wants me to change a couple verses."

Nate shook his head. He knew the demanding pop star all too well. Not only had she been on tour with his band Free Fall, he was currently engaged to her sister.

"Want me to take a look?" he asked.

Relief washed through Melody with such intensity that tears sprung to her eyes. "That would be great. Hunter wants to look at the new verses today. I don't know that they're any good. I'm absolutely drained of all creative energy."

To her relief, Nate didn't scold her, although he sure

looked like he wanted to. Mia was also pregnant, so Nate understood how exhausted an expectant mother could get.

"Give me your notes and Mia and I will put our heads together. Go have dinner with Kyle."

"Thank you."

She'd left her phone in her purse while she worked. It was in the corner of the room under her jacket. As soon as Nate left the room, she went to dig it out.

At two, when she realized the project for Hunter wasn't going well, she'd called Kyle and explained that she needed some extra time in the studio. She hadn't revealed that she was working on something for Hunter. Kyle would not appreciate having his date night usurped by her ex-boyfriend.

Sure enough, there were two calls and several texts over the last half hour. She'd promised him she'd be there at three. Now it was four. No doubt he was frantic. Ironically, showing up late or not at all was the exact sort of thing that had driven her crazy about Hunter. She'd hated how his tardiness had made her feel so low on his priority scale. Now she was doing the same thing to Kyle.

"Sorry, I lost track of time," she said when he answered the phone. "I'm leaving the studio now."

"I'm just glad to hear your voice and know that you're okay." He sounded less tense as he went along. "I don't know how hungry you are, but we might have to bag what we planned to go for something simpler."

She'd been in charge of finding a dish that was straightforward enough for them to handle, but time-consuming in its preparation. She'd settled on a recipe for baked tortellini pie that sounded fantastic. She and Kyle shared a love of all sorts of Italian foods.

Leaving Ivy's song in Nate's and Mia's capable hands, she headed to Kyle's place. Traffic was worse than usual and it took her half an hour to get there. Now, at four thirty, there wasn't time to make all the tortellini from scratch, create the ragu, roll out the pastry dough as well as make the almond soup and the flourless chocolate torte for dessert.

"I was thinking about the shrimp scampi over angel hair pasta we made the first night I stayed over at your place," she said, hoping the fond memory would alleviate some of the disappointment she saw shadowed in Kyle's hazel eyes.

"With some crusty bread and something decadent for dessert."

She had to give him credit for trying to seem upbeat. "Sounds perfect."

They got in his car and headed for the grocery store near his house. It was a boutique market with specialty cheeses and meats, fresh-baked bread and all sorts of fun and interesting edibles. After loading up with angel hair pasta, shrimp, lemons and garlic, they headed to the bakery for bread and decided to buy a tiramisu and a death-by-chocolate cake instead of trying to make something.

She was sampling an olive tapenade when her phone started ringing. Kyle was several feet away, looking at the infused olive oils. She decided to risk checking who was calling. To her relief, it was Mia. She answered.

"I love the changes you've made," Mia said. "Ivy will, too, I imagine. Nate and I tweaked a couple things here and there. Do you want me to send you the updated version?"

As curious as she was, Melody was leery of letting work interrupt any more of her date night with Kyle. "No, I trust you. Do you mind sending it to Hunter?"

"No problem. You kids have fun."

"Who is that?"

Melody whipped around and realized Kyle was standing right beside her. "Mia, telling me to have fun tonight." Her stomach clenched at the half lie, but what Kyle didn't know wouldn't ruin their evening. "Are you ready to check out?"

Fifteen minutes later, they were back at Kyle's house. Melody put classical music on the stereo—Kyle had balked at Italian opera—and together they made quick work of the shrimp cleaning. Standing side by side, they chopped greens, zested a lemon and started boiling the pasta. While their ingredients sizzled in a skillet on the stove, Kyle set the table and poured the basil-infused olive oil into small dishes for them to dip their warmed bread into. In no time at all, plates loaded with pasta and shrimp were heading for the table.

Since he was renting the house, she hadn't expected such a well turned-out table, including china place settings, crystal goblets filled with juice instead of wine and silver candleholders. He'd even bought a bouquet of bright flowers for a centerpiece.

"This is lovely," she exclaimed, feeling slightly guilty that he'd prepared for their date while she'd made it a lower priority.

"You taught me a lot about setting the mood."

In the months they'd lived together, she made sure they had a couple romantic dinners a week. Their schedules were often hectic and she'd wanted to make certain they took time to focus on each other and made dinner a special event.

Sometimes it had bothered her that Kyle didn't seem to appreciate the extra bit of work that went into their dinners. Now, she was seeing that he'd noticed and understood what she'd been trying to do even if he'd never commented on it.

"Is it as good as you remember?" Melody asked around a mouthful of succulent garlicky goodness.

He moaned in response and the sound was so inviting that a fire kindled in Melody's lower half. She should've added the sounds he made during sex to her list of things she appreciated about him. With a sigh, she focused her carnal appetites on the food in front of her. Day six couldn't come soon enough.

"Ready for dessert?" she asked after they'd cleared the table and done the dishes.

She was in a mellow mood from the delicious food and thoroughly entertained by Kyle's Club T's stories about some of the crazy things customers had done. Everything from deliberate wardrobe malfunctions to brawling to couples engaging in sex challenges. As if by mutual agreement, they avoided bringing up anything that would result in an argument. Such as Hunter or their future plans.

"Hmm. Dessert," Kyle murmured, cupping her face in his long fingers and tilting her head to the perfect angle.

As he slanted his lips over hers, sensation shimmered and then spread through her entire body until she felt bathed in joy. He'd always had that effect on her, even before she'd understood that in her subconscious mind he'd crossed from being an old family friend to a man she very much desired.

His tongue slid over hers, relearning her mouth. It was a soft, questing kiss. One meant to draw her out instead of claim her. It made it easy to relax and breathe him in. To absorb the warmth of his hands and let the memories unfold in her mind of all the kisses they'd shared. He asked her for nothing more than to revel in this moment with him.

She almost moaned in dismay when his lips lifted from hers. But he wasn't done with her. His uneven breath tickled her skin as he seized her earlobe between his teeth, awakening a shudder.

"That was nice." Melody breathed in his clean, masculine scent and held on like he was a life preserver and she was a woman in the middle of the ocean.

"So very nice. You taste way better than any dessert," Kyle said, claiming her mouth once again. This time his hands moved over her with deliberate intent, but just as she was ready to surrender to jumping ahead to day six, he lifted his lips from her. "Do you want coffee as well?"

"Coffee?" she moaned as his hands fell away. "Just what I need, to be jacked up on caffeine all night so I can stay awake and think about that kiss."

Kyle's smile grew wicked.

"I have decaf," he said

"Lovely." She exhaled her disappointment. "Brew away."

Her phone began to ring insistently from her purse as she cut slices of tiramisu and chocolate cake. By mutual agreement, they'd put away their phones for the duration of their evening. Unfortunately, Melody had neglected to turn hers off. She didn't realize she'd stopped working and was staring toward the source of the sound until Kyle spoke.

"Do you want to get that?"

"No." She finished putting their dessert on plates and carried them to the living room where Kyle had flipped on the fireplace. "I'm sure it's nothing."

And for about five minutes she forgot all about the call as the chocolate cake melted on her tongue. But when her phone began to ring a second time, she twitched in dismay at another interruption.

"Sorry, I should've turned it off the first time," Melody said, getting to her feet. The screen said it was Hunter calling. She winced and shut the phone down. "There, we shouldn't have any more interruptions."

"Who was it?" Kyle asked with studied indifference.

"No one important." She picked up her plate again. "You know that corner right there would be perfect for a Christmas tree. We should get you one."

Kyle's expression grew serious. "I was planning to be back in LA for Christmas."

"But…" What should she say to that? "I thought you'd want to spend Christmas with me."

"I do," he said, his gaze trailing away from her toward her purse. "In our house. In LA."

"Your house," she corrected automatically, startled by the sudden revelation. Not once had she considered his LA house her home. She'd never let herself settle in. It was almost as if she'd half expected their relationship would one day end. "And all my family will be here."

By that she meant Trent, Savannah, Dylan, Nate and Mia. Even though the last two weren't technically related to her, she'd come to think of them as more than just friends.

"I guess that answers my question as to where you're planning to stay once you have the baby."

"That's not fair." She hadn't made any sort of decision. In truth, she was still running scared. "I don't want to fight about this tonight."

"Who was on the phone, Melody?" he asked again, this time with a tone of calm authority.

With a burst of irritation, she decided to tell him. The evening was falling apart anyway. "Hunter." She debated whether or not she should explain the reason and Kyle's flat expression told her it might damage their efforts to reconnect if she let him think the worst. "Ivy Bliss wants to record one of my songs, but needed some new verses so I was working on them earlier today."

"And the reason Hunter called you?"

"I don't know. Just before I came over tonight, I gave Mia and Nate the song to work on and she sent the updated verses onto Hunter. Maybe he was calling to say he liked them or that he hated them. I don't know." Realizing she was breathing too hard, Melody knit her fingers together and struggled for calm. "Hunter and I have a professional relationship. You're just going to need to accept that."

"Or else?" he prompted in a silky tone.

There was no "or else." She wasn't trying to shove an ultimatum at him. "I'm really tired. Maybe I need to go."

She got to her feet, scooped up her purse and headed for the front door. Silence filled the space she'd just vacated. The temptation to turn around and say something clawed at her. But what more could she say? And then she was at his door. Cool air struck her hot cheeks as she stepped across the threshold.

"Don't go." Kyle's voice came from right behind her. "I'm sorry that I acted like such an idiot about you and Hunter working together."

She was so preoccupied by her thoughts that she hadn't noticed he'd followed her. Melody's heart knocked against her ribs and she tried unsuccessfully to swallow the lump in her throat.

She turned in Kyle's direction and saw the pain in his eyes. That he was being open about his hurt and regret was such a shock. She considered how seriously he was taking these exercises and thought of the romantic table setting. He'd been looking forward to their evening.

"I'm sorry I was late to our date," she said. "Working through our problems is important to me. I don't want you to think that it's not."

"You've got a lot on your plate right now. And that's really exciting news about Ivy Bliss wanting to record one of your songs." He offered her a gentle smile as he took her hand and tugged her toward him "Why don't you come back inside and tell me all about it while I clean up the kitchen."

"I can help with that," she offered, feeling as if she owed him for her tardiness.

"No, you will sit and watch me while I work." When she opened her mouth to protest he shook his head. "You're just going to have to get used to letting me take care of you."

Even as she nodded, she realized that he'd been taking care of her in one way or another for as long as she could remember. The question was what had she done for him in return?

Seven

After how things had gone on day three's date night, it was two days before Kyle reached out to Melody again. Deciding to find neutral territory for day four's communication exercise, he suggested Club T's on Monday afternoon. The forty-thousand-square-foot nightclub wasn't open for business until evening. One perk about being part owner and the current manager was that he had the keys to the place.

"I've never been in here when it's been empty," Melody said. "I kinda like it."

"It's not exactly intimate." Fourteen thousand square feet inside, another twenty-six thousand outside including the pool. "Although there are some nooks and crannies we could sneak off into."

"It's such a beautiful day," she said, flashing a smile. The temperatures had climbed into the midsixties. "I was hoping we could sit out by the pool."

"Of course. Let me grab some drinks and we can head out there."

The first three dates had held mixed results. One thing was for sure: anything having to do with touching, they were going to excel at. It also shed light on the fact that they'd been using physical intimacy as a crutch. They'd moved too fast from dating to living together to being parents.

Circling the pool were side-by-side lounges with thick mattresses and backrests that could be lowered flat. Once Melody chose where she wanted to sit, Kyle spun one of the lounges so that they could face each other rather than recline side by side.

"Are you ready to dive into communication?" Melody asked. After that day-three-date-night debacle, she was demonstrating more willingness to participate in the exercises.

"First question," Kyle said. "How can I love you best?"

Since he'd never actually told her that he loved her, this question made both of them wince. She glanced down at her hands, noticed herself playing with her long sweater and clasped her fingers together in her lap.

"How about you answer first," she suggested.

Kyle suspected she was playing for time. "First off, you've committed to fourteen days of relationship revitalization and that's wonderful. I would like for you to talk to me when you're upset about something instead of shutting down all communication."

Melody's lips tightened minutely, but she nodded. "I want to feel secure with you."

The hardest thing about this exercise was to stay silent while she spoke. Kyle gave an encouraging nod even as his insides turned to stone. He knew what she wanted. For him to tell her he loved her. And he did love her, but telling her while they remained at odds wouldn't give her the satisfaction she believed it would. She wouldn't trust that he meant what he said; she'd just suspect he was mouthing the words to facilitate their reconciliation. The time to tell her he loved her had been before she left on the tour and every day after.

"That doesn't mean I expect you to ask me to marry you or even to tell me you love me. It means I want you to trust me about Hunter."

He should've seen it coming. His distrust was what had created their current situation. After seeing her hand-in-hand with her ex-boyfriend, Kyle had never stopped to question why he'd assumed she'd go back to Hunter.

"Where Hunter is concerned, I trust you completely." What he didn't trust was Hunter and his attempts to worm his way back into Melody's life. "Next question. How do I support you in a meaningful way? How can I support you better?"

"You've always been behind me with my music. Even when it tore us apart, you encouraged me to pursue it. You know how hard it was for me growing up with my dad being so negative about my abilities as a singer and a songwriter. I can never thank you enough for not just letting me go but for welcoming me back."

He nodded. Would he do the same thing again knowing how hard it would be to be apart from her for so many months? Probably. She was developing into such a talented performer that to clip her wings would be a crime. In the last year she'd blossomed, both as an artist and as a woman. No man who truly deserved her love would want anything less than the best for her.

"And how can I support you better?"

"Sometimes I think you're a little too understanding."

"What?" That was the last thing he expected to hear her

say. Especially after the way he reacted every time Hunter's name was mentioned. "I don't know what you mean."

"How happy were you when I went off on tour?"

"For you, very. For me, not at all."

"I think your support of my music is a double-edged sword. On one hand, you're the understanding guy who encourages and believes in me when I don't. That's such an amazing gift. On the other hand, because of how my dad was about my music, you treat me like I'm fragile and don't give me good boundaries."

"What are you getting at?"

"The tour with Free Fall." She wrinkled her nose. "Looking back, I wish you'd asked me to only do part of it."

"You'd have been okay with that?" Kyle wished they'd talked more about the opportunity before she'd signed on.

"Maybe, maybe not. But if I hadn't been gone so long, we wouldn't have drifted apart."

"So are you saying you're willing to make our relationship as big a priority as your career?"

Her fingers fanned over her stomach, the gesture protective. "I think that's something we need to discuss further."

"Fair enough." He was wise enough not to hoot in delight. With her album set for release after the first of the year, he'd been worried that she'd put too much pressure on herself to start touring and take their baby away with her.

"So how can I support you better?" she asked, turning the question back on him.

He'd come prepared with answers to all the questions except this one. He didn't honestly know what he wanted from her in terms of support.

"It's pretty hard for me to rely on anyone," he said. "I'm not accustomed to asking for help."

"And yet you have a therapist you see. What do you get out of seeing her?"

"I don't have to be strong with her."

"Strong? Like confident?"

"Confident and together. I went to see her when I was struggling with depression after I realized I wasn't coming back from the Tommy John surgery. I didn't have to put on a brave face for her. I could be angry and scared and she provided a safe place for me to work through all the emotions my father told me a real man could control. He always said, 'Control your emotions, son, or they'll control you.'"

"Is that something I could do for you?"

It was hard to tell her of his fears when his every instinct insisted he appear invincible. Capable of protecting her and providing everything she and their baby could ever need. Even though she was perfectly capable of taking care of herself, he wanted to be her shelter and her strength.

"I don't know." Immediately he knew it was the wrong thing to say, yet he'd committed to being honest with her. "It goes against everything in me to let you see me as weak."

"I could never do that," she said with a startled little laugh. "You're one of the strongest men I know."

"That's exactly what I'm talking about. You see me as strong, but sometimes I'm not."

Her lips parted. She obviously intended to argue with him further, but something in his expression stopped her.

"I guess that's something else to add to the list for when we sit down with the therapist."

Kyle's lips twitched. "At this rate we're going to keep her busy for years."

The next morning, Melody showed up at his house a little after ten in the morning with coffee and bagels. Kyle was feeling groggy as he let her in. He hadn't gotten out of Club T's until nearly five. There'd been some plumbing issues in the men's bathroom that he'd stuck around to oversee.

Melody handed him a coffee. "You look tired. Rough night?"

"I don't get how Trent can do this day in and day out. I don't think I'm cut out to oversee a nightclub."

"Just party in one?"

"That's different. When I get tired I get to go home."

She laughed at him. It was good to see her infectious smile light up her eyes. Kyle resisted the urge to pull her into his arms and steal a kiss. Day six they got to have sex. He wasn't sure how Melody was feeling about it, but after not being with her for three months, he was fairly certain the anticipation was going to kill him.

But first he had to get through day five's connection exercise: forehead-to-forehead breathing for five to twenty minutes. Kyle had no idea what was supposed to happen.

"You don't look ready to do this." She headed into the kitchen and pulled his favorite cinnamon-and-sugar bagel out of the bag and began preparing it for him with slathers of honey cream cheese. "Good thing I brought sustenance."

"I'll be fine after a dose of caffeine and sugar." He noted a certain edge to his voice put there by sexual frustration. She gave him an odd glance.

"We can postpone until later."

"No." He took the plate she offered him and sat down at the breakfast bar. The moan that came out of him after his first bite made her chuckle. "I haven't had one of these in months."

"Why not?"

"Because it's something you and I do together and it's no fun without you."

His words surprised her. "You only eat bagels with me?"

"These particular bagels, yes. We found them together that morning we went for a run and you twisted your ankle."

"You carried me to the bagel place."

"We ate these." He held up the bagel, remembering how he'd kissed the loose sugar and cinnamon off her lips. "I don't think anything has ever tasted so good."

It was that moment he'd known she was the one. He'd never told her that. Nor did he speak up now. It wasn't the right time. They were starting to find each other again, but the journey was far from over.

They sat in silence eating, each lost in their own thoughts. A few minutes later he noticed her fidgeting. Did she have somewhere to go? Someone to meet? Kyle ruthlessly banished the thought.

"I think I'm awake enough to begin," he said, sliding off the barstool and holding his hand out to her. "Shall we get started?"

"The instructions said we're supposed to do this exercise for anywhere from five to twenty minutes. What do you think?"

"Being that it's our first time, I think we should try for ten minutes. Five doesn't seem to be enough and twenty seems way too long."

"You don't think you could sit still with me for twenty minutes?" She shot a mischievous glance at him from beneath her lashes.

"I'm pretty sure neither one of us is good at sitting still."

She gave up with a sigh. "You may be right."

They decided to try the exercise while sitting on the couch. Melody kicked off her shoes and took a few seconds to get comfortable. Once they were facing each other, the awkwardness kicked in. Kyle made no attempt to secure her gaze and noted that Melody was making eye contact with his shoulder.

"We're supposed to set a timer, aren't we?" she asked, pulling out her phone. "Something soothing."

"How about we end by playing one of your songs?"

"The instructions say something soothing," she murmured wryly, indicating that although she'd put her album to bed, she hadn't made peace with it. "The sound of chimes should work." She set her phone aside. "Ready?"

He nodded and they leaned forward until their foreheads touched. "Step two, synchronized breathing. Why don't you keep breathing and I'll match your rhythm."

"Does this seem like a lot of work?" she asked in a somber tone. "Like maybe we're overthinking it?"

"We're new to the process. By that I mean we haven't really taken the time to get to know each other like this." Their relationship thus far had been more like a mad dash, not a marathon they'd spent months and months training for.

"I guess." She lapsed into silence for a few seconds and breathed. Just as he was finding her rhythm, she spoke again. "Eyes open or closed?"

"It depends if you're ready to try soul gazing."

He hoped she was. This felt important to him in a way he couldn't explain. As if their failure to connect through these exercises would mean their relationship was doomed. Day three's date night had demonstrated that they continued to fail at communicating. If they couldn't connect, they couldn't communicate. At least not on the level they needed to at this time.

"Are *you* ready to try soul gazing?" she asked. Her tentative tone made him want to reassure her.

"Why don't we try eyes closed for seven synced breaths.

Once we're breathing together, see how you're feeling and if you want to open your eyes."

"This New Agey side of you is so unexpected," she teased.

He gave her a playful growl. "Shut up and breathe."

Today was day six of the plan. They were supposed to have sex. Ever since Mia pointed out that this was the day they were supposed to engage in a spoiling session for her, Melody had been both excited and terrified of what was to come.

"You realize you're in charge, right?" Mia had said as they were leaving the studio and heading to their cars. "You can do as much or as little as you want."

"But I'm sure Kyle's expecting sex."

"This is a spoiling session for you. He gets his turn on day eleven." When Mia had reached her car, she opened the trunk, pulled out a tiny bag and handed it to Melody. "A little care package." The contents were wrapped in tissue. "Wait until you and Kyle are together and then open it."

"Is it like edible body paint or something?"

"It's a surprise. I think it will help."

"Thank you." Melody had given Mia a hug and headed off to her car.

Kyle had insisted on a romantic dinner before they got down to her spoiling so at least she had some time to think about what she wanted. The possibilities were endless. She could chicken out and ask him to snuggle her. She could go all in and insist they could make love. Or it could be something in between.

Every inch of her skin tingled at what was to come. Kyle never disappointed in the lovemaking arena. She was in for a fantastic evening regardless of what she chose. But it was asking for what she wanted that was the real sticking point. Why did that make her so uncomfortable?

She texted him before leaving the parking lot so when she approached the front door, it swung open and he appeared on the threshold. Even though he didn't touch her, her body went up in flames from the sheer heat of his gaze. She held out the bag Mia had given her as if something as insubstantial as brightly colored paper could act as a shield.

"What's that?" he asked, snagging the bag from her fingers as he drew her inside.

"Something Mia gave me. It's for both of us. She told me not to open it until I was with you."

"A massage oil that heats up?"

"I guessed edible body paint."

"Painting you with my fingers sounds like a wonderful idea." He brushed a kiss across her lips, leaving lingering traces of his smile behind. "I'll break out the plastic sheets."

His kiss had short-circuited her brain. How could the simple graze of his lips awaken such longing inside her? Her feet moved automatically as he guided her deeper into the house.

"Wait." She put on the brakes and stared at him. "You have plastic sheets?"

"It's Las Vegas." His eyebrows rose as if this explained everything. "They came with the place."

Melody's lips quivered into a smile. Kyle was in such high spirits that her nerves rose up once more. Could she do this? Was she ready to take this step with him? And yet, how could she not?

She wanted him so badly, but they'd rushed their relationship in the beginning, caught up in the intensity of their sexual chemistry. Was letting her body speak for how she felt the right thing to do at this stage in their reconciliation? This was only day six of their relationship revitalization—although in truth almost two weeks had passed because of all the work that had gone into meeting her album deadline.

"What's wrong?" Kyle asked, sensitive to her mood.

Screw waiting. She was only going to get more conflicted the longer she had to think about what she was doing. "Let's have sex before dinner."

Kyle stroked his knuckles over her cheek. "I'm pretty sure that's not what you were thinking just now. Didn't we promise to do a better job of communicating?"

She held his palm to the side of her face and stared at his strong throat. Tonight he wore a long-sleeve T-shirt in dark gray that hugged his torso and hinted at the definition in his arms, chest and abs. No buttons to worry about. She could tear the thing right off him.

"I'm worried about us having sex tonight," she said at last.

He didn't tense or frown. Setting his hands on her shoulders, he gave her a gentle shake.

"So, you want to rush into something you're not ready for?" His tone was fond exasperation.

"I don't know what I want. That's part of my problem."

Kyle caressed down her arms and took her hands. His tender touch warmed her clear to her toes, banishing most of her anxiety. "This is your night." His fingers tightened on hers, offering reassurance. "We will do whatever you want."

"But you want to have sex." She wasn't trying to stir the pot and create discord, but she was sure he had expectations and wanted to be clear about them.

"I'm a guy." One corner of his lips kicked up. "I want to have sex all the time. But I don't expect you to do something because I want it. Especially not on a night when making you happy is my only goal."

Melody relaxed a little at his reassurance. More than anything this made her long to be with him.

"So, no sex before dinner." She paused. "And no sex after dinner."

He gave her a wry smile as if understanding that she was testing him. "If you weren't pregnant, I'd suggest a cocktail to relax you. Instead, I'm going to give you some sparkling cider and feed you all the delicious selections Chef Murray made for our dinner tonight."

He'd brought in a private chef who even now was in the kitchen creating an amazing array of tasting plates for them to enjoy. Kyle led her to the dining room and they took their seats. She couldn't believe her eyes; there were so many dishes to choose from.

Melody lost track of how many things she ate and couldn't decide which of the amazing dishes were her favorite. By the time the chef left them with a half-dozen desserts to sample and share, Melody's nerves were humming with pleasure.

"Time to bring out Mia's gift," she said, moaning over a flourless chocolate cake drizzled with sea salt caramel that melted in her mouth.

Kyle fetched the bag and together they pulled out a card game for lovers. Melody's first reaction was an uncomfortable giggle, but Kyle scrutinized the cards with interest.

"I think she meant well." He set them aside without further comment and rested his steady gaze upon her. "But what do you want to do next?"

Melody turned her hands palm up. "My ideas for tonight ended with the meal."

"Well, we have to do something. How about we go into the bedroom and I snuggle you for thirty minutes. Nothing more. Clothing on," he added as if worried she might think he was pushing. "You choose whether we spoon or face each other."

This was something she could handle. "Sounds good and I want us to face each other. There's nothing I enjoy more than putting my head on your chest and listening to your heart."

"Then that's what we'll do."

Since it was her evening, Melody positioned him on his back and snuggled up next to him. With his arms around her, she settled into the deep steady rhythm of his rising and falling chest. She missed this. It was peaceful and soothing. Tight against Kyle, locked in his arms, she floated on waves of trust and love. How had she forgotten he made her feel like this? She'd been so caught up in being hurt and self-protective that the important stuff had diminished in her mind. Why was it always so easy to be negative instead of positive?

"Is something wrong?" Kyle asked. "You're not very relaxed and that was the whole point of this exercise."

"Sorry. I was thinking about how nice this is and how much I've missed it."

"And that made you tense?"

She sat up and stared down at him. Suddenly the floodgates opened and all sorts of emotions began to pour out of her.

"I'm mad at myself for shutting down instead of fighting for us. I'm frustrated that you didn't trust me." She was breathing hard now and her throat constricted to the point where she could barely speak above a whisper. "And I'm scared that if it wasn't for this baby we wouldn't be making an attempt to save our relationship."

His eyes widened at this rush of information, but he kept his voice relaxed as he said, "I think right now we need to focus on the fact that we are making an attempt to save our relationship."

"Ugh." She rolled off the bed and started pacing. "What is wrong with me that I'm so in my head?"

"There's nothing wrong with you. I'm sorry you feel like we're only trying to fix our relationship because of the baby. That's not how I feel."

"So, if I wasn't pregnant, you'd still be here fighting for us?"

"Absolutely."

He answered so quickly and with such definitiveness that the fear clutching at her heart loosened its hold. Damn it. What was she doing? The goal of days one through five was to rediscover each other and connect through talking.

Tonight was supposed to be about them reconnecting physically. Not just sex, but intimacy. She owed it to both of them to shut down her brain and indulge in some straightforward devour-each-other sex.

"Take your clothes off," she said, setting her hands on her hips and looking him over with a lover's keen eye. "Slowly." Her lips moved into a sultry grin. "Very slowly."

With a nod of understanding, Kyle got off the bed and took up a position at the foot of it. "Would you like me to dance for you as well?" He was obviously willing to give her a show.

"That would be nice." Melody went to sit cross-legged in the middle of the bed. They were too far apart to touch each other. "Do you need some music?"

Laughing with him broke down her walls. She'd put far too much emphasis on them having sex. She'd forgotten how much fun they had playing together.

"Whatever you'd like."

Melody grabbed his phone and cued up Christina Aguilera's "Still Dirrty." Kyle's eyebrows went up at her choice, but he started moving his hips to the beat. For someone who locked up his emotions, he wasn't afraid to get silly from time to time. And the man knew how to rock his body. Her mouth went dry as inch after inch of hard, sculpted muscles came into view. She could definitely get used to this.

Her fingers twitched as he slid down his zipper. She could feel the metallic rasp resonating throughout her entire body and got up on her knees as his pants hit the floor. She was eager to get her hands on the erection straining his boxer briefs. When his fingers hooked in the waistband, she stopped him.

"Wait." She smiled up at him. "Let me."

He groaned as her fingers skimmed down his stomach and dove beneath the fabric. "This is supposed to be about you."

"You don't think I enjoy touching you?" she teased, working her palm up and down his hard shaft. He pumped into her grip and slid his underwear to the floor.

"I know I enjoy having your hands on me." He gently pried her grip free. "Later," he promised. "For now we concentrate on you."

Melody stripped off her shirt and shimmied out of her leggings. Clad in bra and underwear, she scooted backward across the mattress and crooked her finger at him.

"I want you to take these off me," she said, sliding her fingers lightly over her bra and panties, delighted by the way his nostrils flared.

"And then?"

"I'd like you to touch me."

"Just touch?" He crawled up the mattress toward her. "Am I limited to hands only?"

"Of course not."

"Do you want me to take things slow?"

Did she? "Please, no. The only thing I want you to take is me. Now."

The months of separation hit her like a truck. Every inch of her ached for the caress of his hands and mouth.

He shifted to her side, fingers trailing up her thigh. When at last he brushed over the crotch of her panties and lingered over the dampness, her hips lifted off the mattress.

"That's my girl," he murmured. "Tell me what you want."

"This."

She grabbed his hand and slid it beneath the material. They groaned in mutual delight as he dragged his fingers through her wetness. His mouth found hers, the kiss hard and demanding. She opened to the thrust of his tongue and clutched at his head while he worked his fingers against her core and around her clit, the pressure perfect. The months of heartache fell away and there was only this. Always this.

"Don't hold back. Give me everything," he murmured and that was all it took.

An orgasm rushed over her so fast she was barely aware of the upsurge of pleasure before her release.

"More," she moaned against his mouth, smiling as he hooked his fingers in her panties and tugged them off her. She dispensed with her bra at the same time and then she was spread open for him. "I need you to fill me."

"We'll get there," he promised. "But first…"

Eight

She tasted like everything heavenly and memorable and the sounds she made as he spread her wide and set his tongue against her was the most beautiful music. He intended to make her come a second time, harder. Whatever it took to drive the last three months of separation from both of their minds.

"Kyle. Oh, yes, just like that."

He loved hearing her cry out his name. She would grow hoarse screaming it before he was done. He slid a finger up inside her and her hips lifted, angling to take more. He obliged her and his thrusting mimicked what would come later.

"Harder," she panted. "Make me come."

Her cries grew as he fell into the rhythm he knew she loved. She danced against his mouth. His fingers bit into her hips as he held her tight against his tongue and drove her toward orgasm. She was arching back against the mattress, her muscles flexing and straining as her pleasure rose. Gathering fistfuls of the comforter, she arched even farther back and a wordless cry spilled from her throat.

Watching her climax moved him in ways he'd never fully appreciated before. He'd done this for her. And she gave him everything.

When she went limp, he sucked in one breath and then a second. Her eyes were closed and satisfaction curved her lips. He stayed still and watched her, waited for what came next. It didn't take long.

Her lashes drifted upward. Her gaze snagged him. "Come up here." She hooked her finger at him. "I need you to kiss me."

She didn't need to tell him twice. He crawled up her body, depositing kisses as he went. He lingered over her breasts, taking one and then the other nipple into his mouth and running his tongue over the sensitive buds. Her fingers dove into his hair, holding him to her, while a stream of whimpers and cries came from her throat.

"Kiss me," she whispered.

He obliged, shifting until he loomed over her, their mouths gliding across each other in smooth, gentle strokes. His muscles began to quiver as he held himself above her. She spread her legs for him and brushed her hand down his body until she found his erection. He sucked in a sharp breath as she touched him.

"I need you inside me. Now."

"I like you being in charge," he told her, placing himself at her tight entrance, feeling the heat of her waiting for him. "Fast or slow?"

"Fast and hard. I need you to fill me. Until I'm no longer me but us."

Despite her words, he took his time, letting her adjust to their three-month absence, savoring her tight fit. She dug her fingernails into his butt, making him groan, and pulled him to her. He lost it a little on the first thrust. It had been so long. She was so perfect with her flushed skin and the indents in her lip from where she'd bitten down.

"That's it," he murmured, giving her his all, thrilled that she took him so deep and deeper still. It felt so good to be surrounded by her, body and soul. "You're incredible."

She wrapped her legs around him and he began to move. The friction amazed him. Her muscles were tight as he thrust into her, finding her rhythm and wringing a cry from her lips. He leaned down to kiss her and she gave him hunger and wildness. They rocked together harder, faster. Her nails bit into him, urging him on. *Have mercy.*

"Make me come, Kyle," she pleaded. "Again, please."

It was what he'd been waiting to hear. He gripped her ass, changed the angle of his thrusts slightly and her body tensed. He was ready to explode, but he would not let himself go until he saw her unravel again.

"Come for me," he growled, watching as her head fell back and a wordless keening burst from her. He held himself in check for a few more thrusts and when he was sure she was over the edge, let his own orgasm claim him.

He shouted her name, a declaration to the universe that this woman belonged to him. And he to her. His chest heaved. Something hot burned in his eyes. He collapsed onto her and buried his face in her neck. Minutes ticked by as they panted in ragged, sated bliss. It was always more than just sex with Melody. It was a mind-blowing connection that couldn't be denied. Her fingers relaxed their grip on him and he shifted onto his side, drawing her with him. With their legs tangled, his fingertips stroked

damp strands of hair away from her face. He dropped a
kiss on her temple.

Mine.

And no one was going to take her away from him. Not
ever.

Kyle was whistling as he stopped his car in Trent's
driveway and slid from behind the wheel. It was six in
the evening and Melody had invited him for dinner. For
the first time since the day they'd attended her ultrasound
appointment, they were spending time together with no
purpose other than to enjoy each other's company. As much
as Kyle had appreciated the exercises that had helped them
reconnect and learn more about each other, he was happy
to have no agenda.

After reading the note on Melody's front door, he turned
in the direction of her brother's house. As much as he was
looking forward to the intimate setting of the guest cottage,
he understood why she was using the main house to host
dinner. Trent's kitchen was three times the size of hers.

He followed the path through Trent's carefully landscaped backyard and arrived at the terrace that overlooked
the swimming pool. It glowed a soft turquoise amid the
cleverly lit trees and bushes that created a tropical para-
dise. The previous week's temperatures had hovered in
the midseventies during the day, but now as December
progressed, Las Vegas was seeing a nearly fifteen-degree
drop. And with sunset an hour earlier than in the summer,
it was downright chilly.

The scent of cooking beef lured him past the narrow
opening in the sliding glass wall and into Trent's two-
story great room. His friend had bought the enormous
property in a gated Las Vegas community and turned it
into a bachelor's playground. Before he and Melody got

together, Kyle used to love to come to Vegas and hang out here. There had always been a party going on with girls and booze and plenty of distractions.

These days, although Savannah had only been back in Trent's life for a few months, the changes were evident. A playpen sat beside the large sectional. The dining room boasted a highchair. On either side of the fireplace, toys lined the bookcases' lower shelves. And below the coffee table was a basket of board books, perfect for little hands.

He imagined his own house in LA looking much the same in six months. After how things had gone between them the other night, he was pretty sure Melody was ready to move back in with him.

She stood in the kitchen, her dark brown hair pulled back in a high ponytail. She wore snug black jeans, torn at the knees, and a dark gray T-shirt that hid her baby bump. Her only jewelry, a silver guitar pick engraved with Melody + Kyle, dangled from a long chain. He'd given it to her the day she left on the tour.

Looking back, he probably should've put a large diamond on her left hand, but they'd only been living together for three months and he'd been too arrogant. He'd never imagined she'd stray during their long months apart. If anyone was prone to cheat, it probably would have been him. But being with her had changed him. Before she came along, he'd been accustomed to being alone. The minute she walked out the door, loneliness barged in and sat on his chest like an adult bull elephant.

"Something smells amazing," Kyle said, holding an enormous bouquet of pink roses and white lilies out to her. "These are for you."

Predictably, her eyes widened at the sight of so many flowers. He scanned her expression for disappointment. She probably would've preferred to receive red roses from him. But someone had already beaten him to the punch and he didn't want to remind either of them of that fact.

"These are gorgeous," she exclaimed with such delight that Kyle winced.

How long had it been since he'd showered her with tokens of his affection? He scanned his memory and realized it was too long. What was wrong with him? Melody was the most important woman in his life. She was generous, thoughtful and loving. When she'd first gone on tour, he'd taken delight in sending her little things that made her happy. But as the weeks went on and he ran out of ideas, he'd fallen back on text messages, and the romantic gifts had become less frequent.

"But you don't have to bring me flowers." She so obviously meant it that his heart contracted to the size of a peanut.

"I know you don't expect it, but that doesn't mean I should take you for granted. Hunter made that mistake and he lost you."

"That's not really why he lost me," she said quietly as she filled a vase with water and unwrapped the flowers. "I fell in love with you."

"I don't deserve you."

"Probably not." Her cheeky smile came and went. "I hope you have an appetite. I fixed your favorite."

His mouth started to water. "Beef bourguignon?"

"The very same."

It was the dish she'd fixed the night she chose him over Hunter. They'd arranged to have dinner at her apartment, not as part of the ruse, but because they both reached a point where being together—even as friends—had become the best part of their day. She confessed later that she'd created a romantic setting without even thinking about it.

He glanced toward the formal dining room and saw it

was decked out with fine china, crystal glasses and flickering candles. "You went all out," he said softly, hope stirring inside him like the first glimpse of dawn.

"I thought maybe we could both use a reminder of what it was like in the beginning."

"I like that idea." His voice was a husky murmur, the best he could do given the lump in his throat. "What can I do to help?"

The fastest way to Melody's heart was to pitch in and become part of her team. She was everyone's cheerleader and preferred group sports to solo activities. It was another way they differed. He'd grown up an only child, and although he'd chosen baseball as a career because he excelled at it, pitching had always felt like one of the most isolating of positions. Often the flow of a game hinged on how well he performed. It was one thing to stand in the outfield and wait for a ball to come to you. It was another to place pitch after pitch exactly where you wanted it.

Such drive for perfection was what Kyle and Melody recognized in each other. Their disciplines might be different, but their desires sprang from the same well.

"You can open the wine," Melody said. "I pulled a lovely red from Trent's collection."

"You can't drink alcohol and I'd rather not drink alone."

She smiled sweetly and nodded. "In that case, dinner will be ready in ten minutes." She clasped her hands before her and eyed him with interest.

"How shall we entertain ourselves?" He closed the distance between them and slid his hands over her hips, drawing her gently toward him.

"Ten minutes isn't a lot of time," Melody murmured, her nails raking against his scalp in the way he liked. "And I've spent too much time cooking to let it burn."

"Then we'll just have to use the time wisely."

* * *

After dinner, they left the dishes soaking in the sink and Melody led the way to the guesthouse where she planned to offer him the dessert of his choice: a cheesecake with white chocolate and raspberry or her. As she entered the tiny living room, turning on lights as she went, she had a tiny déjà vu moment as once again Kyle spotted the basket filled with baby things she'd left on the dining room table.

"Who is that from?" He demanded.

"I don't know. There was no card." She didn't turn to look at him, afraid to see suspicion in his eyes.

"Okay." But from the tone of his voice, it wasn't okay. "Did this get delivered to the studio as well?"

"No. It was waiting for me by my door."

He froze, eyes widening. "You are in a gated community. You didn't find that strange?"

"Um." She recalled her earlier disquiet, but didn't want to upset him. "I figured someone dropped it off with the guards and maybe they brought it by."

"But they don't have the code to the side gate. How did it get to your door?"

"It came while the crew was working on putting Christmas lights up. I figured maybe one of them brought it in."

"Did you ask them?"

"No."

The delivery method had seemed off at the time, but then she'd called Savannah and got to thinking about Kyle and their future and become completely distracted from the basket's mysterious arrival.

"Melody," he chastised, taking her by the shoulders and turning her to face him. "What the hell is going on?"

"It's not from Hunter."

Kyle's mouth drew into a grim line at the mention of her ex-boyfriend. "Did you talk to Savannah or Trent?"

"It's not from them, either." This would probably be a good time to mention how the CD from her ultrasound had gone missing as well. "There's something else."

"What?"

"Friday, after the doctor's appointment when I went to show Mia the ultrasound, it wasn't in my purse."

"You lost it?"

"I looked all over the studio and asked around but nobody had seen it. And then two days later it was back in my purse. I swear it wasn't there on Friday when I wanted to show it to Mia."

"Do you think someone at the studio took it and then gave it back?"

"No. Why would anyone do that? I just figured maybe it had fallen out and someone found it and put it back. The CD has my name on it."

"This is really strange and I'm not sure it's a good idea for you to stay here alone."

Kyle's concern was causing her anxiety to spike, but she pulled it under control. "Don't be ridiculous. Like you said, this is a gated community. It's all just a coincidence."

"I don't believe in coincidences. There's something weird going on and I don't like the idea of you staying here by yourself."

"I'm fine."

"Humor me."

"Humor you how?"

"Move into my place." He must've picked up on her dismay, because he quickly added, "At least while Trent and Savannah are gone."

"That's not necessary, I assure you."

But the basket's mysterious origin couldn't be denied. She put on a brave face, not wanting Kyle to think she was feeling even the littlest bit anxious. Red roses and baby gifts weren't exactly frightening, no matter what the source.

"I don't like that someone has such easy access to you."

"So I'll call the guard at the gate and let them know that no deliveries for this address should be allowed past them. And then I'll talk to Trent and make sure he doesn't have any more landscaping projects planned."

Kyle didn't appear satisfied with her answer. He crossed his arms and frowned down at her. "Then I'm going to move in here."

"Definitely not. We are not ready to cohabit again."

"I'm not talking about cohabitation, I'm talking about your safety."

"Roses and bibs. Not exactly scary stuff."

"Anonymous gifts."

"So I have a secret admirer," she said flippantly. It took a second for her own words to sink in. The reality of a secret admirer wasn't nearly as delightful as it sounded. "I'm sure it's harmless."

The skeptical expression on Kyle's face matched his words. "You need to take this more seriously. You're in the public eye now. People think they know you. They believe they have a personal connection even though they've never met you."

He'd had his own experiences with such fans. There was the woman who'd posed as his girlfriend and bluffed her way into his hotel room not once, but twice, while he was on the road with the team. Later, she'd bombarded him with letters and presents, making quite a nuisance of herself. Eventually he'd had to get a restraining order against her. Still, she'd threatened to commit suicide in an LA boutique after she spotted him shopping there with a woman he was seeing.

"I'm not famous in the same way you are," Melody said.

"I'm just that girl who opened for Free Fall. I don't have a big following on Twitter or Instagram. Maybe once my album drops it will be different."

"It only takes one person."

Kyle wasn't the sort of guy to try to frighten her just so he could persuade her to move in with him. If he was alarmed, he was genuinely concerned about her.

"Okay, now you're scaring me," she said.

"Good."

"Can you give me tonight to think about it?"

Kyle began sifting through the baby items; she couldn't imagine what he was looking for. The last thing he picked up was the teddy bear. As he turned it over in his hands, he began to frown.

"There's something weird about this." He fiddled with it some more and produced a black box from the back of it. He looked shaken, and alarms started going off in her head.

"What's wrong?"

"This is a camera. One of the teddy bear's eyes is the lens."

"A what?" She glanced around her living room, trying to imagine the space from the angle of the stuffed toy. "You mean like one of those nanny cams?"

"Yes."

He regarded the thing with a frown before walking it outside. She followed him as far as the door and watched as he dropped it into the pool. Her skin felt as if it was crawling with a hundred tiny insects. She shuddered and set her hand against her lips as her stomach roiled.

"I don't know what's going on," he said, returning to the guesthouse. "But I don't like it one bit. You can't stay here a second longer."

He had her good and spooked. Suddenly, the idea of an alarm system between her and the rest of the world sounded pretty great. She half wished Savannah and Trent had left Murphy behind. The French bulldog might not be big enough to take down the intruder, but he was fierce enough to bark and warn her if anyone was trying to get in.

The main house had an alarm system and no creepy, anonymous gifts sitting on the dining room table. "What if I go sleep in Trent's extra bedroom? There's an alarm system and I know no one has been inside. Let me pack a bag and you can walk me over."

"It would be better if you didn't stay alone."

"I'll be fine."

Whatever she'd intended for the evening was now spoiled by her fear of stalkers. While Kyle stood in her living room like a guard dog on high alert, she threw stuff that she'd need into an overnight bag. Her nerves jangled as she stared around her bedroom, seeing the big windows and the drapes she never drew. What would be the point? There was an eight-foot wall around the perimeter of Trent's large backyard. She'd never imagined a stranger would be peering in her windows.

After locking up, she and Kyle returned to the main house and he made the rounds, checking each window and door to make sure it was locked. Melody wore a frustrated frown through this process, but it was mostly to hide her anxiety. She'd planned for such a different end to the evening.

She should ask Kyle to stay, but she'd made such a big deal out of not needing him. She'd asserted that she wasn't ready to resume their relationship so many times that she wasn't sure how to stop pushing him away. What was it going to take for her to give up and give in? If a stalker wasn't the perfect excuse to admit she needed and wanted to rely on Kyle once again, then what would it take?

"Everything seems to be secure," Kyle said, standing in the middle of the great room and staring around.

Melody wrapped her fingers around his arm and nudged him toward the front door. "I'll be fine."

Part of her wanted to take him up to the guest room and tear off his clothes, but it was an impulse born of anxiety and fear of being alone. That wouldn't do. It wasn't fair to either of them. And how long before this real or imagined threat stopped being an excuse for her to turn to him?

Feeling proud of herself for being so sensible, Melody lifted onto her tiptoes, wrapped her arms around his neck and gave him a chaste kiss before sending him out the door.

Nine

As soon as Kyle heard the front door lock click into place behind him, he pulled out his phone and dialed Trent. When his friend answered, Kyle heard a shrieking baby and a barking dog in the background.

"Sounds like a party at your house," Kyle said. Opening his car door, he slid behind the wheel, but didn't start the engine. All at once he realized he couldn't bring himself to leave Melody by herself. He would spend the night in his car out in front of the house. There was no way anyone was getting past him.

"Dylan stole Murphy's favorite toy and thinks it's funny when he gets barked at."

Despite the concern weighing him down, Kyle couldn't help smiling. Was that chaos going to be his life a year from now or was it different having a girl? He couldn't wait to find out.

"So what's up?" Trent asked. "Something going on at the club?"

"Everything is running as smoothly as it can. I'm calling about your sister."

"I'd like to help you, but Melody's got a mind of her own."

"Don't I know it." Kyle rubbed his forehead. "But this isn't about playing go-between in our relationship. It's something more serious."

"I don't think I like the sound of that."

Kyle suspected Melody wouldn't be happy with him for calling her brother, but she wasn't taking this situation seriously enough. "Some weird stuff has been happening to her."

"Define weird."

"I think she's called you or Savannah about some flowers that got delivered to the studio."

"Red roses. Yes, Savannah mentioned something about it. You didn't send them, I take it?"

"No, and she's convinced that Hunter didn't, either."

"You believe her?" Trent sounded relieved and worried at the same time.

"I like to think I've learned a little something these last few months."

Trent snorted. "Yeah, you keep telling yourself that."

"Fine, I'm a jealous fool." And for the first time in three months, it didn't make him feel bad. Because it meant he cared. He felt. A lot. "Your sister is important to me. That's why I've been acting like such an idiot."

"You remember what I said to you when you first started dating her? I said I'd kick your ass if you hurt her. You promised me you wouldn't."

"I'm not overjoyed at the detour our conversation has taken. It's never been my intention to hurt your sister."

"I figured you were both adults and she knew what she was getting with you." For some reason Trent was on a roll. "Frankly, I thought you'd move on before she got too attached."

"I'm committed to making a life with Melody and our child. Nothing about that has changed. She's the one with questions and doubts." By the time Kyle got all that out, he was working hard to get air in and out of his tight chest. "Now, can we please get back to the anonymous gifts she's been getting."

"What else has arrived?"

"A basket of baby things."

"Savannah mentioned something about that. You didn't send it?"

Kyle wished he had. "No. And it showed up on her doorstep. No card. Nothing at all to indicate who it came from."

"What do you mean it showed up on her doorstep?"

"I mean someone got into your gated community and into your locked backyard and put it on the front step of the guesthouse."

"How the hell did that happen?"

That was the same question Kyle wanted answers to. His uneasiness grew with Trent's concern added to the mix.

"I don't know. I had her move into your house for tonight because there's an alarm. It's a start, but I would feel even more confident of her safety with her at my place. She, however, is resisting."

"Do a better job of convincing her."

Kyle resisted snapping at his best friend. None of this was Trent's fault. Taking a few seconds to gather and then expel a long, steadying breath, Kyle said, "That's my plan, but your sister has a mind of her own." Thank goodness. And yet with her safety at risk, Kyle wished she was a little bit more tractable.

"What do you want me to do?"

"I don't suppose you could come up with a good reason for her to come to LA for a visit?"

"I know Nate's been talking about her doing a concert to kick off her album. Maybe we could put something together here."

"Do you want to give him a call?" Kyle asked. "Or should I?"

"I'll do it. What are you planning for the rest of the night?"

"I thought I'd sit in my car and watch your house."

A long pause followed his words. When Trent spoke, he sounded more serious than ever. "Is that really necessary?"

"Maybe not, but she and the baby are the two most important people in my world. I can't risk anything happening to either of them. And it's not as if I'm going to be able to go home and sleep."

"I'll call Nate and let you know what I find out."

Kyle pushed back his seat and settled in for a long night. At least he wasn't going to struggle to stay awake. His nerves were too much on edge to allow him to sleep. With his phone connected to Trent's Wi-Fi, the car filled with live sports talk from *ESPN*. The conversation didn't do much to tax his attention, but the sound kept him alert. An hour into his vigil, Trent called back.

"My sister called to tell me there's a stalker in her driveway." Trent's drawl lacked any tension, so he obviously knew where Kyle was at the moment. "Any idea who that might be?"

"Text her back and let her know that come morning I expect coffee and some of those disgusting frozen waffles you keep in your freezer."

"She says you should come in."

"She wasn't too happy about the idea earlier." Kyle

knew he was being stubborn, but he had a point to make and she'd started it. "I'm fine right here."

"Suit yourself. I talked to Nate and he agrees about you taking her to LA for a while."

"Great." A weight was already lifting off Kyle's shoulders. "Now all we have to do is come up with a reasonable explanation for her to go."

"Already in motion."

Dawn was pushing salmon and gold into the sky when Kyle heard a knock on his car window. He'd been staring toward the street and didn't notice Melody approaching from the house. He rolled down the window.

"I thought you would've given up and gone home by now," she said, setting her hands on the door and leaning down. "You look like hell."

"Good morning, gorgeous," he murmured, surveying her messy updo, the sleepy droop of her lips and the hint of cleavage peeking out between the sagging lapels of her robe. "Sleep well?"

"Not particularly." She gave him no more explanation. "Hungry?"

"Sure."

"Come on in. I fixed breakfast."

"Coffee and waffles?"

"You hate those waffles."

"I didn't figure there was anything else available."

"You forget Trent doesn't live alone anymore. Savannah makes sure the freezer and refrigerator are well stocked. There's bacon, eggs and toast. As well as coffee."

"You didn't have to go to all that trouble."

She gave him an unreadable look before pushing away from the car. "Come get it while it's hot."

Kyle followed her inside, gleefully sucking in the invigorating aroma of coffee and bacon. Instead of eating at the breakfast bar, they brought their plates to the couch in Trent's great room and sat side by side.

Twenty minutes later, Kyle set his finished plate on the coffee table and sat back with a groan. "That was fantastic," he said, glancing her way. "Are you sure you got enough to eat?"

"I'm just starting to get my appetite back so I had plenty." She carried their plates to the kitchen.

"Here, let me help."

Together they rinsed the dishes and pans before loading the dishwasher. They worked in companionable silence while the morning television show updated them on the latest news. Despite her attempt to maintain her outward calm, Melody buzzed with nervous energy.

"I spent a lot of time thinking last night and I really do believe this is all just a huge overreaction." From the rock-solid set of her jaw, she'd obviously decided to go on as if there was no threat.

Kyle was not on board with this. "Feel like heading to LA for a week or so with me?" Maybe once he got her back to LA and into his house, she'd feel inclined to stay there.

"Aren't you supposed to be minding the store while Trent is gone?"

"Nate can take over for a little while."

She leaned back against the counter and crossed her arms. "I suppose if I don't you'll be spending every night in the driveway?"

"It's a possibility." More likely he'd hire a security guy to watch over her.

"I think the neighbors will start to get concerned."

"Yes," he drawled. "Let's worry about what the neighbors think."

She made a face at him. "The thing is, how long do I live like this? Fearing things that may or may not be real?"

Kyle considered. Her point was valid. He hated the idea that she would be looking over her shoulder until she moved back to LA. And he was assuming that was where they were going to end up. On the other hand, he wasn't all that keen on her anonymous gift giver escalating to more personal contact.

"Let's go…" He barely stopped himself from saying *home*. "Get some shopping done for the baby at those ridiculously expensive Rodeo Drive stores and hang out at the beach."

When she immediately agreed, Kyle was a little surprised at her change of heart. Then, he decided it was less about her interest in buying baby stuff and more about getting away from a scary situation. But either way he thought, as he folded her into his arms, he'd take the win.

A couple days after Kyle spent the night in his car outside Trent's house, Melody found herself the victim of some clever manipulations on the part of her brother, Nate and Kyle.

"I'm giving a concert at The Roxy?" She was sitting in Nate's office at Ugly Trout Records. Her emotions whirled in a combination of excitement and trepidation. "When?"

"A little over a week."

"How am I supposed to do that?" The band that had backed her up on the Free Fall tour had all gone off to new gigs. She had no idea what to sing. "I can't be ready to perform that fast."

"It's all set. I've hired the musicians, and they already have the arrangements of your songs. I also leased the practice space. You just need to show up in LA and rehearse."

She crossed her arms over her chest. "Seems like you've thought of everything. Whose idea was this?"

"Several people provided input."

"This is your way of getting me out of Las Vegas and away from my supposed stalker." Melody blew out a breath. "Nothing weird has happened since the basket arrived. We don't even know that there is a stalker."

"A performance at The Roxy is still a great idea."

"You're right. I've got a lot to do. When do Kyle and I leave for LA?"

"How'd you know Kyle was going with you?"

"Because he's become my watchdog for the last three days."

After he'd spent the night in Trent's driveway, it became apparent that Kyle wasn't going to be happy unless he could keep an eye on her so she'd agreed to move into his guest room. They still weren't in a place where she was ready to go back to their former arrangement, but being compelled to spend more time together had sped up the relationship revitalization process.

"You leave the day after tomorrow. That'll give you a week to rehearse."

"It's tight." But she knew a lot more about getting ready for a performance after spending so many months on tour. "But doable."

After leaving Nate's office, Melody went in search of Mia and found the songwriter working beside Craig in studio C's control booth. A few weeks earlier, Nate had brought Mia under his wing and was training her to produce music. The industry was dominated by men and Melody was delighted her friend was doing her part to change that.

When Mia looked over and spotted Melody entering, her eyes lit up. "So? Are you excited?"

"Very. And a little nervous. I've got a lot to do in a short period of time."

"You'll be great."

Craig took his eyes off the studio musicians going to town on the other side of the glass and observed her with interest. "What's up?"

"I'm going to be performing at The Roxy in a week."

Now it was his turn to grin. "That's great. You'll be fantastic."

"I hope so." Melody soaked up her friends' encouragement as she took a seat next to Mia. "It was really nice of Nate and Trent to organize this for me."

"I think you can use a break from Las Vegas," Mia said, her eyes saying more than her words.

They'd all decided to keep quiet about her stalker. As much as Nate trusted his staff, there were all sorts of people coming and going in the studio. It wouldn't do for word to get out. And Melody couldn't forget that the roses had been delivered here and the business with the CD of her ultrasound vanishing and reappearing had taken place in the studio, too.

"It will be good to go…" She'd been about to say home. "Get away."

"How long do you think you'll stay?" Mia asked.

Craig had returned his attention to the musicians, leaving the women to their conversation.

"I'm not sure. It depends on how things go." She stared at her fingers for a second before adding, "Kyle wants us to spend Christmas together in LA."

"How do you feel about that?"

"I'd rather be with family."

"But he's your family, too," Mia reminded her.

"Yes, but I don't want to have to choose between you all and him."

Mia eyed her sympathetically. "I understand how you feel. Ivy didn't exactly make it easy for me when Nate and I were trying to sort out our relationship." Not only were Mia and Ivy twins, but Mia had been Ivy's constant companion ever since the pop star had started her career at age six. She'd even been her personal assistant once they were older.

"But in the end, you chose Nate because you loved him."

"And you'll choose Kyle for the same reasons."

Melody nodded, even as she hoped that when the time came, Mia would be right.

It was day eight, another date night. Melody wanted to do something upbeat and fun after the emotionally exhausting discussion they'd had during the prior day's exercise.

Day seven had been about communicating. Each person was supposed to take twenty minutes to talk uninterrupted about whatever was on their mind. Melody had spoken about her upcoming booking at The Roxy, sharing her excitement and fears about the solo show and how her new songs would be received.

Kyle had spoken about his father, sharing a story about how he'd canceled Kyle's tenth birthday party at the last minute after his baseball team had lost in the final inning of the playoffs. Kyle had missed catching a fly ball and the other team had scored. Kyle's father had declared only winners got to have a party.

Melody's heart had broken while Kyle told his story. She wanted to call his father and scold him on Kyle's behalf, but she knew it would do no good. Kyle's father wasn't going to apologize to his son for such misguided treatment because he thought he was teaching Kyle a life lesson by being so hard on him. Instead, she'd put her arms around Kyle and let him know she'd heard his pain.

The exchanges had brought them to a place of intimacy

they hadn't achieved before and filled Melody with confidence for their future.

For their eighth date, they were supposed to take a class in something that neither of them had done. Melody had been thinking about this for a while and decided she'd come up with an idea that would provide the sort of team spirit they were trying to achieve.

"I want to learn how to tango," Melody said.

Ever since Kyle had treated her to an evening of sexual spoiling, she'd been feeling an increase in her libido. She wasn't sure if it had something to do with the easing of her nausea, the second trimester hormones kicking in, or her album being done at last, but she'd become obsessed with getting her hands on Kyle as often as she could.

"Tango?" He looked more intrigued than resistant.

"It always looks so sexy when people do it on TV."

He laughed. "I'm sure they've had tons of practice. But I'm game. If nothing else the class will be loads of fun."

This was something else she could add to her growing list of things she appreciated about him. He was always ready to take on new challenges. Even ones that pushed him out of his comfort zone.

"I found someone who will give us a private lesson tonight at seven."

"Dinner first or afterward?"

"First, I think." She gave him a wicked smile. "I'm hoping tangling on the dance floor will prompt us to want to tangle in the sheets."

"I'm all in."

Melody was surprised how slowly the rest of the day went. They had a quick dinner at what was becoming their favorite Las Vegas restaurant, a small Italian place with great food. Melody barely tasted her lasagna and when they arrived at the small dance studio, she was practically vibrating with anticipation.

"So you two want to learn the tango." Their instructor, Juliet, was a lithe blonde with the straight spine of a ballroom dancer. "Is it for your wedding?"

"No," Melody answered, glancing at Kyle.

"Tonight it's just for fun." He met her gaze. His eyes contained a somber note at odds with the half smile curving his lips.

It was at that moment that she realized he really did want to marry her. Not because of the baby, or not *only* because of the baby. He wanted them to be together. So did she. And the way things had been going with this relationship revitalization exercise, they might actually make it.

To her surprise, butterflies took flight in her stomach when Kyle caught her hand and led her onto the dance floor. He moved with confidence, following Juliet's instructions, and slid his hand onto Melody's back. They stood facing each other, the upper halves of their bodies touching.

"Okay, let's begin," Juliet said. "Kyle, you are going to step forward with your left, forward with your right, forward with your left and to the side with your right, sliding your left foot as you go."

She demonstrated his steps and then Melody's, before slowly calling out the movement as they imitated what she'd shown them. To everyone's surprise they managed the four steps without mishap.

"Very nice," Juliet said. "Let's practice that a few more times and then move on. Remember to bend your knees as you move and keep your spine straight."

Melody found the experience to be both frustrating and exhilarating. At times her feet didn't go where they were supposed to and she lost her frame when she started thinking too much. Kyle, on the other hand, was a rock. He moved with careful deliberation through each step. His hold on her didn't waver and she learned confidence in the circle of his strong arms.

"You've done this before," the instructor said to him as they approached the end of their lesson.

"Never the tango," Kyle said. "And I haven't danced in a long time."

"How long?" Melody asked, curious at his unexpected talent.

"When I was a kid, my mom put me in dance lessons. From age six to eight I learned how to ballroom dance. I didn't exactly hate it, but it sure wasn't what my friends were doing. She thought it would be a safer activity for me than playing baseball."

"What made you stop?"

"Believe it or not my dad didn't know what I was up to and when he found out, he forced my mom to stop sending me to classes. He enrolled me in baseball instead."

How could a father not know what his son was up to for two years? Melody wanted to ask, but Juliet started the music once again and they took their places to go over the steps they'd learned one final time before the session was over.

"You must come back and dance more," Juliet said. "You are both fine students."

Kyle's fingers tightened around Melody's. "I'd be open to it if you would."

"It would be fun. This has been a great experience." She felt closer to Kyle. Something about having to coordinate their steps had put them in sync. It was a little bit like the breathing exercise they had done on day five.

"It was a great suggestion," Kyle said as they headed out to the parking lot.

"At first I wondered why you were so willing to go along with me. Now I find out you took dance lessons as a kid."

"It's not exactly something that ups my rep as a cool guy."

"No, but it does up your rep as a sexy guy." She put her arm around his waist and snuggled close. "And the way you can move your hips gets me thinking that maybe we should go back to the house and do some more dancing."

"I like the way your mind works."

Ten

With rehearsals done for the day, Melody entered the Bird Streets house she'd shared with Kyle for three short months. At first it had felt a little strange to be back in LA and staying with him in the place where once she'd been so wildly optimistic. When she'd first moved in, they'd seemed to be in sync and she'd pinned her hopes on an idyllic future with him. But as the months went on and she'd grown frustrated with his unwillingness or inability to tell her how he felt, she'd become afraid of being hurt. Afraid that he'd disappoint her the way her father and Hunter had.

But in the past week, as she'd split her attention between preparing for her concert at The Roxy and the daily exercises that were bringing her and Kyle closer together, she'd been noticing a shift in her perspective. Each day it was a little easier to open up to Kyle and although conversations about the future continued to make Melody anxious, they'd recently had a wonderful evening stargazing and spent a day showing their appreciation for each other with love notes and special surprises.

Today they were supposed to have sex. This time, it was Kyle's turn to be spoiled. Melody was ready for this. She had no problem with anything he wanted to do. Their physical relationship had always been comfortable. Much more so than their emotional one.

She found him in the great room with its tall ceilings, movable wall of windows and fantastic views of downtown LA. He was sitting on a barstool, staring out at the pool. His laptop was on the breakfast bar nearby, its screen saver engaged. How long had he been sitting here staring off into space?

"So what's it gonna be?" she asked, stepping into his line of sight. Setting her hands on her hips, she walked toward him with a sultry swagger. "I'm yours to command."

"I'm not really feeling it today."

Seeing him shut down after everything they'd been through these last couple weeks worried her, but she refused to let him see her concern. "Oh, no," she said, setting her fingertip against his chest and pressing just hard enough to drive her point home. "It's my day to spoil you. We're having sex. That's all there is to it."

"Fine," he grumbled, crossing his arms over his chest.

"That's the attitude." For some reason his annoyance sparked her libido. "It's your day. What do you want me to do?"

He scowled at her. "I suppose you could start by taking your clothes off."

His grumpiness flowed off her like water cascading over a well-waxed car. "Do you want me to just get naked or do you want a show?"

Her words got through to him because his eyes flared briefly before narrowing.

"What sort of a show?"

"I'm yours to command." To further unsettle him, she put her palms together and bowed her head. "How may I be of service?"

When she peered up at him, he was regarding her in helpless amusement. At last she'd gotten through to him. To further tickle his funny bone, she gave him a silly little shimmy of her shoulders, her version of the burlesque dancers of old. And then, inspiration struck. She began to sing.

She strutted around the room, dropping her T-shirt off her shoulder in a parody of seduction as she sang "Let Me Entertain You."

It was working. His lips were twitching uncontrollably. She grabbed a pillow off the white sectional, put her back to him and stripped off her top.

Setting the pillow against her chest, she turned and faced him. One at a time she slid her bra straps down her arm as she kept singing with an exaggerated swagger.

The gleam in his eyes gave her the encouragement she needed to pop the clasp on her bra and slip the thing from her body. She twirled it around her finger a few times before launching it in his direction. He caught it and draped it over his shoulder.

"If the album tanks," she said with a sassy grind. "I may audition for a burlesque show."

"I'll be in the front row opening night."

She beamed at him. "'I'm very versatile.'"

Once again she turned her back to him. This time she held the pillow out from her chest while she unbuttoned her pants one-handed. She spun, grabbed a second pillow, spun, held the second pillow over her backside while she awkwardly skimmed out of her pants and then with a laugh turned to face him holding both pillows over her body.

"That was quite complicated," she said, breathing hard from her exertions.

"You did a great job."

She did a great bump and grind all the way to his chair. When she was standing before him, wearing a big smile and a couple of pillows, she finished her song.

Then she tossed the pillows to either side and threw her arms around him. Her lips found his and a second later his hands coasted over her skin. He got to his feet, fingers sliding beneath the elastic of her underwear. Cupping her bare bottom, he lifted her against his erection.

She moaned and scraped her nails against his scalp. She opened for him and his tongue swept in to devour her. The kiss started hot and became incendiary as he skimmed her underwear down her thighs and lifted her into the air. She wrapped her thighs around his waist and let him carry her to the bedroom.

He lowered her to the bed and quickly stripped off his clothes. Even though tonight was about spoiling him, she took pleasure in his beautiful, powerful body bared to her greedy gaze.

Naked. Aroused. Male. It just didn't get better than this. Color darkened his cheekbones as he set his knee on the bed and came toward her.

"Tonight is all about you," she reminded him.

Her fingers ached to touch him, so she reached out and smoothed her palm down his chest, over his washboard abs, before clasping him in a firm grip. He sucked in a breath through clenched teeth. Now that she had his full attention, she gazed up at him.

"What would you like me to do?" She hadn't intended

to pitch the question so seductively, but her own aroused state gave her voice a husky purr.

Kyle hesitated, seeming to fight for the words. They'd always been very good at giving each other pleasure, each sensing what the other would like without having to be told. But their goal with the relationship revitalization project was to learn to communicate and she intended for him to tell her what he wanted.

"Your wish is my command," she prompted.

His lashes lowered and he watched her through half-slit eyes. "I'd very much like to have your mouth on me."

"Of course." She'd expected this and didn't need much encouragement. "Can you point to a specific spot?"

He looked positively grim as he pointed to his cheek. She gave him a sweet peck before looking up at him with wide-eyed curiosity. Next, he drew his finger down his neck to the base of his throat. She obliged him by trailing her lips to the spot where his pulse throbbed. Nipping at his skin rewarded her with a surprised exhalation.

She wondered how long he'd last at this game. He surprised her by taking her lips on a tour of his entire torso before arriving at the destination they were both eager to reach. She took him into her mouth, loving the silky texture of him, his salty taste and the deep, long groan that rumbled from his chest as she rolled her tongue around and over him.

Without knowing what else he wanted from her, she settled in to make him crazy. With tongue, lips and hands she worked him to the edge of orgasm and held him there. Occupied as she was, she had no way of asking him what was next. It was up to him to tell her.

His fingers bit into her upper arms, drawing her attention. "Not like this. Not tonight. I want to come inside you."

That's all she needed to hear. Shifting position, she kissed her way up his body until she straddled him. Judging from the intense light in his eye, he'd had enough of her taking care of him. Now, he reached between their bodies, positioned himself and drove into her. The feel of him filling her was a joy she could never get enough of. His hands on her hips told her the rhythm he wanted. Guiding her into a fast, steady pace, Melody found her herself rushing toward her climax sooner than she'd expected.

"Come for me," Kyle said to her. "I want to watch."

Melody pumped her hips, increasing her pleasure. Knowing he loved it when she touched herself, she slipped her hands over her breasts and played with her nipples. His hoarse curse made her smile. A second later, her head fell back as her orgasm claimed her. Kyle's fingers bit into her hips as he pumped almost frantically into her. She rode him to a second climax, and cried out his name.

"Yes," he rasped, his heart thudding wildly beneath her palm. "That's my girl."

She was his. In that moment of perfect clarity she recognized he'd own her heart forever. Was that why she'd been so afraid? Why she'd kept her distance? Because she belonged to him and that didn't seem fair when she couldn't claim his heart as hers?

Distantly, she heard his shout of release and her own name pouring from his lips as he came inside her with a final deep thrust. His fingers bit into her skin as if he was trying to make them one body instead of two. She gazed down at him, watched as unfettered joy replaced concentration on his strong features.

Chest heaving, he opened his eyes and the look there stole her breath. He gave her everything in that single moment of contact, of connection. But as she held her breath, waiting for the words to come, he only cupped her face between his palms and brought her head down for a sweetly sensual kiss.

"No woman has ever made me feel the way you do."

It wasn't *I love you*, but she'd take it. What choice did she have? She'd given him her heart and had to trust that he would take good care of it.

"I love you," she murmured and sighed as his arms tightened around her.

The afternoon of her performance, Melody headed to The Roxy for her sound check. Kyle had offered to come with her, but she was in such a state of anxiety over her first solo concert that she turned him down. She'd rather have him see her in her element tonight instead of having him witness the meltdown she could feel brewing.

She needn't have worried. The group of musicians backing her up were professional and fantastic to work with.

As she and the band were finishing up an hour before the doors opened, Hunter strolled in. She was surprised to see him and as the stage cleared, she sat down on the edge with her feet dangling.

"What are you doing here?" she asked.

"Nate mentioned you were performing tonight so I asked if I could introduce you. I thought you could use all the support you could get."

"That's really nice of you." Her stomach knotted as she wondered how Kyle would feel about seeing him here.

"I hear congratulations are in order," Hunter said. "Nate told me that you and Kyle are back together."

"I guess we are." Things between them had been going pretty fantastic this week. Being in LA had brought back all the great times they'd had together and Kyle had gone out of his way to make her feel special and adored.

"You don't sound sure." Hunter came to stand before

her, one hand resting on the stage on either side of her hips, not quite touching, but suggestive all the same.

"It's been a challenging few months since you and I were in New York that night." In all the weeks that they'd worked together at Ugly Trout, Melody had kept things as far away from personal topics as she could. But for some reason, now that she felt more secure in her relationship with Kyle, she wanted some answers. "He has this crazy idea that you want to get me back." She wanted to hear him deny it.

"It's not so crazy." He took her hands and gave a gentle squeeze. "You know I'll always be there for you, right?"

She didn't know that, but nodded anyway. Kyle's words came back to haunt her. Hunter couldn't possibly want her back. But staring into his eyes, she could understand why Kyle was so insistent. The vibe rolling off Hunter reminded her of how she'd once felt so desperate to be loved by him.

"I feel the same way about you." She pulled her hands free and forced a smile to her lips. "But Kyle is my future. We're going to be a family." And after this past week, she was really starting to believe it.

"You have a full house out there," Nate said, popping into her dressing room shortly before she was to go on.

"I don't know why I'm nervous." Melody puffed out a breath and shook her hands to ease the tension in her muscles. She couldn't go out on stage looking like a wooden soldier.

At least it wouldn't last long. She was always besieged by preshow jitters. Yet, as soon as she stepped onto the stage, all her doubts faded away. It became about the music and the lyrics.

He gave her a quick, fierce hug and then smiled down at her. "You're going to do great."

"Thanks."

Together they walked through the backstage area. Out on stage, the group of musicians she'd been rehearsing with for the past week settled in while Hunter warmed up the crowd. Melody focused on the people in the audience who would be rooting for her with everything they had. Kyle, Nate, Mia, Trent and Savannah. She would sing for them.

And then Hunter was gesturing in her direction and Melody stepped on stage. She smiled and waved as if her stomach wasn't doing cartwheels and stepped up to the mic.

"Hey, LA, how is everybody doing tonight?"

The crowd came back to her with an enthusiastic howl that made all Melody's problems fade into the background. She started the first of her planned ten songs, reassured when her voice sounded strong and pure, unaffected by the anxiety attacking her nerves and making her hands shake. During the nine months on tour, she'd faced thousands of fans in huge arenas. They'd been a faceless sea, undulating as they'd danced to her music.

Tonight's crowd was different. She could feel their energy surrounding her, inspiring her performance. The intimacy thrilled her. She connected with them, recognized familiar faces. They were here for her. She wasn't an anonymous opening act for Free Fall, she was Melody Caldwell, rising star.

As she came off the stage, it seemed as if her feet barely touched the ground. If she'd been worried about how her new album would go over, tonight's crowd set her mind at ease. They'd been wonderfully receptive to every song. And she'd poured her heart and soul into every note.

"You were fantastic," Hunter called over the wild cheering.

To Melody's surprise he caught her up into his arms and

spun her around. The shadows of doubt and fear creeping over her these last few weeks had been burned away by the strength of the spotlight. She laughed and hugged him back, glad he was there to share the moment with her.

Hunter set her back on her feet. And then suddenly his lips were on hers. For a second she was too surprised to move. In the back of her mind Melody recognized that this was New York City all over again. A different club. A completely innocent moment between friends. Utterly open to misinterpretation. A heartbeat too slow, she pulled back and broke the kiss.

"What the hell do you think you're doing?" she demanded, her delight crushed by Hunter's actions.

Hunter gave no sign that her distress registered on him. "Do you have one more song?" he asked eagerly, motioning toward the wave of sound rolling in from the audience. "They seem to want more."

It was then she noticed the trio that stood less than ten feet away. From the expression on Savannah's face, it was pretty obvious they had seen her embracing Hunter. Trent looked surprised, but it was Kyle's stiffness and the betrayal lurking in his gaze that told her she'd screwed up again.

"Not one the band knows," she said. "But I have a song I can do with just the keyboard."

Turning her back on Hunter, she stepped back onto the stage. With a tentative wave at the audience, she approached the keyboard player.

"Can I borrow this for a song?" She asked over the cheering crowd, her gaze straying backstage in search of Kyle.

"Be my guest."

She adjusted the keyboard mic and smiled at the crowd. "This is a little something that I've been working on with

a very talented songwriter friend of mine, Mia Navarro.
I hope you like it."

The crowd quieted and she began the first bars of the
song. It was something near and dear to both women, a
song of love and longing. Of hope and fear. Written during a time when neither believed they could ever be with
the men they loved. Melody cracked her heart wide open
and sang with everything she had. What poured out was
vulnerable and poignant and as she finished the last note,
the room was utterly silent.

A tear slid down her cheek and she brushed it away.

The room erupted.

As she bowed and waved at the audience, grateful for
the outpouring of love and approval, she cast glances toward the wings. She'd sung for the man standing backstage. The lights blinded her and she couldn't see past
Trent and Savannah to where she assumed Kyle was standing in shadow.

Instincts told her to get to him as soon as possible, but
she had an obligation to her fans as well. At long last, she
could resist the pull no longer and made her way offstage.
This time, instead of rushing to Hunter, she went past him,
eyes darting around the people gathered to congratulate her.

First Savannah and then Trent hugged her. Their trio
was joined by Nate and Mia, but when Melody looked
around for Kyle, she didn't see him.

With her heart crushed by disappointment, Melody
fought back tears and tried to appear normal. She gave Mia
a questioning look. "Was it okay that I played our song?"

"Okay?" Mia's eyes were overly bright. "It was fantastic. As many times as I've heard my sister sing one of my
songs, it was always spoiled by the fact that she was taking credit. You are the first artist to sing a Mia Navarro
song. And you killed it."

"I might've been the first, but I'm not going to be the last."

As the group made their way back into the club for a celebratory drink, Melody slipped up beside Savannah and leaned close. "What happened to Kyle?"

"He said he had to make a call." Savannah linked her arm through Melody's. Her reassuring smile wasn't having the right effect.

"He saw me with Hunter, didn't he?"

"Yeah." Savannah drew the word out, obviously reluctant to put a damper on the evening. "He didn't look happy when he left."

"I've screwed up again. What is wrong with me?" Despair flared as the full impact of her mistake flooded through her. "We've been over this and over this and I put myself into a situation."

"Look, I'm sure he knows nothing is going on between you and Hunter."

But it probably hadn't looked that way. She had to explain what happened. "Any idea where he went?"

Savannah screwed up her face and looked everywhere but at Melody.

"What's going on? Where did Kyle go?"

"He might have hustled Hunter outside when you went back on stage."

"Which way?"

"Into the alley."

And with a curse, Melody headed for the stage door.

Eleven

As soon as Melody headed back on stage, Kyle grabbed Hunter and propelled him in the opposite direction. Rage dominated his emotions and fueled his strength as he made a beeline for the stage door. The kiss between Melody and Hunter had brought every one of his fears to the surface.

She'd looked so damn happy in his arms. In those seconds before she'd shoved Hunter away, Kyle had been stripped down to the raw core of his psyche. In the instant that he'd watched another man swing a laughing, joyful Melody off her feet, every primitive elemental cell in his body had screamed for him to rip them apart and put his fist into Hunter's nose. And then the bastard had kissed her.

Even though he knew Hunter was the one to blame, that Melody didn't love him, something tore inside Kyle. He hadn't done a good enough job loving her, hadn't given her everything he was, the good and bad. While he no longer feared losing her to Hunter, he wasn't sure he'd ever be able to win her love if he couldn't stop believing she'd leave him.

The heavy door gave beneath his onslaught, dumping the two men into the alley. A second later the door clanged shut, leaving them alone in the cool night air. At the far end of the alley a single light pierced the darkness, but where they stood it was as if the walls absorbed the light. The indistinct sounds of nearby traffic were barely audible over Kyle's harsh breathing.

"Where the hell do you get off kissing Melody?" he bellowed, his voice reverberating off the alley's walls. He shoved Hunter against the brick, venting every bit of rage and fury on the man.

"Screw you. You don't own her." Hunter's arrogant, conceited grin flashed in the dim alley. "Let me go."

"Why can't you just leave her alone?"

"Because she doesn't want me to." Hunter shoved at Kyle and bought himself enough breathing room to tear free.

Fists clenched, Kyle growled. "You're not going to get her back. She loves me. And that's my baby she's carrying. Plus, you don't strike me as the sort of guy who wants to play daddy."

"I could say the same about you."

"My wild days ended before Melody and I got together. We're going to be a family. She needs stability and consistency."

"Has it occurred to you that maybe she doesn't want what you're offering? Did you see her out on stage tonight? She's a star. She shouldn't have to settle for your limited vision of her as your wife and the mother of your kid."

Hunter's words came at Kyle with all the speed of a fastball and caught him off guard. That wasn't all he wanted for her. She deserved to have whatever career she wanted. And if that career took her away from him? True, the nine months they spent mostly apart while she was on tour had created an enormous rift in their relationship.

But should she be expected to give up her career for the sake of their family? Was that what he was pressuring her to do? Kyle thought over their last few conversations surrounding the future. She'd offered up vague answers about how she intended to promote her new album.

"This isn't any of your business," Kyle growled.

The stage door opened and Melody appeared. She took in the tense scene before stepping into the alley.

"What's going on?" She gazed from Kyle to Hunter.

Hunter spoke first. "I was just telling your boy here that you're too talented to take a step back from your career right now."

"Was he arguing with you?"

"He has some old-fashioned expectations when it comes to you."

"And you are setting him straight?"

Kyle repressed a grin at Melody's mild tone. Hunter had no idea how much trouble he was in at the moment. It almost made Kyle feel sorry for him. Except he figured as soon as she was done with her ex-boyfriend, her sights would be set on him.

"Yes," Hunter said. "But I only have your best interest at heart."

"If that was true, you'd know that not only can I make my own decisions, but I've been doing a good job of it for a long time." There were icicles in her tone.

"I was merely trying to help."

Melody nodded toward the stage door. "If you don't mind, I'd like to speak to Kyle alone."

"Sure." With a quick glance in Kyle's direction, Hunter headed back into the club.

"Was that necessary?" she demanded as soon as they were alone.

"It felt pretty damned necessary to me."

"Why?"

He didn't understand how she'd managed to get him on the defensive. She was the one hugging and kissing her ex. "Do you seriously need me to answer that?"

"I rather think I do." She crossed her arms over her chest and fixed a steady, determined glare on him.

"You and Hunter."

"He hugged me. I hugged him back."

"He kissed you."

Some of her righteous anger dimmed. "I certainly didn't plan for that to happen. And maybe I shouldn't have hugged him, but I was excited."

"Has it occurred to you that you're encouraging him?" The accusation might not be fair, but Kyle couldn't hold it in.

"That's not true." She sucked in a shaky breath. "Okay, maybe it seems that way because he's been there for me a lot lately."

Kyle raked his fingers through his hair, struggling for calm as he absorbed her statement. "Meaning I haven't been?"

"Meaning Hunter and I have music in common and I value his opinions." This last she finished lamely as if she recognized that throwing her connection with Hunter in Kyle's face was sure to inflame their argument further.

"Did you know he was going to be here to introduce you tonight?"

"I didn't ask for him, if that's what you're thinking."

She paused, and then said, "I'm pretty sure we're not fighting about Hunter."

"I'm pretty sure we are." He ground his teeth together. "I'm not accusing you of cheating."

"Well, thank goodness for that, because I wasn't and I haven't and I'm not going to."

"But it feels as if you like having it both ways."

"What is that supposed to mean?"

"You won't agree to marry me. Why is that?"

"Honestly, because you've never told me you love me."

"I do."

"And yet you can't bring yourself to say it. I get it, your father instilled in you the compulsion to repress your emotions because he thought they made you weak."

He had no argument and stared at her in frustration and anguish. His father had made him outwardly tough while his mother had made him inwardly weak. He could see every possible thing that could go wrong and it terrified him. But he couldn't bring himself to tell Melody that. She expected him to be strong, but being that for her also diminished his ability to be vulnerable.

She sighed and her voice calmed. "You say I want to have it both ways. I really only wanted one way. I want to feel safe in a relationship."

"That's why I asked you to marry me. I want you to realize that I'm committed to you and our daughter." Was there any better way to demonstrate how he felt about her than to make her his wife?

From Melody's expression, her consternation had grown as he spoke. "I don't want us to get married for the wrong reasons."

"We wouldn't."

"If I hadn't gotten pregnant, would you have asked me to marry you?"

"I believe we were heading there." He wouldn't have asked her to move in if he hadn't been going down that road. But he couldn't say for sure whether she'd been all that keen on the idea. "Or at least, I was."

"I don't believe you."

"I'm not the one who's skeptical about marriage. My parents might not be perfect for each other or even happy all of the time, but they've honored their vows and I don't doubt they'll stay married until death." Now it was her turn to answer some tough questions. "Did you see marriage in our future?"

"Honestly, I never imagined you'd ask me, so I never saw us married."

Her answer struck him hard even though it didn't surprise him. "Why were you with me at all?"

Her eyebrows rose in surprise. "You are fun and sexy, strong and sweet. You know how to make me laugh and can turn me on with a look. I enjoy being with you." She looked as if she wanted to say more, but then shook her head.

"That sounds like a description of how any number of men could make you feel. In fact, I think when I asked you what it was about Hunter that you couldn't live without, you said something similar."

"That's not true." But she frowned and he wondered if she was second-guessing herself.

"When I look at you," he said, "I see my future."

"How can you say that when you can't tell me you love me?"

"I have offered you everything I am. If three words are all that stands between us, then you can have them. Just don't be surprised when they don't bring you the happiness you expect."

Kyle paused, but it wasn't as if the words hadn't resonated through his thoughts a thousand times. He didn't want to say them like this. In the middle of a fight. To prove a point. He'd wanted the moment to be romantic and as perfect as he could make it. Yet, maybe love wasn't about the big moments, but rather the small ones.

He pulled in a breath, took control of his voice, and then spoke from his heart. "I love you."

I love you.
Damn him for being right.

Despite the truth in his eyes and the gravity with which he spoke the words, she didn't feel better. The problems between them weren't based on an unspoken declaration, but rather on unrealistic expectations. She'd thought that if Kyle broadcast his love for her, she would feel safe and secure. What she hadn't realized was that the true treasure of love was in being able to receive it.

And thus far, she'd proven herself a poor receptacle.

"You're right about needing to think," she said. "A little bit of time apart would be good for both of us."

For a split second he looked crushed by her decision and then he gave his head a sad shake. "I wasn't looking for more time apart. I think we've had too much of that already."

Once again she was the one retreating. What was wrong with her? The man had told her he loved her. She should be throwing herself into his arms and smothering him with kisses. Wasn't this what she'd been craving from him since the beginning? An admission of how he felt about her so she could feel protected?

"Look," he tried again. "We haven't done day twelve, communication, uninterrupted listening."

Had Kyle memorized the entire fourteen days' worth of exercises? It was infuriating that he remembered each activity, both the day and the detail. Melody couldn't seem to keep anything straight anymore. Before she finished her album, she'd blamed her lack of focus on that. Then she'd blamed the various changes her body was going through. The stress of potentially having a stalker. And this past week on rehearsing for the concert. But was any of that really the cause of her distraction?

"I just don't have the energy to talk or to listen right now," she said, knowing that for the last two weeks Kyle had been putting more effort into their relationship than she had. Maybe she wasn't good enough for him. Tears sprang to her eyes. She cursed the pregnancy hormones that made her want to cry at the worst times.

"That's fine," he said, his tone calm and reasonable. "We don't have to say another word. It's been a long week and you're exhausted. Let's go home. After a good night's sleep, both our heads will be clearer."

Except she didn't want to go home with him. She wanted to slink off somewhere and lick her wounds.

Aware that she was once again avoiding him when she should work on their relationship, she said, "I can't leave now. My friends came out to support me. Go if that's what you want to do."

And before he could answer, she turned on her heel and returned to the theater. She'd charged through the backstage area and reached the house before she noticed that Kyle wasn't behind her. She shouldn't be surprised. How many times could she push him away and expect he wouldn't get sick of it.

When she found Trent, Savannah, Nate and Mia, they'd been joined by Craig and a pretty blonde woman he introduced as Sasha. Savannah glanced in the direction Melody had come, obviously looking for Kyle, before shooting her a questioning look. Melody shook her head. Nate bought

her a soda while Craig and Sasha congratulated her on
the performance.

Her joy in the evening was severely reduced by the argument she'd had with Kyle and his subsequent absence.
Had he gone home? Should she have gone with him?

The party started to break up after an hour, with Trent
and Savannah leaving first. Melody walked into the lobby
with the other two couples, hugging Nate and Mia before
saying goodbye to Craig and Sasha.

She headed backstage to collect her purse and change
into street clothes. Before she left the theater, she decided
to give Kyle a call. She wasn't surprised when she got his
voice mail and hung up without leaving a message. Obviously he was shutting down communications after she
told him she didn't want to talk tonight.

On the way out to the parking lot, she dreaded the idea
of returning to Kyle's house and risking another fight.
Maybe she should just get a hotel room. Some space would
probably be good for them. As she neared her rental car,
she pulled out her phone and shot Kyle a quick text, letting him know her plan.

"You okay?"

Melody whirled around and spotted Craig approaching
her across the lot. "I'm fine. I was just sending Kyle a text."

"How come he left?"

"He had another commitment tonight." She didn't want
to get into the details with Craig. "Where's Sasha?" she
asked, giving him a tired smile.

"She went home. We came separately."

"So where are you headed now?"

"Back to Las Vegas."

"Tonight?"

"Yeah, I drove down this morning to catch your show
and now I'm heading back."

"You're driving?" As tired as she was, going home held a lot of appeal. She could be in her own bed by morning. "How long will that take?"

"About five hours."

"I was thinking about heading back to Las Vegas as well, but it's probably too late to catch a flight."

"You can ride back to Las Vegas with me," Craig said.

"I'm so tired, I doubt I'd be much company. And I have to drop my rental at the airport."

"I could follow you there."

"Okay." This was crazy. She should just find a hotel or better yet, go back to Kyle's house. But something elemental was driving her to run.

Maybe she was overwrought or just too tired to think straight, but an hour and a half later they were clear of LA and she was staring out the window at the darkness of the desert, her mind strangely numb. With her album done and her future with Kyle up in the air, she felt like a bit of dandelion fluff caught in a breeze, blown this way and that. She had no idea what she planned to do when she got back to Las Vegas or what she intended to do about her relationship with Kyle.

After last night, one thing was clear. If she didn't stop running he might give up chasing her. And judging by his lack of response to her earlier text, maybe he already had.

Twelve

Melody woke to daylight and blinked her eyes. As she lifted her head from the passenger-side window, her neck screamed in pain. She rubbed at the cramped muscles. It took her blurry mind a few seconds to orient her to their location. Still on I-15, moving parallel to the Strip. She glanced at the dashboard clock and saw that it was close to seven.

They'd stopped in Barstow for gas and something to eat, giving Craig an opportunity to rest and load up on coffee. Once back on the road, she'd been unable to keep her eyes open and managed a couple hours of sleep. But it wasn't enough. When she got back to the guesthouse, she intended to crawl into bed and sleep the rest of the day.

"How'd you sleep?" Craig asked.

"Not bad."

"Another twenty minutes and you'll be home."

"I can't wait." Silence filled the car as Melody yawned.

"I know I already said this, but it was really nice of you to drive all the way to LA to hear me sing at The Roxy." She chuckled. "Especially when you hear me singing all the time."

"It's different when it's a concert. You have no idea how much you shine on stage, do you?" His eyes lingered on her, bright and filled with admiration.

"You're right about singing being different in front of an audience," Melody said, her gaze returning to the road ahead of them. "The energy was fantastic last night. Over the last few weeks, I'd been considering giving up my singing career and just going back to songwriting. But last night gave me hope."

"I suppose Kyle would prefer that you quit performing."

"No. He's always been supportive of my career."

But he had shared his concern about her going on another major tour like the one with Nate now that she was going to be a mom. And in truth, she couldn't imagine leaving her baby for any extended period of time. Yet, life on the road would be hard on kids with the constant moving from one city to the next.

"You shouldn't stop singing. You could be a great star."

"That's never been one of my goals. I love music, but there are sacrifices involved with becoming famous. You give up your privacy." She supposed that was already the case since she'd started dating Kyle. He had a pretty high profile lifestyle as a former pro baseball player and partner in the LA Dodgers.

"It must be hard having so many people love you."

"I don't know about love me." She gave a self-conscious laugh. "I like to think they love my music."

"But you're so wonderful," Craig went on. "Not only are you incredibly talented, but you're really nice. People around the studio are always talking about how you know everyone's name and how you help people out all the time."

He was making her sound a lot more impressive than she actually was. It was a little embarrassing.

"That's sweet of you to say. I guess I remember what it was like starting out. If it wasn't for Nate I wouldn't have considered singing professionally. He encouraged me to get on the stage. How can I not pay that forward?"

"It's more than just that. You are a truly kind and thoughtful person."

Melody needed to turn the conversation away from her. "I really enjoyed meeting Sasha. You two make a very cute couple."

"We're not dating." Craig's voice had gone cold.

"Oh, I thought you were." Melody shook her head in bemusement. Sasha mentioned they'd been going out for a year. Maybe Craig was like Hunter and taking Sasha for granted. "She's really nice. And she really seems to like you."

"She isn't the woman I want." He smiled at Melody.

Suddenly she became aware of a certain sort of vibe coming off Craig and it made her a bit uncomfortable. She'd always thought that Craig liked her, but now she wondered if his feelings for her were more involved than she'd realized.

"You might want to sit down and have a conversation with her," Melody said, knowing how hard that could be for both parties. "She seems to think you guys have a future together."

"She's wrong." There was rising irritation in his clipped tone.

Perhaps she'd pushed too hard. "Sure. Of course."

Since there didn't seem to be anything else to say, Melody lapsed into silence. As Craig made a left-hand turn, she realized she hadn't given him any directions since the first one. And yet he seemed to know exactly where he was going. She frowned. She'd given him the address to Trent's house. Had he fed it into his phone without her noticing? Her thoughts had been caught up in what she'd left behind in LA.

She started to pull the gate key out of her purse, but Craig rolled down his window and waved a card over the electronic lock. The gate arm began to rise.

"You have a key?"

"My aunt has a house in here. When you mentioned it, I recognized the name."

Had she mentioned the name of the gated community to him? She could have. Her brain had been pretty scattered these last few weeks.

Or maybe she was just being paranoid. Wasn't it possible that he'd heard things in passing from conversations she'd had at the studio with Nate?

"In fact, if you wouldn't mind a quick detour, I need to pop in and check on the place. Water her plants. Look around to make sure nothing's wrong."

All Melody wanted to do was get home and crawl into bed, but Craig had been kind enough to drive her home. The least she could do was accompany him on a brief check of his aunt's place.

"Sure. As long as it's a quick stop." She hid a mighty yawn behind her hand. "Sorry."

"I get it. You've had a busy few months. What you need is to take some time off and rest. I can't imagine all the stress you've been under is good for the baby."

"You, Nate, my brother and Kyle. Everyone's worrying too much. I'm fine. The baby's fine. And it's early. It would be different if I was in the last month or two of my pregnancy."

Craig pulled into the driveway of a large home similar in size to Trent's. "This is my aunt's place."

Melody glanced around and recognized where she was from her frequent walks around the neighborhood. "Wow! She and my brother are really close. His house is a couple doors down on the street behind this one." In fact, she guessed there'd be a partial view of Trent's backyard from the second floor here.

"You don't say." Craig gave her a friendly smile and turned off the engine. "Would you mind helping me? Plant watering will go faster with a second set of hands."

"Sure." Anything to get this task done sooner.

Craig led her inside and toward the kitchen. As with Trent's house, the open floor plan offered unobstructed views of the pool and the beautifully landscaped backyard.

"This is a really nice house," she said as she took a watering can and headed for the plants near the stairs. "What did you say your aunt does for a living?"

"She sells real estate in LA."

"So this is a vacation property for her?"

Craig nodded. "She likes to gamble and Las Vegas is a quick flight."

While Craig headed upstairs, Melody poured three cans of water on the plants downstairs. She was dragging by the time she slipped the watering can back under the sink. She cast out for some sign of Craig, but couldn't hear him. This quick errand was stretching out longer than she expected.

"Craig?" she called out. "Are you about done?"

When she didn't hear anything she wandered into the formal living room just off the foyer and perched on the closest chair to the door. Her lashes drooped. She rubbed her knuckles over her eyes. In another five minutes she would fall asleep right where she sat.

"Craig," she tried again. This was ridiculous. She was

just around the corner from Trent's house. She would just walk home. "I'm going to get going. I'll just walk. Thanks for the ride."

Silence greeted her. While half of her wondered what had become of him, the other half was burning with frustration. She headed out to the car, but when she tried the door handle, she realized it was locked. Unable to get her bag out, she returned to the house.

"Craig?" She headed up the stairs and was halfway to the top when she heard a sound coming from below. Turning, she spied him. "There you are. Look, if you still need to do things around here, I can walk home. I just need to get my bag out of your car."

"Why don't you stick around? I'll make us something to eat."

"I'm really tired and not very hungry." And growing more irritated by the second. "I just want to go home."

"Just a little while. Please."

As she retraced her steps down the stairs, he moved to cut off her exit through the front door. His demeanor was casual and relaxed, but for some reason the hair on Melody's arms stood on end. Why wouldn't he let her go?

"I'm really tired." She couldn't see a way to get past him and reach the front door.

"Please sit down."

"I don't want to sit down. I want to go."

He advanced toward her and Melody backed up. He herded her into the living room and gestured toward the couch. During her earlier assessment of the backyard, she'd noted that there was a tall concrete wall around the entire area. No way to escape there. She'd just have to play along until he decided to take her home.

"I am afraid I can't let you," he said.

Exhaustion and anxiety were blocking her ability to think clearly. "Why?"

"You need someone to take care of you and as you pointed out, you don't listen when people tell you to slow down and take care of yourself and the baby. So I'm going to do that."

How could he look so rational and say such outrageous things?

"What are you talking about?"

"You liked everything, didn't you?" His smile was overly personal. "The roses. The baby gift?"

Fear burrowed into her muscles, rendering them useless. "That was you?"

"Yes. I wanted you to know how much I love you."

"Those were very nice things, but you shouldn't have sent them. I'm with Kyle." Only she wasn't with Kyle. She had left him in LA. And come back to Las Vegas with Craig. And now she was in terrible trouble.

"In time you'll see he wasn't good for you. Not the way I will be. We are going to be so happy."

Kyle sat on the couch in his LA home and stared at the phone in his hands, willing Melody to call or text him back. He kept going back to her last message about spending the night in a hotel and cursing himself for not responding right away. At the time, he'd been so damned angry that he'd been afraid of what he might write back. But as night dwindled into morning, he'd sent her an apology and asked for her to call him as soon as she could. Now, lunch had passed without any response and his anxiety prompted a call to Trent.

"Have you and Savannah heard from Melody since last night?" Kyle said after Trent picked up.

"No. Haven't you?"

"She left me a text last night saying she was spending the night at a hotel. I've called her several times today, but she's not picking up." Maybe he shouldn't expect her to given the way they'd left things last night. She'd made it pretty clear she needed some time to think. "Could one of you try her?"

"Savannah's trying right now. Have you checked with Nate?"

"I haven't called him yet. He and Mia were heading to visit his mom in Texas. They left first thing this morning. They should've arrived by now."

"Savannah said she's not picking up."

Or she can't. Kyle banished that thought from his head. She was fine. It was all a case of him overreacting. But there was a sick feeling twisting in his gut. Why hadn't she reached out to anyone?

This was all his fault. He never should've let her walk away. Had something happened to her? Kyle supposed the next step would be to check the hospitals, but he was sure if there had been an emergency, he or Trent would have been notified.

"Could that security friend of yours in Las Vegas run her credit cards? Maybe we could figure out what hotel she's staying at." If Kyle knew where she was staying he could stop worrying.

"You don't think that's a little extreme?"

"May I remind you that someone sent her a teddy bear with a camera in it. Not to mention that her being out of contact for this long is unusual."

Trent paused for a couple seconds after considering Kyle's words. "I'll give Logan at Wolfe Security a call."

Feeling no less agitated despite their plan, Kyle shot Nate a message and then began to pace. Twenty minutes later, Trent called back.

"Logan ran her credit cards, and got a hit on a couple charges in Barstow. One of those was at a gas station. Which wouldn't be unusual if she drove back to Las Vegas, except it seems she turned in her car at LAX last night."

"She turned in her rental, but she didn't get on a plane." How had she gotten to Barstow? "What's going on?"

"What if she had her wallet stolen?" Trent suggested.

"Then she wouldn't have been able to get a hotel room and I'm sure she would've called you or Savannah."

"Maybe she got a ride from someone back to Vegas."

"Who?" And why would she do something like that? Especially without telling anyone? Kyle grabbed his keys and headed for the door. "I'm catching the first available flight to Vegas. It has to be where she was going."

"Are you sure you're not overreacting?" Trent asked.

Was it crazy to think something might have happened to her? That her stalker had tracked her down in LA and kidnapped her? Maybe this was all just a huge misunderstanding, but Kyle's gut told him something was wrong.

Kyle shook his head. "There are too many weird things going on."

After a brief pause, Trent asked, "Should we call the police?"

And tell them what?

"I want to," Kyle said. "But it hasn't been forty-eight hours and Nate hasn't responded to my text or voice mail. As soon as I hear from him, I'll let you know. In the meantime, can you send me Logan's number?"

By the time Nate called back half an hour later, Kyle had spoken with the security expert and had been reassured that they'd check into video footage from the Barstow gas station and send a car to Trent's Las Vegas house to see if she'd arrived there. Despite Logan's calm demeanor and crisp efficiency, Kyle wasn't at all reassured.

"Neither Mia nor I have heard from her," Nate said. "How long has she been missing?"

"She texted me last night that she was heading to a hotel. That was around midnight." He went on to explain how Logan had tracked her credit card to LAX and then Barstow. "It's as if she's heading back to Vegas by car. We just don't know the exact circumstances."

The slow pace of traffic on I-405 south had given him ample time to work himself into the beginnings of an anxiety attack.

Nate latched onto Kyle's concern. "You're thinking she's been abducted?"

"I'm thinking the logical explanation is whoever's been stalking her finally made his move." Kyle let that sink in for a second. "It's not like her to disappear without saying anything to anyone."

"No, it's not. Have you thought about calling the cops?"

"Yes, but she hasn't been gone long enough for them to start looking for her."

At the moment, Kyle was regretting not reporting the previous strange incidents to the cops, but with all the crime that happened in Las Vegas every day, who could say if they'd even look into something as obscure as a few anonymous gifts?

Damn it. He never should've left her alone last night. He'd thought she was safe in LA. What had possessed her to take off for Vegas without saying anything to anyone? It just wasn't like her, making the possibility that she'd been kidnapped much more likely.

One thing was clear. He'd failed her, and that was completely unacceptable. No matter what the cost, he would do everything in his power to get her back.

Thirteen

Melody perched on the edge of the living room couch and contemplated her situation. Craig was obviously not ready to let her leave and she was not going to be able to get away from him. But he couldn't be vigilant all the time. At some point he would have to sleep or leave her to go to work and that was when she could escape.

Of course, the problem was what he intended to do with her in the meantime.

"I knew you and I were meant to be together the first time I heard you sing," Craig said, smiling at her with all the eager enthusiasm of an ardent lover.

"Craig, you know that I'm with Kyle." It was nearly impossible to keep the fear out of her voice, and she worried how he'd react if she got hysterical.

"He isn't going to be able to make you happy the way I can."

"Maybe not," she said, wondering how a seemingly normal guy could turn into a stalker. "But I love him."

"I don't think you do. You were leaving him after all."

She'd been so wrong to confide in Craig. "I just needed some time to think."

"Think about what?" Craig frowned. "He accused you of cheating on him."

"How did you know that?" She thought about the nanny cam teddy bear Kyle had found and barely repressed a shudder.

"I heard it around. That's why I knew he didn't deserve you. A woman like you would never cheat on the man she loves."

"No, but you mentioned that you saw the picture the paparazzi took of Hunter and me." Melody forced herself to say. "You could see where in the moment we looked like we were together."

"That's because Hunter wants you back."

Damn. The guy knew way too much about what was going on between her and Kyle. Was the teddy bear the only thing he'd bugged? She shuddered.

Craig continued, "He went to New York when you were there to see if there was a chance."

"That's crazy." Melody knew she'd chosen the wrong word when Craig's eyes widened. "What I meant to say was that Hunter didn't come to New York to see if we could get back together. He knew I was in love with Kyle."

"Yes, but you were in love with Hunter once, too."

Melody shook her head. "I only thought I was in love with Hunter. Once I started seeing Kyle, I understood that I was following a pattern with Hunter. Being with him stirred up the same insecurity that my father makes me feel. Growing up, my father barely had any time for me. I was always seeking his love and approval. I equated love with deprivation. Kyle's love made me stronger not weaker."

As much as she disliked digging out her emotional baggage for this virtual stranger, Melody sensed that keeping him talking was going to be the best way to convince him to let her go.

"Your dad is a terrible person. I've worked with several artists who used to be on the West Coast Records label. They told stories about how he ruined careers of people who tried to stick up for themselves. And I don't think he was any better with his own family."

Again, Craig knew way more than the average person. "How do you know all that?"

"I listen. Sometimes I record stuff. You'd be surprised what goes on in the studio when no one's around."

Melody's thought scrambled through the hundreds of hours she'd logged at Ugly Trout's studios. What sorts of things had she talked about in the recording booth, imagining herself safe? Some of that time Melody had spent with Mia, sharing romantic angst in the days before Mia and Nate had sorted out their issues. Melody suspected Nate would be furious at what his employee had done.

"Why would you do that? Those were private conversations."

"I need to know what's going on. The last two places I worked went out of business and I wasn't prepared to be out of a job. I swore that wouldn't ever happen again. I wanted to make sure I knew exactly what was going on at Ugly Trout."

"Why would you record me?"

"It wasn't you specifically. I just bugged the studios."

Melody noticed Craig had grown agitated as she put him on the spot and needed to calm him down. "Okay, I get it. Being out of a job is really scary and I promise if you let me go that I won't tell anyone."

"I'm not sure I believe you." Craig regarded her with a frown. "You'll need to stay here for a while."

"How long?"

"Until I know I can trust you."

Here were her worst fears realized. "How long do you think that will take?"

It was on the tip of her tongue to ask how he intended to keep her here, but she wasn't sure she wanted to put that question to the test. What if he tied her up or locked her in a room?

Her mind began to work overtime. She'd left LA without telling Kyle where she was going. He knew she was upset with him. How long before he'd wonder where she'd gone? Based on what had happened after the paparazzi incident with Hunter, it might be a couple weeks before he cooled off. And the argument in the alley last night had been so much more damaging than the previous incident because she'd pushed back.

But, even if she couldn't count on Kyle to look for her, surely Savannah, Trent or Nate would check in and after not finding her, start to worry. Should she warn Craig that this might happen in hopes that he'd let her go? Or would it backfire and her situation become even more dire?

"I don't know." Craig looked less confident and his expression grew more menacing. "I really want us to be together. I guess once I know you love me as much as I love you, then I can trust you."

His words roused her panic. How was she supposed to prove that she loved him? Would he expect her to sleep with him? A chill swept through her. Would he force her if she refused?

"I'm not feeling very well," she said, overwhelmed by the need to put a door between her and Craig. "Can I use the bathroom?"

"Are you sick?"

"Just morning sickness from being pregnant."

"Oh, sure. I've heard of that."

Wonderful, Melody thought, feeling nausea starting for real. "The bathroom?"

He pointed the way and she gratefully escaped to a small powder room. To her dismay, Craig camped outside the door and continued talking to her through the door.

"How long do the symptoms last? It's almost noon. Does that mean you'll stop feeling sick?"

"It depends. Sometimes I don't feel well all day." She sat down on the closed toilet seat and dropped her head into her hands. "And it's worse if I don't have anything in my stomach."

"I don't have any food in the house."

"Could you go get something? It would really help."

"I don't want to leave you here alone."

"I'll be fine."

After a long pause, he said, "I gotta take care of something. I'll be back in a minute. Don't come out until I tell you to."

Afraid of the consequences if she disobeyed him, Melody sat in the bathroom and glanced between the closed door and her watch as the seconds ticked by. Where had he gone? It would be too much to hope that he'd left her alone in the house. Dare she make a break for it?

Summoning all her courage, she opened the door a crack. The sound of drilling came from somewhere in the large house. The bathroom door had muffled some of the sound. The pounding of her heart had blocked the rest. While he was occupied, she should make a break for the front door. It couldn't be more than thirty feet from where she stood to freedom.

But before she'd taken more than three steps, the drilling sound stopped. Melody glanced up, but couldn't see Craig. Did she still have time to make a break for it? Terror gave her the strength to try.

She had her hand on the front door knob and was turning it when Craig spoke.

"Where do you think you're going?"

"I just wanted some fresh air. Sometimes that makes me feel better."

"I think you're trying to leave. You can't do that." He seized her wrist, hard enough to bruise, and twisted her hand off the knob.

"You're hurting me," she protested, yanking her arm back in an effort to free herself. "Let me go."

He was strong, but adrenaline raged through her, fueled by her narrow escape. She kicked out at him, continuing to demand that he release her. Panic took ahold of her, turning her into a mindless, desperate animal. She needed to get away.

And then he let her go. Melody had a moment of searing relief before the left side of her face exploded in blinding pain. The impact of his hand against her cheek sent her stumbling backward. Her shoulder struck the wall leading into the living room and sent more pain blasting through her body.

Her father had struck her once. Not long after her mother had left. Melody had gone into a frenzy at the realization that she was being left behind and had screamed at her father, blaming him. At first he'd argued back, telling her to shut up and then to go to her room. But she'd been wild with grief and afraid of being abandoned. Looking back, Melody could barely remember what had been the exact trigger that caused her father to lash out and strike her.

It was all a blur of fear and pain. She'd never forgiven

him, but probably as he'd intended, she respected his authority from that moment until she left LA to attend Juilliard at age eighteen.

"You made me do that," Craig said, grabbing her arm and pulling her toward the stairs.

Melody refused to respond. Her face stung, but she kept her spine straight, unwilling to let him know how hurt and afraid she was. This was not the moment to aggravate him further.

Instead, she retreated to that same place inside her where she'd gone the day her father had hit her. She went there to survive and plan.

As Kyle stepped out of the gangway and into the Las Vegas airport, he received a text from Melody.

Everything is fine with me. Not ready to talk yet.

This should've eased his mind, but he couldn't shake the anxiety as he texted her back.

Where are you?

Staying at a hotel. I don't want to see you.

And right there he knew it wasn't Melody.

His phone rang as he was contemplating how to respond. It was the security expert, Logan Wolfe.

"We've got her at that Barstow gas station with someone," Logan said to Kyle. "We're having trouble reading the license plate on their car, but we have a good picture of both Melody and the guy she's with from a camera inside the station. I'm texting a photo to you. Do you recognize him?"

Kyle glanced down at his phone's screen and saw the photo. It was off security footage and not the best quality, but something about the guy seemed familiar. One thing was clear: Melody wasn't afraid of the guy.

"I don't. I'll forward the photo to Trent and Nate. Maybe they'll have better luck. In the meantime, I got a text from Melody saying she's okay, but I'm pretty sure she's not sending the message. She claims she's staying at a hotel."

"And we know she was on the road between LA and Las Vegas last night. You think it's the guy she's with?"

"It would make sense if he's got her." Kyle was surprised how steady he sounded.

Damn it. Who was this guy? When Kyle got ahold of him, he was going to put him down.

Kyle's hands shook as he sent off the photo to Trent and Nate and hoped they were both standing by.

"Thanks for all your help, Logan."

"We'll keep at the security footage. My guys have some pretty sophisticated software. Hopefully they'll make some progress on the license plate."

"I'll let you know if Trent or Nate recognizes the guy." Before he could sign off, he had a text back from Nate. "Wait a second. Nate says it's Craig Jameson. He's a sound engineer at his recording studio." Kyle tried to picture the guy and couldn't.

"We'll check him out and get back to you."

Kyle was staring at the picture when his phone lit up with Nate's number. He answered immediately. "Who is this guy?"

"Nobody. I mean he's totally normal. Dull even." Nate paused and Kyle could imagine him shaking his head, equally baffled. "I'm racking my brain, but can't think of a single instance when he said or did anything inappropriate. Around Melody or anyone else."

"So he just snapped?"

"We don't know that he did anything," Nate said, but he didn't sound all that convincing. "Logan thinks he and Melody drove back to Vegas together?"

"It appears as if they were friendly and she obviously feels comfortable with him." Kyle's gut tightened as he imagined what might've happened to Melody since. "Right before Logan called, I got a text from her claiming she's staying in a hotel."

"You don't think it's her?"

"No. I think it's this Craig guy."

"So, we're assuming he offered her a ride back to Las Vegas," Nate said, sounding puzzled. "And then we think he what? Kidnapped her? This just doesn't make any sense."

"Why would he have been in LA?"

"He was at The Roxy for her performance."

Kyle was liking this less and less. "So obviously he's interested enough in her to make that trip." Could Craig have been her stalker? The roses that showed up at the studio. The ultrasound video that disappeared and then reappeared at the studio. It made sense.

"We don't know that's the only reason he was in LA," Nate said. "Maybe he had something else to do and since he was there decided to catch her show."

"Why are you defending him?" Kyle demanded, fists clenching.

"I'm not. I'm just trying to look at this from all angles. We don't really know what's going on."

Acid ate into Kyle's gut. "I know that Melody is missing and Craig is the last guy she was seen with. That's good enough for me."

Nate's tone grew conciliatory. "Hey, I get it. We're all worried."

"Sorry." The breath Kyle hauled in didn't calm him, but he knew nothing would be gained by lashing out. "I didn't mean to take anything out on you."

"It's okay. You did the right thing getting Wolfe Security involved."

"From the way Trent talked, they can dig into whatever we need to find her."

"If you need any information on Craig, just call the studio and ask for Reggie. He can get into the personnel files. Whatever you need."

"I appreciate it."

Kyle hung up and stared around the airport gate area without seeing any of it. Curses rang through his mind as he contemplated what could possibly be happening with Melody right now. He began making his way to the exit. He couldn't just sit around and wait. He had to do something. The phone rang as he left the terminal and was heading toward the parking lot.

It was Logan, calling him back. "We've got the guy's address and phone number. We tried calling, but it rolls straight to voice mail. I have a three-man team heading over to his house right now. They'll let me know what they find."

"Should we call the cops?"

"At this point we don't have any evidence of a kidnapping. Let's see what my guys find. It's possible we're barking up the wrong tree."

Logan didn't say what Kyle was thinking. That time was of the essence if Craig actually had abducted Melody. The cops would be slow to investigate, especially with the question of whether or not she had a stalker. Roses and a nanny cam weren't all that conclusive.

"Give me his address," Kyle said. "I want to be there."

"That's not a good idea." Logan's tone brooked no argument. "Let my men handle it."

"Please tell them to be careful." Kyle could imagine too many ways this scenario could go wrong.

"Don't worry, they're trained in this sort of operation. Just sit tight and I'll let you know what they come up with."

Kyle couldn't just sit around waiting to hear. "That's not good enough. I need to be doing something."

"At this point there isn't much to do. I promise I'll let you know as soon as I hear anything."

Kyle headed to his car. He could go to Nate's studio and get Craig's personnel records. There'd be an emergency contact. That person might know. And he could talk to the sound engineer's coworkers. Surely they would know something that could shed light on what made Craig tick.

Half an hour later, he was sitting in Nate's office at Ugly Trout. Logan had called a couple minutes ago and said that they'd struck out at Craig's house. Kyle's jaw ached from clenching his teeth. The only thing keeping panic in check was a lifetime of repressing his emotions.

Before him on the desk was Craig's personnel file. He typed the guy's address into his phone, and then scanned through the paperwork for an emergency contact. Craig had listed his mother in California. Kyle dialed the number, unsure what he planned to say.

Hello, Mrs. Jameson. Do you happen to know where your son might have taken the woman I love?

When a woman answered, Kyle began the conversation with more tact. "Mrs. Jameson, my name is Kyle Tailor. I work with Nate Tucker at Ugly Trout Records where your son is employed and I was wondering if you've heard from Craig lately."

"Not since last week. Is something wrong? Has he been hurt?"

Not yet.

"Nothing like that. He isn't at work today and we had some questions for him. He's not answering his cell phone. He mentioned spending some time with a friend. Any idea where they might have gone."

"I don't know how I can help you. I haven't heard from him. Have you tried him at home?"

"Yes, it doesn't appear as if he's been there for a couple days. I believe he was in LA to see a concert last night and he was supposed to come back to Las Vegas sometime today." Kyle left out the part where he'd been caught on the gas station security footage in Barstow. "What I'm wondering is if he hasn't been home, maybe you know someplace else he might have gone."

"I can't imagine. Sometimes he likes to gamble at the casinos. Not that he's a big gambler or anything. Maybe that's where he is and he's turned off his cell phone."

"I guess if that's what he's done, then we're out of luck. Would you happen to know a favorite hotel he likes to gamble at?" It was a long shot, but it was possible that Craig had taken Melody to a hotel.

"No. I'm sorry. Oh, wait. My ex-husband's sister has a vacation home in Vegas. Craig looks after the place when they aren't using it. Waters the plants, makes sure the air-conditioning is working, that sort of thing."

"Would you happen to have the address?"

"No. I'm not on good terms with my ex's family. But I can't imagine Craig being there. Why would he when he has a perfectly nice home of his own?"

Why indeed. An empty house would be the perfect place to stash the woman you kidnapped.

"Maybe I can look up her address. What is her name?"

"Minerva Brooks. But I'm pretty sure she's not listed."

"I guess it never hurts to check." And Kyle had access to the sort of people who knew how to get information. "Thank you for your help."

As soon as Kyle hung up with Craig's mother, he called Logan. "I have the name of Craig's aunt. Minerva Brooks. She has a house in Las Vegas that he has access to."

Kyle heard the keys click while Logan input the name on his computer. "That's interesting. She has a house in the same gated community that Trent lives in."

Understanding lanced through Kyle. The mysterious gifts. The nanny cam with the short range. Melody had thought she was safe in the gated community, but her stalker had full access. Kyle cursed.

"That has to be where he has her."

"You sit tight." Logan's deep voice was edged with warning. "I'll send my guys over there."

"Sure."

But this time, Kyle didn't have to sit back and wait for Logan's men to make their move. He had a location, maybe not an exact address. The neighborhood wasn't all that extensive. How hard was it going to be to spot a couple black SUVs and a security team?

Fourteen

Like a caged tiger, Melody paced the bedroom Craig had locked her in. The afternoon had faded into evening, taking daylight with it. She stared out the window at the surrounding homes, so near and yet, thanks to the large lot sizes in the gated community, so far. As the western horizon had gone dark and lights began to appear behind the curtains of the nearby houses, she'd barely resisted the urge to throw open the window and start screaming for help.

She'd been afraid to draw Craig's attention. From the look of the padlock he'd affixed to her door, he had no intention of letting her escape. But he hadn't thought of everything. The bedroom was on the second floor and the drop to the ground was daunting, but she'd already decided she was less afraid of the height than staying in this house much longer.

But she had to wait. She didn't dare risk trying to escape while he was still in the house. He'd already demonstrated his willingness to punish her once. She was scared how far he'd take things if she tried and failed to escape a second time.

Her stomach growled. She hadn't eaten anything since they'd stopped in Barstow, over fifteen hours earlier. He'd said there was no food in the house so he had to go shopping at some point. He claimed he wanted to take care of her, so he wasn't going to let her starve. The problem with where the bedroom was situated in the house was that she couldn't see the driveway and determine if his car was still parked there. She'd spent some time with her ear pressed to the door, but couldn't hear anything.

After taking all this into consideration, she'd decided to make her break in the wee hours of the morning. Like the escapees in any good movie, she stripped the bed and made a rope of sheets she could tie to the bed leg and dangle out the window. To her relief Craig hadn't thought about nailing the window shut.

A quick glance at the clock radio on the nightstand showed her it was nearly seven in the evening. Had anyone wondered why she hadn't checked in? Nate had taken Mia to visit his mother in Texas this morning. They would be too busy to think about her. As for Trent and Savannah, Craig had her phone and could have texted them that everything was fine.

That left Kyle.

The way she'd treated him the night before, she wouldn't be surprised if he never wanted to see or speak to her again. Except that wasn't his style. Especially now that she was carrying his daughter. But how long before he reached out? And even if he did, what sort of vile messages would Craig send in her stead? Would Kyle believe them? She hadn't exactly fallen into his arms after he told her he loved her.

In the long hours that she'd paced this room, she'd realized just how stupidly she'd been behaving. Why hadn't she listened to Kyle when he told her that Hunter was interfering in their relationship? Damn. Why had she let Hunter kiss her? Kyle had every right to be furious.

She had so much to make up for. She only hoped when she got out of this mess, he would be willing to give her another chance.

A faint noise sounded downstairs. Melody began to realize how she'd attuned herself to the silence, searching for anything that would indicate Craig was still in the house, until she heard…voices? Someone was here. She ran to the bedroom door and began pounding on it. Were her frantic cries loud enough to penetrate the door and reach the people below? Regardless of who they were, surely they would be curious about the noise.

She barely heard the sound of the padlock being removed, but then the door was opening. Heart pounding, terrified that it was Craig and not someone who could help her, she retreated. When Kyle's face appeared in the opening, pale and haggard with worry, she covered her mouth and then rushed at him.

His arms came around her body, crushing the breath from her lungs. Burying her face in his neck she held on for dear life while he soothed her with gentle reassurances.

"It's okay," he murmured, stroking her hair. "You're safe."

"Where's Craig?"

"Some friends of mine are taking care of him downstairs."

"I can't believe you found me." It was hard to get the words out between gulping breaths.

"I'm sorry it took so long." His hands drifted up and

down her back while his strong body absorbed her shaking. "Are you okay? He didn't hurt you, did he?"

She shook her head. "No. I'm fine."

As if not believing her claim, he held her at arm's length. His gaze immediately went to the side of her face where Craig had struck her. She put her fingertips over the spot and couldn't meet his eyes.

"Did he do that to you?"

"I'm fine. Really." She touched his face, her eyes pleading with his. "I love you. I'm so sorry for what happened last night."

"Last night?" He blinked as if he couldn't figure out what she was talking about.

"You told me you loved me and I ran away." She swept tears from her cheeks with the back of her hand. "Again. I've been so stupid. I love you."

"I love you, too." He cupped her face. "I've been in love with you since that day at the bagel place when you twisted your ankle and I kissed cinnamon and sugar off your lips. I'm sorry I haven't told you that every day since."

He'd always treated her with such devoted affection. Why had it been so important for her to hear the words? How much heartache could've been avoided if she'd just believed they truly belonged together.

"Let's get out of here."

Melody nodded her agreement and let Kyle guide her down the stairs. Four large men dressed in impeccable black suits and black shirts watched her approach.

"These men are from Wolfe Security," Kyle explained as they neared the bottom.

One of them stepped forward as she and Kyle moved into the foyer. He stood significantly over six feet tall. "You okay, ma'am?"

"Fine." Melody couldn't help glancing at Craig.

He was seated on the floor in the archway that led to the living room, hands bound behind his back, staring into space. Melody shrank against Kyle as Craig glanced toward her.

"Make them understand I did it because I love you," he said.

She felt Kyle tense and dug her fingers into his arm. "Don't."

The muscles beneath her hand didn't uncoil as Kyle urged her toward the front door. When they got outside, Melody sucked in a lungful of night air.

"Come on," Kyle led her toward his car.

"What about the police?"

"The security team is handling that call. We'll wait for them out here."

Once she was tucked into the passenger seat of Kyle's car, the little bit of calm she'd achieved vanished and she began to shake in earnest. Kyle got behind the wheel and pulled her into his arms. Safe with him, she gave in to the overwhelming anxiety and fear that she'd bottled up these last terrifying hours.

By the time the police arrived, her trembling had subsided and she felt her strength coming back. Kyle handed her a packet of tissues for her to blow her nose. Smiling her gratitude, she dabbed away tears.

With her breathing finally under control, she said, "I must look a mess."

"You're the most beautiful thing I've ever seen."

Not only had the cops shown up, but also the paramedics. They checked her over and pronounced her okay except for elevated blood pressure, but because of the baby, they wanted her to go to the emergency room and be checked out. Before she left, the police took her statement and she got to hear how Kyle had found her with the help of Wolfe Security.

At the hospital, they photographed the bruise on her face and then checked out her and the baby. Both received a clean bill of health and Kyle took Melody back to his house. On the way, they swung through a drive-through and she wolfed down a hamburger and large fries in record time.

She was half-asleep by the time he tucked her into bed, but she seized his hand before he could move away.

"Please don't leave me," she said, tugging at him. "I need you."

To her relief, Kyle lay down beside her and pulled her into his arms. The steady beat of his heart beneath her cheek should've been enough to ease her into sleep, especially because the adrenaline of her misadventure had long ago worn off.

"I had a lot of time to think today," she told him. "I have made so many mistakes in the last few months. I don't want to make another one."

"We've both made our share."

Melody silenced him with a finger to his lips. "This last fiasco is on me. If I hadn't been so blind to Hunter's motives for spending time with me, and then not believed you've loved me all along, I wouldn't have run away from you in LA and ended up with Craig."

He grabbed her hand and kissed her fingers before pulling them away so he could speak. "I shouldn't have overreacted when I saw you with Hunter."

"I'm glad you did. I don't know why I've been so blind. I wanted you to say that you loved me, but I was too blind to see that if you didn't care, you wouldn't have been bothered that Hunter wanted me back." She paused. "And I set him straight, by the way. I told him you're my future."

"I love hearing that." Kyle sealed his vow with a reverent kiss.

"And I want that future to be in LA. I've had enough of Las Vegas." She gave a small shudder and snuggled closer.

"Oh." He sounded surprised.

"Oh?" She echoed, looking up into his face. "What?"

"When you seemed conflicted about where you wanted to live, I started looking for a house here."

"You don't want to move."

"No, but I thought we could go back and forth. With your family living here, I know you want to be close."

"Did you find a house?"

"I found three. I intended to get your opinion on them before I bought anything."

"Before *we* bought," she corrected him. "I think it's time I stopped renting and mooching and become a homeowner. I want this to be our home."

It was important to her that she'd realized it, but now that she'd said the words out loud, she wanted nothing more than to buy their home.

"I love that idea." He kissed her again. This time with focused passion, tempered by gentleness. "And can we go get married tomorrow? I don't care if you want to have a big wedding down the road, but right now there's nothing I want more than to make you my wife."

"I think that's a great idea." Coming so close to losing him a second time had finally driven home how much she adored him. "I don't need anything, but you."

And with a smile on her lips, she proceeded to show him exactly how much.

Epilogue

Day fifteen. Hire a professional photographer to take pictures of you as a beautiful memory of your commitment to and completion of this relationship revitalization challenge.

It took them ten months to reach the final exercise, but Melody had wanted a photo that reflected how blessed they were and insisted on including her entire family in the picture. Kyle had hired the same photographer who'd done Melody's album shoot and Nate and Mia's wedding photos. They were gathered at the home Kyle and Melody had bought in LA.

After Melody's abduction, she hadn't wanted to stay in Las Vegas any longer. She'd returned with Kyle to LA, only returning to Sin City to prepare for and then testify in Craig's trial. Both Kyle and Melody had decided that their new family needed a house with more yard for their daughter to run around and sold Kyle's Bird Streets house, opting for a sprawling Monterey colonial sitting on nearly a half acre with glorious gardens, sun-drenched rooms and a guesthouse.

Kyle balanced sleeping four-month-old Lily on his arm and watched Trent wrangle his active toddler back into the shot. Beside him, Melody let her head fall onto his shoulder. He felt as much as heard her soft sigh.

"Is ours going to be that bad?" Nate was on Kyle's other side, glancing from Trent and Savannah's bundle of energy to the bright-eyed infant in his wife's arms.

"I hope so," Mia murmured, kissing her son's bald head.

He'd been born a month premature after she'd displayed signs of preeclampsia and the doctor induced labor. Although there had been a few tense hours after Mia had been rushed to the hospital, Aiden Tucker had been born without incident. And to hear his father tell it, the boy was perfect.

"You hope so?" Nate asked his wife as Trent tucked Dylan under his arm and carried him—with loud protests and flailing interspersed with giggling—back to the photo shoot.

Mia sounded amused. "Boys are supposed to be active."

"There's active," Nate said, shaking his head in bemusement as Dylan settled like an angel onto his mother's lap after being promised a cookie, "and then there's wild."

"Chasing after him will keep you in shape," Kyle said as Melody adjusted the bow in Lily's soft brown hair and smoothed the skirt of her pale pink dress.

He wasn't sure how he'd been blessed with two such beautiful women in his life, but he wouldn't trade his current happiness for all the no-hitters in the world.

"Are you sure you don't want me to take her?" Melody asked, unable to stop fussing over her daughter.

"You know I have this."

"You are the most awesome father ever." She gave him

a wistful smile. "It's just that I'm going to be gone for two days and I'm going to miss her terribly."

"We could come with you," Kyle offered for the umpteenth time. "I can clear my schedule and we can all go up to San Francisco for your show."

"As much as I'd love that, I need to see if I can handle these short weekends away from you and Lily."

After releasing her first album, Melody had been booked into several small venues before her pregnancy advanced to a point where she complained that no one wanted to see a woman give birth on the stage. Once Lily was born, she'd let Nate talk her into performing three times over the course of three months. The first of those performances was this upcoming weekend.

"Maybe it would be better if you took both of us along and that way you will see we can make taking your act on the road work for our family."

Becoming a mom had inspired Melody and she'd been writing furiously for the last several months. Nate was encouraging her to get back into the studio. Mia was excited to produce her friend's music. So far Melody had refused to go forward while she and Kyle discussed how best to balance her career with their family life. Both were conscious of how an extended separation had affected their relationship last time. Kyle was confident that after the lessons they'd learned and the relationship work they continued to do each day, they wouldn't fall prey to the same problems this time around. Still, he wasn't all that keen on living without his wife or daughter for even a day.

Trent had taken a break from his business to spend several months on location with Savannah. There was no reason Kyle couldn't do the same. In fact, he was looking forward to watching his wife live her dream.

"You don't know how stressful all the travel can be," Melody said.

"I know exactly how it is. I spent twelve years in the majors and we were on the road half the time."

"You didn't have a baby to worry about."

"Are you kidding? I had a clubhouse full of big babies that were never happy," he joked. Seeing she wasn't convinced, he leaned down and kissed her lightly on the lips. "I want us to be together and I want you to become a huge star. Whatever I can do to help make that happen I will do."

Her eyes grew luminous. "Stop being so wonderful. I can't cry. It will ruin my makeup and we haven't taken a single picture."

"Is everyone ready?" the photographer asked.

This brought everyone's attention back to the business at hand. From his position behind Savannah, Trent and Dylan, Kyle beamed with pride and happiness. Next to him, Nate radiated a similar joy. How odd that a year ago all three owners of Club T's had been involved with the three women who sat or stood beside them, but each couple had been struggling to find their way.

Since then, Trent had released past hurts and reconnected with the only woman he'd ever loved. Nate had fought for and won the woman of his dreams. And Kyle had learned that sharing his deepest thoughts and emotions with Melody made his life so much richer and joyful.

"Thank you for making all my dreams come true," Kyle murmured to Melody as the photographer announced that he was done with the photo shoot.

"Your dreams?" Melody echoed in surprise. "I think it's me who's lucky to have you." She gazed down at their daughter. "Both of you. I never imagined I could be so happy."

"How about our dreams?" he countered. "You, me and our daughter. No matter what the future holds we are going to have each other."

Melody's eyes shone bright. "And it doesn't get better than that."

* * * * *

*If you liked this story, pick up these other
Las Vegas Nights novels from
Cat Schield!*

*AT ODDS WITH THE HEIRESS
A MERGER BY MARRIAGE
A TASTE OF TEMPTATION
A GAME OF SEDUCTION (novella)
THE BLACK SHEEP'S SECRET CHILD
LITTLE SECRET, RED HOT SCANDAL*

Available now from Mills & Boon Desire!

MILLS & BOON®

Desire™

PASSIONATE AND DRAMATIC LOVE STORIES

A sneak peek at next month's titles...

In stores from 7th September 2017:

- **Billionaire Boss, Holiday Baby** – Janice Maynard *and*
  Little Secrets: Secretly Pregnant – Andrea Laurence

- **Billionaire's Baby Bind** – Katherine Garbera *and*
  Fiancé in Name Only – Maureen Child

- **One Night Stand Bride** – Kat Cantrell *and*
  The Cowboy's Christmas Proposition – Silver James

Just can't wait?
Buy our books online before they hit the shops!
www.millsandboon.co.uk

Also available as eBooks.

MILLS & BOON®

Join Britain's BIGGEST Romance Book Club

- **EXCLUSIVE offers every month**
- **FREE delivery direct to your door**
- **NEVER MISS a title**
- **EARN Bonus Book points**

Call Customer Services
0844 844 1358*

or visit
nillsandboon.co.uk/subscriptions

* This call will cost you 7 pence per minute plus your
phone company's price per minute access charge.